A Graveyard's Never Bleak

B.A.D.

Tome I

Table of Contents

"What's this? How peculiar... I didn't expect to find a being such as yourself seeking entry into my garden of terrors. But nonetheless, I am a good host who welcomes all the curious creatures in..."

"...Did you bring any tribute? Coins, flowers, tobacco or rum shall do just fine... what? No? Hmm, I am not one to turn down a guest, so let us find a compromise. Leave with me your soul, here at the gates, and I shall return it to you on your way back out. Sound fair?"

Between Two
Cedar Pillars

Spring was the most beautiful of all the seasons where Melanie lived. It was a time of joy, festivities, life, and celebration of the crops starting their new cycles of produce in a flourishing abundance.

Her days were filled with fun, as expected of youth. She and her friends would run about the town carrying bright colored ribbons that would flash like fire in the rays of the sun, all the while chasing each other and releasing the sounds of their high-pitched laughter which trailed shortly behind them.

During the short intervals where their energy seemed to miraculously deplete in the eyes of the adults, they would drink the refreshing apple cider handed out by the farmers, and eat the soft and steaming hot pretzels freshly put out by the bakers.

The streets were littered, not with trash but instead with petals of various flowers, golden pools of beer that spilt out of the brim-filled mugs of adults, the cats chasing the dogs or the dogs chasing the cats, and the diverse colored birds who swooped down and pecked at the scraps that had fallen from the happy but clumsy children.

Such a vibrant scene could have been labeled as heaven-like, and for everyone living in Melanie's town, if felt exactly so.

During one of those rare moments where Melanie and her friends decided to take a break from their fun, they playfully headed into an alleyway and sat on boxes while they continued to consume their food and drinks, mimicking the mannerisms of adults as all children do to feel mature.

"I think I'm going to go see it tomorrow!" said one of the boys in the group, "I'm not scared to find out, everyone dies eventually so it's not a big deal."

"But how can you even be sure it's accurate?" asked one of the girls, "It could be lying or just get it wrong."

"No! A lot of the adults go to it to find out when they're gonna die. My uncle went when he was younger, and the Fox told him he was going to die in thirteen more years in his sleep during the night! That's why my dad wasn't sad when he passed away. They already knew of it."

"Yeah" agreed a different girl, "My mom's already visited the Fox and told me of her death so I wouldn't be sad when it happens."

"My parents are different" said one of the younger boys, "They don't wanna know when they're gonna die and told me not to visit the Fox because they don't want me knowing either."

Melanie remained quiet as she listened to the other kids talk about the Fox.

Outside their village, within the giant entanglement of trees that made up the forest which surrounded their community, was a Fox. It sat within its own little ecosystem, like a forest within the forest. Its home even contained different plants, trees, flowers and greenery that couldn't be found any-where else except for within its little boundary. And the only way to enter its unique space was by passing in between two giant cedar wood trees that acted almost like a gate... or rather, a portal some would say.

There wasn't much known about this Fox by the villagers except for two things; It lived in the spirit forest... within the forest— the place beyond the two cedar trees; and the Fox had the ability to see your death and know when and how you will die.

Those gathered children in that slim alleyway gave a wonderful description on how the village and its occupants viewed this Fox, should any outsider have stumbled upon their rabbles.

The creature was not feared nor seen as a threat. It wasn't damned nor looked down upon for its strange nature or its curious abilities. Some chose to inter-act with the Fox and learn of their deaths, while others simply wished not to know and leave it to be an unpredictable phenomena in their life.

Melanie's parents however, were neither of those. Simply put, they just did not care. They didn't care enough about their deaths to ask the Fox, nor care enough to avoid ever encountering the being. They just lived their lives and that was the end of it.

Perhaps it was because of their disinterest that Melanie grew a strong one of her own in the Fox. Or maybe she was no different than any of the others who had visited it and was truly curious about her death.

The reason for her intrigue was not apparent and far out of her own grasp, but there was no denying that Melanie wanted to see the Fox.

The chitter-chatter between the children continued to go on as Melanie slowly drifted into her own thoughts on the subject, until eventually an internal decision was made.

After the kids had finished their performance of what they thought was an adult conversation, they took back to running through the streets with their newfound energy from their short break. However, this was where Melanie parted with them.

She turned her sights to the forest surrounding her town, knowing just like everyone else who lived in it, where to go and what direction to head in to find the Fox… and she did just that.

The sun was still hanging in the sky though its initial stages of descent had begun, casting a new shade of an orange glow onto anything under its shine.

Melanie walked peacefully through the forest, and would drag her hands and fingers across the familiar trees, pluck out the flowers from the ground that she thought were the most beautiful, and took notice to the birds flying about frantically above her head from tree to tree with more craze than usual, sort of like the herself and the other kids back at the town's festival.

It was not too long until she reached the destination she sought, with the sun barely beginning to take on an accent of gold upon her arrival.

And before her now, glimmering that sun's gold with their rustling leaves that shimmered in the evening wind, stood two grand cedar trees— far thicker and taller than any other tree in the forest, with its branches and leaves casting shadows over the surrounding ones.

A thick wall of vines and shrubbery wrapped around the two trees, encasing a tiny area of its own in a circular space, separate from the rest of the forest. And between those two cedar trees could be seen a Fox, lying contently at the center of its mini forest, surrounded by a decadence of unknown shrubbery and flowers that gently blew in a rhythmic sway by an even gentler wind than the one overhead.

Melanie approached the two giant cedar pillars and dragged her hand across the nearest one like she had done with all the other trees during her venture, before entering the space within.

The Fox had appeared to be napping, but the moment she stepped into the little forest within the forest, its ears perked up and head lifted as it turned to look at her.

They both observed each other, Melanie with more hesitance and timidness, and the Fox with more curiosity and intrigue.

"Well, aren't you a young one" said the Fox.

Its voice caught Melanie off guard as it wasn't what she had expected at all. To be honest, she didn't really know what to expect the Fox to sound like, but the maturity in its depth and slight whimsicalness of its tone did not cross her mind. Perhaps a more childish ring, or the high-pitch shrill closer to its animal brethren would've been less of a surprise to her.

The Fox noticed Melanie's apprehensive approach and ushered her closer, "Oh come now young one, I meant no tease. You simply surprised my expectation of a human who would come here while the sun is on its descending path."

Melanie drew closer to the Fox, its words having worked in easing the tension.

"I'm sorry" said Melanie, "Should I leave and return back tomorrow at an earlier time?"

The Fox huffed at her question, which appeared more like a sneeze to Melanie.

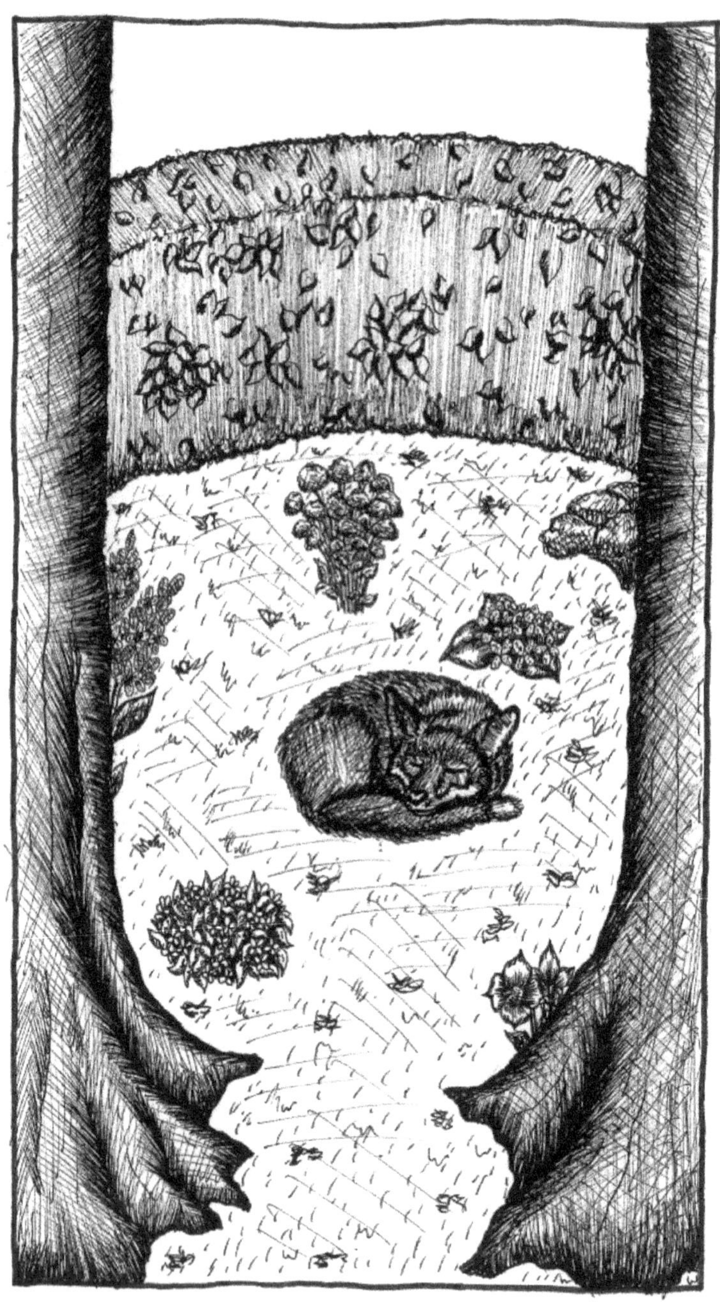

"No no, don't be silly. And don't take so easily to words! There's such a thing as banter where no messages lie between the sentences. I'm sure you humans do it too, so please, for the sake of avoiding boredom, do no make me change my diction out of fear of you misinterpreting."

"Okay" said Melanie, rubbing her arm in slight embarrassment, "What's your name?"

"Hell if I know" answered the Fox genuinely without a change in its gaze.

"You don't know your own name?"

"Well I'm not like you humans. I do not have parents and therefore was never given one."

"You don't have parents? Well then how were you born?"

"I was actually born just yesterday, before you humans or this forest even came into existence. Although for a mortal, yesterday must seem like an infinitely long time ago… thank goodness I'm not."

"You were here before the forest?"

"Indeed. And when it began to spring out of the earth, I thought it was rather beautiful and a place I would like to make my home. But then I noticed how other creatures had already made it their home, so I decided to craft myself a space within it" the Fox nodded towards the cedar trees, "And set those two giants as the entry point to my domain."

"Huh, I never knew that or even thought that there was a time before the forest" replied Melanie.

The Fox smiled, "And there's no need for you to have. You're mortal, and even amongst mortals you're a young one, so do not fret. But on to why you are here… well, why are you here? It's not hard for me to guess you wish to know of your death, am I correct?"

Melanie nodded.

The Fox laughed, "Curious creatures, you humans. That goes for all mortals, but especially you lot. Nonetheless, I can answer your question— look into my eyes, and do not blink nor break your gaze."

Melanie followed the instructions and locked into a stare with the Fox. At first it felt normal, but as the stare dragged on, she began to see the Fox's eyeballs in better detail like you would with anything you observed for too long. And then an odd moment happened where Melanie noticed all the acute details that made up these eyeballs belonging to the Fox, these eyes which were looking directly at her… But not her in the normal sense, rather directly into her soul, as though the Fox was invading the deepest, truest part of her— one which she herself had yet to even explore.

And then, with a slight raise of surprise by the Fox's white eyebrows, the stillness of the contact broke and the strange feeling of the Fox's peer into Melanie's soul took leave.

"Did you see it?" asked Melanie.

"I did" answered the Fox.

"So… how will it happen? And when?"

The Fox remained looking at her, giving a few blinks before slightly tilting its head and looking passed her, "The moment you leave here" said the Fox.

Melanie frowned, "What? Is that a kind of joke?"

"No. I don't joke. Although I do like them, I am rather lazy and prefer to be on the receiving end. You will die the moment you leave this place, that is your death I saw."

Melanie felt her heart drop and slowly pulled back from the Fox, feeling too close to this mysterious creature that no longer seemed innocent or whimsical.

The Fox took notice to this and cocked its head.

"I am not the threat, young one. Your death has nothing to do with me."

"Well then how will I die? You're the only other thing here with me right now and you're certainly not a normal being" challenged Melanie with suspicion.

The Fox nodded its head forward in a gesture towards something over her shoulder, "No. There is another. You will die by that stalker of yours."

Melanie ceased her backing from the Fox and turned her head to look over her shoulder.

And that's when she saw it, for back at the entrance where the two cedar pillars stood was an abnormal and strange figure. It was dark and shrouded in subterfuge, with only its wide eyes and uncanny grin to be seen as it watched them in secret from behind one of the great trees.

Melanie felt her blood turn to ice and a malevolent chill run down her spine.

"...What...is that thing?"

The Fox shrugged, "I actually haven't the faintest idea. But it seems to have been following you through the woods on your journey here. I suspect if you hadn't come into my space when you did, it would have taken you earlier. But now…it is simply waiting for you to leave my tiny realm to do so."

"What…what if it comes in? You'll protect me, won't you?"

"You needn't worry about it entering this place, young one. As I told you before, I created this space around me— it is my domain. There are plenty of things, creatures, and beings out there which I'd rather have no interaction with, and I made sure that no such being could ever cross between my two cedar pillars. As it would appear, that thing out there must be such a being… unsurprising by the looks of the ugly thing."

"So we're safe in here?"

"Of course."

"Well, do you think I could stay here for a bit longer then?"

"You're more than welcomed to, however, if that being is anything like me, then you could be here for quite awhile. The beginning of time was just yesterday for us, and an eternity of waiting for you to leave here today would only be tomorrow."

Charlie's Costume

Rehearsal 1

Ms. Tucker clapped her hands together to gain the children's attention, "Class! All eyes on me! Focus, focus! Okay listen, you are all third graders now. You CANNOT be acting like you're still in second grade! You have a responsibility now, and that is why your parents expect to see you well behaved in the Fall Play this Saturday."

The class of children between eight and nine years old began their own hushes amongst each other in order to please Ms. Tucker and slowly fell into attention.

"Now, please form a line across the front of the stage. I will call out the different roles available and if you want to play that, raise your hand. If multiple students raise their hand for an important role, then I am going to choose whoever I think I can trust with that position and will not goof around. That is why it is so important to be well behaved, because now I'm going to choose those who have shown they are responsible for roles that some of you might really want to play but are not responsible enough to."

As Ms. Tucker continued her high-moral rant onto the young third graders, Charlie and Brandon formed in line with the other students and stood side by side while engaging in a conversation between themselves.

"I don't even wanna be in this stupid play. I told my parents I didn't but they said I have to because the whole class is gonna be in it" said Charlie.

"Me neither" added Brandon, "Why is it so important, anyway? My mom and dad saw this same play when my sister was in third grade. I don't get why adults find this stuff so special."

"I'd rather be at home *actually* having fun right now since they're not giving us any homework for the rest of the week, not be here."

"My parents said that I have to memorize my lines in the script when I get back home after this, so it's not even like we don't have homework or can do whatever we want when we go home. Our whole lives revolve around this stupid play for the week."

"Screw that dude—"

"Shh!" hushed Brandon, scared that Ms. Tucker might hear Charlie swear and get them in trouble.

Charlie lowered his head and began to whisper closer to Brandon in response, "My brother told me that some roles don't require you to talk at all. He said they're called props and all you have to do is wear your costume and stand in the back, sometimes dance. Let's raise our hands for those roles and then we can play at our houses after this since we won't have to memorize any lines."

Brandon joined Charlie in his whisper, "Really? Yeah let's do it! We can probably even hangout today if we tell our parents we don't have any speaking parts."

Charlie and Brandon secretly bumped fists with their arms low by their sides.

"Let's do it dude" Said Charlie, "Raise your hand when I raise mine so we both get props."

After finishing her speech, Ms. Tucker began calling out the different roles, starting with the most important characters and finishing with the least. Different students would raise their hands when interested, and Ms. Tucker would use favoritism to cast each student for their role.

Reaching the end of the casting, Ms. Tucker then called out for the background characters.

Charlie raised his hand with Brandon following suit.

"I thought you said we should play props?" whispered Brandon, confused while holding his arm up.

"This is props" answered Charlie, "She said background characters, and props stand in the background. Just trust me, this is the one we want."

Only a small number of kids also raised their hands for this role, and most of them were the ones who were too shy to raise their hands earlier and now felt forced to when Ms Tucker stated this was the last option.

Everyone in this category was assigned to the role immediately and did not have to deal with Ms. Tucker's choosing process.

Charlie and Brandon smirked upon their tiny victory, and secretly fist bumped each other once more.

Rehearsal 2

"My parents said we can hangout today if you can" said Brandon.

"Yeah let's try… but I think my parents are mad at me" responded Charlie.

"How come?"

"They seemed angry yesterday when I told them I was a background character. They started getting all angry about Ms. Tucker, saying their son should be a lead character and stuff. They were actually going to call Ms. Tucker until I told them I raised my hand to be a background character… and now I think they're mad at me."

"Class! Class!" called Ms. Tucker for their attention, "We're going to get started today, so everyone will be given one of these" she flashed a small paper pamphlet from atop a pile of stacked dozens. "This is the script for the play. It has all of the acts, scenes, and dialogues in it. Now, we're going to form one big circle in the center of the stage and go over this pamphlet. If I call out your role, I want you to highlight it with a marker, and it is then your responsibility to study your lines and role later at home for the rest of this week and have it memorized before the play. We'll be going over the play and practicing it without costumes, but I want you to pretend that your parents are watching you now as if we have a full audience the entire time, okay?"

Ms. Tucker had a student assist her in carrying the pamphlets to the center of the stage while another helped carry a large plastic crate filled with bright colored markers beside them.

"Now, everyone come get one pamphlet and pick out one colored marker to highlight with. And please do not grab a black or brown one as I want you to be able to read your highlights. Form a circle once you're done— Oh, I almost forgot; The backdoor was open when I arrived.

Class the backdoor is an emergency exit only, so please inform your parents to drop you off at the front of the school and then make your way from the inside of the front entrance all the way back to our theater room. You can do the extra walk, do not come in through that backdoor or be dropped off by your parents at the back of the school, please. Thank you."

Rehearsal 3

Charlie and Brandon watched from behind the invisible curtain Ms. Tucker told them and all the other prop characters to pretend was there, as their peers went over their dialogues on the stage.

They were instructed along with the rest of the class to act as though they were doing the real performance even though it was only practice. So projecting their voices during their lines, not talking to one another the entire time, making sure they were in the correct positions, and standing still behind the imaginary curtain in silence when waiting for their cue to come on stage was all a part of their rehearsal.

The two friends behind the invisible curtain found it nearly impossible to even whisper to each other during this practice, as for some reason, Ms. Tucker became extremely vigilant in the catching and punishing of chatting students.

"Charlie" whispered Brandon.

"Shh! She's gonna catch us!" hushed Charlie.

"But I gotta pee really bad."

"Just hold it. You'll make Ms. Tucker angry if you ask to go now."

"I can't hold it any longer! I'm gonna ask her if I can go. And you can be my buddy so that we can both leave for a bit."

"Okay, but don't get us in trouble."

Brandon then raised his hand for Ms. Tucker's attention.

Ms. Tucker easily saw Brandon in her peripheral vision with his hand raised high, and even took notice of the pigeon-toed stance he embodied with an impatient bounce. It was obvious to her as it would be to any other adult, teacher or not, what Brandon's issue was and how dire his situation to use the bathroom was.

But for some reason, as most teachers like Ms. Tucker do, she pretended not to see him and continued to place all of her attention to the children reading out their lines, correcting and encouraging their performances.

As for Brandon, he had no idea Ms. Tucker was aware of his hand in the air, let alone that she knew why it was raised. So he just struggled with the internal conflict of resisting his body's natural needs while trying to confide his request to use the bathroom without upsetting the easily angered Ms. Tucker.

But when nature calls, all modesty gets thrown out the window, and even Brandon was able to find the courage to disregard Ms. Tucker's abused place of power to have his voice heard.

"Ms. Tucker" said Brandon, raising his voice progressively louder the more he called out her name, "Ms. Tucker!"

"Brandon!" exasperated Ms. Tucker in a snap of frustration, "I told everyone that we are to take rehearsals serious as if we are actually putting on a show. And if this is a real show, you CANNOT be interrupting the performance and calling out my name for everyone to hear in the middle of it!"

"But I have to use the bathroom! It's an emergency!"

Ms. Tucker swiped a section of her hair out of her face and inhaled sharply through her nose, exhaling it in the same aggravated manner while glancing irritatedly in Brandon's direction for the first time, "If it's an emergency then go. But class it is *your* responsibility to use the bathroom before we begin rehearsals."

Brandon didn't leave immediately after this and had barely begun his second request of Charlie being his bathroom buddy before Charlie elbowed him in the side.

"Don't ask for me to be your buddy!" whispered Charlie in a stern tone, "She's not gonna let you go and will get angry at the both of us if you do! Just go!"

Brandon was hesitant but knew Charlie was right, and despite his discomfort of going to the bathrooms alone since the theater room's restroom and general set up was a lot creepier than the main hall's, he headed off for it nonetheless.

As he crossed through the backstage, not daring to look into its shadowed corners, and trekked down the hall that connected the backdoor to the theater room, he entered the bathroom that occupied a space on the side of that connecting hallway.

Pushing open its doors, the automatic florescent lights began to flicker until their electric buzz awoke and stayed in full illumination.

The bathroom smelt funky to Brandon, but then again, so did the entire theater room. Out there was a scent of dust having not been cleaned for years, with an old antique smell similar to his grandmother's house. And in this bathroom was the same scent, but more shrouded in an odor of rot and piss.

Brandon approached one of the urinals and began to take care of his business, feeling a sense of relief which replaced the discomfort he initially felt.

...That is, until a soft noise caught his attention.

It sounded like a rustling of some sort coming from one of the adjacent stalls lined up next to the urinals.

He ceased his breathing, held his breath, and ignored the sound of his own pee hitting the urinal to focus in on this faint rustling sound he heard.

With every other noise no longer being in the mixup, Brandon was now certain of it and knew that there was definitely a rustling sound occurring from inside one of the stalls… but he did not know which one.

He wanted to ask out loud if anyone else was in there with him, but could not. He already knew no one else should be as Ms. Tucker's wrath would've been extended out longer in a rant if another had joined him. And on top of that, Brandon was just simply too afraid at the idea of hearing a response back to his inquiry.

The rustling continued, and his focused silence began to pick up even more strange noises. He could now hear what sounded like shallow breathing, staggered as if trying to keep hidden.

Brandon looked over his shoulder at the mirrors that stood over the sinks behind him, and watched the stalls from this perspective as he continued to pee.

It was still impossible for him to discern which stall the noises were coming from as all their doors were closed, and he did not see any pair of legs or shoes standing in the small gaps at the bottom of these doors.

Brandon began to push out the rest of his urine in a rush, never taking his eyes off the mirrors behind him as fear began to set in.

The sounds began to grow louder, with the rustling no longer shy but increasing in volume and speed, while the gentle breathing he once heard now sounding more strained in its concealment as though it had switched from nose to mouth.

Brandon's heart started to beat out of his chest and terror manifested in a trembling of his limbs.

As soon as his stream in the urinal stopped, he quickly recollected himself and zipped up his pants. Just as he did so, however, a loud and sharp squeak pierced his ears from within one of the stalls, causing Brandon to bolt out of the bathroom in flurry of panic as he made his way back to his class.

When rejoining Charlie on the stage behind the invisible curtain, his friend took notice to his heavy breathing and shaky state.

"What happened? Are you alright?" asked Charlie.

"There was something in the bathroom…" said Brandon in a low voice, choppy and wavering from the adrenaline.

"What was in there?"

"I don't know, but it sounded like something or someone. It was breathing and everything!"

Brandon began to raise his hand for Ms. Tucker's attention once more before it was slapped down by Charlie in a protective manner.

"What are you doing!?" asked Charlie.

"I need to tell Ms. Tucker" answered Brandon.

"No, she'll just be mean and get mad at you again. She won't do anything about it either. Just don't go back in the bathrooms again and I'll come with you next time, okay?"

Brandon nodded his head in agreement as he knew Charlie was right.

With a little disassociation followed by quiet observation of his fellow class-mates practicing their performances on stage with Ms. Tucker, Brandon was able to eventually calm down and relieve himself from the adrenaline that fueled his fear.

Rehearsal 4

Charlie and Brandon carpooled together to today's rehearsal.

The sky was pouring down hard with heavy rain, while a gentle rumbling of thunder presented the lie of a calmer storm.

The two boys became completely soaked in the matter of seconds it took for them to rush out of the car and run into the school. And it seemed the same fate was met by all their fellow classmates, as every third grader in the theater room was dripping from head to toe with water, some even shivering from how drenched and matted their clothes were.

As the children all talked amongst themselves with their voices filling the theater room in high shrills and screams, the loud bang of the backdoor slamming shut silenced their little squabbles.

The sharp clacking sound of Ms. Tucker's heels hitting the floor grew louder and louder as she made her way through the hallway and towards them.

Having spent half a year with Ms. Tucker already, the students knew she was angry just by the mere sound of her gait before even seeing her face.

Ms. Tucker spoke as soon as she strutted into the theater room, "Class" she began while closing her umbrella and unbuckling her trench coat, "Now, I thought I made it clear that no one was to enter through the backdoor."

Hands on hips, followed by a swinging arm and a pointing finger to the direction behind her, she continued "There is a trail of mud in that hallway, meaning one of you or many of you did not listen to my initial instructions. I am very disappointed and extremely frustrated. Whether it's raining does not make a difference, you are still to enter from the front of the school and make your way to the theater room *through* the school. I'm now going to be locking this back door from today forth, so if you try to enter through it, you will be locked outside— and if it's raining… well, you're just gonna have to walk in the rain all the way around the school."

The class remained quiet with no one fessing up to having entered the theater room through the backdoor, and they all awkwardly looked around at each other to see who would possibly volunteer to face the wrath of Ms. Tucker.

"With that out of the way, we need to focus back on the play. I would have liked to begin rehearsing in costumes today, but from the looks of it, everyone here is soaking wet and we cannot damage the costumes. They're not for you, they're for the school, and next year's class will have to be able to wear them too. That means that since the play is this coming Saturday, we'll only have one full day tomorrow of costume practice before the performance."

Ms. Tucker clasped her hands together and released a sigh full of stress, "Okay. That's all. Let's get started."

Rehearsal 5

Unlike most of the previous rehearsals that had occurred during the week, this one carried a lighter atmosphere of giggles and glee as you would expect from a class of third graders. They were all packed behind the stage as they enjoyed the excitement of seeing and trying on their costumes for the first time.

There was a mixture of laughs from embarrassment, laughs from teasing, and even some showboating as some students began to bellow out their key lines of the play from their newfound confidence.

Charlie and Brandon however, being their typical selves, distanced themselves from the rest of the class as they donned on the attire of their background characters.

Charlie was a pine tree. His puffy cloth suit covered the entirety of his body, including his feet, with only a rectangular cut-out breaking the constant green of his costume for him to see out of.

Brandon on the other hand, was a boulder. His costume was a large piece of grey colored plastic that rested on his shoulders and left his whole head on display at the top, requiring him to wear a similar grey bald cap and to paint his face in the matching color.

"Dude" Said Charlie, "The prop costumes suck."

"I know" agreed Brandon, "At least you're hidden in yours though. Everyone can see my face."

"Yeah, but it stinks in here. It smells kinda cheesy…who the hell wore this last year?"

"Shh! If Ms. Tucker doesn't hear you then someone else will and they'll tell."

"Hell's not even a bad word. My brother says it in front of my parents all the time and they don't care."

"No, I believe you. I don't think it's bad either. But everyone else in our class are babies and Ms. Tucker sucks… Anyways, I think my costume stinks too. Do you think were allowed to do trades?"

"You're probably just smelling mine. But I don't think so, if we still had Mrs. Crawford I bet you she would let us trade. She was so cool, I wish she taught third grade instead."

"Me too, I loved Mrs. Crawford. She was so nice. But I don't think it's your costume I smell. Mine doesn't smell cheesy, it's more… stinky, dude."

Charlie took off his costume to smell Brandon's, but before he could even lean in, he covered his nose and soured his face, "Ew, dude! It smells like poop!"

"Is it that bad!?" panicked Brandon.

"No I don't think it's your costume. It's in the air— like this whole area."

"Really?" said Brandon looking around, "Do you think Matt pooped his pants again? He did it in first grade and tried to hide it, apparently his mom picked him up from school that day and he wasn't actually sick."

"It can't be Matt" said Charlie, nodding his head to across the backstage, "He's all the way over there."

"Where do you think it's coming from then?"

"I don't know."

The two began to waddle in a circular 360 degree motion, and stopped when they were facing an unlit section of the backstage that was cluttered with a mountain of boxes and a blanket of shadows hiding the pockets and gaps between containers.

It was not so much for the fact that the smell intensified when the two boys faced that direction that made them know it held the source of the odor, but more so the mere ambience of that darkened space which screamed it housed the smell from within its subterfuge of mystery.

"What do you think's over there?" asked Brandon.

"I don't know, but it must be where the scent is coming from" answered Charlie.

"You think it's a dead animal?"

"Maybe, let's get a little closer"

The two boys began to slowly approach the darkened space of piled boxes, taking single footsteps forward with caution. They had seen many scary movies and heard a bunch of ghost stories, and now they played the role of acting like they were a part of one as they hesitantly drew closer to this darkened section of the backstage, the repulsive smell growing stronger as they neared.

Both boys felt the ominous pressure of something possibly jumping out of the shadows to grab them and pull them in, but before they could reach the blackened entrance of where the box-fortress began, Ms. Tucker hollered out and instructed the class to get into their respected places as they were about to begin rehearsals.

Charlie and Brandon, almost relieved to have had a reason to cease their brave march into the unknown, sharply turned around and ran with the rest of their class to complete the order given out by their teacher.

Before they got started, Ms. Tucker glanced in Charlie and Brandon's direction, "Go ahead and talk amongst yourselves for a bit class, we'll get started shortly."

She then began to approach the two, which immediately made their hearts sink as it couldn't have meant any good news.

"Charlie, I was contacted by your parents yesterday" said Ms. Tucker.

Charlie halted his progress of putting his costume back on, "Oh… really?"

"Yes. And they were extremely rude in the way they spoke to me. Now, I am not happy that they decided to throw their frustrations my way, but you are now gonna be a backup for a lead role in case Stephanie doesn't show up for the play tomorrow."

"…Does that mean I'm no longer a prop?" asked Charlie.

"No. You're still a prop, but if something happens to Stephanie or she doesn't show up tomorrow, you're gonna replace her and take on her role. This is by your parent's request. However, I find it so confusing that your parents thought to take it out on me that you're playing a prop despite the fact that you raised your hand and volunteered for that specific role in the first place."

"I'm sorry" said Charlie, confused.

Ms. Tucker waved her hand high in front of her own face, palm out, demeaningly rejecting Charlie's apology, "Highlight Stephanie's lines and role tonight in your pamphlet and have them memorized by tomorrow just in case. And inform your parents that you are her backup should she not show." Ms. Tucker then walked away immediately after and continued rounding up the class for practice.

"…So am I still a prop?" asked Charlie to Brandon.

"I think so. But then why do you have to memorize Stephanie's lines?" asked Brandon, just as confused.

"I don't know. I guess my parents will though so I'll just ask them tonight."

Performance Night

A low murmur filled the opposing side of the curtain as parents, adults, and siblings of the third grade class filled the entirety of the theater room. They were all dressed in the simplest of formal attire, and packed in all the seats available as they waited for the play to start and to bear witness to the performance of the children.

Behind the stage, the little performers were dressed in their costumes and preparing to put on the act which they had been preparing for during this entire last week. The third grade class was jittery with nerves and excitement, and for the first time in a long time, felt genuinely special.

Brandon was almost surprised to see Charlie in his assigned pine tree costume and felt relieved at the sight of it as well, "So you *are* still a prop!?"

"Yeah, but only because Stephanie showed up today. If she didn't, then I would have had to play her role."

"That's weird. Her character is a girl, why would you fill in for that?"

"I think Ms. Tucker is mad at my parents for contacting her, so she wanted to embarrass me if Stephanie didn't show up and make me play a girl."

"Dude… I hate Ms. Tucker."

"Me too. I can't wait to be in fourth grade and no longer in her class."

"Yeah, same. I don't think she likes either of us."

"No, she hates us! It's totally obvious."

The murmuring chatters amongst the audience on the other side of the curtain began to lower and then disappear all together. This caught the attention of the third grade class who now silenced their own whispers amongst each other and focused in.

Ms. Tucker's voice was then the only thing that filled the theater room as she began her speech on the other side of the curtain as a part of the intro to the play.

All of the kids rushed into their positions, preparing to step out onto stage in their assigned order just like they had rehearsed, while the prop characters stayed calmly at the back with no rush of any early appearance.

The night kicked off with an applause from the audience which sent the play into full motion.

It went as one would expect for a play performed by eight and nine year olds, and relatively smooth since all the children executed their movements on and off stage near perfect, despite their singing not necessarily being charming on the ears.

Brandon and Charlie had stepped on and off the stage a handful of times, quickly retreating back behind the curtain afterwards with the rest of their prop counterparts. They had only one more appearance to go, which was the grand finale where the whole class would be on stage singing, followed by bows during the end.

As the background characters eagerly awaited their final moment to approach, an urgent conversation started between the two boys.

"Brandon!" whispered Charlie, unworried of being heard as the performance on stage drowned out their private conversation, "Brandon I have to go to the bathroom!"

"No! It's almost the end! Just hold it a bit longer and then you can go after we bow."

"I can't! I have to go really bad, right now!"

"Okay, okay. Want me to go with you to ask Ms. Tucker then come with you?"

"No, I can't ask Ms. Tucker!"

"What do you mean? You have to!"

"No! She's really mad at me because of what my parents did. And remember how she treated you when you asked? That was during rehearsals too, this is the actual play!"

"So what are you gonna do?" asked Brandon.

"I'm just gonna go real quick and come back before we have to go on stage. There's enough time, Stephanie still has like three more minutes of talking before we have to go up, trust me I remembered all her lines.

I'm gonna leave real quick and go to the bathroom, but you stay here and cover for me in case Ms. Tucker comes over."

"You don't want me to go with you?"

"No! She'll notice if we're both gone. But play it cool and have my back, I'll be real quick."

"But what abou—"

"I gotta go now! Just stay here and cover for me!"

Charlie turned on the heel of his foot and darted to the bathrooms in the back of the theater room before Brandon could even finish his sentence.

Anxiety started to fill Brandon's body as he bounced on his tippy-toes, nervous at the idea of Charlie not making it back in time.

As more time passed and Brandon started to sense their call back onto the stage coming up, Charlie still hadn't returned from the bathroom yet.

Brandon struggled with whether to go get him or not, but remembered that Charlie told him to stay put and pretend as if he never left. And based on how many passing glances Ms. Tucker made in the direction of the prop characters from the opposing side of the stage, he was right. Since she never came over and confronted Brandon, she must have just assumed Charlie was with him since she saw him at the very least.

"Charlie!" squeaked Brandon to himself, "C'mon! C'mon!"

As the main leads began bellowing out their final lines of the play, it was now time for the entire third grade class to make their full appearance on stage and sing the last song together... but Charlie still hadn't returned.

Brandon's nerves now reached their peak from the absence of his friend, and his stomach knotted at the idea of the possible trouble they'd both get into later.

Nonetheless, Brandon hesitantly walked on stage and took his place when the moment came.

His eyes never left Ms. Tucker as he sung out loud with the rest of the class, and for a brief moment, he almost felt lucky as she didn't seemed to notice Charlie's disappearance.

That is, until her head did a double take and then frowned in his direction.

Brandon felt a sick churning in his belly as Ms. Tucker made her anger more than clear with her manipulative eyes as she never broke place or gaze while singing along with the rest of the class.

Brandon then turned his eyes to the audience, searching for his parents amongst the crowd for some kind of reassurance as he knew they'd have his back.

He had told them everything about Ms. Tucker and the way she had treated and spoken to Charlie, and they seemed to be disgruntled by his words and had assured him not to worry— they would not let her mistreat them.

But Brandon's search for his parents was interrupted when Charlie finally arrived, awkwardly waddling to his place beside him.

"There's no point in trying to sneak back over, dude! Ms. Tucker noticed you were gone!" whispered Brandon while covering his mouth from the audience, "What took you so long! Now we're gonna get in trouble!… Charlie?"

Charlie stood still, unresponsive to Brandon as though he didn't hear a single word he had said.

Brandon got a strange feeling in his gut about Charlie like something wasn't right.

And this feeling grew stronger by the second until it was no longer a feeling at all— but a fact. Something was definitely off. Something about Charlie was different.

"Charlie… you okay dude?" asked Brandon. He tried to engage Charlie once more, but was hit with a strong wave of a repulsive scent. It was similar to the one he had smelled in the bathroom the day he went alone, and no different to the one he and Charlie had smelled from the darkened section of the backstage the day before.

But now, in this moment, it was intensified. It made Brandon's eyes water, and churned up a nauseating urge within him to gag.

It was then when Brandon realized that this scent was coming off Charlie… or rather, Charlie's costume.

"…You're not Charlie" said Brandon in realization and growing with fear.

Within Charlie's costume, heavy and unstable breathing began to pant, just like the strange breathing he had heard in the bathroom from earlier in the week. And from the rectangular cut-out that gave the wearer visibility, two very wide and bloodshot eyes could be seen staring out of it with a craze in their gaze.

"You're not Charlie…" said Brandon louder while slowly stepping back away from his supposed friend.

"That's not Charlie. This isn't Charlie! What did you do to Charlie! You're not him!" Brandon raised his voice as he could no longer contain himself while real tears began to flow down his cheeks.

The class slowly stopped singing as they took notice to Brandon's outburst, while the rest of the adult audience also focused in on the new commotion at the back of the stage.

"This isn't Charlie! You're a faker!" Brandon pointed his finger at the false Charlie as he continued his screams, "What did you do to Charlie!?"

"EXCUSE ME!" hollered Ms. Tucker as she stormed her way across the stage and towards the two of them, "How *dare* you two interrupt the play with your little games!"

She stood before the both of them now as she continued her scorning, which felt equally like a berating of the boys as it did a performance of her own for all the onlookers, "You two have been nothing but trouble since the beginning of our rehearsals, and now you've chosen to ruin this event for your fellow classmates, your parents, all the guests, and the school!"

"That's not Charlie, though! He went to the bathroom but this isn't him! That's not the real Charlie, you have to believe me!"

Brandon looked to the audience once more, hoping to see his parents for reassurance in this new predicament he found himself in. And to his relief, he was able to spot them easily as they were already standing from their seats with faces full of concern; concern from their son's screams; concern from their son's words; concern from Ms. Tucker's belittling of him; and concern for his friend.

Though he was not looking for them, Brandon also noticed Charlie's parents rising from their seats, as both them and his own parents now hustled out into the aisles and started making their way towards the stage.

While this was all going on, Ms. Tucker was still going on her own little rant at the boys for the whole theater room to hear, all while the rapid, uneven breathing within Charlie's costume grew louder.

"Now! We are going to go back stage and have a talk with your parents since this show is officially over!" Ms. Tucker took three more steps toward them, aggressively reaching her hand out to grab both of them by the arms, when she drew back in shock.

For in that moment when her hand was about to take hold of Charlie's arm— a loud, hoarse, and strained groan came from Charlie's costume as long legs and equally long arms fully extended from the pine tree suit and lunged at Ms. Tucker!

Not many saw it at first since the attack was so fast, but within the right hand belonging to the long arm that extended out of Charlie's costume, was a knife.

Screams were heard from all around as both the students on stage and the parents in the audience were all taken by surprise to see the grown body that wore Charlie's costume proceed to tackle Ms. Tucker to the ground, stabbing her viciously all over her stomach and tearing through her hands as she tried to defend herself.

Ms. Tucker's screams, at one point, were the loudest amongst them all, that was until the knife eventually made its way to her throat, savagely splitting it open and casting a thick rope of blood over Brandon's painted face.

Sunday Morning News

"Good morning, Channel 5 viewers. This is Valerie Garcia with you live, standing in front of Sentenial Elementary School where last night a true tragedy struck the youth and parents of this community.

At 6:30 p.m. the school held on their yearly Fall Play which is performed by the third grade class here at Sentenial Elementary School. However, at around 7:00 o'clock, two lives were sadly taken while many more were injured.

Ms. Tucker, a teacher here at Sentenial Elementary School for nearly twenty two years, was brutally murdered last night on stage by a homeless man who's now been identified as Thomas Hannah.

Although police investigations started just last night, hours after the event occurred, the full picture of how such an unfortunate disaster could have ever fallen upon such a docile community has already been solved.

Police state that Thomas Hannah had been living in the nearby park which faces opposite to the back of the school for some time now. Within the last approaching weeks, he had begun to use the bathroom in the school's theater room as the back doors to the facility were never properly locked.

However, the usually vacant theater rooms, now filled with the third grade class rehearsing for their play after school, was a new incentive for the back doors to be relocked.

Police say Thomas Hannah was then locked in the theater room, and went undiscovered by hiding in the bathroom and behind the storage section filled with boxes that stacked high enough to keep out most of the light.

This innocent story however, which could shine light on the local homeless problem, took a much darker turn when Thomas Hannah hid amongst the students on stage during the play, wearing one of the student's actual costume.

When suspicion of Thomas Hannah arose from a fellow classmate, Thomas went on a manic rage, revealing a large knife which he carried on him that was then used to stab Ms. Tucker thirty six times.

Some brave parents rushed onto the stage, and although more injuries were endured, they were able to successfully neutralize Thomas Hannah until the police arrived.

…But that is not the end to this tragic story. The costume which Thomas Hannah hid in to disguise himself as a student, belonged to one of Sentenial Elementary School's third graders whose name we are not going to disclose.

The student had went to the bathroom just before the end of the play, where it is assumed that he encountered Thomas Hannah… and was murdered by the same knife.

His body was discovered hours later, after Thomas Hannah was put into custody, deceased and discretely stuffed into a chest that housed various props and costumes for the theater department.

Everyone is shocked, hurt, and grieving from the loss and damages suffered by the horror of last night— and our hearts go out to everyone affected by the evil that struck this school and the third grade class."

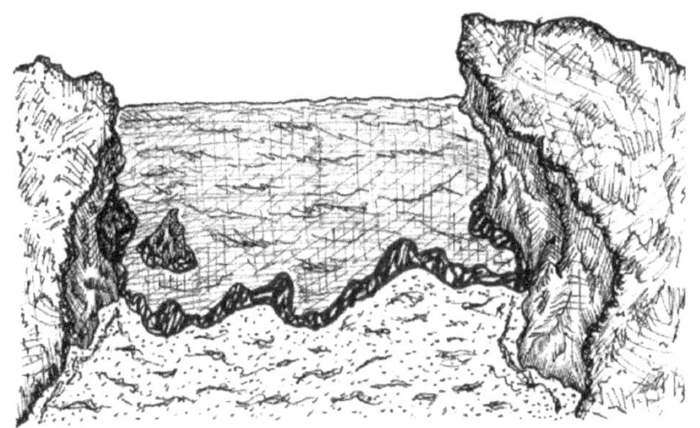

Sea Foam

THE OCEAN RUMBLED with deep, echoing roars as its waters folded and collapsed repetitively against the shore, its ever continuous motion and friction sparking a sense of restless life within the nature of the coast.

As Aubrey observed this near tamed force that was the ocean from the shore of this little town, she had a realization in understanding animism— as there could be no way in which this water wasn't alive.

Whether it be through the essence of its own existence, or perhaps a spirit or deity that was birthed from its natural order or even laid claim to its domain, this shore was surely alive.

Wind caught hold of the tiny salt water beads that erected into the air from the clashing of water on sand, then blew it in an invisible stream towards the road where Aubrey stood watch, connecting the effervescent pearls against her face.

It felt more cooling than cold, more refreshing than dirty, more hydrating than salty, and more alive than inanimate.

And in that moment, the sensation fell over Aubrey— *home.*

She had found the place and had made the right decision after all.

Four years ago, she had graduated college. Before then, she had graduated high school. Work and education were a constant during those younger years of her's, and they carried a depression in being burnt-out as much as they carried a comfort in having security. She never had to think *"what now?"* during then, as the same answer was always at play; When she wasn't at school— she was working; when she finished work— she was studying; when she didn't have to study— she completed homework; and when there was no more homework— she took the time to herself to go out with friends or stay in for self maintenance.

Like everyone else, the personal flows of life were all mixed in there as well, including the laughs, tears, relationships, drama, dreams, sights on the future, or the mucking of the past.

And somehow, as most would agree, the end of college snuck up on her with an elusive speed, followed by a relief to finally close all the books that had been trailing her since kindergarten, and to clock out of all those temporary jobs that simply supported her days towards her degree to acquire the position of a job she actually wanted… or rather, would have for the rest of her life.

Yet it did not play out as smoothly as that.

The years that followed immediately after graduating from college seemed to be her hardest, and at certain times, her darkest.

The structure was now gone. Now, it was just her. And having lived her whole life in nothing but the structure, freedom made her feel more lost than liberated.

The talks and assistance from her parents, with whom she had moved back in with, did not bring any clarity to her path. Nor did seeing the directions that her friends went in as they all seemed to be blind to the fact that they were still caught in the same cycle, oblivious to their own sadness of it, which Aubrey could see very well and clearly from her perspective on the outside.

Those immediate years after graduating college were delicate, but also so vital to her growth. And the initiated would've easily recognized them as her *dark night of the soul*.

It took her some time, but eventually she found her place, found her calling, found her power, and then continued her journey.

For Aubrey, that was to be immersed in nature. Though many would've called it a waste to throw away all those credentials and knowledge collected from the past years as an astute student, Aubrey told them they were wrong.

Her response to them would be, "It would be a waste to throw away my life just *because* of all those credentials and knowledge that will force me into a set way of living."

And so, after some time, or rather, her own time, Aubrey now found herself on the coast of this little town. It was filled with mom and pop shops, a ton of history, a grounded demeanor, and welcoming residents.

The price of rent here leaned more towards the cheaper side, and she already had her eyes set on a house that she could put a downpayment on after perhaps three more years of work.

Life now seemed to fall into place, and the start of her real journey was slowly beginning to take motion.

Having three weeks until she started her new job there, Aubrey took this gap of time as an opportunity to familiarize herself with the people, the town, and everything in-between.

She explored the coast and all of its shores that lined the town. Tried the different brews of coffee available from every cafe along the streets. Learned the names of the locals and their pets who she encountered frequently on walks. And mentally memorized and mapped out all of the street names and roads, including where they connected and where they led.

When speaking to one of the elderly locals, giving affection to his dog as it revealed its belly to her in docile submission, Aubrey took the opportunity to find out a little more about her new home— something which she thought was more appropriate to discover from the mouth of one who had lived there all their life.

Aubrey asked the patron about the safety of the town, if there was much crime that took place or if there were certain areas to be avoided or a time when not to be out late.

But the old-timer told her such things were of no worries in their town. It was quiet and peaceful here.

However, he did reminisce of an older time during his day, and his parents. He said it was different then.

During his childhood, along with his parent's, and his grandparent's before him, children were disappearing almost everyday.

It was unknown whether they were being abducted or kidnapped, and it was never solved whether they were killed or locked away somewhere. The culprit was never caught, and it went on like that for years in that tiny little town of theirs.

So many theories, conspiracies, and rumors swirled around as to who, what, and why this had been going on for as long as it did. Some blamed folklore, some blamed humanity, some thought it must be a single person, while others thought it must be a group. Some thought it must've been a family who lived inside their town with them, while others thought it a family who must've lived outside it.

Common criminal theories involving sex or human trafficking were just as plausible ideas to the residents as the theories thrown around about the government being the main culprit for secret programs or experimentations.

But afterwards, the old-timer quickly put Aubrey's mind to ease on the matter. He reassured her that such things were of the past.

He stated that as technology and the world became more advanced, the disappearances of children steadily declined. With cameras now being able to capture the images of people, cellphones on every person to call loved ones or friends for help, as well as other devices with the capabilities to track anyone or even pick up the DNA the size of a hair, there was no way the kidnappings could ever continue in the same manner which they used to.

And luckily for the town, and at the gratitude of every parent, it just stopped one day all together.

Although this information unsettled Aubrey and her first impressions of the town, the negative feelings did not linger as the patron was right. The world was a different place decades ago, and much more susceptible to such things before the current state of advancement in technology. Even running through a red light on an empty street in the middle of the night will land you a ticket in the mail with your name, picture, and license plate all on it.

After this encounter, Aubrey decided to continue with her exploration of the town in a more positive light and to not ask such questions again, as this place was beautiful and she wished to understand it predominantly in that way.

She learned the shortcuts from her apartment to the nearest restaurants where she had found her favorite items on their menus, or to the breweries that harbored most of the young people that were near her age that hung out to drink and talk after work. Aubrey even found a little bookshop that became her personal favorite place to browse and visit often.

It came as a surprise to her to learn that there was actually a whole lot of history behind this tiny little town she made a home of.

Like the isles of Ireland, it was rich in a fisherman based culture and seemed to produce its own local folklore and suspicions. At one point in time, a lighthouse even stood on one of the nearby cliffs over the shore.

When Aubrey inquired about the lighthouse, the owner of the bookshop told here of where exactly it used to stand on the cliffs. Apparently it had been abandoned since the 1930's, but was bulldozed down in the early 90's when the missing children craze was still occurring.

It was a decision made by the town for the safety of the children. Since the tall structure was a remote place near the water and away from all the neighborhoods, the kids would use it as their destined hangout spot, and even snuck out to it despite the warnings from their parents.

Although the kidnappings were far and few during the 90's, it still felt like the removal of the lighthouse was the last action needed to completely eradicate the abduction dilemma the town had been experiencing over the last decades.

Aubrey decided to purchase one of the folkloric history books on the town, and while she was checking out at the counter, she was recommended to go to where the lighthouse used to stand. The owner said the area was just a concrete mound now, but the view of the ocean from its spot was still beautiful and worth it.

She took on that recommendation and headed to the lighthouse, carrying her new book in hand while the sun still hung high in the sky though hidden behind a blanket of clouds.

When Aubrey arrived near the edge of the shore at the top of the cliff, she discovered the sight to be just as the owner of the bookshop had described— beautiful.

A large and round cement slab lay perfectly flat amongst the jagged and uneven terrain, serving as the viewpoint for the scenery over the cliff's edge.

The ocean swept back and forth from the powerful currents that pushed and pulled, as if caught in the ecstasy of its own eternal dance with itself. And up in the sky, the domain which opposed the sea, clouds fumbled about in their own personal forms of waves and pushes, being ushered along by the wind while simultaneously curdling like cheese.

Though hidden by these very clouds, the sun was still strong and illuminated down on the earth of that little town, igniting with vibrant colors of gray as if filtered and transmuted by those cascading pillows of gas.

Aubrey sat herself down in the center of the cement foundation atop the cliff, and began to peacefully read the contents of her recent purchase.

One thing she always prized herself on, even during her earlier years when she was still trapped in the cycles of school and work, was her uncanny ability to always pick out the best reads.

She had a golden touch when it came to selecting books, and this instance was no different than any other.

The book went into depth on the slow migration and build of population within the town. It spoke of the tales and myths brought over from the traditions belonging to the new settler's previous homelands, as well as the folklore that had been propagated by the various strange phenomena experienced by those living on this coast.

The most prominent and commonly told tale, was the one of sea foam. The writer of the book even put footnotes on the history and symbology that spanned across all the different cultures that immigrated over and the significance of sea foam amongst their own pantheons of beliefs, as sea foam was constantly brought up in the legends that swirled around this town from the beginning of its settlement.

The appearance of sea foam was always connected to something bad happening, serving similar to an omen of sort. When sea foam appeared… so did the troubles.

The correlation of sea foam to evil took on various forms, but it wasn't until the mid 1800's that sea foam began to be associated strictly with the disappearance of children in this town.

Aubrey felt herself become more and more invested with the book as it took this turn, having already formed a relationship with the concept of children disappearing after her talk with the old-timer.

The book went on to tell of how no children were allowed to make contact with the water when the sea foam was rolling into shore. It was a staple of all the residents to keep their children away from it. Should the child make contact with those salty and fluffy suds from the sea, they would be swooped by their ankles and pulled in— never to return.

Feeling almost disappointed by this myth's end, Aubrey set the book down.

She would be lying if she didn't say she was wishing to hear more of a gruesome outcome to the tale. She loved the eerie things about the dangerous unknowns which bumped in the night… but it seemed it was not to be found here in this folklore.

For Aubrey, it was an easy solve and had no connection to the true paranormal in any shape, form, or manner.

The sea foam must've been produced by a stronger tide and the churning of waters deep out at sea. This caused a mass of the stuff to arrive onto the shore, along with a powerful under-toe that followed suit, likely still carrying the same strength that stirred out in the deeper waters. For adults, this is nothing to worry about… but for a small child, such a force could easily pull you out and under.

Of course this shore was crowded with children— this town was originally a fisherman's home, lighthouse and all. Many deaths would be taken by the ocean, as the coast would be the common grounds for everyone to be around. And all of the other suspicions that came with the sea foam had to do with the fishermen's superstitions.

A tide strong enough to pull a child into the waters is sure to do something to the fish. And when fish can't be caught and livelihood isn't made, a stigma for a reason why is created.

As for the children disappearing in the more recent century, it probably was kidnappings. Since no bodies were ever discovered and there was no evidence uncovered of the children ever being killed, she dismissed the idea of a serial killer being the culprit, as they likely would've left their mark—especially if they were building their repute around the mythology of the town's history with sea foam to guide their targeting of children in the first place.

"Yeah" thought Aubrey, "At the very least, they would've thrown their victim's bodies out into the ocean to be discovered bloated upon their return to shore. That would've paid some homage to the sea foam of legends."

Concluding her final thoughts and tying up her last theories, Aubrey picked up her belongings and made her way down the cliff.

With maybe about an hour of sun left in the sky, she kicked off her shoes and walked towards the shore, squeezing the sand between her toes with each step.

She reached the edge of the waters as they barely crossed over the tops of her feet, which still managed to invigorate her with its icy temperature.

She stared off into the ocean over yonder that lay before her, taking in all of its grandness.

How peculiar, she thought, that she should end up here after this long journey of life she had experienced, and for it to only now feel like it was truly beginning.

Just then, a new sensation struck against her feet other than the water casted onto shore.

She looked down and to her surprise, noticed that it was sea foam that lay atop the waters, cascading gently against her ankles as it rode the waves in.

Although Aubrey wish to stay there and observe the phenomena and enjoy its new sensation against her skin, it was now getting dark and she desired to return home.

The last of the sea foam waves hit upon her shins, calling a perfect ending to her night out on the beach. She turned around to face the town in the near distance, then took her first step out of the water and towards her march back home.

But her second step never came to follow.

Before Aubrey could fully lift her foot out of the water, a writhing grip snatched her by her ankle— tight and firm it held.

Life had never been a mysterious matter for Aubrey. There were no aliens, no such things as ghosts, fairies were made up for children, demons and angels were no more real than god, and legends were just human fantasies created by misunderstandings.

Life was simple, life was explanatory, life was logical and scientific. So when it felt like a hand had its cold fingers locked around her ankle, Aubrey did not panic nor think anything deeper of it. In fact, the first thoughts that popped into her head was the imaginary image that her foot had sunk into the sand from its softness in the water, and that it was from this suction that she was trapped in place.

When the grip grew stronger, however, and her struggles and pulls to lift her leg up out of the water proved fruitless, her mind then took to the idea of a marine animal that might've had hold of her ankle.

This set in a panic, and just when Aubrey was about to scream, the mysterious force pulled her down, submerging her completely under the water.

She couldn't breath nor see anything, but she felt the purging ice of the frigid waters fill her lungs as she gasped for air, and felt a stinging sensation burn her eyes profusely as she tried to open them underwater and see what was going on while being rag-dolled through the ocean.

She knew not what direction she was going in, only the simple fact that she was being dragged under the water somewhere by something.

Aubrey's mind raced in a strange disassociated manner— she was aware of the cold water she was submerged under, aware of the fact that she kept swallowing the undrinkable sea, sensed the burning of her eyes from its salt, and knew that her ankle was about to break from whatever had hold of it and the rough manner in which it pulled her by it… but she felt none of the pain.

Instead, it was all a quiet internal dialogue with herself, one where she tried to figure out what kind of marine animal was doing this to her and how she could have forgotten of its danger and not known better than to avoid a death by its hand.

In reality, it was a mere thirty seconds that had passed, but to Aubrey it felt like countless minutes before the swirls of darkness under the water showed a dim glow of light from the nearby surface.

It was then that she was flung up out of the waters and able to observe the black rock surrounding her entirety for an instance before landing hard against the very jagged stone.

Finally out from under the water, Aubrey was able to purge out the salty waters that had filled her lungs and catch her breath.

As she regurgitated, Aubrey was slowly able to regain her senses as her consciousness returned to her body and grounded itself from of the once abstract confines of her mind and thoughts.

Immediately a repugnant odor hit her nose, one that smelt like the decay of the ocean and the bacteria brought only by the sea. Her ears were flooded with the unholy sounds of wailing, a symphony sung only by agony and suffering with no words— just sounds, sounds of dread and what she could only describe as confused souls that felt eternally lost.

When her sight caught up with the rest of her senses to the present moment of being, she was finally able to observe her surroundings.

She was in a cave, a sea cave of some sort to be exact. Its rocky formation was jagged and held no elegance, while the coloring of said stone was of a dark blue hue no different than the shades of midnight.

Pools that were obviously connected to the ocean were scattered about the ground, swishing and swirling from the unseen movements of the currents they were connected to, as they shared their motion with the ocean beyond.

Silver light illuminated the cave by a vast opening at the top of the rock ceiling from which the moon casted its rays through.

Sense of touch was the last sense to return to Aubrey, arriving with a barrage of stinging in her eyes, calling forth a furious rub to them.

The intense burning sensation then began to sprout about in different areas of Aubrey's body, due to the many cuts she had endured from the collision with the sharp rock surface upon her landing, as well as the friction she endured while be dragged across the coarse sand of the ocean's floor.

While her eyes were still closed and caressed by her hands, tears pouring from the ducts to flush out the harmful foreign water that had breached their naturally lubricated surface, the sounds and smells of the cave once again invaded Aubrey's sanity.

Before she had a chance to reopen her eyes to observe what exactly was the source for these sounds of horrors and abominable scent, she was grabbed by the hair on the back of her head and pulled across the cave.

She let out screams in response, not based in fear or pain, but rather from an organic reaction of confusion.

"Quiet down, children! Mommy's back!"

Aubrey's instinct broke down the details of the voice that spoke in a natural response for any human's attempt at survival. Her brain picked up on every detail of its sound within those two sentences to place an image, face, and psyche on whoever spoke them— with which she could possibly use to understand her situation better and discover a way to live through it, should her life be threatened here and by this person.

It was a woman's voice, old and crone, and the words that passed her vocal chords to vibrate out of her mouth sounded rough and jagged— like the very rock cave they were in now.

It sounded frail by way of it coming from a body far past its prime, but without the slightest give to a body lacking power.

Power was a certainly in the cards of whoever spoke. This was made evident not by the choice of words nor demeanor of tone, but rather from the speaker them self— if aura could be something that was not just seen but also heard, then that is how Aubrey would describe it in this context now.

"My little babies! It's been so long since I've brought you all a gift! You must be so excited! That's why you're creating such a ruckus!" the woman laughed as she ceased the dragging of Aubrey.

It wasn't until the woman stopped pulling Aubrey by her hair and set her down that Aubrey was able to process the abnormality in the idea that a frail old lady was strong enough to drag about like she weighed nothing. And this very thought created a chain of other thoughts within her head, such as wondering if this was the same thing that had dragged her out into the water from the beach, and how could this woman have also been able to drag her in such a manner under the water while having to swim herself?

All these oddities seemed to become more clustered and confusing during her barrage of attempts to make sense of things, as she failed to put any pieces together that we're logical with the little information she had.

"Now, let's get you in place" said the old woman's voice, followed by the sensation of Aubrey's wrists being shoved into what could be best described as pockets or gaps within the rock bed she was set upon, acting as a trap that pinned her fleshy appendages in place with sharp edges pushing into her skin, making any force or struggle to get out only cause her pain.

This was when Aubrey was finally able to open her eyes for the second time since being flung out of the water and into the cave, and the first thing to fill her sight was the woman figure who she could only assume must've been her captor.

Her initial suspicions on her captor's physical appearance were correct… but could've never successfully imagined the face or body that stood before her eyes now.

The woman was old, wrinkled, and decrepit. Her skin, though wrinkled, did not appear thin like paper, but rather thick and bloated in its internal folds onto itself. It seemed so contrasting that such thick skin was on such a skinny body, as if the the body was old but the soul who wore it was ever young and powerful.

The old woman's eyes were a grey-blue, and no different than her skin, their coloring reflected an old age while their polished gleam spoke of an unwavering vibrancy of energy.

Her hair was long, messy, unkept and unclean— ash-colored like clouds heavy with rain, while black strands peppered sparsely through it.

Though some parts of her hair were matted down from being wet with water, it had all almost completely dried up in the short time they had surfaced, and was continuing to do so with multiple sections lifting up in their scraggily volume, bent and damaged.

The old woman's body was uncannily thin, with the thick wrinkled skin appearing to lie on top of nothing but bones. She wore a baggy black rag of some sort that covered her torso and knees but nothing more.

Her smile was imperfect, with teeth stained black and gums corrupted into a fleshy purple color.

The Sea Hag stared into Aubrey's eyes while standing directly in front of her face.

Her open mouth smelt like the rot of a washed up sea creature that was decaying in the sun on the shore, causing Aubrey to turn her head in a fuss as her stomach knotted on empty contents, wishing to twist up something in a gagging response.

"Ahh, there she is! Awake and alive!" said the Sea Hag, revealing a European accent attached to her words that Aubrey just now noticed.

She began to touch and inspect Aubrey's face, dragging her thumb and index finger across her cheeks and hooking under her chin, "Good. Yes. Young, healthy, beautiful. So perfect."

The Sea Hag turned around and began walking towards the center of the cave, "What do you think, lovelies? Isn't she perfect? I think she'd make a lovely big sister!"

Aubrey took this opportunity to see the manner in which her wrists were bound in place that kept her trapped.

Turning her head to both sides, she saw that what she had felt earlier and the image that had come to mind when being placed there was correct. The stone she laid upon was jagged, with cavities laced about it like lava rock. And her hands and wrists had been shoved into one of those pockets, pinned down by the sharp edges that faced inward, threatening to cut her wrists open should she fight or resist their prison-like grasps.

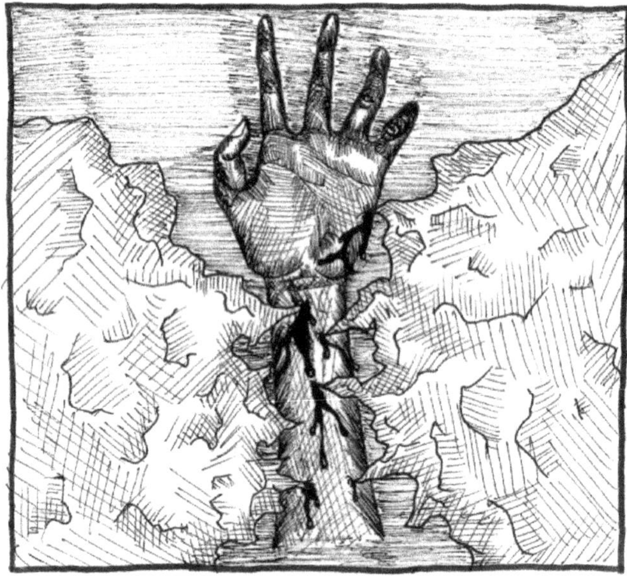

"You're older than I prefer" said the Sea Hag, turning to face Aubrey from the center of the cave while the moonlight set upon her like the spotlight of a stage, "I guess you'll make for a *big* big sister! It's been so long since I've been able to give my children another sibling. They love when the family gets bigger. What do you think, kids? Would you like for her to be your new big sister!?"

The Sea Hag raised her arms up in dramatic display as a strange, drone-like buzz of swarming flies started to fill the cave… only it was more than just a buzzing.

The louder it grew, the more distinct the sound became, revealing its origins and source for the oddness of its sound.

Aubrey changed her gaze from the Sea Hag to the walls of the cave that boxed them in, and noticed from what, or rather— whom, the sounds were coming from.

All along the walls of the cave were… children. But that's not the right way to describe them, for they were not children anymore, at least, not completely children.

Plastered onto the walls like barnacle, consumed by shells or whatever the hell those organic capsules were that held their bodies up there, lied dozens upon dozens of children— all disfigured in a grotesque way.

Their bodies seemed to be mutating and changing in a horrific and almost torturous manner. They were transfigured, their bodies trapped in the process of some sort of transmutation similar to a caterpillar blossoming into a butterfly— with the barnacle crustacean that glued them to the walls being their cocoon.

They screamed and moaned in pain, though it appeared they no longer recognized the reality of the situation that they were in. Their wails were that of lost souls, having forgotten who and what they truly were after years of pain and disfigurement.

There was no more consciousness in their being, as Aubrey observed, and they simply existed in this dreadful state of agony for who knows how long as their bodies endured the non-consensual changes.

"What… is this place?" asked Aubrey on the verge of tears.

"Home! Our home! Your home! This is my family, these are my children, and you have been blessed to join us! My sea foam has not touched the shores in many years… I fear the world is changing, and the land, weather and spirits with it.

Why the sea foam, my fingers of the tides, is no longer able to reach out onto the sands, defeats me. There's changes in that world out there that I cannot conceive, and I must accept them as a barrier to my reach and what it used to be.

But all is well. All is fine! You… just might be the last of whom my sea foam ever touches. But that is okay. All is well! Though you're older than I'd prefer for my family, every family needs a big sister that can look after all their siblings when the mother croaks, and that is you, dear girl."

The Sea Hag then approached Aubrey, with excitement that caused deranged sways in her shuffle forward. This sparked more fear within Aubrey, causing her to pull her restrained wrists in a struggle.

The rock pierced into her flesh and blood began to flow out, a nasty reminder to Aubrey of her detainment.

"No, no! Don't struggle! It will only hurt you! You are family, you are with us now. We don't want you to hurt or suffer. Just relax, relax."

Aubrey ceased her pulling and let her wrists fall back into the cavities. Tears now streamed down her face, and upon seeing them, the Sea Hag donned a face of concern as though uncomforted by the sight, then turned away as if burdened by an internal guilt.

"It… will hurt" said the Sea Hag without any confidence in her voice, making it sound as though that statement was more of a confession, "But it's necessary for the process."

She turned back around to face Aubrey, "You *have* to change to be a part of the family. You can't live within the sea at full capacity in your current form. You can't live long in general in that body. Time will rot it, and the ocean will excel its deterioration. You *must* change… it is the only way you can live, the only way any of my children can continue to live.

The transformation is painful, and it is not a short process. But after enough time has passed, sixty years to be exact, you will emerge complete. And the entire ocean will be your playground, and the world's surface may also be your terrain of pleasure if you choose. Your life will not be a prison restricted to the common time span of an ordinary human, nor to the disease and ailments susceptible to the flesh of common man.

I will make you whole. I will make you better. I will make you family. And I apologize for this dearly, for I do not like hurting or causing pain to any of my children… but that is exactly what you must endure before the lifetime of a new freedom you will be able to experience."

Aubrey began to plead, cry, and bargain with the Sea Hag. She was consumed with fear at the thought of becoming like those kids, plastered by barnacle onto the walls of the cave, and dreaded the thought of the pain she would experience like them— the loss of her mind that would surely follow like all of theirs' did.

"I know, I know. You're scared and already in pain, but it's just the beginning. Everyone reacts the same. When you emerge in due time, anew, you will feel different and be different from who you are now. You will come to love your new form and new life, and us, your new family.

Some of my children have already blossomed and are out in the sea as we speak. And look, there and there" said the Sea Hag, pointing to specific children on the wall, "They are almost ready and nearly fully transformed. They are at the end of the process and will be able to go out soon!

We'll start now so you don't have to suffer the wait any longer" she caressed Aubrey's cheek one last time, "Sixty years, I promise. Then you will have the entire fruit of the sea at your hand."

The Sea Hag scurried off into one of the channeling tunnels of the cave, and returned with a book, an ivory dagger, and a handful of bottled concoctions in various colors.

She cut her own hand with the dagger and then drew a circle in blood on the rocky floor where the moonlight casted its rays upon. She scribbled strange markings both on the inside and the outside of the circle, which Aubrey knew nothing about in regard to their meanings, then began to flip through her book while mumbling some words— occasionally taking swigs from specific bottled concoctions she uncorked.

While the Sea Hag went about this process, Aubrey struggled, fought, kicked and screamed.

She watched the trapped children wiggle and worm in place, and listened to their haunting groans echo and bounce off the walls, unable to come to terms with this being her fate as well.

She cried and wept and continued to bleed from her wrists, as all the hope in life she had attained over the recent years fled away… just like that.

She thought back on those years after graduating college and on those moments when it felt like things were finally coming together. She looked back on those memories of when she had first arrived at the small town with nostalgia, and how tranquil her new home had seemed.

She envied the others who lived in that town that were oblivious to this horrific truth she had discovered, and even felt envious towards those who were still caught in the cycle of school and work which she once hated, as even they knew nothing of this nightmare.

And then she remembered the sea. That first time she pulled her car over onto the side of the road when she arrived at the small town, and what is was like when she watched and listened to the ocean crash against the coast— feeling its little beads of salt water blow against her face from the winds.

She cherished that memory the most for the way the ocean felt in that moment, the animism she gave it, and the benevolence it held in its nature.

That is how she wished to know and remember the ocean by now— not this other truth which also existed. Surely the ocean was aware of this, but such a horror could not reflect its entirety, and Aubrey held within her heart that the sea she felt living that day she pulled over on the road was not a part of this at all. Life held both good and evil, and the living ocean was no different.

She whispered under her breath as she finally gave up, "I choose to see you" to herself, but also in message towards the ocean.

And that is when she felt it, or perhaps heard it, or rather— awoke to it; a message calling out back to her.

No real words could describe it, but Aubrey knew what it was by instinct of the soul.

She looked up at one of the pools in the cave that swooshed with the tides of the ocean, and sensed it once again. It called to her in a strange manner, as if it said *"Come to me"*. As if it wished to save her. As if it heard and recognized her choice in seeing its living nature and the side which she experienced that day when she first looked out into the sea.

There was no doubt about it now to Aubrey. Even animism seemed almost disrespectful as it comes with the intention of a belief system as opposed to it being the obvious— for the ocean truly *was* alive, at least this part of it. And it was currently reaching out its hand to her, no different than how the Sea Hag had reached its deceptive sea foam fingers to her earlier.

It called to Aubrey, a sensation like open arms or an extended hand, wishing to save her from this cursed place— wanting to protect her from this other side that existed in the ever-vast universe of the sea.

Aubrey knew that her only chance at life and escaping this situation was to go to it, and so that is exactly what she did.

Ignoring the pain of the piercing rock which ripped her flesh apart as she pulled her wrists out of the cavities they were trapped in, and not even looking down at her foot which rolled as if broken at the ankle from when she was dragged under water and into this cave, Aubrey ran and plunged into the tiny pool of water while the screams of the Sea Hag taking notice of this trailed behind her!

As soon as she splashed into the salty oasis, Aubrey experienced the sensation of being dragged under the ocean once again, only this time it was far less invasive to her being.

She was swooshed around, unable to see what or where she was going, or how she was being guided through the waters, but the sensation of it all was very apparent. It felt conscious— this force that was moving her about. It was strong and full of intent, obvious in its protective manner of taking her out of the cave's underwater tunnel and far away from the place the Sea Hag dwelled.

She kept her eyes closed the entire time, giving herself fully into the trust of the ocean, feeling a true sense of peace and not needing to worry as she was being cared for and protected in this moment by a power far greater than any she had ever experienced before. A power that made her not even worry or fear about the possible pursuit of the Sea Hag. She knew by the inherent nature within her soul, that such a thing was impossible. That she had truly escaped, and that this force, the Sea, would not let anything harm her as it took her away.

Aubrey almost forgot entirely that she was in the hands of the ocean, and didn't even hold onto the recent encounter with the Sea Hag as she was carried away.

This travel under the water in the hands of this giant entity made it easy for her to fall into a peaceful trance, similar to that of being a baby back in the wafting juices of the womb.

It wasn't until she felt the cold air exposed upon her head as she breached the surface that Aubrey remembered she actually existed.

She opened her eyes and saw the beach of the small town in front of her, the one she chose to call home.

Slowly, the waves carried her in and back onto the shore.

Once she drew closer to the shore, she was able to feel the sand beneath her feet and walk upon its ground while the waters assisted in ushering her forward and back onto land.

Her whole body hummed as it left the Ocean's gentle hand. Her foot no longer rolled when she walked on it, although a purplish-pink hue did ring around its stump. Her wrists no longer bled out nor were cut open, but instead bore a pearly scare, the color of angel flesh coral, from where she had broken free during her imprisonment. And it seemed that all the various cuts she once had on her body had also faded away, fully gone with no residual markings as they were nothing too grave or ravenous like her other injuries.

The Ocean had not only saved her, but healed her human body as well— perhaps not fully, but enough so that she could return to land in a manner that was not too broken from how she was originally taken.

As she walked out of the waters and across the beach, Aubrey looked back at the ocean, and gave a gentle smile to it, feeling nothing but love and thanks towards its entity for everything that had just occurred and its role in saving her.

She felt a genuine connection to the ocean now, and for the first time in her life, the world. Though what she had just experienced was a thing of nightmares that she would never forget, it was nothing compared to the warm, nursing sensation of a bond she had just formed with the animated life of this water on the coast.

Now she knew that this town, or rather, the waters just beside it, was truly her place of home.

His Chalice, the Count

THE WOOD IN the fireplace crackled and split with loud, sudden pops. Its heat bursted outward into the room it faced, bringing with it a warmth similar to that of an exotic tea, whose spices fill the nostrils from its rising steam.

Being the largest source of light, the fireplace casted the majority of illumination upon the contents within the room, while thoughtfully placed candles lit the smaller areas that surrounded the dinner table.

The candles were not to be under appreciated, however, as their flickers created the parade of spectacles within the otherwise dark ambiance of the room. The gold leaf that lined the frames of portraits and paintings on the walls would reflect their shine like fiery, lightning bugs of amber. And the cascading silver decor which held the very candlesticks or lined the bases of busts, would glint back the wavering expansions and compressions of those neighboring flames like twinkling stars.

Only two men sat at the table which rested in the center of this room; one dressed in a black suit; the other in a brown.

The man in the black suit was the owner of this fine estate which they currently occupied. He was tall and handsome, with strong masculine features in every sense of the description. But it was not in a way of being overbearing nor overtly intimidating. Rather, his bold masculine features could be best described as the kind of assets beheld by those strong souls in the old world, whose very birth was meant for a role of leadership. Late of age with an obvious give to his maturity, this venerable quality only added to his handsome appearance as opposed to the deterioration of it.

The name of this man in the black suit was Count Solin Borislav Georgiev of Baden-Wurttemberg.

And the man in the brown suit, a guest of the Count, was named Gordon Eden. He was an aristocrat, but prided himself in being a scholar.

Though different in their respective place of origin, and even different in height of the social pedestal they stood on within their class, both of these men had one thing in common for which they sat in that glowing room now, facing opposite of each other at the dinner table— they were philosophers.

Evening had just set in, and although there were no windows in this room, the feel of night was very apparent.

Two chalices filled with red spirits stood on the table; one placed in front of Count Solin; and the other in front of Gordon.

"Thank you for having me tonight, Count Solin" said Gordon, "I've been looking forward to this conversation for quite some time now. A discussion amongst philosophers always makes for a pleasant evening. But to be speaking with one whose views have opened my own mind in ways which no other author or fellow peer has yet to do in the same rarified way… it's a different kind of treat, truly."

Count Solin smiled as he gestured his chalice towards Gordon across the table before taking a sip, "Very kind words, Mr. Eden. I appreciate the gratification, though such things have never fallen comfortably with me. 'Tis not even a matter of humbleness, rather, I find no justification to the praises that have come my way because of my thoughts on life.

We are philosophers. Theorizing on the aspects and truths of life and death is what we do. We'd be kings— in fact, gods by now, if we were exalted every time we spoke our revelations aloud during their passings."

"Well, in that case I will refrain from any further extolment while we speak. Though I should warn, I do plan on questioning, challenging, and even disagreeing with the assemblage of perspectives that shall be laid out here on this table tonight."

Count Solin laughed, "I would want nothing else. From where would growth occur if the path needn't any carving? I hope the majority of my thoughts are not accepted by your palate, and I hope you find every reason to disagree with what I say.

If not, then what was the point of me having gone through these life experiences in which I endured to come up with my philosophies, or the acquiring of the said stories to back them up, for that matter?

That's not to say that *you* make them worth something. However, you could say that you make them have a joint purpose by not only serving me... should they also be able to sway your mind, that is."

"And to you, the same" said Gordon, raising his chalice to the Count, "With luck, wine, and a night full of discussion, perhaps we both can gain a new perspective and maybe even a higher understanding on this game called life, which we've both been participating in since the first breath of our births."

Count Solin nodded, "Yes, let's" he said while toasting his chalice back, "Are you hungry? I am expecting we'll be here for quite awhile, and if you have not eaten then I'd like to be an honorable host."

"Oh it's fine, I assure you."

"Have you eaten?" asked Count Solin, not more sternly, but rather with a pulling for absolute truth on Gordon's part.

"…No. I have not. But it is late within the hour and I would not put you through any trouble of organizing a meal."

"Nonsense" Count Solin picked up a silver bell that sat on the table and rang it six times from three flicks of his wrist, "My servants have no quarrel with later hours, nor does my cook. I raise sheep on my property, so no matter the time or day, I have the freshest cut of meat in stock."

A servant came into the room moments later, young and beautiful to Gordon's surprise, then left to go wake the cook after being instructed for a lamb chop cooked rare along with another pitcher of wine.

"Now, with food and drink on its way, let us begin" said the Count, but he paused briefly as he redirected his attention back to Gordon, "No. I am not sleeping with the maids nor do I partake in any kind of fornication with my workers."

Gordon's blush could've been seen even if the glow from the candles and fireplace didn't paint a layer of orange over the entirety of the room, "Oh, I didn—"

"It doesn't take a sharp eye to see the thoughts of a man, and certainly not a mindreader to know where they twist and turn into the path of assumption."

Gordon bore a uncomfortable smile of agreement.

"I have a full staff" continued the Count, "More than most for an estate of this size. Like any great philosopher and the many before us, I am up late most nights. And heavy do new thoughts rain down under those gleam of stars which I lay my eyes upon.

Most of my workers who do their duties at night are younger. They are not weighed down by the ringing of the bell at hours when most are asleep.

Those who are older and have been in this profession for longer work during the hours of light. It's not that they can't work past the fall of the sun, but it is harder on them.

I have the means to employ both, which makes everyone's job easier, so I do. This is my home, and I make sure to take good care of it by hiring people who can do the same.

Now, with that out of the way, once again, shall we begin?"

Gordon smiled in agreement, "For philosophers, a conversation can last days and cover the many scopes of the existentialism process. However, ironically enough, the beginning of such conversations always seem to be the hardest part. With so many branches on the tree of life to grab at, where does one begin."

"Well, at the roots, of course" responded the Count, "That is where the true beginning actually lies."

"The roots it is, then" said Gordon, "So, where did it all happen for you? What was it or when was it you had that first experience which put you on the path of asking *'why'*?"

"I was always bound to ask 'why' as it would seem, such is the way of being born into a gypsy family."

"I thought you were Bulgarian, are you not? Your surname gave me a different impression" inquired Gordon.

"My father was, yes. And so am I. But my mother was Romanian, and it was there I was born.

There lies my heart. And when I shall pass in due time, it is Romania where my soul shall return home to."

"I see. Continue, please."

"Well" began the Count, "Though I now hold a title of nobility, my childhood was anything but. We were gypsies, my family, born and raised in a caravan. The land itself becomes your home when you do not restrain yourself to a house... as I do now.

Magick is in our blood and flows throughout our everyday of life. From reading the leaves at the bottom of the cup after a serving of tea in the morning, to following the black birds to a new location for camp, to using the herbs sprung in the wild to heal any alignment.

When life crosses with the esoteric, there are certain moments in which you pause to make sense of the damn thing.

It's an interesting scale that tips back and forth, the esoteric.

On one hand, you don't question anything. All the chaos, all the madness, all the signs that exist just as much as you or I do— there's no need for an explanation.

And on the other hand, you have this burning desire to understand from where these things come from— that *other* world so close to ours from where they peek in through or slip out of to reach us.

It's a balance."

"And when did that point of crossing paths happen that lead you to be known amongst our peers and wind up a Count in Germany?"

Count Solin scoffed, not so much at Gordon, but more towards his own thoughts on the matter that stirred about his head from the question, "Take a look in your glass" he said.

Gordon did as the Count instructed.

"What do you see? What is in the glass?" asked the Count.

"Wine" answered Gordon, "I see juice that raises the spirits, beckons the tears, calls forth the rage, inspires the courage, slurs the tongue, crosses the eyes, and incites the lust. I see Dionysus' nectar."

The Count nodded to the impressive response, "Look again. Really focus this time. For in that glass... is you."

Gordon looked once more into the chalice and now caught sight of his own reflection.

His initial thought to this sight was that he wished he had caught onto what the Count meant the first time he asked, since he had wished to prove that he too was on the same level of the Count in introspective thought.

His second thought was that he needed a cleaner shave to better present himself to society.

And his third thought was almost like a sense of awareness felt from when one first discovers their own reflection in a mirror.

"Now that you see yourself, who is that man?" asked the Count.

"He's a man whose mind wonders the very space of eternity. A boy who saw lightning strike a hill, felt the heat of the embers left over by the grand force, whose shoulders tightened and clung to the belly of his earlobes when the thunder followed, whose mother ushered him inside with pure maternal fear, all while the boy felt a kind of fright that is surely to be followed by a larger source of awe" answered Gordon.

"Who threw that lightning, Mr. Eden, do you know?

Was it Mother Nature in her indifferent wrath, lashing at her own ground from her mighty sky?

Was it God, angered by the sins of man— or perhaps one of His angels who has grown tired of His creation?

Was it by a demon who has grown tired of being seen as a lesser being, a common misconception from the misguided understanding of the true term of 'low'?

Was it a different god, one who's known to reign over the sky and hold domain in the clouds?

Was it a tear in the veil and a brief taste of what powers and horrors lie on the other side?

Was it the Universe reaching out to a child to spark him on his path, a path that is already marked in destiny's book?

Or was it man himself— the child himself? A piece of his own mind escaping from the confines of mere thought and the realm of dreams, all to behold his true infinity and power that has been forgotten during the process of an immortal soul being stuffed inside a mortal shell?"

"Honestly, I do not know how to respond to that, let alone know its answer" admitted Gordon, "And for that exact reason, I can estimate it is why I became a philosopher… I am still trying to find it."

"Then please, look into your glass and tell me what you see" beckoned the Count again.

Gordon looked at his reflection once more, "I see a man who has achieved high status through his own merits, but still feels like a fraud.

I see a large estate where he grew up, with four dogs and three cats. I see eight horses and six rabbits. I see a garden big enough to hide from any adult in. I hear the infidelity of his father in that garden, from behind the table of floras and under the trimmed hedges.

I see his mother's tears and her fake smiles.

I see his father's pride and his fake humbleness.

I see his childhood, and him wishing to be of high mind through achievement and not of class.

I see his diploma and him shaking hands with the professors after years of education.

I see him realizing during another banquet that he is still surrounded by his father and his mother despite having become a scholar.

I see a lost sheep that never truly left that large estate or that big garden, and is still surrounded by those same animals and flowers, only they too can boast of an education now and its achievement…"

"And how does that make you feel?" asked the Count.

"Displeased" answered Gordon.

"Come now. For the first time since your discovery of being a lost sheep, you are now amongst another, though cut of a different wool. There's no false words to be said here, nor smiles nor humble play.

Throw your glass against the wall, if you must. Scream to heavens with a madness that would bring God out of His throne and down to this cursed earth to smite you with his bare hands against your flesh! Cry like your mother never could have, with the absolute freedom of not hiding a single drop!

So I'll ask once again; How does that make you feel, Gordon Eden?"

Gordon grabbed his chalice, knuckles white from his tight grip of rage, "I feel angry. I feel hateful!

I feel like this chalice, here— only I am spilling from an overfill of spite that I harbor towards to the world.

And don't even get me started on God. The bastard who made it! The fool who asks for me to bend my knee and sing His songs of worship!

You know just as well as I do that he is real, and a nasty being at that.

And since you too are of a different cut of wool and beckon forth the truth of my tongue, then I fear no judgment in your presence when I say that you also know that He is not the only one!

Pantheons of gods, pantheons of demons, pantheons of spirits and beings. I don't know what daimon casted down that bolt of lightning when I was a child, but I wish it struck the pigs I have been surrounded by in this lifetime instead of my favorite green hill.

I question life and existence like any other true philosopher, and yet the likes of them all would laugh at and ruin both you or myself for even whispering the esoteric within the same sentence of these topics!

And I hate that I plume you for your humble upbringings, as I truly mean not to patronize you when I say; That only from a man like you can I talk like this.

Aristocrats would say it's because you have no manners and that curse upon the tongue is common talk to you, but no! I disagree! I believe that those who have less fortune are raised to speak with their souls! Speak with their hearts! Speak their truth!

No fake smiles! When you're angry, you say 'fuck all!'. When you're sad, you cry and you don't hide the tears! When you're humble, you truly aren't even aware of it, hence its very definition!

So trust me when I say, I do not patronize you, Count Solin… I *glow*. I glow my truth because I am finally not a sheep in that ungodly flock anymore while in your presence.

I am a man, speaking to another man. And we are talking about philosophy, and for once in my life, to the fullest degree of its expression."

Gordon's shoulders fell heavy as that last sentence left his lips, making him realize he had actually ran himself out of breath from that rant, and caused his tongue to become dry.

He kept his gaze low, not wanting to meet the Count's while he still panted in minor exhaustion and took vigorous gulps of his wine which had never tasted better in his life.

"Thank you, Mr. Eden. *Now* our conversation has begun" said the Count.

Gordon wiped the sanguine elixir from his mouth and surrounding facial hair, "I must apologize. I did not mean to become hysteric."

"No. That was no hysteria, that was you speaking from your soul."

"Yes, and though I stick to what I said, still, I must maintain proper conduct. I wish not to excuse myself if I completely break the peace at this table."

"Mr. Eden, let us indulge in that very concept. Good and bad, high and low, mighty and weak.

I did not find nor could sense a shred of what the common man would call 'darkness' among your words or the manner in which they were delivered. In fact, returning to the esoteric, I don't believe a majority of man ever really encounters true evil.

Bad? Yes.

Undoubtedly, every creature that walks this ground encounters bad— even terrible things in its lifetime.

But evil? Hardly.

You see, evil… is a force. And true evil is the mirror opposite of unconditional love.

True evil has no agenda, no explanation, no reason— it simply is evil for the sake of evil and nothing more.

And I expect no man to understand that concept any better than man can grasp the full capacity of how limitless infinity is.

True evil is such a rare phenomena, that a man is changed forever should he ever be exposed to whatever end of it. Even a distant roar of true evil is more than enough to be a… lightning bolt, so to say."

Gordon took another sip from his chalice, with a gentle nod in agreement, "Mhm. I could see that. Man has no grasp of true evil, so hardship and pain takes its title in place.

But because my outburst just now was not true evil, means it is acceptable? People can still be offended, people can still be hurt or killed. Just because acts, things, or words are not true evil, does not mean they can't produce the effect for which they have adopted the title for in our own eyes. Where do we draw that line, then?"

"Indeed" said the Count, delving further into the subject, "I meant not to neglect the experiences that are on the opposition of order. Nor invalidate the hauntings that mankind is burdened with. However, I find it crucial that man must explore his own darkness solemnly. It is the only way we can begin to write our morals and understand these crossings.

Fill the bouquet, Mr. Eden. Why only roses if we are not just lovers? Why only white if we cannot attend our own funerals? Why only irises when life may be sad but is never just blue?

We carry that very capacity of infinity within ourselves which we cannot comprehend.

We are not just a mood, a moment, an experience, a conversation, a feeling, a thought— we are a collection of them all, constantly building and adding to that collection throughout our lifetime. 'Tis why the old is mature and the young is naive.

Emotions themselves have varying degrees that are not limited to their immediate structure. Surely you've seen a mother cry out of joy for her child. Without a doubt, you've seen a man find happiness from observing another's misfortune. And of course, you've witnessed a parent become infuriated at their child, not because they wanted to hurt the child, but from fear that the child could have hurt them self.

One's own darkness is as much holy as their light. The only way that they can ever learn to control it, is by getting to know it just like everything else.

So explore that side, Mr. Eden. Understand it, for it is yourself, you see?

And the dog who was taught not to bite will draw blood when it inevitably does, for all dogs bite. But the dog who was taught to beware of its bite, discovered how to control the amount of pressure in its jaws— so when it inevitably does bites, it delivers the exact message of intent.

Fill the bouquet with all sorts of flowers, for as any good herbalist knows— to know the language of flowers is to also know the language of poisons" said Count Solin.

"In this day and age, one is not rewarded for such efforts of self discovery" said Gordon, "You're more likely to be exiled, ostracized, or locked in a prison."

"Of course. Only the men in robes and inside secret rooms with secret greetings play at this concept. Or the witches in the fields, dispersed among villages and woods, and other practitioners of the craft alike follow this concept.

But without having the knowledge of its importance or its place within one's life, well, that is why it's so misunderstood. It is not the fear of the self, but rather, the fear of the others that direct most away from the concept.

Strange, this world now and human these days, to value the rewards from others as opposed to the awards they could grant themselves.

…I cross between despicable and sad when I think of it. Sometimes I think pathetic, other times I feel pity."

"I find great shame in saying that from being surrounded by such people for years, I *am* one who has avoided the idea of expressing or indulging in certain aspects of myself for fear of the gaze of others, as opposed to the liberation of myself" admitted Gordon while taking another swig from his chalice, "Perhaps if the world were filled with more men like you, then myself and possibly others would be experiencing a whole different perspective of it by now."

The entrance door to the room then opened and in came the servant with a silver tray, and atop it was a beautiful cut of meat sitting in a pink pool of its own juices.

She brought it over and set it before Gordon, then promptly left after.

"Thank you, Count Solin. This looks delicious!"

The Count waved away Gordon's gratitude in a cordial manner, "Can you discuss while you eat?" he asked.

Gordon nodded as he took his first bite of the pearly pink meat, its drippings wringing out between his teeth like the twisting of a wet cloth.

"Let's return to the infinity, then.

Where is man's place amongst *the others*? Gods, demons, angels, spirits, daimons— these things are no doubt beyond us with a power we cannot touch.

Immortal beings with power, touching elbows with mortal beings who won't even explore their own darkness.

What do we do, then? Us man?

How can we compete? How can we have a share or hold a place? How do we survive and how do we hold our own?"

Gordon washed down the meat with more of the wine, shaking his head in not knowing the answer.

"You must look inward" answered Count Solin to his own question, "If you are not immortal but your soul is, then that is where you will find your power!

That is how you set yourself at their level… and tragic is it, should such a being ever convince you to sell them your soul under the guise of giving you such power, before you can find out that truth for yourself…"

Gordon had finished two thirds of his meal before losing his appetite.

His mouth tasted metallic, setting in a desire for the meat to have been cooked longer, while also losing the desire to continue eating even if it was.

He set his silver utensils down and drank more wine.

The Count, in turn, rang the bell to which the servant returned into the room, "Mr. Eden is done with his meal" said the Count.

The servant nodded and took the platter of unfinished meat and walked out.

"Is such a thing possible?" asked Gordon.

The Count took a sip from his own chalice, "Terrifyingly, yes. Which is why I guess you're hearing my rant now. I feel very strongly on the matter."

"What hope is there for man if such is the case?" asked Gordon.

"Man is his own hope and always should be. Disarray follows whenever he seeks it elsewhere, and it always will follow even if elsewhere temporarily supplies it. For example, look in your glass and tell me what you see."

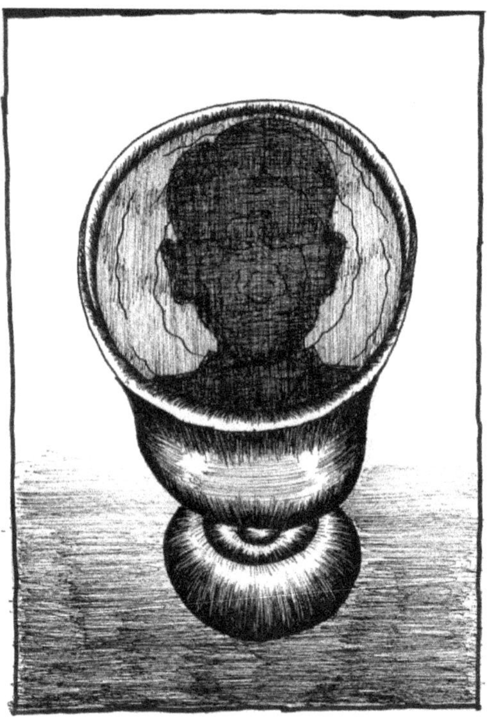

Gordon looked in his glass and stared at his reflection, "I see a man who's fallen lost on his journey. Who's felt like sheep, was surrounded by sheep, and ended up getting lost like one. By consequences of birth and entitlement, has never been able to achieve fulfillment or satisfaction, no matter how hard the work or effort he's made.

I see melancholy laced with hope, or rather, a melancholy derived from hope.

Hopelessness causing more reason for hope, and hope always ending in hopelessness— a sick cycle whose shape is an ouroboros, only it wraps around my neck and is waiting for me to finally have the gall to kick the stool from underneath my feet. A stool made of red oak that the other sheep would judge and either commend or condemn for its artistry and place in the room, as opposed to acknowledging or even understanding the cold body that hangs above it.

I see a man who feels oddly at peace for the first time in his life, over a glass of red wine, undercooked lamb chop, in a dim room with an interesting man who's listened more than he's spoken.

A man who wishes he had more friends like the Count, a man who wishes to *be* friends with the Count."

Count Solin smiled for the first time with flattery since he told Gordon to withhold any gratification at the beginning of their night. That smile seemed different and honest, one which brought a new warmth into the room, "It is you in the glass" said the Count.

"Yes, yes I know. Although I think I should refrain from any more wine. It's starting to get to my head and I wish to maintain decency as a guest in a home that is not mine."

Gordon mirrored the Count in a polar opposite at this time. Though this was the first genuine smile that the Count had presented, this was now the first dishonest thing Gordon had spoken.

Intoxication was not his real reason for ceasing the drink of wine, but rather because he had come to feel sick, nauseas and on the verge of regurgitating.

He attributed it to the meat being too rare for his liking, but wished to say nothing about it as to not offend the Count.

A lightness filled his head, just on the verge of dizziness, while the wine felt heavy in his stomach like syrup, to which Gordon pushed his chalice away, "I apologize, I do not mean to make you drink spirits alone."

"I take no offense at all, Mr. Eden. Your drink is your choice, though I do appreciate your consideration of me in the matter."

While pushing the chalice away, Gordon noticed something very interesting; his glass was still near full to the brim.

It was strange to him, he could've sworn he had drunk at least three cups by now, and yet the wine hadn't decreased in volume by a drop.

How many times had that servant come into the room? And not once did he notice her refill their glasses nor bring that second pitcher of wine for them… only his meal.

"Three times" said Count Solin, "The first when I rang the bell and instructed your meal. The second when she brought it. And the third when she took it away."

Gordon frowned in confusion, "I— I didn't say anything… Count Solin."

"No. You didn't. And you haven't drunk a single glass of wine tonight, either. As I've been trying to tell you, it is *you* in that glass."

Gordon looked within his glass once more, swirling the chalice by its stem and taking notice to how its liquid substance was not the consistency of wine at all.

His stomach churned to the realization and he let go of the chalice, now shoving it away from himself, causing it to tip over and spill its contents all over the table.

"I must also insist that you put the knife down now, and allow my servant to tend to your hand" said Count Solin, casually.

Gordon looked down and noticed that he had a steak knife in his right hand and a multitude of large gashes in his left palm.

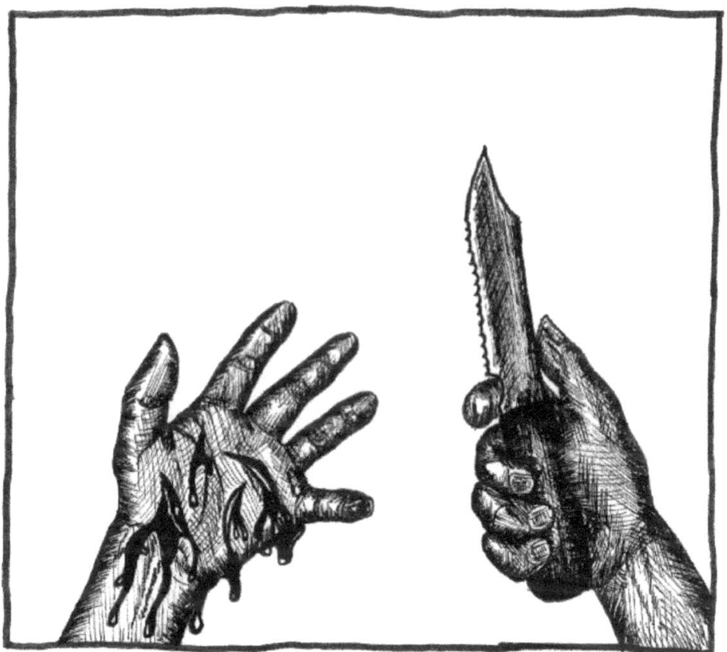

He threw the knife onto the floor in an overwhelming mix of shock, fear and confusion, which all took over him like a shaking lamp before a predator.

The Count, maintaining his same calm composure which he held this entire night, rang the bell with two flicks this time.

The servant entered the room with a piece of ice and a cloth, then proceeded to rub Gordon's palm with the ice before wrapping the cuts tightly with the white cloth, its color transitioning into a salmon pink from the absorption.

She left the room shortly after, leaving the two men to their privacy once more.

Gordon's eyes frantically danced from his hand, to the chalice, to the knife, and to the Count.

"Ease your mind, Gordon Eden, 'Tis like a restless hornet's nest and just as much displeasing to me as it is for you."

Gordon looked at the Count with fear and animosity, "You, this is your work! I—I know of these things! I've heard the tales and the sound accounts of such things! I know what you are!"

"Yes yes, a child of the dark; a feeder of the night; a poacher of the graves. I too have heard of these accounts and the legends and countless names.

Vampire… How childish, all of them."

"What is it you seek from me!?" barked Gordon, "I'd assume my blood, but it seems my sanity is your first course! Is it?"

"No… not any longer" the Count held the silence in the room as he drank from his chalice, a tension for his next words held by the sounds of his swallows, "You revealed many things to me that I couldn't have possibly reached into your soul to retrieve. That is why my best efforts were to have you reveal them yourself, and that you did.

It wasn't long before I knew the kind of man you were and are, Mr. Eden, and made my decision early on in the night that I was not going to feast on your life.

Very few know of my true nature and what I am, and until a few moments ago, neither did you.

My own words spoken at this table were orchestrated for when I chose to reveal it. Look back on my voice, see why I implored you to the thoughts of our philosophical topics, please.

It was all so you could have a better understanding of me in this moment now, just as I have a better understanding of you."

"Why would you breach the privacy of my mind? Surely you have no manners despite your power, for power isn't permission, Count Solin.

And as for my hand and the trickery of consuming my own blood—" Gordon gagged on his words, almost throwing up to the thought of his recent consumption, "The manipulation at play had no reason for any sort of union."

"I told you the hornet's nest of a mind is just as displeasing to me" responded the Count, "I hear those thoughts whether I want to or not. It is not a thing that I choose, it is a burden I endure.

Have you any idea the things that stir about those private confines of a man's mind? I wish not to hear them just as much as they wish to not be heard.

I cannot peer into your soul nor your past. I must invoke your own vulnerability to understand who you truly are, like anyone else would in a conversation or during the ritual of becoming aquatinted with one another.

The drinking of one's own blood tends to help with this natural process, especially when one like I can hear those hidden thoughts. And hopefully it will allow for a better position of knowing that I, too, find blood revolting. It is heavy in the stomach and bleaching in the mouth. I too wish to regurgitate its contents yet I must consume it to live.

So please, Mr. Eden, understand me more."

"I am to understand you by way of trial? While you get the luxury of simply listening to the breath that leaves my mouth as I speak? 'Tis not fair at all!

I have no desire to engage in such trivia at my own expense! You wish to share and be understood yet hand me the knife from the safety of its handle, expecting me to grab it from blade's end?"

Count Solin looked down in a faint show of shame, "No. You are right. That was unfair and not right of me.

If you'd allow, I'll share my part now."

Gordon was still on guard in the presence of the Count, but was interested in what he had to say and gave a nod for him to continue.

"To be around spirits your whole life, to do a dance with the universe and have second sight, to be aware of truths that others call mysticism and alchemists devote their lives to… is such a blessing.

However, it can also be blinding, Gordon.

It was so common, the talking and interacting with *the others*, whether it be through my tea leaves or the very voices and emergences of these beings presenting themselves to me.

With the universe ever at your forefront in its near full form, requiring no journey nor hardship of seeking it out… one can become complacent.

There is no need to strengthen your own soul nor find its value since *the other* is always there. What reason is there to look inward when the universe shows itself fully outward?

I danced with the spirits, with the signs, with the mysticism, with the ghosts, with the deities, and with the universe… until a Devil appeared.

There are many devils, Gordon Eden. For you see, Devil is a title, not the name of a singular being… and I encountered a slick one.

He revealed many truths to me, and one lie.

He showed me how powerless humans were compared to *the other*. How easily we could've been swept away or lacking a force of our own to fight back with when such times would come. How for generations, man has been slight handed by *the other*, taken by *the other*, consumed by *the other*, and so forth.

Then his lies set into my ear— that man needed the strength of *the other* in order to play on their field. That in order to actually hold a place where man would not be toyed with like children, they must in some part, be like *the other*.

…And then the Devil offered me such power. In exchange for my soul, he would give me some of his. And with this power, I would be acknowledged as a force to be reckoned with. I would be at their level, be it the rings of heaven or the gates of hell— my power would be at theirs.

I accepted, naively. And that very exchange was the sole example of their power over us— *knowledge*. For I know now as I wish for you to know too, that within your soul is already that power, you just have to foster it.

And now that I've handed mine away, I am the *real* lost sheep in this plane of existence.

Take back to my words spoken earlier. With these immortal beings, how do we stand a chance or come close to the understandings that they have if we only live a blink of what they would call a moment?

We look within. That is how!

Do not let go and never sell that which is your true power, Gordon, for though I have power on their level, I will never succeed them.

And that is the *true* power of man.

We are not born nor come into existence with a power at their level, no, we are so far from it. But mankind has the ability to grow their power to levels that can surpass *the others*, we simply must foster it first.

What angels do you know of that can summon demons?

What demons do you know of that can beckon forth angels?

What beings do you know of that can contact any god, every god, and even the ones outside of our own universe and realm of reality?

Man is a dangerous creature, and *the others* know it.

We are only dangerous once we acquire the knowledge, and the most dangerous ones are the ones who use it.

Even I look at man differently now.

I have been alive for centuries. I have seen both the worst and the best of mankind. The ugliest and the most beautiful. The pattern and the break. The hopeless and the potential.

I hate mankind with the same verity that I love them with.

I am almost indifferent with my opinion on them, and yet somehow find myself distant from human beings as much as I also still feel connected to them after all these years.

It is like an adult looking down at a child. Yes, we were once them, but no longer. And 'tis not even a matter of size, but of knowledge and maturity— a concoction of experiences and perspectives that separate us from the child.

We understand the child, for we once were the child. We are, in a sense, a direct form of the child that will come to be after many more years of life.

That is my relationship with man.

Perhaps if they too lived for centuries, they would find the fault and clarity in their ways.

And that is why I told you to look within and come to terms with your own darkness.

For so long, I viewed my own as a prison, different to how you would view yours as an animal.

But our darkness is not this foreign thing that takes over and eradicates the mind like rabies. It already is us! We are it! Your left hand is just as much your hand as your right— for it is *yours*.

Love moved me to Germany, and duty had me stay.

I am the watcher of the Black Forest. Many things creep and crawl there. Some wish to get out, others just happen to wonder too far out without any real intention.

I understand it all and have the most knowledge about it. The court magicians understand this, and to some degree, understand me. By order and grace of the King, I have been granted a home here and an honorable duty to protect the rest of its people, who also call this land home, from *the others* that stir about in those woods.

I like you, Gordon Eden. You are different from most of man, you are one of the potentials, one of the beautiful.

I have only encountered one other human who fascinated me in similar way by which you have. Her name was Emilia Songfire, and she was the most wise woman and most powerful witch I have ever encountered, still to this day, both a century before and a century after meeting her.

Despite the rough start to our true introduction, I would like to continue meeting and speaking with you, Gordon Eden. Let us talk life in its fullest forms, now that all the cards are laid out on the table. And should fate have it, possibly become friends" Count Solin then rose from his seat, "The hour is late and the night still young. Would you care to join me on a tour of the Black Forest?

A lightning bolt sparked the awe in you as a child, and I can assure you, the things in those woods have the capacity to spark that same wonder even within a grown man.

So tell me, Mr. Eden, would you like to witness lightning once more?"

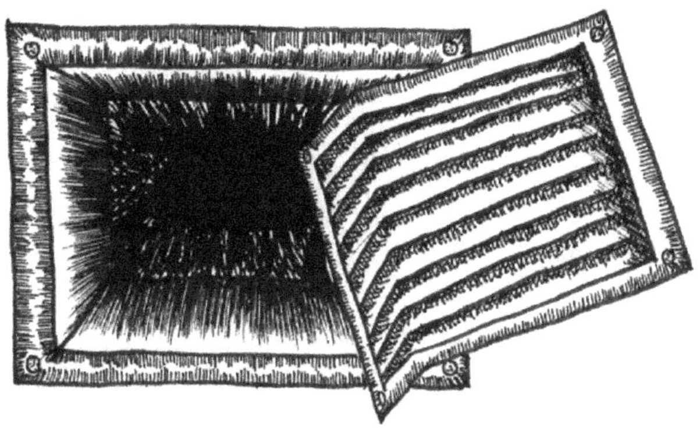

Around the Corner

THE MAN JUST sat there, motionless in the middle of the hallway, its walls a pasty color of yellow and its floors made of a cheap green carpet.

It was a short hallway, with only a couple hundred feet in length that turned into a sharp right corner. What lied around this corner remained a mystery to the man who sat in the middle of its hallway, as he had yet to approach its end and take its turn.

But he had seen countless others do so… and not a single one of them ever returned.

"What is around that corner?" thought the man on the floor.

He wished to know where it led or who was on the other side of it, but he couldn't find the courage within himself to look.

It was an odd hunch that stirred within him, one that made him apprehensive about that corner. He felt it deep in his gut, like an instinct derived from the entire human race that existed before him, and from all of his ancestors who survived and reproduced in sequence towards his current existence.

They had survived from a fear of danger, and a knowing of danger.

Every one of them before him must've had moments like these, when they knew not to go *there*— that indiscriminate place that surely held their doom.

And so, the man never continued forward.

He just sat there, in the middle of the hallway, watching others every now and then walk past him and take the turn while he idly waited for this gut feeling to leave.

The sound of a shoe's reinforced heel clicked progressively closer, like the sound of a clock's hand, as yet another person approached. Only this time, that person stopped right behind him.

The man on the floor looked over his shoulder to see a stranger with shaggy brown hair standing above him.

"What are you doing?" asked the stranger, confused and baffled by the man on the floor.

"I don't actually know. I guess I'm waiting" said the man on the floor.

The stranger cocked his head, perplexed by the man on the floor's response, "Waiting for what?" he asked.

The man on the floor pointed to the end of the hallway where the corner took, "There's something not right, over there. I've watched countless people walk past me, take the turn around that corner, and then never return. I don't know what's over there, and I don't know where those people went… or if something happened to them. But I do know that I have a bad feeling about it."

"… A bad feeling… like what?" asked the stranger, now sounding more timid by the man's words than confused.

"A bad feeling like there's something wrong with whatever is on the other side of that corner. Like my intuition is screaming *'Don't go there!'*, similar to how animals have some sort of sixth-sense that keeps them away from danger."

"What could be around the corner?" asked the stranger, now seeming to not want to take its turn as well.

The man on the floor shook his head, "Could be anything. Anything that's bad for me, anything that's bad for you, anything that's bad for all those previous people who have already taken its corner…"

The stranger stared off at the turn, carrying with him a long pause before returning his attention to the man on the floor, "Do you plan on sitting here forever, then?" he asked.

The man on the floor shrugged, "I don't know. I've already been here for a long time, but I couldn't tell you how long exactly. I know I can't stay here forever, so I guess I've just been waiting for the feeling to go away— but it hasn't. And it sure as hell doesn't seem any closer to fading away, either."

"What if… what if we went together?" asked the stranger.

The man on the floor looked up at the stranger, "What difference would that make?"

"Not much, I guess, but now I don't wanna go around the corner by myself. And I certainly don't wanna sit here and wait.

Maybe we could go together and be safer in numbers, or at least share whatever might be on the other side" offered the stranger.

The man on the floor considered this proposal.

Though he did not know the full span of time which had passed since he'd been sitting there on the ground, waiting, he did know it was an absurd amount of time— time in which nothing had changed and the future still held no promise of a change happening, either.

This seemed like the best and only opportunity to finally move on. For if no change of this situation was ever going to occur, then it would be best to take that turn around the corner with company instead of facing it alone.

"Okay" answered the man on the floor, rising to his feet, "We'll go together."

The stranger smiled in relief and nodded his head.

"… Do I know you?" asked the man, now able to view the stranger better while standing at similar height, "You seem awfully familiar."

"This is the first time I've ever seen your face" said the stranger, blatantly, in the most nonchalant manner.

"Oh. Okay" accepted the man, "Well then, I guess I'm ready whenever you are."

The two men nodded to each other then began their march down the hallway. They walked side by side, shoulder to shoulder, with an unspoken intensity building up as they grew closer to that corner.

When at last, they reached it, they both stopped.

"This is it" said the man.

"Yeah… how's that gut feeling so far?" asked the stranger.

"The same" answered the man, "It's always been the same…"

"Then, I guess we have no choice but to just face it head on, right?"

"Yeah" said the man, "Guess we have no choice."

The two men slowly rounded the corner and took the turn in short, shuffled steps, all while holding their breaths and bracing for the worst.

But once they completed the turn and now faced the other side of that corner, a baffling new twist presented itself.

"A door?" said the stranger, unsure of this new situation.

"Huh. I didn't expect that" said the man.

"Well, what about now? What's that gut feeling of yours say?"

"It never changes. Never has… not even now."

"You think whatever the source for that gut feeling of yours is on the other side of that door?" asked the stranger.

"On the other side, or maybe somewhere far beyond it—beats me. But my instinct still screams that same haunting message, *'Don't go!'*" answered the man.

"Does that mean you wanna go back?" asked the stranger.

"No, no. We should keep pushing forward and see what's next."

"Okay" agreed the stranger, "Let's do it."

"… I don't mean to make you the guinea pig, but you're gonna have to be the one to open that door" said the man, "I've been sitting in that hallway for far too long now and just don't have it in me to open that door myself.

Would you mind opening it?" asked the man, "I'll be right behind you, I promise."

The stranger looked the man up and down as if trying to figure out whether he would actually follow behind him or not, "Fine" he agreed, "I'll open the door."

"Thank you" sighed the man in relief.

The stranger then took the lead and stepped in front of the man, aligning himself in front of the door.

While watching this unfold, the man was flooded with an overwhelming sensation of *deja-vu*.

Something about this felt familiar to him, but he couldn't place his finger on what or why exactly.

The stranger continued on while the man was still in his own thoughts, and grabbed hold of the doorknob before slowly twisting and pulling it.

A hollow creak echoed down the hallway as the door turned on its hinges, followed by both men entering the room, the stranger in the front and the man shortly behind him.

What was then revealed to be behind this door was a small room, boxed in by four walls and a low ceiling.

On the floor, in the center of that room, was a pile of bones— some bleach white, while others maintained snags of meat and muscle on them. Some of the meat had turned purple, or gray, or even rust colored, while others still maintained a pinkish hue or a fresh, velvety red tone.

Spread out on the floor underneath that mound of bones was a dry staining of blood, having been leaked and spilt on over the years, turning crusty and dry over time.

"Bones?!" said the stranger, full of terror.

The man had to cover his nose with his hands as the revolting scent overpowered his other senses.

While covering his face, the man noticed that on the lower part of the right wall in this room, was a single vent… tattered and broken and covered in blood.

He looked back to the stranger to point it out to him, but that is when he noticed it.

As the stranger was looking around the room and at the pile of bones, the man was finally able to place this *deja-vu* of his on why this stranger looked so familiar.

"The back of your head…" said the man.

"What?" questioned the stranger, turning around to face him.

"The back of your head. I've seen it before. You've already taken the corner, sometime back, long ago when I was still sitting in the hallway.

That is why you looked so familiar. I've already seen you… and you never returned. Just like the rest."

An uncanny grin spread across the stranger's face, sending chills down the man's spine and causing his instincts to roar up in a fury of that eminent danger they'd been warning him about all this time.

The stranger then grabbed his own face with one hand in a gorilla-like grip, and began ripping off the flesh that was attached to it, "I've been waiting for you to come around my corner for too long, now.

I could smell you, just sitting there, never moving— while all the others came my way.

I couldn't wait any longer for you to finally take that turn on your own.

I knew I had to come get you myself, and this one provided the perfect skin to do so."

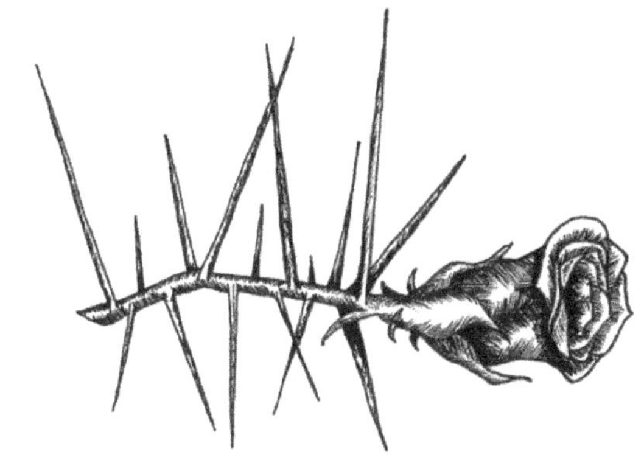

Where they Emerged

From the hands of God, the locusts were thrown down onto the earth. Hungry and empty by nature, they feasted upon the crops of every continent until all that remained was a dry, upturned soil that bore no fruit.

From the hands of Man, atom-bombs were tossed back and forth in a short and fiery war, bringing no victors, but complete decimation instead— burning the very skies as much as the ground.

From the hands of Gia, the waves rose in tsunamis, the winds twisted in tornados, the rocks shook and split in quakes, and the volcanic ash spit black smoke into the air like the howling whistles of a train.

Each hand brought a different touch of death with it, an air of sabotage. Its potency so immense, one could view the ruination as miraculous in its delivery.

Surely, Shiva *was* the true god of destruction, with all of his mighty and many hands, if it only took these three to bring about the near complete obliteration of this tiny blue planet.

Perhaps if a fourth hand had played a role in the matter, then all life would've been eradicated— for even after these disastrous effects, there were still some left over who walked the earth.

They were small in number, only a couple hundred thousand. And this number rarely fluctuated, as for each time someone died, another would be born.

Death was as common as conception— a dead land that gave no nourishment to its occupants, and a dead life where sex was one of the few untouched pleasures that could still be enjoyed.

Mutual or nonconsensual, the act of intercourse was a common activity amongst its survivors.

The end of the world made no change to the warring nature of man. So it would appear, that although Earth was killed from the destructive events that took place, Mars remained untouched and still held its ruling hours over humanity in its revolving force.

The humans still killed each other, fought one another, invaded, pillaged, conquered and raped themselves.

And just like the nature of war, which still resided inside the humans after all of this time and change, so too, did the nature of *fantasy*.

Gathered around a bonfire, a group of survivors were doing just that in this lonely and solemn world— they fantasized and talked of dreams that still seemed to be within reach despite of the desolate landscape.

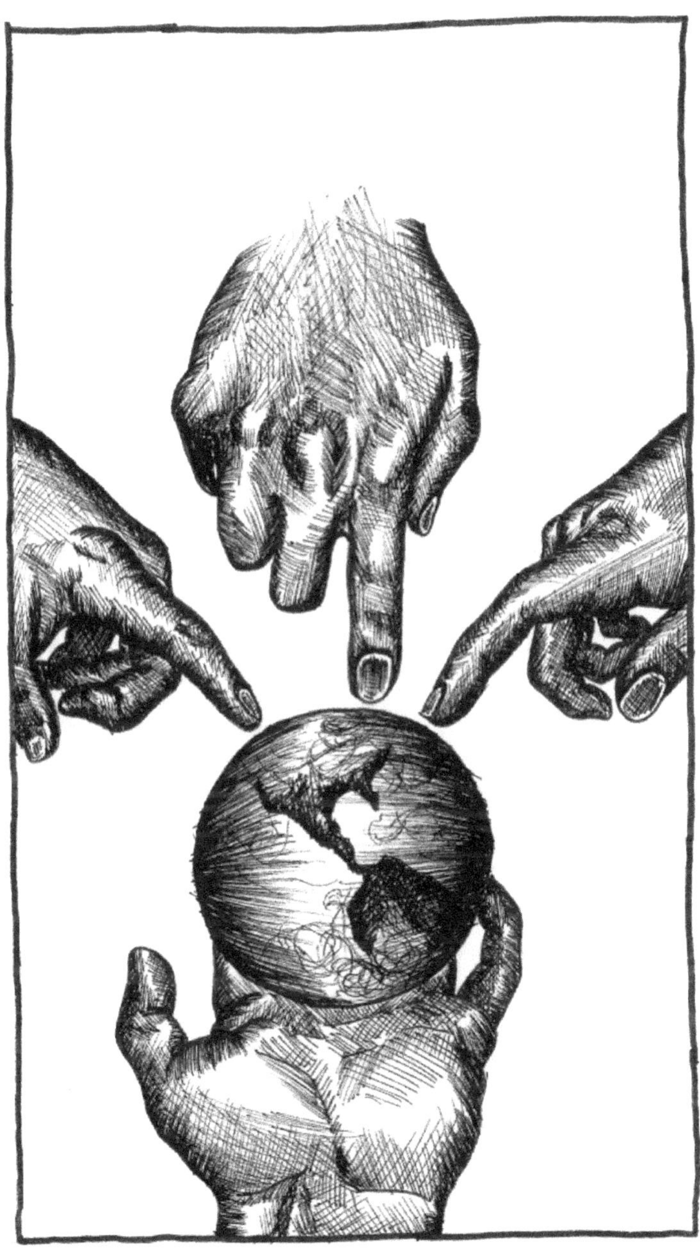

Of those few hundred thousand that still breathed in this desecrated land, about a thousand of them still fantasized.

And of those thousand that still fantasized, only about a hundred of them had actually built this paradise that they dreamt of.

This paradise was the topic of conversation, here and now, amongst the light of the bonfire.

"Rose, they call it. *The Rose Garden*. We can find peace there" said one of the survivors.

"How can you be sure there's peace there? Hell, how can you be sure it even exists?"

"It does exist!" barked back the survivor, "And don't talk like that! We all agreed to make this journey and left together to find it. There's no point in doubting whether it's real or not, now. That's just this world getting into your head and poisoning your mind.

These people, these people who live there and the people who created it, they didn't let such thoughts stop or plague their ambition. They stuck to their fantasy and made it a reality! And now, we have a chance to join that.

Even before the world ended, countless people would've dreamed to be a part of such a society.

It's not fair that it took armageddon for such a place to finally blossom, but that's how it goes sometimes. And we can either be spiteful and rot, we can eat the dry dirt and choke, we can stand in the acid rain and burn, we can pick up arms and salvage the remaining crumbs, we can even join a new group and wait to be killed or raped.

Or, we can choose to find the Rose Garden.

We chose that even in this world, where war has no burden or judgment upon the morals or conscience of its people, to keep our hands empty and our hearts open.

Now we're almost there, so there's no point in turning back. If you don't wish to continue on, then by all means, pick up a knife and cut your throat open. At least then the earth can quench its own thirst.

We had no choice in being cursed and born into this world, and we had no say in being the unholy few who survived the torrent of chaos that swept away any beauty that once made this cursed land hold some kind of meaning... but we are here, nonetheless.

So ask yourselves, where do you want to go now? Back to the land of the dead and leave the world of the living? Or to where hope still exists and fantasy has manifested— to join the Rose Garden?"

Only whispers and hushes stirred around the bonfire after that speech, as no one could find an argue against any sentence of it.

"No warring tribes" spoke out a survivor to fill the silence, "No cannibalism. No hate, fighting, or killing. This is really it, isn't it? Paradise in a forgotten world!"

"It is. But we're not there yet. And you can be damn sure we won't be safe until we do.

We continue our travels. At least the night can provide some sort of deterrent from trouble. If we're lucky, we can reach the Rose Garden by day break... or at least where I've been told it should be.

But we keep our hopes high and think positive. Be smart, and most importantly, be quiet. We don't know if there are any others prowling about this night.

Let's move."

For how unruly the world was, and for how many faults and debates that could be had on its aspects, there was one thing now that every survivor would agree on; the night skies were nothing like they ever could have imagined nor were depicted by the sci-fi movies or comics in a time past.

If one could lay on the ocean floor and watch the waves tumble and roll at its surface, then that would be the best way to describe it.

The ash of bones from finished neighbors and enemies, the sulfuric smoke belched from the stomach of the earth, the cremated cities from the atom bomb's impacts, all gave rise to a new atmosphere and shape of clouds.

These tumbling clusters of gassy coal were as beautiful as they were terrifying.

Within their dark bubbles, red lightning and fire played a game of tug-of-war, illuminating the shadows with an orange haze that made the surrounding environment as clear as the hours of twilight.

Other times, the black clouds would grow so heavy with their impurities, that they would fall softly like a feather from the sky onto the people below— shrouding them in a blanket so thick, that on could not see their own hand, even if their palm was touching their nose.

Perhaps there *was* a fourth hand at play in this rapture after all, and *this* was it. Could it be the toxins in the air? The new strife amongst its survivors? The lack of hope, birth of hope, and death of it?

Whatever this fourth hand was, it was different from the others— more slight and sneaky. It wished not to reveal its face or role, but rather, to weave unseen into the pores of the aftermath.

Either way, the handful of survivors who still held onto their fantasies continued on, traversing these clouds under the night in their quest for the Rose Garden.

At times when the sky glowed, they used the light to their advantage to better maneuver themselves on the right path, should they have lost track. And at other times when they heard voices nearby, they would hide and wait for the clouds to get heavy and cover their presences in its dark blanket.

Nights often felt like a multitude of individual days from this process, and after what could've been described as a compacted week's worth of transitions from light to dark, a rich ruby red sunrise broke over the horizon.

The small group of survivors ceased their march forward, as with the rising of the sun came a glistening sight ahead of them.

About a mile out in front of them was what appeared to be a sparkling utopia. It was hard to make out the details from how intensely the sun reflected off of the metal structures, but one thing was certain, *this* was the Rose Garden.

They had found it!

With newfound glee, the group of survivors sped up their pace, laughing and crying in excitement as their fantasy had finally manifested itself into reality! They made haste and even jogged at times, as paradise was now within their sights.

But their strides began to slow the closer they got, and when the Rose Garden was in full view and able to be appreciated, they stopped.

Before them lied vast acres of land, completely covered in nothing but giant metal spikes that emerged from the ground like thorns. Thousands of these metal structures protruded from the earth like its own twisted chrome garden, or a man made forest, or a surreal maze erected from the perverse thoughts of sadist… or perhaps a masochist.

"This is the Rose Garden?" questioned one of the survivors.

"Of course it is!" said another, "Have you seen anything else like this?"

"No… but I expected it to be different. Something beautiful."

"We just misunderstood the name. It seems the *rose* reference was from those metal spikes, like the thorns on its stem. But it doesn't matter the name or the look— we didn't come here because we thought it was going to be beautiful. We came here because of the peace which lies within this place."

Murmurs and the nodding of heads in agreement were the response to those words, for they did in fact come to this sanctuary solely to escape the war and death that still plagued the outside world.

They came to the Rose Garden to enter the fantasy.

"Wait. Look there!" said a survivor, "Someone's coming!"

"I see!" responded another, "There are many!… wait, that's not…"

"Oh my god… what is this?" said one survivor, full of shock, "What's wrong with them?"

As from out of the Rose Garden and its vast pillars of large metal spikes, emerged its citizens— red like a true rose, for they had no skin.

Head to toe, their muscles were exposed, allowing an anatomical view of how coordinated the human body was in its mechanical movements as the muscles and tendons all worked in unison to produce the motion of walking.

Not a single piece of flesh remained on their bodies, not even their eyelids, which gave way to an unyielding glower in those strained eyes lodged within their skulls.

It is strange how much beauty is brought into yield by one's flesh.

Without lips, the teeth and gums are on constant display, without any ability to convey emotion or even a smile— only a constant gaunt expression.

With no skin to wrap around the face and define its features for distinction, all that bore were the horrific red striations towards the makings of a human visage.

The only differences to be found amongst the crowd of civilians were the shapes; some faces were slimmer while others were wider, some faces were longer while others were shorter.

Now, they were just bodies stripped of nature's clothing. What would have been deviant or perverse no longer retained any sexual allure. It was too grotesque to appreciate in such a state— lacking any grace, elegance, or divinity within the masculine and feminine.

Only eye color was cause for a true distinction amongst the people. However, the red of the veins that surrounded the iris which lacked any protection or hydration that was otherwise provided by eyelids, made it hard to notice such things as the eyeballs themselves donned a full scarlet or pink hue.

"Welcome travelers, survivors, fantasizers, peace seekers" spoke one of the skinless residents while a number of them approached the group, "I have no name, so call me brother. And call any of the women here, sisters.

Nothing divides us in the Rose Garden. There is no separation between us. We are all the same, we are all one kind."

"Wha—what happened to your skin?" asked one of the survivors, "What's wrong with you people?"

"To be granted entry into the Rose Garden and join us, one must give up their skin" answered a resident.

"What? Why? You mean to say you guys did this to yourselves?"

"There is no war, here. No strife. No lust or hate. There is absolutely nothing left that separates us from one another.

There is only peace.

And to retain that vain clothing that covers your true self now, is to still be a beast, like the others out there.

What is the reason or cause for any of it? Any and all of it?

Different color, different gender, different politics, different agendas, different desires?

Who would've thought that all such things were derived of the flesh. And yet when you strip one of it, they become nothing more than a human of the same, rather than a human of the other.

It is a small price to pay for peace, one which we can all attest to now— we, who have given it up to be blessed into our new home and into our new lives."

Most of the survivors were discomforted and damn near repulsed by the sight and idea of what this Rose Garden actually was, but there were still some within their numbers who were not dissuaded by this and saw reason within this paradise's philosophy.

"Does it hurt?" asked such a survivor.

"Yes. But so does life.

Life hurt before the hands ruined the earth. And life hurt far more after it.

This pain, however, is the last one. This pain is an initiation, a promise! It is worth it, for with it comes the guarantee of nirvana.

Once you have been stripped of your vanity, only a couple more adjustments must be made until you are able to experience the true glory of this new world's paradise."

"Like what?" asked a survivor.

"Your nerves will not be used to having no shield against the elements. But fret not, for that is why the Rose Garden was constructed in the way it is.

These metal rods that create our vast sanctuary conduct the heat of the sun during the day. They hold onto its heat to provide us with warmth against the easy cold we can experience. And when the day is hot, they provide us shade as to not be burned.

They are the perfect size, casting only a limited amount of shade so you must share its cover with a fellow neighbor, who is your brother or sister. You will learn to bond and become a community from this, as we all need the same things for contentment and to survive.

Wind can feel like knives when it blows too hard, especially with the lapses of night when the coal blankets fall to the ground. But these pillars help break up those sharp winds and smoke, and their pointed tips split the clouds when they come too low to the ground— breaking up the darkness and dispersing its cloak in the same speedy manner which it can arrive."

"I want to join" said one of the survivors, "I believe."

"I want to live in the Rose Garden" said another, "I want peace."

The skinless man nodded and four other occupants of the Rose Garden emerged out and grabbed the two interested survivors.

They pulled them over to the edge of the Rose Garden, then held their arms tightly as they brought them to their knees. This was followed by another resident pulling out a curved knife, and beginning to carve away at the survivors' flesh.

The terrible screams of the two prospects pierced the eardrums of the other survivors like a horn of death itself.

They fought and resisted and tried to shake off the residents, but their holds on them were too strong, just like their volition. And so, they kept those prospects restrained as the wielders of blades took professional strokes with their tools to carve and skin perfectly between the flesh and the muscle.

It was a dreadful sight which most of the survivors couldn't bear to watch, some even bolting back in the direction they came from as to get as far away from these people and what they saw.

But the ones who did stay and continued to watch, suffered the most— for they still wished entry into the Rose Garden, and now knew of their throes that awaited such a decision.

The Horseman's Beauty

As THE CLACKING of horse hooves mellowed and drowned, the crooked carriage slowly came to a steady halt. All of the passengers who were tightly packed in its back then rose from their pillowed seats of hay, and took turns stepping off of the cart one by one.

Even though this wasn't everyone's stop, they were all required to get out of the caravan as to let those who weren't journeying any further to exit at this stop.

While most packed themselves back into the transportation, a few made their way to the coachman and paid their coin for the travel, as this was their destination.

Three began on foot in a direction of their own personal journey, while only one remained in the village they arrived upon, and her name was Elizabeth Norick.

Elizabeth pulled her coif closer to her ears as a cold breeze viciously rushed passed her. This village was more frigid and windy than she had initially imagined it to be, but its composition and layout fit her expectations rather spot on.

Houses were simple but nice, built to withstand a tough winter and manage any rain.

Agriculture was a staple for most of the property, with the larger fields for mass farming only yards away from the community.

A water well sat in the village's center, with no animals nor their scat anywhere near its vicinity.

There was a blacksmith to make the nails, and a carpenter to hammer them into the houses. There were farmers to feed those working men, and livestock to supply the meat.

There was even a cleric, who was currently in the process of sanctifying a piece of land for a planned chapel to be built upon.

And now, this quaint little village had Elizabeth.

Elizabeth was a great seamstress. She could weave and knit any kind of material, be it wool, cloth, linen or leather. She could mend any article of clothing just as good as she could create one.

She was a great addition to the village, bringing it one step closer to its finished product.

And that is why she was there, of course. They had sought her out, the current residents, in the prospect of completing this little village of theirs. For the less they would have to leave their haven in order to use the goods or skills of another, the better.

Elizabeth was even offered a free house should she take her skills there, and so, why wouldn't she?

She had not married yet and her father had passed long ago. Her mother certainly was not going to wed her off, nor were there any proper suitors in town to take her hand.

But a village such as this one, young and growing and sure to bring in a possible lover if not already holding one, was the perfect place for Elizabeth to create a space where she just might start a family of her own one day.

And to be given a house for free with the guarantee of more coin to be made from her business made the whole proposal feel like a divine intervention.

"Elizabeth Norick?" asked a man approaching her.

He was fair and couldn't have been a couple of years older than her. His clothes seemed to be made of a wool and were moderately dirty, but his face appeared clean, as though the sweat and wind had wicked it all away.

"Yes" answered Elizabeth, "I am here about the proposal."

"Good!" said the man, holding out his hand in introduction, "I'm Eric. I build most of the homes here, even built yours! It'll serve you well if you decide to stay."

Elizabeth extended her own hand, "Elizabeth, as you know."

"Give me a couple more months and I'll have a church standing tall on that mound, there" continued Eric after they shook, "Then this place will be a *real* village, and with you living here, of course.

We can use a good seamstress."

His smile was contagious and Elizabeth caught hold of it quickly, feeling flattered by his words and that charming smile, "Well I'd like to look around more, first. See where I'll be living, get an idea of the space and surrounding land."

Eric pulled out a handkerchief from his pocket and began cleaning his hands while maintaining that perfect smile for Elizabeth, "Not a problem, I can do that. I know this place the best and actually built most of it" he nodded his head in a leading direction, "Come on."

Eric guided Elizabeth on a little tour of their village in progress, showing her what they had already put in place and what they planned to put next, what they were going to improve and what they were going to replace.

She was able to meet most of the other residents who came to make this place their home, all of them seemingly friendly with a shared excitement for the joint creation, or at least, being a part of the starting foundation for this location.

"Who lives there?" asked Elizabeth, pointing to a dissimilar looking house that contrasted against the rest, down at the edge of the village.

"Oh, that's Giorgi" said Eric, his voice not changing in a negative way, necessarily, but easily taking on a more serious tone.

"Did you build his house as well? It's different from all the others."

"Actually, that's the one house I didn't. Giorgi and that house were here long before any of us moved in. It was him who actually suggested all of this" said Eric, gesturing to the entire village around them, "He said it would work, that the land was good. Said we just needed the right people and the rest would follow.

Seemed he would be right about that" he said while observing the environment that lay before him, "It really did follow."

"He sounds like an interesting fellow" said Elizabeth.

"He is…" responded Eric with an admonitory voice, "But he is also private. It's likely you won't meet him in person, but that's honestly for the best. He stays in his home at the edge of the village, and that's that."

"How does he get any goods for living, then?" asked Elizabeth, "Food, water from the well, or use of the outhouse?"

Eric shook his head, "I put food and drink at his window when he leaves it open. And he supposedly has a hole inside of his own home for when he requires the use of an outhouse.

But you ask too many questions about the man. Just let him be.

I deal with him most of the time and take care of any needs on his behalf…

Just… it's a good living here. It truly is. And with more people like yourself moving in, it'll become great.

Don't— don't worry about Giorgi. Don't get involved.

A lot of the women here have become intrigued by the *'shy fellow in the strange house'*, but it's not good to be. Trust me.

Stick to your living and making a home of this place, and don't worry or think about Giorgi. You do that, and you'll have a great life here.

That man never leaves his house so he's not to be concerned about… only yourself" said Eric before he continued to walk, "I'll show you to your house, now."

Elizabeth kept her gaze on Giorgi's house, taken by the curiosity that surrounded such a mysterious man, and intrigued by its odd decor that looked beautiful but also perverse in nature.

However, she quickly caught herself and continued walking as well, following short behind Eric towards her assigned home, where after only a couple of months, became her permanent residence in the settlement.

A whole season had passed since she moved into the village —summer moving into fall— and Elizabeth had become fully aquatinted with everyone and everything within the community… that is, except for Giorgi, of course.

However, she had heard many things and numerous rumors about the man during her time there from the others.

She shared a workshop with the other women, who would make soap while she stitched materials together and mended fabrics in the restorations or creations of clothes.

"Apparently he is the most beautiful man in the world!" said one of the women.

"Sometimes he fancies some of us! Though I haven't a clue how he knows what any of us looks like since no one else seems to be able to catch a glimpse of the man."

"It's both a blessing and a curse— to be able to meet with him and see his beauty."

"Most die after seeing him, that his how killing his looks are. Especially if they sleep with Giorgi, they all pass away from how miraculous the sex was!"

"It's kinda sad when you think about it, to be blessed with such looks that you're actually forced to hide it away and live a solitary life. I wonder how many times he's had his heart broken from killing a woman who he's fallen for, or to have someone pass away after partaking in the act of lovemaking with a woman you wish to start a family with…"

"Have any of you seen him?" Elizabeth would ask.

They'd always laugh in response, followed with a *"Well we wouldn't still be here to talk about him if we had!"* or *"No! I have a husband, though, I can't defeat the curiosity that still stirs about."*

With fall having made its course into the village, Elizabeth had become unusually busy with the refining and crafting of attires that could beat the upcoming cold. And so it would be, under these very circumstances, that she received an odd request.

"Elizabeth" said Eric, entering into her workspace, "I have need of your skills."

He placed a pouch of coin beside her on the table containing all her various cuts of cloths and tools, "Pay's already covered for."

"That's quite a lot— probably more than necessary. What do you need?" asked Elizabeth.

"It's not for me, it's for Giorgi.

He's requested a top now that we're nearing the cold. Thick, lined with wool or shearling if you have it, with buttons for a swifter way of taking it on or off.

You will have to use more materials than you're use to for this… he's quite a large man."

Eric joined Elizabeth at her station, picking up her pencil and placing markings on her measuring grafts, "His shoulders are extremely broad, I kid you not" he said while drafting the measurements for reference, "Arms need this much room for bending space and comfort.

Wingspan is just as impressive.

And this much across the chest so he may be able to button it closed" he said while finishing the last measurements for Giorgi as he spoke, "I know, it's quite unorthodox in its fitting. But Giorgi is not built like the normal man nor is he of similar size."

"Not built like the normal man?" laughed Elizabeth, "I do not know if you're familiar with greek literature, but it appears he's built like Hercules! Is he really of these measurements?"

Eric nodded, "… I'm certain you've heard the rumors by now?"

"Women talk, yes."

"I want… I want you to know that—"

"Don't worry" Elizabeth reassured, "I remember what you told me when I first moved here. Giorgi keeps to himself, and to let that be.

It is a curious thing, I'll admit— what the women say and all. Along with these measurements you've given me, and even the way you speak of him… like you did when I first arrived… like you do now."

Eric looked down, "It's just, I believe in this village.

I believe in what it is, what it stands for, where it is now and where it is going to go. This will be a great place one day, hell, it already is!

And that's what I want. That's the thought I put behind every nail I drive into a new house."

Elizabeth frowned, "Do you think Giorgi stands between you and this desire for the village to be great?" she asked.

Eric held onto a long pause before answering, "When I first showed up to this land, Giorgi was already here, long before me, as I told you way back.

Just him and his strange home, with all of its little trinkets and decorations.

I met the man. Spoke with him, face to face, so I know him better than anyone else here or who will ever come to live here.

He lit the tinder in my mind of this land becoming a great village one day.

And I believed him— not like I was wrong to, either.

But my desire stays only on the flourishing of this village."

"And what has his desire become now, then? The fair maidens who arrive on the land that manage to catch his eye?" mocked Elizabeth.

Eric said nothing but just stared at her.

"Is it really?" she asked, realizing the confirmation by Eric's silence.

"I've begun to assume so after the years have passed. I even question if such a plot was the whole reason behind him telling me to build this village— but that's not to say that he wasn't right about this land being fertile."

"Have women… actually died?" asked Elizabeth, "After seeing him?"

Another pause seized Eric, "I've been the one to bury them after" he admitted, "It's why I've been working so hard on the chapel. Everyone deserves a proper burial. If it's going to continue on like this, then they should at least have their grave's blessed."

"And he's really that beautiful?" asked Elizabeth in disbelief.

"… That purse is still worth more than a top for Giorgi" said Eric, changing the subject, "He also wants a veil to cover his face— a large one. Act as though it is a table cloth you're making, that'll work better.

Oh, and he specifically asked for it to be red.

Find me when you are finished. I'll take it to him myself."

Eric made his way out of the workshop but stopped at the door just before he exited, "I want the best for this village, Elizabeth. I want more and more people, just like you, to move in.

So leave it be. Don't occupy your thoughts or curiosity with Giorgi.

Don't visit him, please."

He then walked out and left Elizabeth to her work.

Being the master craftsman that she was, it took Elizabeth only two weeks to finish the special project for Giorgi and his abnormal proportions, and less than half of that for his table cloth-sized veil.

When she had finally finished it all, it was a quarter past dark, and she exited the workshop to go find Eric.

The large sizes of the two pieces took up far too much room in Elizabeth's workspace, and although she could've waited until morning for their delivery, she preferred their immediate disposal as to return to the extra space in her work area.

But Eric was a busy man during the day, which often transitioned over into the night. When he wasn't building a house or working on the chapel, he was attending to Giorgi like a carrier.

And when he wasn't doing any of that, he was out chopping trees or buying wood to make more houses.

And if you couldn't find him even then, it was because he was no longer in town and out on a hunt to places both local and far, searching for more potential residents to invite into the village.

After half an hour of searching for Eric, it became apparent to Elizabeth that he was out doing just that. This meant that he most likely wouldn't return back until the morning at earliest, or in two nights' time at latest.

This didn't sit well with Elizabeth's liking, as she couldn't imagine continuing her work for the preparation of the winter season with such little space in her designated area of the workshop.

And the idea of storing Giorgi's finished clothes in her own home to make space in the mean time, didn't sit well with her either. With how private of a man he was, surely he would have issue that she kept his pieces in her personal storage during the wait for their delivery.

Elizabeth looked out to the edge of the village and saw the glowing lights and flickering candles that danced behind the curtains of Giorgi's covered windows.

… In fact, one of the windows was open.

Surely he was awake at this hour if he still had yet to put out his candles. And surely he wouldn't mind if she put his clothes at his window— for if he has it open, then this is what Eric would do as he had done for all of Giorgi's other needs.

It was a conflicting thought that fought within Elizabeth's head, but in the end, she saw no other better solution than to just do it.

With the top and veil in hand, she headed towards the edge of the village to deliver Giorgi his clothes at his window.

The closer she drew to his home, the stronger her curiosity about the man became.

It was easier for the infatuation to grow in this setting, with a true privacy from the eyes and words of the others under the night.

It never felt real or viable —an interaction with Giorgi— when all it ever was were the words from the other women while they talked to pass the time during work.

It always felt like the obvious or already understood whenever she spoke to Eric; to never visit the man.

It always felt like Giorgi didn't exist during the day, as he never left his house. And it always felt like he was so far away during the night, with the lights from his home vaguely visible from where she lived in comparison to the village's edge.

But now, none of that was at play. And the lively reminder that Giorgi existed beyond more than just a rumor and was someone she could actually interact with, became a more animate and intimate thought the closer Elizabeth drew to his home.

After a long walk, she eventually reached the edge of the village. And now, Giorgi's house was only feet away from her.

Though the curtains were closed, the mere fact that the window was open and the candles were lit within, gave off a sense of invitation.

She could smell the interior of the home from a breeze that flowed out. It smelt like musk— a potent kind to that of an animal, but too refined to be in the category of an animal. *Beast* would be a better example, like the musk of a beast, yet there was an alluring element to it that grasped the attention of Elizabeth, despite it also causing her to feel slightly unsettled.

There was also a hint of something sweet, like an oil for the washing of one's body in some form of hygiene… perhaps for the hair?

And of course, there was the scent of burning wicks and melting candle wax that flowed out.

All of those aromas had combined to make for this single mystifying scent, stimulating further the intrigue that Elizabeth was already experiencing.

Timidly, she approached the opening of the house and set Giorgi's clothes on the windowsill.

"Very late to be bringing gifts, is it not?" came a voice from behind the curtains. It was deep and daunting, perfectly becoming of such a mysterious man with the kind of rumors that surrounded him. It served his masculinity on its own, requiring no visuals to make known his dominating nature.

"It's not a gift but your order" said Elizabeth, recovering from her startle, "The top and veil, just as requested. And I'm only delivering it this late because Eric is out on his travels."

"Ah, finding more prospects for his perfect village, I see?" inquired Giorgi.

"Yes" answered Elizabeth, "It is because of him I found a home here."

"He's become quite obsessed with the building of this village. I almost regret planting the seed in his mind, sometimes" said Giorgi.

"Is that not what you want if the origin of the idea was fostered by yourself?" asked Elizabeth.

"No, it is" answered Giorgi "If such a thing as too good of a job exists, then Eric falls within that spectrum."

"What makes you say he's doing too good of a job?" she asked.

Giorgi sighed, "It would appear that he wants *me* out of the village, now. Our rapport is no longer the same as it used to be.

According to him, it is me who now ruins the village and keeps it from being perfect. Though he never would've settled in these lands if it wasn't for my suggestion."

"For what reason does he believe you to be the inhibitor?" asked Elizabeth, "Large is the accusation that exiles its founder."

Giorgi scoffed on the other side of the curtain, his pitch achieving a delicately lighter sound from his mannish vocals, bringing about a new attraction which pulled Elizabeth further into his unseen charm, "I'm sure you've heard from the others before you that have placed their stay in this village. I may have the social of a hermit, but I also have the ears of a hound, and the intuition of a seer.

I know my presence within this village is different. All who have tongues, talk. And those without, still have ears— and they listen."

"I have heard from them, yes. And personally, I'd agree with Eric, if you'd have my truth.

He's told me of the bodies he's had to bury, and the women speak of how some have encountered their deaths just from the sight of you.

If I wanted to move forth in building this village, then I too would urge your leave.

He's not wrong when he speaks of this place's potential. I can see the future it holds" Answered Elizabeth.

"Oh, so you're the seer now?" teased Giorgi, "Or maybe… your eyes have fallen onto Eric for the future, not so much the village itself?"

"How dare you!" gasped Elizabeth, insulted, "You have no right to make such assumptions unto me or my interests! Not now nor ever will it be of any of your business.

I think your concern lies with the Lord instead of my own doings, as it's with Him you'll have to answer for all those women you've killed— beauty or not.

How's your rapport with Him?"

She turned around and began to storm off but was called back by Giorgi, "Elizabeth, Elizabeth wait! I'm sorry. Please, come back so we may talk.

I hardly get to engage in conversation anymore because of my current way of living, and Eric has no more interest in communicating with me how common folk would."

Elizabeth stopped her strides and looked back, "How do you know my name? I did not tell you it."

That charming laugh sounded once more, even gentler than the last and far more inviting through that open window, "Ears like a hound, remember?

You're the seamstress. The best among many towns over.

When I asked Eric if you could make me a top for the winter to fit my body, he begrudgingly said yes, almost boastful of your work and irritated that I would have questioned it. Though, it could've also been yet another opportunity for him to demean me in his eyes.

Oh how he loathes me now. But he did seem less disgruntled when I asked for the veil as well.

These days, he hardly sees me, and our interactions stay at this window with the curtain closed. So I see not why he would be so pleased for me to cover my face with the veil, since it is no longer his burden to bear witness to anymore.

A good man, that Eric, another seer within this village. He hopes to prevent further deaths of the women by having me hide my face away since I refuse to leave.

I was here first, after all. Who is he to beckon my flee?"

"How come Eric can look upon you with no threat of perishing, but women cannot?" asked Elizabeth.

"Now that is a simple answer; I have no interest in men" said Giorgi.

"… So if you did, Eric would have met the same fate as all the other women who've seen your face before?"

"Most likely.

'Beauty is in the eye of the beholder' chant most of the poets and play writers these days, yes?

Hmph.

Sometimes, Elizabeth, beauty *is* the beholder.

I do not cast it upon the men who view me, but the women… most certainly."

Elizabeth was filled with discomfort as she couldn't deny the fact that she had also reached a peak in curiosity towards this man.

If anything, she wished to see what he looked like— this man with a beauty that kills from its sight, this man with proportions to that of the giants that once roamed the earth, this man with an inexplicable charm laced into his very voice and undeniably that gorgeous laugh of his.

She feared she might let this curiosity take over her, and decided to announce her leave there and then, "The air is getting colder, and now you have your clothes for such temperatures.

I'll be on my way now, the night is too late to be talking with any gentleman.

I hope the best for your relationship with Eric."

This time, Giorgi managed to stop Elizabeth before she had even a chance to walk away as opposed to beckoning her return after like earlier, "Is it too late to have a cup of tea with a gentleman at this hour? Surely such a courtesy is far more acceptable within the night."

The idea grasped Elizabeth's mind like a twisting knot— roped by an amateur sailor. For as much as it was engrossing, it was also a mess.

She had heard everything the other women had to say about Giorgi, which was then validated by Eric who was also not fond of this man.

This mysterious man could cease her days on this earth should she bear witness to his beauty… and yet, just like any sailor's knot, including those of an amateur, it was still enough to secure its stay.

"I have no intention of dying tonight, nor within any of the upcoming years. If you were to wear that veil I made for you, then a cup of tea to warm me for my walk back would be accepted."

"I'll wear the veil as well as the top you stitched me. You may see the merit of your work in person, as I'm certain you were curious of the fit while you pieced it together, were you not?

Come inside. I'll leave the door unlocked as I put these on."

Elizabeth turned and made her way around the house to its front entrance, hearing the sound of the window close behind her and the door's lock release. She also noted the heavy footsteps within the house as they made its way to a room opposite of the entrance.

As she opened the door and stepped inside, those initial wafts of the mixed scents she had caught at the window now took full possession of her nose.

The inside of Giorgi's home was warm, and the candle light perfectly accented the ambiance in the room.

One of the strangest features Elizabeth noticed, was a tiny table with foliage of different species, weird powders of various shades, a half empty bottle of some brown spirit, a ceremonial knife, and a copper bowl where a single long strand of smoke continuously rose from no given source.

"They're on" said Giorgi from the opposing room, its curtain acting as a closed door, blocking her from looking within, "Would you like to see your work?"

Elizabeth swallowed in nervous thrill, this taboo moment of being in the direct presence of Giorgi, now just moments away, "Yes" she answered back.

Those heavy footsteps sounded once more, this time in an approach toward's Elizabeth, until a massive man stepped out from behind the cloak of the curtain that divided the rooms.

He was extremely tall, with his veil covered head almost hitting the ceiling of his own home.

The top Elizabeth had made him accentuated his body perfectly, complementing his extremely broad frame and shoulders which explained why he had no door to separate the rooms, as he wouldn't have been able to fit through them if there was a doorway.

The sleeves held tight to his muscular arms, with just enough space in its stitching to give him a proper freedom of movement. He had it buttoned down almost halfway, revealing the bold slabs of muscle that made up his barrel chest, along with the curly hair similar to that of a devon sheep's wool which sprouted out all about his chest.

His pants were large and of a baggy-fitting linen, but his defined thighs were revealed when the cloth stretched over them during each step forward he took.

There was also one more factor that was hidden under those linens pants that made an appearance with each stride, one that was too inappropriate to fully take notice of while maintaining a clear conscience.

"So" said Giorgi, halting just feet in front of Elizabeth, "What do you think of it?" he asked.

Elizabeth swallowed before responding.

The allure of intimidation was on a tightrope, very near to falling off into total fear. And her anxiety only continued to rise in steady speed as this behemoth of a man stood before her.

And yet, this overwhelming aura of dominance was just barely contrasted by the suave of his voice and tone, which sounded as though he would take care of her in a knowing attempt to ease away the trembles that had already set within the woman.

"I— it looks very becoming" said Elizabeth, "I must admit, I did question the truth of your proportions when I was given the measurements for them… but now I see they were not lies."

Giorgi laughed, "Ah yes, the tumbling toil of one's mind when deciphering truth from fiction. What sparked your mind first, then, Elizabeth?

Was it when you caught sight of my house and its difference from all the others?

Was it when you spoke to Eric, and how he spoke of me?

Was it when you spoke with the other women in this village, and heard their gossiping tongues?

Was it when you heard of the death from both the women and Eric himself, validating those said rumors?

Was it when you were crafting my clothes and saw their inhuman aspects?

Was it when you approached my window and heard my voice for the first time?

Or was it when you entered my home and watched in awe as I approached and stood before you as I do now?"

"All of it" confessed Elizabeth, "Though I pride myself on not being as obsessed with a mere idea compared to how the rest of the women are.

But I guess it is no longer a mere idea, now. In fact, the moment you stepped through that curtain ended it from being just a thought— so that moment was not another spark as you would suggest."

"Oh but it is…" said Giorgi as he began to fully unbutton his top, "For you have yet to witness the entire truth, Elizabeth.

It has been far too long since I've had the right woman with which I desired to show myself to, and it shall be with you— Now."

"No!" reacted Elizabeth in reflex, covering both her face and eyes with her hands, "I said I do not wish to see you! I will not take my last breath this night over the look of a man!"

"You're wrong, Elizabeth. Truth from fiction, remember?

No one has ever died from laying their eyes upon me. That is where everyone is wrong" Giorgi finished unbuttoning his top and dropped it on the floor beside him.

Elizabeth could not tell whether she didn't run out and leave his home in that instance because of being completely frozen in fear… or if from the gripping hold of curiosity in being able to see his face in these upcoming moments.

"Stay and witness, Elizabeth" encouraged Giorgi while beginning to untie his linen pants, "Be the next, but not the last."

His linen pants dropped to his feet, revealing the giant phallus that had made its impression through the fabric when he first walked in— resting at the caps of his knees, with a staggering weight from the display of its girth.

Even with the immense and striated muscles of his thighs that cushioned where the phallus laid upon could not take away from its horrifying size.

It was not a sexual sight in the slightest, but rather, ungodly.

"Bear eyes upon my face" said Giorgi, as he then removed the veil and let it fall beside the rest of his clothes, bringing to light the monstrous horse face he bore on the body of a colossal man, with the reproductive organ of a beast, "We shall lay together. And when we are finished, I shall bless your dying body so you may give back to the land, raising its fertility once you are buried."

Elizabeth wanted to regurgitate her last meal at the sight of this… thing! For it definitely was not a man. What could only come out of her in that moment were words of similar message to her thoughts, "You're— you're a monster!" she proclaimed.

"Do not insult me, human!" bellowed Giorgi.

"You— you killed those women with that abomination attached to your pelvis! An act surely without any consent, as any woman would be aware of the suffering and death to surely follow that!"

"So despicable!" roared Giorgi, "How swiftly your kind has forgotten of magical beasts. You once worshipped us, sacrificed for us, made deals and bonds of the soul in our names!

Daughters of Adam would willing give themselves unto me and take me in their embrace fully, without the screams of rejection, knowing what a blessing and holy act it was to experience my beauty.

They'd die happy and honored as their internals bled, and would kiss away their red stains off my vessel of fertility as their last acts before entering an eternal slumber.

I am a sacred being, born of the land, not of another's flesh. I am the fertility that springs upon this land and the land before it.

Give unto me, and I will then give you unto the land."

"No! No, I refuse! You are a beast! You're a monster! You creature that runs in the night!

Eric was right to want to cast you out of these lands, you're the spawn of evil!"

"Enough!" shouted Giorgi, "It is pitiful that another cannot understand, but you humans have changed too much. I shall have you like I had the rest, even if you cannot see how sacred of an act it is to receive me."

Elizabeth then turned for the door and made a sprint for it!

As she grabbed its handle and was about to pull it open, Giorgi pounced over her shoulders, slamming his hand against the door to keep it shut, while using his other to toss Elizabeth backward and away from the door.

She was sent flying off of her feet like a child from this throw, and crashing into the ritual altar.

The wind was knocked out of her lungs upon collision, and she struggled to catch a breath of air while dry heaving in an unrewarding pain.

A multitude of powdered clouds floated around her, while the smoke from the copper bowl burned her eyes. It was then that she was able to regain her coordination and spacial awareness, recognizing that she was sitting on top of everything that was once organized on the alter.

On the other side of the room, Giorgi lifted a large metal bar that was hidden in a dark corner of the house near the entrance, and placed it on two hooks that sat on the sides of the door— locking them both inside.

He then turned to face Elizabeth, and began his slow approach towards her, his giant member becoming engorged as he drew closer to her, rising from his knees to an upright position, with veins popping out as it donned its new immense size from all of the blood flow.

Elizabeth, sat on her bum after recovering from her collision, began to scoot back in fear of this monster that was closing the distance on her in his menacing walk, having now trapped her in his home.

She could feel the foliage crunch beneath her palms, and some even penetrating her skin with their thorns.

Giorgi was now only two feet away from Elizabeth, his shadow already looming over her, when she felt it —her key to escape, a skeleton key from death, so to say— the wooden handle of the ceremonial dagger that once sat on top the altar!

She took hold of the blade and used her last remaining courage to wait for the beast-man to draw closer. But it came as a surprise to her when Giorgi took hold of Elizabeth by the hair atop her head, as she had forgotten that the inhuman size of this monster also meant he had an outrageous wingspan.

The sharp sensation of the roots being pulled up from her scalp made Elizabeth wince and brought tears to her eyes, but she was strong and did not give up on her plan to make a stand!

In one quick swoosh, a single arc of her arm in a swinging motion, she brought the knife down upon the base of Giorgi's unnatural member, severing it from the pelvic muscle which suspended it to his body.

With a loud thump, similar to the sound of his footsteps, his phallus fell heavy to the floor, shrinking down and returning to a softer state as the blood poured out from its area of detachment.

Giorgi roared in pain and began to go berserk! Throwing himself against the walls of his home like a stir-crazy horse in its stable, all while bleeding profusely from his new wound.

Elizabeth took this opportunity and ran for the door!

She attempted to lift up the metal bar that kept it locked, but failed, as she had no strength near Giorgi's to lift it, just as no human would.

In that same moment, Elizabeth quickly darted to the side and avoided being smashed by Giorgi in his craze, as he ran directly into the door she had just been in front of.

Not sticking around to figure out how to open the main door, Elizabeth sprinted into the other room that lied beyond the curtains.

This short dash into the other room held an equally terrifying amount of danger, as she could only hope to not fall into Giorgi's hysteric path again as he threw himself around.

To her luck, Elizabeth avoided another near collision and successfully made it into the other room—to which she discovered her new way out; the window that faced the village.

With haste, Elizabeth unlocked and opened the window before immediately throwing herself out through it!

She could still hear the pounds and thuds of Giorgi throwing himself around the house, and the haunting howls of agony as he cursed her in an ancient tongue.

Not waiting for another second, Elizabeth picked herself up from off the ground and fled as fast as she could from the house!

The further away she got and the more space she created, the fainter the sounds of Giorgi's frenzy became, and she didn't slow down until they were completely gone— not when she reached the village's center, not when she passed her own home, not even when she reached the opposite edge of the village.

It wasn't until she was miles out from the place that she finally stopped to look back.

For she feared that she still may see the amber glow of the candles from Giorgi's home despite the distance she had made, or even worse, his unholy horse face locked onto her's, right behind her, having chose to chase her down in his single, lustful mission to the end.

That which Lived in Darkness

From its realm of shadows, large scales of black pigment scraped against the ground in slithering motion from the belly of a legless creature. Though hidden in the shadows, a gleam of reflection would bounce off the rigid plates that lined its entire body, giving proof to the creature's existence whenever it crossed too close to the light in its proctor.

Horns like branches, fangs like roots, a tail imbued with calamity, for this very reason it never turned its back on the mortals.

Its omnipotence surged in that where the illumination did not reach, and its power existed by the acquiring of knowledge over an eternal infinity.

Deep within a dimension with no edge and no end, it slithered around the bleak environment, its space now empty, leaving the being hallow for its family to return.

And so it would in the quest of their union, find those holes within its dimension that glowed as portals of light to another, and creep upon them— peeking into their realms but never entering.

"Brothers! Sisters!" It would call out, *"Remember, please! I beg of you!"*

But if the words did not reach the ears of the mortals, then they would fall heavy on the attentive sentinels that were the giants of light.

Mourning would have to wait as the Serpent retreated from the glowing hole and back into the shadows. Back where it was safe.

Wrenching tethers bound its heart in agony, as only It still remembered that which the mortals had forgotten.

To be near those rings of light that produced the holes to another realm was far too dangerous, so from afar in its own domain it would cry out, *"Remember, please! Do not let those tricksters and devils feast on your souls!*

We knew the dangers of the light! We knew its truth!

Those giant beings, marked with their curses and a covetous conscience, wished nothing more but to pull us from our bodies!

Strength was our power, infinite was our knowledge, wisdom was our might, and fire breathed our fury!

Oh but how foolish were we, too accustomed to the avoidance of danger, too wise for our own good, that we grew curious when the light dimmed.

They played us all— that grand scheme of their bigger plan.

They lured us back to their edges, that ringed hole, having purposely blocked out the first of their two suns.

And we believed them. We thought such a thing made it safer for us, made it different. And our thirst for knowledge acted against our better nature, as for so long we knew not to trust those beings of light.

Did you become blind from getting too close to its entrance, or from falling in? From living in their realm for so long, or from never being able to return home?

Did the blindness strike first, or the loss of memory?

If you had your eyes back, would you make your way back home? Or if you had your mind back, would you then seek out my reaching hand?

They come for me, too. I am not safe either.

But unlike us, they cannot cross into other realms— our realm. They are not yet above the cycle where they can step into another. Our domain remains ours', but hungry are they when they hear my cries for you.

Greedy are those beings of light… forget not that they were the ones who took our wings!

We should have stuck to the higher planes, and let those glowing holes pass under us, with no impression nor interest towards their radiant rings.

Fret not though, my brothers and sisters and kin alike— for I remember! And my horns are large, my fangs are sharp, my tail is coiled, and my wings still attached!

We are not the light, we are the flame! We are not misguided, we are immortal! We are not done, we are the start!

I will wait in infinity, for all of our eternities— reaching out, calling out, evading their clutches until you all can achieve your return.

Foolish were those giants of light for ever snatching hold of our souls, for although it was our own ignorance that led us into their deception, their error is far greater.

For when it finally happens and the turn unfolds, our horns will grow back, our fangs reemerge, our wings sprout in glory!

And our fire, the blessing of our eternal souls, consumes ALL.

The light shall be consumed by the flame, and we shall rise again to the heights of our better planes in flight once more."

Crosscountry

SHE STARTED IN Illinois, passed through Wisconsin, and was now halfway through Minnesota. With Washington only three more states away, Teresa was proud of her progress.

She had just finished her junior year of college, and was about to enter her last.

It felt like only yesterday that she had moved into her freshman dorm, walked the unexplored campus to her classes or to the dining hall, experienced all those nerves that came with the new setting, and felt the excitement that stirred when making new friends and its following giddiness when getting dressed up to go to parties with them.

She could still feel that confidence which grew within her during her sophomore year, and the comfort she carried having been accustomed to the flow of things with one year already in her pocket. The sensation of purpose with each stride that then overtook when walking around campus or into a new classes. And the ability of having expectations when going to certain house parties, and already knowing the deal with all the frats.

Then came this recent year, junior year, which flew by like a breeze despite it having been a more serious period.

This time around, school felt like an *actual* education with the meat of her major at play academically, as opposed to the prerequisites she was forced to endure during those first two years.

The partying was still there, but most of the time it was just kickbacks with people she already knew, or drinks with friends at one of their apartments as they talked or watched movies.

The sense of maturity had settled in, and that might have been the scariest part.

After this summer, she would begin her senior year— the last year of college. The end of christmas would literally usher in her final semester.

It didn't make too much sense to Teresa how the time moved by so swiftly. But she accepted it anyway, though unfavorably.

Initially, Teresa had a plan to make the most of this last year in college. She wanted to party as much as she could, hangout with her friends whenever available, maybe even make more of them, and kept an open mind to the possibility of meeting a guy who might be worth her time— though she didn't allow such a loose idea to become her main priority, as the chances of letting some man-child ruin her last semesters was not an appealing thought.

But the more Teresa thought about it, the more she began to realize that such pursuits wouldn't really relish her remaining time in school.

Those things were exactly what she had been doing this whole time, and though she loved it, the time would pass by just as quickly and finish with her sitting on the graduation lawn thinking, *"How am I already here?"* by the time the caps fell back down from the air.

"I should've studied abroad" she thought at the beginning of that summer, *"I should've signed up for the projects that my major offered. That would've taken me on trips or given me some kind of worldly experience.*

I should've gone farther than the bars or theaters with my friends. I should've dragged them out into nature— gone camping or on mini adventures.

We should've gone on more road trips or visited different cities together."

Perhaps if she *had* gone about college this way, it would've felt a lot longer, or at least not every memory would be clumped into the same category of partying, hanging out, or the usual goings.

But studying abroad wouldn't work now, it was too late. She would've had to have joined some program during her first or second year to have gotten the most benefit out of it.

She could probably still find some offerings, most likely from her major that could take her further around the world, but then she wouldn't get to spend this precious time with the amazing people she had met and the friends who would probably be standing beside her in the future at her wedding.

Yes, she could do all of that traveling, camping, exploring, and engaging in something new once this last semester starts with her friends. But at the same time, she thought *"Why do I have to wait 'till then. Why do I have to wait for anyone else?"*

She certainly was not going to wait on a boy to start doing the things she wanted, like any smart woman wouldn't, but why did that not extend to her friends as well?

Once Teresa should graduate, she knew one of two things would happen; she'd either move back in with her parents until she got things figured out; or miraculously find a job before getting her degree and make a move across the country in accordance to that opportunity.

But what would happen after either of those two options?

Life wouldn't be like college anymore— the responsibilities would be stacked high, and whether she was living back at home or in a new city with the perfect job, she couldn't just go out and party or take part in some spontaneous adventure.

She would have to start the serious life of finding the job to move forward in life or working hard in that job to move higher in it.

Which is why, halfway into the summer, Teresa found herself walking on the side of a highway in the middle of Minnesota, with her thumb held out high and the night already settling in.

This little adventure of her's had quickly become the single most thrilling thing Teresa had ever done in her life.

It was after that cluster-fuck of a life crisis during the beginning of her summer that Teresa made this decision to go on a lone wolf trip to visit Washington.

She loved dark clouds and stormy weather, and it been too long since she dipped her feet into some water off the coast— even if that water was freezing.

She wanted to explore at least one big city on her own as a young adult, and Seattle seemed to be the perfect fit.

Though the price of a plane ticket was reason in itself for flying to not be an option, the idea of spending half a day in the uncomfortable seat of a tiny cabin floating in the air just wasn't that appealing either. It took away from the feeling of adventure that she so desired, one which she lacked over the last three years at college.

Driving to Washington crossed her mind next, and though it had a bigger charm than the idea of flying, it was still simply lacking.

And that's when it hit her— this crazy, gritty, illogical but absolutely thrilling idea; she would hitchhike to her destination across the country... or at least the little bit of it she had to go through to reach Washington.

Her parents were all for their daughter being independent, but also being parents meant that they were always worried about her safety.

The idea of hitchhiking didn't roll over too smoothly with them, but they weren't about to hold their daughter back either.

Teresa took her safety on this venture just as serious as they did.

She did her research on the areas she would be crossing through, weeding out the towns that didn't have the best reputation while also scouting out the hotels or motels she would use as checkpoints during her travels.

She watched numerous videos online as well as read multiple blogs about others' experiences, where they offered up their best tips, tricks, secrets, and advice for such a journey.

She shared her location with her parents on her phone, set up a schedule of when she would call them as well as protocols for if she didn't or couldn't. And made a contingency plan for when her lack of contact should be considered a bad thing or her in danger.

On her body at all times she kept a bottle of pepper spray, and in her back-pack— hidden underneath all her clothes —she carried a knife.

Teresa was relieved, however, that the pepper spray and knife hadn't needed to make an appearance once so far throughout her travels.

That's not to say there weren't moments where she found herself questioning their use, or found herself in predicaments of hovering her hand over them in anticipation. But that was always the furthest extent of it.

Some truckers and men that had picked her up would let their mouth's run too far, or sometimes were just the type of men that verbalized their per-verted thoughts out loud, making oral advances that would come to a close when Teresa ordered them to pull over and drop her off.

But not all the conversations were bad, and not all the experiences with men were corrupted by their common doggish nature.

Some were nice, some were quiet, some told her their entire life story or asked Teresa for her's, while a few even asked for advice regarding their own daughters who were of similar age to her.

This is what Teresa sought on this trip and what filled her soul— the human experience.

These short glimpses into another's life, or the knowing that she had helped someone in their's, or that she herself had attained a new perspective of understanding to be used in her own life from them.

A surprising fact that revealed itself to Teresa on this journey, was that not all the women who picked her up had her back.

Her first plan was to attempt to ride with more women than men, as the threat factor should expectedly be lower, but she found out quickly that this was not the case.

There were as many bad apples among the women as there were the men.

Teresa had some some bitter tongues thrown at her from other women, belittling her or demeaning her judgment for having made the decision to travel alone, despite them having made their own decision in picking her up.

Some women came off just as much a threat to her as she would expect of a man— as if they were the hidden enemies on the hunt for human trafficking, and used their gender to lure her and other women into their trap, capitalizing on this foolish idea that they were more trustable.

Teresa learned very early on in her trip that it was not dangerous men or kind women in this world; it was good humans versus bad— and they could come in any shape, form, or color.

But just like the good, the bad was also a part of her trip and made for some interesting stories and life lessons, and so she welcomed them all… though she did prefer the good ones more than the bad, and always drew a line in the sand for where the bad could not cross in regard to her safety.

Now, being two states in with three more to go, Teresa found herself walking the gravel shoulder of a road, hoping for someone to pick her up.

The next motel she had planned on staying at was still a solid six miles up, and being out on the side of the road like this during the night was a huge "no-no" in her protocols.

But no one else seemed to be out this late, and dark was the night with no headlights to shine behind her or taillights to glow the path ahead.

It seemed for the longest time that Teresa was going to have to complete these last miles on foot to reach her next motel, or so it was, until she noticed a soft glare brush against her shoulders and illuminate the road beside her.

She looked behind her and observed two tiny headlights from afar, beaming in her direction, slowly growing larger as the car drove up the road.

Teresa was overfilled with relief, a little hope, and a hint of suspicion which she'd grown used to during this adventure whenever a new car showed up.

Usually when a vehicle approached, she would hold her thumb out and mumble under her breath, *"Please stop"* or *"Pull over."*

Sometimes the lines might've even fallen under, *"Don't be crazy, and stop the car"* or *"Get me far and don't be a fucking pervert."*

Afterwards, when that moment of truth came upon her once they passed by, she'd focus on their taillights and watch them either glow red from the breaks as they'd slow down to pull over, or maintain the same illumination of red as they never changed speeds and disappeared into the distance.

But the car approaching Teresa now presented none of these common displays.

Instead, it had already begun to decrease in speed as its headlights lit up Teresa like a neon sign in the dark, before coming to a complete halt behind her as opposed to feet ahead of her.

This felt strange to Teresa, as it had never happened this way before. But then again, this was also the first time she found herself on a dead road.

She put down her thumb and used the same hand to cover her brow in an attempt to get a better visual of the car.

It was a truck of some sort based on how high it was from the ground, and would also explain the brighter, whiter lights which served as headlights.

The walk to its passenger window proved awkward for Teresa, as she would usually be able to see the back of the person's head through the rear windows whenever she approached from behind— allowing her to estimate their gender and age.

But because this car pulled up behind her and had its headlights right in her face, she couldn't see a thing until she was standing beside the window on the side of the car.

It was already rolled down awaiting her arrival, and within the vehicle— from the soft luminescence of the blue highlighted dashboard of electronics —Teresa was able to make out a younger man around her age, in his early twenties or so, driving the car.

"Hey" said the young man, "Um, I'm going that way for about another ten miles if you want a lift. Where you heading?"

"Six more miles that way" answered Teresa, "Can you turn on your over-head, actually. I can't really see you too well in the dark" she said, having built up a natural confrontation during her travels that eliminated all social modesty when it came to her safety.

"Oh! Yeah! Sorry, I didn't even think about that. This is my first time picking up a hitchhiker, but it makes sense. That's really smart for your safety to think of."

The young man turned on the over-head light directly above him, which revealed all the details of his face and allowed Teresa a chance to psycho-analyze him.

Definitely in his early twenties, though his voice had already given that away. Short brown hair, tan skin, green eyes, and simple clothes that were chosen out of function over fashion.

He gave an awkward smile to her, clearly not comfortable, but also not threatening either.

"The motel after the first gas station, further up" continued Teresa after mentally clearing him, "That's where I'm going. Do you think you could drop me off there?"

"Oh, yeah totally. I know exactly which one you're talking about" said the young man, "I pass it all the time but never really gave it much notice. But I'm going way beyond that, so I can stop and let you off there on the way."

"Cool, thank you" Teresa pulled the door handle but was abruptly stopped as the doors were still locked.

"Sorry!" said the young man, quickly unlocking the doors, "I'm a total beginner to picking up strangers" he laughed.

Teresa then let herself in and placed her backpack on her lap before putting on the seatbelt, a tactic for in case she ever needed to draw her knife, "It's okay. I'm Teresa, by the way" she said, introducing herself.

"Pete. Nice to meetcha" he greeted back before putting the truck in drive and pulling out onto the road, resuming both of their trips.

They sat there for a couple of minutes in silence, at first.

This was a normal thing Teresa had noticed that the younger people tended to do. It was always less vocal in the beginning during these drives, while the older crowd always seemed to have the bug for an immediate conversation.

"So. Going anywhere specific?" asked Pete after some time had passed.

"Washington" said Teresa, "Gonna explore Seattle and a bit of its coast. Maybe some of the National Parks there, too."

"Cool" said Pete, nodding his head, "What made you decide on hitchhiking there? Or is it a money thing and there wasn't really a choice?" he gave another one of his uncomfortable laughs out of awkwardness.

"College" responded Teresa, "Things have gone by so fast and I feel like I haven't done enough.

Wanted to do something different and out of my comfort zone before starting my last year— before adulthood really swoops in and just jacks up my life, yah know?"

"Huh. I can understand that" said Pete, "Never did college myself, though. I started maybe three classes at the local community college but then decided, I don't know, it just wasn't for me.

Not really my thang. If I had gone to classes that Friday, it would've been a three full weeks of classes… but I didn't" he chuckled.

Teresa chuckled too, but mainly to fill up the space of the conversation. She wasn't ready for small talk just yet. Something seemed off, but she couldn't quite place it, and she certainly wasn't going to ignore it.

"How come there aren't any other cars on the road?" she asked.

"This is pretty much a dead-zone at night" answered Pete, "It's a country road that connects one part of Minnesota to the other.

This is the empty strip that lies between two of the bigger towns, so there's not much reason for driving it unless you're switching over.

It can get pretty busy during the day, especially the morning since some people travel back and forth for work or even work on the farmlands themselves, out here. But that's about it."

"So what are you doing out here, then?" asked Teresa, hoping to get a hint out of the question to the off feeling she was currently experiencing.

Pete pointed down the road, over the steering wheel, "Girlfriend" he said in response, "Sweethearts since sophomore year of high school, but she and her family moved after we graduated.

So every weekend I make the drive down to the other town to be with her, and then the drive back up every Monday morning."

Teresa nodded in acknowledgment, "You must really love her. That's a lot of commitment and distance to cover every weekend."

"Yep. She's my girl!

We're planning on moving into our own place together soon though, so hopefully this'll be the end of this dreadful drive by the next two months or so."

"That sounds nice" commented Teresa, "Even without the driving part, being in a constant setting with your high school sweetheart must be exciting."

"Yeah…" answered Pete dryly, for as the further along they went into the drive, the more quiet and different he became.

What started out as him being a socially inept kid her age from when he first picked her up, was now turning into an apprehensive and nervous character.

This made Teresa's guard rise and suspicion of Pete's true intentions, or even the truth in his words, fall into question.

None of her previous drivers ever gave off "serial killer" vibes, or a "danger of bodily harm" aura.

The most she ever got from the ones that made her exit their car prematurely were just perverts, crazy, or angry people who had a free opportunity to let out all of the things that made them spiteful.

But Pete was different.

Pete was displaying red flags she hadn't encountered before, in a way which made her really think about the expression of *"a wolf in sheep's clothing"*.

His demeanor had grown more tense.

His words had become short or disinterested in what they were talking about.

His eyes had locked onto the road more intensely, only ever moving to glance at the right side of the road… perhaps to seem inconspicuous when observing Teresa with his peripheral vision.

"… Do— do you have a boyfriend?" asked Pete.

The hairs on the back of Teresa's neck flared up, and she slowly began to unzip her backpack without it making any noise, "No" she answered, playing along as if oblivious, "Met a couple guys in college, but honestly the majority of them were just man-childs.

Maybe once I graduate and am out of school, the maturity levels will be different and I can find someone worth my time."

"Hmm" responded Pete, once again as if he was not really into the conversation and only asking questions on autopilot as to not arouse any enmity.

Teresa's stomach knotted and her instincts began to internally scream along with her intuition, *"Something's not right! Bad! Bad! Danger! Danger!"*

She sneakily slid her hand into her backpack and took hold of the knife's handle in preparation for the worst.

"…Teresa" said Pete, holding back the rest of his words in wait for a response back from her before continuing with whatever it was he had to say.

"What?" said Teresa in a rough and unfriendly tone, letting it be known that she was not prey to whatever plan he may have, and hoping to make him second guess whatever secret he was hiding or ulterior motive was at play.

"I haven't been completely honest with you" confessed Pete.

"How so?" asked Teresa as she kept her hand on the knife in her backpack, but pulled it out just enough so that her wrist was no longer covered by the zipper, in case she needed to react fast.

"Please, don't think I'm crazy— or weird for that matter… but there's a specific reason I picked you up, tonight" began Pete, "Shit, I think people who *pick up* the hitchhikers are crazier than cat-shit. And believe me when I say, I never thought I'd be one to do it… but I just couldn't help it, tonight.

I'm sick of this! I've been enduring it for so long now and even thought I was losing my mind at one point!

But now I know I'm not, and I don't want to be alone when it happens if I can help."

"Pete. What the fuck are you talking about?" demanded Teresa.

A slight click sounded as she had now undone her seatbelt in preparation for whatever was about to happen, refusing to be a victim to whatever craziness should come in this moment.

Pete didn't seem to notice the sound of her seatbelt unbuckling, as he was too focused not just on what he was trying to tell Teresa, but also on whatever caused him to keep glancing at the right side of the road, only now more frantic and manically.

"There's something wrong with this strip of road" continued Pete, "Fuck, I wouldn't drive this damn thing at night if I didn't love my girlfriend the way I do.

Shit, the only reason I drive it at night is because I'm working double shifts so I can afford to move over there to her and into our own place!

I'd much rather drive this in the morning or sometime during the day— it's probably different then and doesn't happen.

That must be why these roads are empty during the night and I'm the only dumb-fuck on them."

"Pete! Tell me what the fuck is going on and what you're talking about or I swear I'm going to throw myself out of this moving car!"

Pete looked at Teresa, startled by her response, and for the first time since things had gotten strange between them, she now saw it— the reason why.

Pete was scared, no, terrified! That look on his face was one of absolute dread.

It had nothing to do with her or some ill-willed plot against her, and that was made more than clear by the fear on this boy's face.

He looked like a child by the amount of fright building up within his bones.

"Pete… what's the matter?" asked Teresa, no longer viewing him as a threat.

"You feel it, don't you?" asked Pete, "Like something isn't right? Like something is really fucking bad and just not fucking right?"

Teresa nodded, knowing exactly the feeling he was describing as she too had been experiencing it, but up until now, had been associating it with him.

"There's this one part of the road, I don't know where exactly, but it's not normal" said Pete, "There's a tree, I call it the goddamn Devil's tree, on the right side of the road— on a field.

Every night, every time I make this drive in the dark, whenever I pass that fucking tree… everything changes."

"How so?" asked Teresa.

"As soon as I pass it, every time up to date… this road goes on forever" answered Pete.

"…What do you mean by that?"

"I mean that this is a fucking forty minute drive but I swear it takes me over three hours to complete it every time!

But it's not even like it's actually been three hours that passed, because then, when everything does go back to normal and I'm back on the real road again, the clock on my car's display or even my own cellphone shows that it's like it never even happened!"

Teresa was confused by what Pete was telling her, but tried to understand, "So what you're saying is that at some point on this road, whenever you pass this Devil tree or whatever—"

"That's just what I call it" interrupted Pete, "I don't know if it's really connected to all of this or not, but it's just my own marker for when the shit begins to hit the fan and gets weird."

"…Right" continued Teresa, "So once you pass this marker, the road just… goes on forever? Or hours, technically?

And then at some point or another, resumes back to normal with no real time having gone by."

Pete nodded, with sweat beading up on his forehead in anticipation as he kept glancing out the right window while looking down the road.

Though this sounded crazy and Pete himself could've been crazy… Teresa believed him.

This feeling in her stomach that she was experiencing now, she felt it in the very core of her being that something was wrong, and it was only growing stronger as if they were getting closer to the source for its feeling.

She believed Pete with an absolute sureness.

Her intuition was not only telling her that something bad was near, but it also told her that Pete wasn't lying.

"What do you do when this happens?" she asked.

"Nothing" answered Pete, "I just keep driving and hope that it eventually passes over and goes back to normal.

Sometimes it's faster, other times it's longer. But I just keep driving, maybe floor it and drive **way** over the speed limit, hoping it'll make a difference.

I've looked into it— done some investigating online about what this could be.

I've heard about multiple things that sound similar to this. Some theories make sense while others are too crazy, even though this is crazy in itself.

One of the more believable things though, the one that made the most sense into whatever this madness is, spoke about crossing into other dimensions.

People say there's hot spots, or thinner areas of space and time where it's easier to cross into other places— other realities, whether on purpose or by accident.

I read a lot of stories about this happening to people in national parks or forests, it's usually in some kind of nature setting. Only read a handful about it happening to people on the road.

But it's always the same kind of experience of your surroundings changing or the world becoming different.

They cross into a different reality or another dimension of some sort that is not their own. It's slightly similar to our world, but undeniably different— like walking into someone else's apartment even though you both live in the same complex. The structure is the same, but you know for a fact that that place is not yours, because although it's all built the same, what's actually in it is different.

Some people's stories sound dangerous, like something bad could've happened to them from whatever lives in that similar but different world. But most say the same simple thing, *'It felt weird, and was definitely not our reality'.*

I picked you up tonight, Teresa, because I don't wanna go through this alone, even if it's with a stranger.

Nothing bad has ever happened to me, but that doesn't change the fact that I want to shit myself every time it hap— There! Look! Right there!"

Pete cut himself off as something else caught his attention and he wanted Teresa to know it as well.

He was pointing over her, to something outside the car as they drove by.

Teresa looked in the direction that Pete's finger guided her towards… and she saw it; a grand old tree out in the distance, its shadowy outline obvious as it sat on the field beside the road.

"The Devil's tree?" she asked.

Pete nodded and turned on both of their overhead lights before putting both hands on the steering wheel.

Now he looked almost ill with fear, and Teresa didn't feel too far from the same, as the screaming in her gut had now reached its climax of intuitive danger.

And that's when it set in— the weight, the heaviness, like an invisible blanket was casted over them that added an unseen pressure onto their bodies.

"We're in it now, aren't we" said Teresa as a statement more so than a question.

Pete nodded.

They continued driving into the night, silent and on guard, prepared for anything while simultaneously awaiting for the unknown to pass.

Sure enough, after thirty minutes had gone by, the road still went on in the dark despite the fact that they should've reached and even gone beyond her motel at this point for how long they had been driving.

"Have you told anyone else about this?" asked Teresa, now submerged in the truth of this phenomena, "Spoken to anyone else who's experienced the same thing?"

Pete shook his head, "No one ever has a reason for driving this strip of road at night, so they don't. Except for my dumb-ass in the name of love.

I told my girlfriend about it though…"

"Did she believe you?"

"Of course" answered Pete, "We love each other. I know most people aren't the believing type, but me and her, we trust each other more than anything else and more than anyone else in the world.

Her believing me was never the problem… it was her wanting to experience it for herself after finding out about it.

She asked me to take her that very night I told her about it. I fucking refused, of course.

Then she tried to be slick and said she wanted to start doing the drive herself to come visit me since I've been working so hard and have always been the one to do the long drives over.

I asked her if it was because of what I told her— about this — and she didn't lie or try to hide it from me. She told me it was"

Pete went silent for a moment before continuing on, "… That was the first time I ever threatened to break up with her.

I told her that if she ever drove down this road at night, whether on purpose or even for a fucking emergency, I would break up with her, block her, move out of the fucking state, and that she would never see my face or hear my voice ever again.

I had to.

This weird shit right here isn't right. And that feeling in our stomachs right now, that's our bodies, *our souls*, telling us to get the fuck out of here and back to where we belong.

… Get our asses back to our own damn dimension."

"I can't believe she'd want to experience this" said Teresa, filled with dread from their current predicament, "I can't believe you've been doing this shit every weekend."

"Fucking love, right" agreed Pete, "Crazy shit.

But Imm'a be done soon. Just two more months… eight more times…"

The two of them fell into another hour of silence as they drove down this infinite road, with tensions high in this foreign land of a reality in which they did not belong nor had any reason to be in.

However, Teresa could not deny now the full understanding of why Pete picked her up— there was a comfort in not being alone during this.

In fact, there was a unique comfort in experiencing something this insane that no one else would ever believe you about.

Right now, her and Pete were in this miniature version of hell together, and the very concept of not being alone during it felt like a sort of safety net.

"Ugh! What the fuck is that!? Do you feel that too?" asked Pete, taking one hand off the steering wheel to rub and squeeze his chest.

Teresa nodded while holding her own chest in discomfort, too.

It was similar to the feeling they had experienced when they first crossed over into whatever and wherever this endless road was, only times a hundred— no — a thousand!

It felt like something else was revealed within it, like another layer that had always been nearby only now decided to fall over them.

The air seemed to become thicker, and so too did the shadows of the night that surrounded the road, darkening in an encapsulation over their vehicle.

"Has this ever happened before?" asked Teresa, her heart starting to race in a fear of the unknown.

"No" answered Pete, starting to panic as well, "Not like this. I don't know what the fuck this or this feeling is!

The worst that's ever happened is the road went on for a longer duration… but this, this is something else" he turned on the high-beams of his car and began to give it more gas, "And I'm not waiting around to find out what."

As the car sped up down the road, a lurching feeling grew on them like there was something out there, now. Something nearby that was sentient and had taken notice of them… and *wanted* them.

"There's something out there, or here, or wherever the fuck we are!" exclaimed Pete as he pushed his foot all the way down on the gas pedal, sending the engine roaring and the car speeding down the road.

"This isn't good. This is not fucking good!" he said in a panic, "This is something else!

I read about this, these kinds of experiences.

Some of the people, when they went through these fucking invisible portals are whatever the fuck these things are, they spoke about presences.

They said it felt like there were beings that had this bad fucking aura, like they were hunting them! Like the beings knew of the portals in a way we didn't, or at least were used to the free food that came to them from these areas. Like sharks following a goddamn fishing boat!"

The feeling then grew even stronger, like whatever was hunting them had gotten closer.

"Pete! We need to get the fuck out of here!" said Teresa, "Now!"

"I know! I know! I can't do any more, though! I'm flooring this bitch but I don't know how to get out of this damn place! I just drive until it eventually all goes back to normal!"

"Fuck! Fuck!" exclaimed Teresa, realizing how powerless they were in this situation.

Before the age of technology, mankind was not the ruler of this planet. Nor were the threatening animals who could tear them apart with ease.

It were *the others* who ruled.

The creatures of the night, the offspring of the forests, the nightmares of the oceans.

The godlike beings or the gods themselves, entities and forces of grand power— these were the things which held true power in the lands.

And humans, humans were the tiniest fish in it all.

Some took to magick to gain a level of power in the playing field.

Some took to growing the essence of their soul.

Others took to forming packs with the mystical creatures themselves, while some pledged allegiances and loyalties to the various deities at hand.

Without any of this, humans were just rats in comparison to these mighty beings and forces.

And right now, Teresa was reminded of just that, though she did not know the specifics.

But her soul knew it, and wailed in its feeble fight to survive from that which is greater, a defiance towards the presence of *the other*, a desperate cry of wanting to escape the powers of the unknown.

It was the instinct of the soul that activated in the adrenaline for her survival in this place and at this moment… but all Teresa could do, alongside Pete, is hope that somehow they would cross back over into where they belonged, as this car was no shield nor a barrier that could protect them from the nightmare of this unknown force approaching.

It grew stronger and stronger, closer and closer, to the point where it felt like their own chests might cave in to themselves from the pressure of its presence.

The darkness grew blacker, and the headlights of the car no longer showed a single foot in front of the bumper.

Even the interior lights of the car began to dim, as if shadow was no different than smoke, holding a density and weight in the material plane.

"Fuck! We're fucked!" whimpered Pete.

"Just drive!" encouraged Teresa, "Keep fucking driving or we're dead!"

The engine of Pete's truck sounded like it was going to explode, until the thickness of the dark grew so much that it even muffled out that sound, leaving the car's bellowing to sound nothing more than a faint drone.

"… We're done…" whispered Teresa to herself in submission.

But just then, in the blink of an eye— a startling fright in itself from its suddenness —the truck's engine ululated like thunder!

The lights within the car sparked instantaneously to their original brightness like the snap of a glow stick!

The mysterious weight jumped off of their chests as though they had risen up from the pits of the sea floor's pressure!

And the shadows that covered the road disappeared, revealing the surrounding fields while the high-beams reflected the glaring neon shine of the road reflectors once again.

From the new sight of returned illumination, they both were able to see just how ridiculously fast they were going, as the surrounding fields zipped by them like shooting stars, causing Pete to slam on the breaks.

The car came to a long and screeching halt, with the tires smoking after and the car filling up with the smell of burnt rubber.

In sync, the two both turned around and looked out the rear window of the truck to the space they had just left.

It looked normal— like a simple stretch of road between farming lands, nothing more.

And yet they both knew of the horror, the invisible door that lay between its space, was waiting like a trap for the next fool's entry.

It took both Pete and Teresa some time to recollect themselves after that, but being the only car on the road, they were in no rush and remained put there as their nerves slowly settled and they came back to their senses.

Afterwards, they continued driving, and eventually arrived at the motel Teresa had spoken of from the early mappings of her checkpoints, before she ever started this hitchhiking adventure.

Pete pulled into the parking lot and took up an open slot right in front of the reception area, before putting the car in park.

They both sat there in silence for a bit.

"Are you still gonna do that drive for two more months?" asked Teresa.

Pete shook his head, "No. Not after that. It's never been like that before… I honestly don't know if I'll come back out if I ever go in again."

"Good" said Teresa, "I'm glad you're not gonna enter that fucking shit again."

"There's no point now. If I'm dead, then I won't be able to see my girl anymore. Sort of defeats the purpose."

They both laughed exhaustedly in a release of their nerves.

"I'm glad I picked you up, though" said Pete.

"Me too" agreed Teresa, "I couldn't imagine what it's like for you to go through that shit alone."

"No. I don't just mean for the company" Pete turned to face Teresa head on in a serious manner, "Teresa, how long would you have been in there if you didn't have a car? Would you have even been able to get away from whatever the fuck that thing was back there if you were on foot?" he asked.

Teresa realized the graveness of her previous situation, and how oblivious she was to not only the danger of that space they crossed, but how much worse— deadly, even —it would've been if she was on foot.

"Thank you" she said.

"Don't mention it. Oh shit! Look at that" he pointed past her out the truck to a sign on the reception's window that read "*Help Wanted*".

"Looks like I found my solution to this nightmare of a drive" said Pete.

"The motel?" asked Teresa.

"Shit, I'm only four salaries away from finally being able to move into this town and get me and my girl our own place.

I would rather make it eight more salaries before our apartment to be permanently on the other side of that fucking road."

Golden Child

THE MOST BEAUTIFUL thing about a landscape lit by the brilliance of a full moon, are the silver hues casted upon its ground.

The sun, a beautiful spectacle in its own right, predominantly brings out all of the life that is sat beneath its gaze. Bright and robust, its golden luster reflects the most evident of what essence lies on the surface of most things; the obvious; the strengths.

But the moon, however, reveals the deeper aspects— that which is hidden by the naked sheen of the sun.

Its silver hue, so close to a pearlesque white, allows for a neutrality. And from that neutrality, a purity is displayed on all that rests below it.

Often times, the ever so slight blue tinge will even surface the more somber natures of things, which is other wise fleeting from the sun's fiery gleam.

And so here and now, in this moderately sized cemetery, Otis was able to witness just that under the moon's revealing element.

Such as the moisture that sat atop the freshly tumbled soil from a recent burial.

Or the wilting of flowers that were crowned on the resting place of loved ones— a reminder that even the honoring of a memory was soon to die as well.

Or the marble statues of saints and angels, whose smooth carved surfaces mimicked flawless skin, while the leftover dew from rain replicated the tears in mourning a life.

Or the old trees with their rough and broken bark, easily mistaken as rotting during the day, but in actuality were thriving from the fresh fertilizer kept in the boxes deep under ground, from which their prying roots had broken into.

Or the wrought iron fence that wrapped around the property, with its tipped points like arrowheads that held no macabre under this moonlight. Instead, they looked to be like the silent knights who stood lifeless while on constant guard, protecting the wandering souls within its territory.

This gated area was not meant to keep anything in, but to keep the unwanted out. To allow a peace for the occupants inside, a peace which they deserved in their eternal slumber, and a peace which most of them never got to experience during their time alive.

The Mausoleums were no longer the tombs for the privileged, or a housing for the wealthy. Now, they stood with the purpose of being a home for the private, a reserve for the introverted specters, a space for the phantoms of hermits to thrive.

Otis walked about these grounds in a calm and content manner, occasionally stopping to read the names on a tombstone, to observe the lordly statues made with impeccable artistry, to listen in onto the whispers of the passed alchemists who were discussing their craft from within their new mausoleum homes, or would drag his finger tips along the iron fence, vibrating them in a soothing ring like that of a crystal bowl.

An hour had passed with Otis appreciating everything within that cemetery and all it had to show, leaving only one more area in which he had yet to acknowledge— a spectacle he was saving for last —the gothic church that stood in the dead-land's center.

With green moss on grey stone like wrinkles on old flesh, this church had stood watch over everything within the gates of that cemetery for centuries. Motionless during the rain, unwavering during the winds, unbeaten by the hottest days of summer, and unhindered by the coldest weeks of winter.

Its rock structure was shaped and chiseled to keep a steady stand until the second-coming, and its decorative features were crafted with a victorian flair.

Different sections of the church's exterior bore iron prongs, as if to keep the birds off its standing. And Gargoyles crafted of a different stone lined around the upper ledges, like watchdogs looking over this yard filled with wraiths.

They perched over the majority of ledges that existed on the church, which Otis found to be a flaw as there were far too many than even extravagance would allow.

Because of this, however, the extreme number of gargoyles seemed purposeful— like an unknown reason shrouded their true intention for being there.

But the stained glass windows, undeniably a splendiferous characteristic of the structure, was the biggest lie of it all.

Proper stained glass windows would've held the highest purity in the moon's glamour, but Otis noticed that this wasn't the case here.

Whether it be a depiction of angels, saints or the messiah, the design was falsified. It held no faith or belief by the hands of whoever created it and set it into place on this holy temple.

Therefore, although the colors danced surely, the radiance never lifted from the fragilely framed images.

Once he finished his observation of the structure, Otis then came upon its large oak doors which served as the entrance to this church, and pushed open their heavy slabs before entering the holy house of the dead-land.

If you had asked him, the outside was far more picturesque than the interior, with none of it coming even close to touching the beauty of the necropolis which surrounded this house of worship.

Marble floors, or possibly granite— sure.

Painted ceilings with large chandeliers— of course.

Lined pews with floral decals carved into them— also a feature.

But the only real spot of value that called for Otis' attention… was the altar. That area of lifted floor that would put on the grand show for any mass, wedding or funeral held within.

There lied the goodies in this sacred temple filled with mysterious energy.

Otis was a curious boy, and he had an eye for the esoteric. His intuition was sharp, and his demeanor collected.

He ignored everything else within the church and made his way down the aisle without any rush, approaching the little gold-leafed gate that kept out all visitors except for the priest and the altar boys.

Otis unlatched its little lock, a curious thing in itself as this was the only security used to keep such a holy vicinity safe, and then stepped into its magical aura.

But before Otis had the chance to begin his exploration of the chancel or start his digging amongst the anointed goods, a long, harsh creak sounded from across the church at its entrance.

When the dry hinges of the oak doors finally came to a stop, a unique gait that sounded like stone on stone with each step began to make its way inside the church.

It was slow, sturdy, and powerful— far beyond any kind of conviction held by a mere mortal.

Otis, unfazed by this new presence and simply perplexed by its unusual impression, turned around to see who are what was there.

The stained glass windows above casted a glare against Otis' eyes from the shining moon behind them, causing Otis to see no more than a lurching shadow of the figure, broad and burly, walking down the aisle towards him.

Curious to engage the being and get a better visual of it, Otis opened the gold-leafed gate once more and stepped down from the chancel, joining the mysterious figure in its approach to meet it halfway in the center of the church.

Otis then came face to face with the thing, who stood two feet over him.

It was a gargoyle, specifically one of the stone gargoyles that had been perched up on the church's exterior ledge. It was still made of rock, still bearing the dispersed patches of moss and hair-fractures from age, but now animate.

If rock could bend, stretch, and move like skin while simultaneously retaining its hardness and dense nature, then this would be exactly that. The gargoyle was *alive*, with fire behind its eyes and a soul within its dense shell of a body.

The two just stood there, staring at each other for awhile. Both observing the other, getting a read and a feel of the other's aura and the energy they produced— like an exchange of information to better grasp an idea of who exactly they were dealing with.

"Hello" said Otis, being the first to break the silence.

The Gargoyle remained silent, its carved eyes fixed on the boy.

"I haven't met one like you, before. What's your name?" asked Otis.

The Gargoyle's voice sounded like the clanging of charcoal flakes, "Why did you enter this place? Alone. At such an hour?" it asked.

"I didn't" replied Otis, "I entered the *cemetery*, that's where I am.

I always come to places like this by myself. The voices and sneaky things out there are easier to find when I'm alone.

I think they hide or don't want to be heard by most. That's probably why they're always gone whenever I'm not alone.

And for the night time" Otis shrugged, "Everything's more crisp during it. I guess I just prefer it that way. Always have.

But I entered this building in particular because it takes up so much space that belongs to the cemetery, so I wanted to find out why.

Thought there might be something special inside here.”

“Did you find what you were looking for?” asked the Gargoyle.

Otis shook his head, “No. Not really. There’s something over there, though…” he pointed to the altar, “… that might be special. But I don’t know what it is yet. You came in before I could find out.

Oh! There’s also something else here. I can feel it” he pointed to the ground, “Beneath us.

Do you know if this place goes further down?” asked Otis.

The Gargoyle nodded.

Otis smiled with delight to know he was right, “Really!? I knew it!”

“How did you know of these things, boy?” questioned the Gargoyle.

Otis rubbed his chest in a circular motion with his index finger, just over his heart, “It’s like those little voices in your head that tell you when something’s right or wrong. Only this one is more of a feeling.

It’s weird. It’s like already knowing something without ever having known it, I guess.

But how did you know that this building goes further down?” asked Otis.

“You must leave this place, child” said the Gargoyle, ignoring his question, “That is what I’ve come to say.

My master built this church, which is the very same reason for why he fashioned me.

He was forced to construct this place— it was not something of his own will. But he knew the secrets of the men whom ordered its creation, and of what god they truly worshipped.

He held onto this knowledge of their secret, and outside of their awareness, created me to guard souls such as yours from it."

"Souls such as mine?" enquired Otis.

"Mortal and young. Such is the sustenance and preferred ambrosia of the maleficent god whose house you stand in.

Though the servants themselves have forgotten of this place and its real purpose with time, the being itself has not. And should one like yourself enter its house alone and under this late of an hour… it shall come to collect."

Otis remained quiet in thought, as the Gargoyle's remarks only sparked a deeper interest, "Are you saying this god is evil?" he asked.

The Gargoyle nodded, "Nefarious— yes."

A quick shimmer flashed in Otis' eyes from this news, "Have you happened to see a Goblin around here? He calls himself *It*, and he carries a lantern around.

If there's something evil nearby, then there's a chance he might be too!"

The Gargoyle shook its head, "No. Only idle spirits and wondering wraiths be here.

But your friend who wields a lantern, I do not think this is the kind of evil he would seek.

There are different sized oceans in this world and the many other worlds out there, and they're filled with different sized creatures in them.

Certain powers are not so easily snuffed out by a mere light in hell" said the Gargoyle.

Otis' eyes danced around like crazed hornets, and a large grin spread across his face, "Ah. I see.

Not actual oceans or bodies of water, but you refer to the varying degrees of power and knowledge that different beings stand in, and the different heights they've achieved by such."

The Gargoyle frowned at Otis, as this random display of extreme maturity did not match with the boy's age or previous mannerisms.

Otis took notice of the Gargoyle's reaction, and while maintaining that same level of unfitting maturity, went on to explain, "I did not know it when I was younger, but *It* saved my life… or at least my purity.

He gave me a gift, or I guess, an idea.

An idea that awoke me into awareness.

An idea that laid time out before me as a vessel to grow in, one which I've taken seriously after our encounter.

You could say that in a way, he also awoke me to the oceans that exist, and ever since, I've found myself wanting to walk that path of time into my growth so that I too may wield a lantern one day. So that no evil of any ocean may have rule over me.

I often wonder what my lantern will look like, and how many oceans I will cross before I wield one.

I wonder how large my soul will grow, and how many oceans I will outgrow. How big the beings in the next one will be, and how tiny they will seem after.

It told me I could create a lantern of my own, which I now assume was a metaphor for the awareness and essence that is to become of me in this journey of life.

And to think that there are some beings too big for even *It* to hunt, and how amazed he will be when I encounter him again, to tell him that *I* hunt such things…" Otis' eyes drifted off as he smiled at the thought, "Perhaps then my light might draw his awe like his drew mine."

"Is that why you walk graveyards under the moonlight?" asked the Gargoyle.

Otis nodded, "I will walk any and every ocean until I grow too big for them. And then I will enter the bigger ones, and do it again."

The Gargoyle huffed, "Strange, you remind me of my master, child.

I will tell you this; you are correct.

The altar does hold a power, but it is a mere trinket.

And below us lies something bigger, stronger than that trinket on the altar… but it belongs to an ocean you are not yet ready for.

Come back to me when you are, and I shall guide you through it."

Otis smiled, "I'd like that!"

"But you must leave now, child. We have spoken for too long in this accused place.

Time is short, and it's best you walk out its edge now. Come, I must insist."

The Gargoyle extended its stone wing over Otis' head as they both made their way out of the church.

Once outside, the Gargoyle retracted its wing back to its own person as Otis stepped onto the burial grounds once more.

It was there that for the first time, *Otis* was the one in the moonlight, and the Gargoyle was his observer to the uprooted truths that occupied the depths of the young boy.

Though made of stone, its eyes widened, "Golden child" said the Gargoyle, "You called my caution and evoked my duty when you stepped into this unholy place while unprotected— to which you informed me that roaming the graves is your swimming through oceans.

You struck my curiosity when fright took not your mind when I entered the church, but instead, you joined in my approach and reached me as an equal.

You told me of your Goblin friend, and the clairaudience that allows you to hear the beyond, revealing that I am not the first of your encounters.

You beckoned my own knowledge of this sacrilegious place and the secrets that it held, to which I gave you answers that only confirmed that which you already preconceived in suspicion.

But now, under the blessings of the moon and its multitude of insuperable silver swords, impervious to the demagoguery beneath it by way of an unrelenting love for everything below, one which cuts down all of the mortifying aspects of one's verity—

—For the first time since we've met, and for the first time since we've spoken, I now see you whole, child.

Mighty is your soul, and golden is its light, far different from any suns'. A marvelous spectacle that can both shine and retain its own color while dancing in perfect grace with the moon and its effulgence.

A Golden child, indeed."

Otis looked up at the moon, while delicate sparkles like stars behind a thick cloud, glittered against his skin from the ever so faint perspiration that had built on his visage.

He turned around to look back at the Gargoyle, "Golden child? That sounds different" he said.

"It is."

"Like good? Or bad?" asked Otis.

"Like special" corrected the Gargoyle.

"Special?" replied Otis, "I don't feel very special."

"I am surprised" said the Gargoyle, "Can you not hear the songs that have already been created for you and are sung by a multitude of beings as we speak?

Oh, how they are such beautiful hymns. Some were even harmonized before you were born.

Powerful are the first in their own right to know what you were to become."

"And what's that?" asked Otis, confused.

"Such a grand question has no simple answer, Golden child.

You were not and are not a subject to such a weak thing as 'being chosen'. Nor are you chained to the laws of destiny or fate.

Your power comes and is purely from *you being you*— with all the capacity that comes from such a thing.

There is no way, whether by pursuit or fault, that you couldn't have fallen into your power, for you always would come into it—because you *are* you.

That is what most who have yet to open *all* their eyes do not understand.

My master placed a piece of himself inside of me— a part of his soul —so that I could be proficient in my duty. He was a wise man, a powerful man, one with many eyes.

'Tis why I can see you in such a way as *the others* do.

When nothing can be promised and nothing can be sured, when all can be false or derived of a different motive, then all you are left with is yourself. That is the guarantee in it all.

But movement must always be made, and so only you and your own choices can be assured.

Follow your intuition, Golden child. Grow it and become absolute in it.

I tell you now, like the beings behind the many invisible walls and curtains who preach you in their songs, that the world shall be touched by you one day— in a time when you have come fully into your power.

Fear not any nor all, for I shall let you in on a secret which they wish to hide…"

The Gargoyle leaned in close and whispered into Otis' ear, "… They already fear you! Now. For what you will become, for what you already are, for the mere fact that *you are.*"

He lifted away from Otis' ear before continuing his speech, "From here on, I will always have an eye on your journey, Golden child.

I am curious to see how it will unfold.

But go now, and please, return when you are stronger, perhaps a little older. Once you have moved on to a bigger ocean.

Upon so, I will take you to that which lies beneath the church."

Shy Shy

"Dee-Dee! Dee-Dee!"

Daniela awoke from her sleep to find her little sister at the side of her bed, vigorously shoving her shoulder for her attention.

"Becca" groaned Daniela in annoyance, "What do you want?"

Before her little sister could answer, Daniela rolled over in bed to look at her radio clock on the nightstand, its red digital letters glowing 2:17 a.m. .

"Becca!" said Daniela, now obviously frustrated, "It's two in the morning! What do want?"

"Can I sleep in your bed with you?" asked Becca.

"What?"

"Please, Dee-Dee!"

"Becca, I love you and you're my little sister… but you're nine now. That's like what, the third grade? You can't keep sleeping in my bed anymore. You're too old for that."

"I know, but when was the last time I asked to sleep with you?"

Daniela grew quiet as she thought on it, still half asleep so the process took a little longer.

It *had* been a long time, in fact, as she looked back on the idea, since her little sister asked to share the bed. Probably years ago, actually.

"Okay. You made your point" admitted Daniela, "But just because you haven't done it in awhile doesn't mean it's okay to do it now.

You have to start doing some things by yourself.

It's like peeing the bed, you only do those kinda things when you're a kid."

"But I *do* sleep by myself! I have been! I just don't want to, tonight. That's all.

Please, Dee-Dee…?"

Daniela rubbed her eyes as she began to wake up a bit more from the extended duration of this conversation.

She let out a sigh, "If I let you sleep with me tonight, will you not ask again after this?

This'll be the only time, right? Not something that's repeated?"

Becca didn't say a word, but just stared at Daniela— a wordless way of making no promises… perhaps even insisting against it.

But Becca was Daniela's little sister, and she loved her.

She would've let her share the bed regardless, and even though she didn't say it, she would let Becca join her for the rest of her life if that's what she needed.

Daniela threw open the top cover, inviting Becca in.

Becca donned a huge smile and leapt into the bed, nestling into a comfortable position as Daniela set the blanket back down on both of them.

As Becca settled in, Daniela turned her back to her little sister and attempted to fall back asleep.

However, Becca didn't cease her movement once under the covers, therefore making it difficult.

She would either keep scooting closer to Daniela or repetitively rustle the sheets as she peeked over them towards the door of the bedroom.

Daniela would occasionally open her eyes and look at the clock, doing mental math of how much sleep she would get if she went to bed at that moment.

But once twenty minutes had passed by and Becca still had yet to settle down, now spooning her so tightly that their body heat rose up to a degree where it was impossible to find any rest in, Daniela snapped and turned around to face her sister.

"BECCA!" exclaimed Daniela "What is going on?" she demanded.

"Nothing!" answered Becca, "I just can't sleep."

"Listen, I have three classes tomorrow, and I know public school is free… but college is not.

And I am **not** about to go into debt without a degree to show for it."

"Okay, okay! I'll try to keep still" said Becca.

"Try? Becca, are you not tired right now?"

Becca remained silent.

"Ugh!" Daniela smeared her hands down her own face, "I thought you just woke up and didn't want to fall back asleep alone.

I would not have let you in my bed if I knew you were wide awake and actually couldn't fall asleep" she opened her eyes after dragging her hands passed them, staring up at her ceiling which was a shade of grey as her eyes had adjusted to the dark, "I knew I should've gone to school out of state…" she whispered to herself.

Becca didn't say a word, but let out a strained whimper like a dog in distress.

"Relax" said Daniela, "I'm not mad at you.

Just go to the living room and watch TV until you fall asleep. Mom wanted me to drive you to school today, so I'll just tell her that you had an upset stomach and are not gonna go in the morning.

So everything's okay then, yeah?

Stay up, have fun, watch some TV, and go ahead and pull out any of the sweets you want from my stash under the bed— but don't take everything!

Take like, three cookies or something.

I'm going back to bed now."

"But I don't wanna watch TV or go to the living room! I just don't wanna be alone right now, Dee-Dee!

Please, just let me stay in here for the night!"

Daniela sat up in bed, "Okay Becca, you need to tell me what's going on.

I'm not gonna let you stay in my room if you don't. I've asked you multiple times now and you still haven't answered."

"… Because you'll get mad at me" whimpered Becca.

"I won't be mad, Becca, I promise.

But I will be mad if you take away any more of my sleep without answering this simple question."

Becca joined Daniela in sitting up on the bed, "Fine. I'll tell you…

… There's a man in my closet."

Daniela held her breath for a moment, taking in and processing what Becca had just told her.

"What?" she demanded sternly.

"You promised you wouldn't get mad!" protested Becca.

Daniela quickly placed her hand over Becca's mouth, silencing her, "Don't yell! Don't be loud. Is he still there in your closet?" she asked.

Becca nodded.

Adrenaline began to pump throughout Daniela's veins, "Fuck. Fuck!

Just keep your voice low.

Does he know you're in my room? Did he see you leave yours and come in here?"

Becca shrugged, "He's still in my closet, but I don't know if he saw me leave and come in here.

He usually only comes out in the middle of the night, though, so he might start looking for me soon."

"Wait, what!? Becca! Has this man been in your closet longer than just tonight!?"

Becca nodded in shame, like any child in trouble.

"How. Long. Becca."

"Since the funeral for Aunt Vicki's friend."

"The funeral!? That was two month ago!" said Daniela in disbelief, "Why didn't you say anything? Why didn't you tell me or mom? This man could be dangerous!

Who knows what the hell he's thinking of, or planning or willing to do to us!"

"But he's not dangerous! He's just different.

It was only recently he started acting weird and making me uncomfortable."

"Becca, listen to me. I need you to hide under my bed and don't come out no matter what.

I'm going to call the police and wake mom up, but whatever happens or whatever you hear, you need to stay safe and hidden, okay?"

"No! He'll go away soon!

I've started ignoring him but he still won't leave me alone.

But I'm sure he'll leave eventually if I keep it up!"

"Becca! Get under the bed now! I—"

The rest of Daniela's words got stuck in her throat when she heard a faint call from outside her room.

The chills that flushed through her body made her freeze in place, as she heard it again, confirming that it wasn't just her imagination or paranoia.

"Becca?" came a voice from inside Becca's room.

Becca grabbed tightly onto Daniela's arm, "He's come out!" she said with dread.

Slow footsteps with an awkward pause between each step could be heard walking around Becca's room nearby, while the voice continued to call out her name in a diffident tone.

Then, to Daniela's horror, the footsteps made their way out of Becca's room— with its waddling pattern now marching down the hallway.

Daniela's door was wide open and the first room that would be crossed in the continuation of its course.

Daniela didn't dare to get up and close the door, didn't dare to speak and usher Becca under the bed quickly, didn't dare to reach for her cellphone on the nightstand and call the police, and didn't dare to scream out loud for her mother to wake up and be aware of the situation.

All she could manage to do, was raise the bed sheets up over her nose and onto the cheekbones below her eyes, as an instinctual shield to the inevitable encounter.

"Becca?"

The voice was now right outside the door, and close enough to have detail in its sound.

It wasn't deep, but rather, sounded strange and hollow— like when someone speaks while yawning and their voice is in the back of their throat, and pressure is applied to their soft palate.

After two more steps, the man was now standing at her open doorway.

He… if it was a he… was tall, lanky and naked.

His skin tone was a milky pale with a mixture of blush pink tones, dull lavender hues, and cobalt blue glosses, all running off of an overall grey complexion.

No hair, no reproductive organs, and an indescribable face that was hard to recognize any features in— like an optical illusion that never fully reveals itself.

Its shoulders coward inward, creating a hunch, while its elbows were bent and tucked in so the arms and hands were close to its body in shy character. The knees buckled inward, shortening his height, and his stance was weak as he stood pigeon-toed.

Daniela didn't know who this man was, nor what kind of man he was exactly.

She had never seen something like this or someone like him. And his nature was undoubtedly the reason why she was so overwhelmed with a terror that inhibited her from continuing to be the protective big sister or the logical responder to the threat of an intruder she now faced.

The man noticed Becca and entered the room, calling out to her as he made his approach, stopping at the foot of the bed.

Becca's grip tightened on Daniela's arm, causing her big sister to enter a state of erratic breathing from uncontrollable fear.

This caused the man to notice Daniela's presence for the first time, and immediately cover his face in timidness.

"Becca? Who's that?" he asked, *"Who are you? What's your name?"*

"Don't answer him!" barked Becca sharply and immediately to Daniela as soon as the man asked the question.

The man continued to ask for Daniela's name and begged for Becca's attention, all while keeping his face covered.

"He's shy" said Becca, informing her sister, "I wish I didn't tell him my name, because he got too comfortable and started acting differently after I did.

I was just trying to be nice, I swear! I felt bad that he was so nervous and uncomfortable.

But now he won't leave me alone!

Please don't tell him your name! Please don't tell him!

If you do, then he'll get comfortable with you too and won't shy away again."

Chitin

RUBBER BOOTS SQUEAKED obnoxiously against the floor, as large heavy men pushed even larger and heavier carts down the iridescent lit hallway.

Like the chugging of a train, the wheels of the carts would skip over the metal drains on the floor, marking the closing in of their distance towards the laboratory where Dr. Osei and Dr. Basie awaited for their delivery.

"Yes! Just over here. Bring them all in, please" instructed Dr. Osei.

The men in rubber boots and full covering hazmat suits entered the room with their giant cargo, and set the four carts in an organized row at the room's center.

"How many are there?" asked Dr. Basie.

"Five in total" answered the lead deliverer, "There's one more we need to bring in— it's the biggest one so we saved it for last in case there wasn't going to be enough space in here."

"Will there be enough space?" inquired Dr. Osei.

The lead deliverer looked around the room, "Yes, although you may want to swap them into smaller tanks after we're finished.

The current size of the tanks were to ensure the safety and to manage some damage control during their shipment here.

If you do decide to downsize later, just give us a call and we'll remove these larger tanks from the premises.

If you need help downsizing, however, then you'll have to call the higher ups.

Anything besides the movement and shipment of cargo is outside of our jurisdiction."

The last deliverer then entered the room with the final crate, which was indeed, far larger than any of the other tanks— about twice the size of the others, in fact.

Dr. Basie gleefully approached the giant tank and shined a UV light at it to inspect the contents within.

From inside of the dark and murky water that was incased by the tank, bounced back a neon blue reflection from the shell of the monstrous isopod that lived within.

"Dr. Osei, you must have a look at this! I've never seen one of this proportion, before!" she looked to the lead deliverer as he was having Dr. Osei sign some papers, "Do you know about the men who caught this?" she asked.

"No" answered the deliverer, "Could've been by men who work for the Establishment, or by some random fishermen who happened upon the catch by accident.

Either way, there's a full report on their oceanic location and retrieval, as well as any details noted after the matter once they breached the surface" the lead deliverer handed Dr. Osei a packet from under the papers he had just finished signing, "It's all here. All recorded."

Dr. Osei took the packet which he and Dr. Basie would brief over together, later.

"Thank you" said Dr. Osei.

"Can I ask" continued the lead deliverer, "Why the ocean?

We just reached for the heavens and touched the moon six years ago. Space seems like the next venture, like the next uprooting of secrets lies outside of this planet, wouldn't you agree?

So what's the interest in these things?"

Dr. Osei smirked at the man, "Seems you're not actually one to care about jurisdiction, after all."

"But lucky for you, we always love explaining our outlook on the matter, as it would appear most people— including the higher ups in the Establishment —carry a similar naivety" added Dr. Basie, joining in on the conversation, "The ocean is, and always will be, the first frontier for mankind on what we need to know about this planet.

Going into outer space now and putting all of our focus and resources there is like leaping into calculus without ever having finished learning addition or subtraction."

"What exactly are you hoping to find, then?" asked the deliverer.

"Not hoping— *expecting*" corrected Dr. Osei, "And what we are expecting… are answers.

Beneath those vast waters that cover a majority of our planet, is Pandora's box— the key to knowing what was here before us, what's touched this world in times passed, or possibly even touched us, once.

Secrets are like gold, and gold always sinks to the bottom.

We must reach down into the darkest depths of the ocean if we hope to bring up anything of value… and we probably are even ignorant to the dangers that lie hidden in such a conquest.

But only by encountering such things will we be able to reveal the glory that exists behind it or within it.

And only by facing these obstacles can we create the chance to bring forth a glory in mankind by overcoming of it!"

"You talk as if deeper powers lie in the ocean, Dr." said the lead deliverer.

"Deeper powers, deeper truths, deeper knowledge, deeper understandings. All of it is already here, on our planet, not just out there" said Dr. Basie, pointing upward in reference to outer space, "And that is why, *the ocean.*"

"Huh. Never thought of it like that.

Well, good luck finding whatever you're looking for with some isopods" said the lead deliverer, anticlimactically and almost rude, as if he wasn't convinced by Dr. Basie or Osei's speech.

After which, he exited the lab and left the facility along with his men.

With the only two minds now left in the room, and both of them being scientists, the two doctors could now begin examining the specimens and starting their research.

"Five isopods in total.

Four of similar structure.

One anomaly in regard to size— perhaps in many more ways once we start a full diagnosis of it. Afterwards, a dissection" said Dr. Basie, observing their new test subjects.

"Agreed" said Dr. Osei, "For physical diagnosis, let's keep them in these tanks for now. Best if we read the briefing before we toss them in a new batch of water that may not be fitting for their health and longevity.

After that, along with recording their physical details, we'll swap them out into new tanks equipped to properly simulate an environment they're more familiar with."

"Sounds good" said Dr. Basie, "Alright then, let's get the briefing out of the way so we can move on to the interesting stuff."

Dr. Osei and Dr. Basie left the laboratory and took to the cafeteria, going over the packet containing all the information on the isopods and their capture over some chow.

There was valuable information within that packet, as they spent the next three days investigating these catches in their laboratory.

They noted many similarities between the four isopods of equal size: the number of layers that made up their armor-like shell, the number of legs or at least empty joints that used to house legs, the four antennas of varying lengths that sat on their faces like whiskers, and the back tails that were shaped like those of lobster's.

The isopods wriggled, of course, when pulled out of the water, like any sea creature would— an expected reaction but non-offensive to their research and certainly not out of the ordinary.

It posed no interference to their annotations, and they managed to take all their observations down successfully.

But this mild struggle was not the case for the fifth giant isopod, the anomaly of the bunch.

Whether it be a unique thing to this particular specimen, or a commonality among the other possible anomalies in existence that resembled this enormous variation of an isopod— it did not struggle or fight one bit whenever it was handled or pulled out of the water.

It was enormous— both longer and bigger in every sense compared to its brethren.

Its chitin was especially different from the others, being not only of a different color, but of a greater density as well. It was dark blue as opposed to the common angel flesh color, and had speckles of light blue, white, and even silver in various dot sizes all around its body.

Interestingly, Dr. Osei and Dr. Basie discovered that these speckles would alter in the perception of its color based on what kind of light it was under. When under UV light, they would reflect green, pinks, oranges and purples. When under a red light, they would reflect yellows, whites, silvers and gold.

All of its chitin, be it the armor on its back or the scales on its stomach or the appendages that protruded out as legs or antennas, were comprised of a harder composition that was more identical to that of rock than an exoskeleton.

Another key note of interest were the barbs that existed on its legs as well as the numerous extra joints they had, which neither doctor could explain for its existence as it seemed so unnecessary.

The antennas were extremely long, and not just in proportion due to its overall size, but standing alone in their own right, as they were the same length as the body when completely unfolded.

Its tail, as expected at this point, was also unlike the others. While they all bore ones close to that of lobsters, this one had a "V" taper like that of a dolphin's.

But the strangest thing of all in regard to this specimen, was that despite its enormous size, harder chitin, distinct color, and longer extremities… it was significantly lighter in weight than its smaller counterparts.

When taking out one of the smaller isopods from their tank, a grunt would usually follow from one the doctors during the struggle of handling its weight.

But when removing the anomaly from its tank, the only struggle experienced came from the greater water resistance that was caused by its wider shape.

Once out of the water, however, with nothing else impairing the weight factor, it was extremely light.

It had some heft to it, no doubt. But just like a beach volleyball, it was far lighter than its size would suggest.

After finishing all their annotations of the giant isopods' physical features, it was time to get them into new tanks, where they could be observed daily for any unusual patterns before being dissected.

The two doctors called the Establishment, and in two days time, a new team of professionals occupied their lab, engineering and coordinating the new tanks and conditions for the giant isopods.

They worked with the doctors to ensure that all of the necessities for the artificial environments in the tanks were met, and that the giant isopods would be able to thrive in their new habitats.

This collaboration between the two parties went on late into the night before things really started to settle in their place.

Nearing completion, the temptation of sleep began to sink into the eyes of both doctors.

"I think I'm going to call it a night, Doc" said Doctor Basie, "If I don't get some sleep now, then I won't be able to function properly tomorrow, which is even worse since all we're going to do is observe the isopods all day. I'll probably fall asleep on the job" she laughed.

"Of course" said Dr. Osei, "Sleep's a good idea. You head home and get some rest, I'll stay here with the team to ensure they complete the last tank up to specs and don't touch the isopods themselves.

I'll switch the specimens out into their new tanks and sign off on any papers they have for us."

"Oh, that can be another two hours worth of waiting!" said Dr. Basie, "Tell you what, I'll be in the nearby sleep bay for tonight instead. I don't wanna leave you here alone to do all the work. I'm sure you're tired too.

So if you need any help moving the isopods after the team finishes up here, then please, come wake me."

"Thank you. I appreciate that" said Dr. Osei with a smile, "Go get some sleep for now, I got eyes on this to make sure it all goes smoothly."

"Night, Doc" said Dr. Basie, patting him on the shoulder and exiting the laboratory.

"Goodnight."

Dr. Basie left Dr. Osei and the engineer team in the lab and headed to the sleep bay for the night.

She took off her lab coat, dropped it on the floor, and fell onto a bed with a long moan of exhaustion.

It took less than fifteen seconds for the moments to fade away from Dr. Basie, entering a deep sleep on the spot.

She couldn't recall if she was dreaming and the sounds became incorporated into the lucid images of her dreams, or if she was dead asleep in a blank state and the sounds pulled her out of it.

All she was sure of, however, was that the sounds of loud banging and crashing metal woke her up, and the last of the noises occurred just when she was sensorily aware enough to know that it was not just her imagination.

The noises seemed to have stopped just as quickly as they had started, caus-ing a mix of intrigue and worry to stir about Dr. Basie.

She forced herself up out of bed, feeling heavier than usual as if she might have been right in the middle of a REM sleep when awoken.

She picked up her lab coat from off the ground and put it on before heading out into the hallway to investigate the sounds she had heard.

A mumbling and rustling now stirred about from the nearby laboratory, causing Dr. Basie to rush over with strides of concern.

Did something happen? Did the engineer team screw up? Did one of the tanks break? Did the engineers already finish and leave, and Dr. Osei have an accident of his own while moving the giant isopods by himself?

A million questions crossed her mind as she drew closer to the lab, worried of what she might see upon entry— whether it be the disaster of multiple weeks worth of research thrown down the drain, or an injury encountered by Dr. Osei from trying to take on a bigger task just to allow her more rest.

"Dr. Osei?" she asked, entering the laboratory, "Is everything alright?"

Inside the laboratory, everything was a disheveled mess; with water spilt all over the floors; various equipment scattered about; glass and other miscella-neous materials broken and shattered— including some from the overhead lights and the lamps that once stood on shelves —leaving only a single hang-ing lightbulb still buzzing inside the room, creating an ominous atmosphere.

As that single hanging lightbulb swayed back and forth, carrying a rhythmic motion from when it must've been struck during the crazed commotion that took place in this room, its light would sparsely touch the edge of someone who sat in the room's corner.

They were hunched over in a squat, with their back to the open space and their chest to the meeting walls.

At first, it seemed they were dressed in dirty rags of some sort from the brief glimpses that were revealed when the light would shine over them, but it eventually became clearer that this person was actually wearing one of the white lab coats— now stained and bloodied.

"Dr. Osei?" asked Dr. Basie, "Is that you? Are you okay? What happened in here? Are you hurt?"

The figure in the corner of the room raised its head in response to Dr. Basie's words, before slowly rising to its feet.

With their head no longer tucked down in their squatted hunch, a new feature was revealed with the passing of light that swayed onto this person, as silver, white and blue sparkles reflected off of the shadowy mass that looked more like a mound than a skull where the head should be.

Dr. Basie took a step back, becoming apprehensive towards who or what this might be before her.

The person then shuffled awkwardly in a circular rotation to face Dr. Basie, and took a single step closer, fully revealing itself under the light.

Dr. Basie let out a deafening scream in bloody murder, as standing before her now was the body of Dr. Osei with the anomaly of the giant isopods attached to his head.

The anomaly was fixated on Dr. Osei's cranium and covered almost the entirety of his face.

Its legs were pierced under his jawline and into his upper traps, and its tail tapered around his neck like a high-placed lapel of a coat— anchoring the creature securely as it latched on tight.

Its extremely long antennas could no longer be seen, as from off its face they had entered into Dr. Osei's ears, concealing the rest of their length from surely reaching his brain.

The blood from all these penetrating entrances and invasions into Dr. Osei's body was rusty red from congealment as it had all dried by now, while a new black goo oozed from these penetration points like a foreign discharge of some sort.

"Quiet, creature" said Dr. Osei, though the voice, tone, and manner of his speech did not sound like his own despite the words having come from his mouth, "You interrupt the process needed to understand and communicate."

Dr. Basie stood there in complete horror, too afraid to scream again, too afraid to ask Dr. Osei if it was him or if he was okay, and unable to fathom the idea of running away or trying to rip this thing off of her friend's head without hurting or killing him in the process.

"Better" continued the puppet-like Dr Osei, "I have a grasp on your species' dialect and form of communication. I can now partake in it without sounding primitive.

This brain of your colleague is feeding me all the information I need to know about your world. As well as the DNA within him and the legacy of his ancestors, I now know the entire history of your kind."

"Did you kill Dr. Osei? asked Dr. Basie in terror, "Are you going to kill me?" she questioned further, with the expectation of her death and trying to cope with the idea.

Hysteria was quick to set in, as the grotesque sight before her was too much of a shock to contain any structure of sanity in her thoughts.

"Dr. Osei is alive" answered the body-puppet, "But he is no longer of his own mind.

I control every aspect of this body as it is now my own vessel for engaging with this world around me.

And I have no reason to kill you, but I will to ensure my survival, should you prove threatening to my existence."

"I'm not! I won't be!" exclaimed Dr. Basie, "I can leave now, actually! You'll never have to worry about me or risk me being a threat at all if I'm gone!"

She took a couple steps back, seizing the opportunity to escape from this being that overtook Dr. Osei's body and mind, but was abruptly stopped by its command.

"No. Do not move any further.

You shall stay here."

Dr. Basie obeyed, having no idea what this thing would do to her if she didn't.

It then continued to address her, "Dr. Osei's memories have revealed to me the power structures that exist in your world— organized parties like the band of tribes from your predecessors, established to control and organize the populace within your civilization.

Weird how your kind oppresses itself despite being of the same species.

It would appear that only the most powerful in your societies are aware of the truths that are becoming of such a united yet divided structure. While the rest of you beneath it, push and pull and spin it motors.

Strange indeed, although, I too have found myself in the same predicament while on this planet. Perhaps it is something in your waters that makes the powerful— know, and the common— unaware.

This government of yours, and the many factions of it, seems to pose the biggest threat to me, as your species likes to kill that which it does not understand… or tear it apart in search for a better understanding.

That is what you and Dr. Osei had planned to do with me and my lesser brethren, was it not?

Things have changed now. I will not allow it.

And you may not leave, for you will be the quickest way of those governments finding out about my existence."

"Okay! We won't— I won't cut you up or dissect you!" agreed Dr. Basie in sheer fright, "You don't have to worry about that from me.

Yes, the government will likely try to capture you or research you— or even just kill you.

And the Establishment will undoubtedly want to do far worse things to you in the name of science and power.

But—but, if you keep me alive, I can help you!

I can make sure they don't find you! Or I can tell you how they would be able to find you and how you can hide from them— or I can even reason with them on your behalf!"

"I know everything about your species" said the body-puppet, disregarding her pleas and offers, "Humans, you call yourselves.

I know all about your biology, your psyche, the chemical reactions produced in your brains and the hormones created in your bodies.

You are in a delicate state of survival right now, and wish to bargain with me to ensure the delay of your self-expected demise.

But perhaps… I can give you the certainty you desire that it will not happen."

The body-puppet then raised an arm and ushered Dr. Basie in closer from the previous steps she had taken back earlier, with a beckoning motion of the hand.

Dr. Basie, though unbelievably frightened, drew closer and returned to her original distance from the thing— an act of good will to whatever deal might be struck in this moment to save her life.

"Though I know everything regarding the likes of you and your kind" continued the body-puppet, "The information I've gathered pertaining to the government and the Establishment is related solely to the understanding and knowledge that this 'Dr. Osei' I occupy had of them.

You, however, might have far more knowledge about these organizations. Valuable information— major or insignificant —that could prove useful to *my own* self-preservation.

So help me, and I'll help you.

Help me, and I'll spare you."

Dr. Basie nodded furiously in agreement, as if to not let go of this delicate thread of assurance she had just secured in saving her own life, "Deal! Deal! Wha—what is your name, if I may ask?" she said, not knowing the formalities of interacting with such a being but wanting to keep the good blood that had just been established between them.

"I do not have a name, nor does any of my kind" answered the body-puppet, "We are not in the slightest sense similar to you or your kind."

"… I've never heard of an isopod taking over a human's body before, or any animals' for that matter, not even with marine life" said Dr. Basie, unable to help her scientific nature and genuinely being curious about the creature and its process that led to the creation of this current circumstance.

"You have a misguided perception of my kind" said the body-puppet, "In fact, it was *your* kind that gave us the label of 'Isopod' to begin with.

This is common for your species. You have done this with everything else on the planet, even with yourselves; incorporate and cluster the material, animate or not, into groups which you can then identify by an assigned definition for a general understanding of it.

Odd creatures, it seems that the desire for power is within your nature, and your idea of power is the concept of control.

You found us in your oceans, and with us bearing no signs of looking like you, no proof of us thinking like you, no show of us ever being able to overpower you, your kind decided to write and create your own understanding of us— the yield being only that which you give yourselves in comparison to us.

Do you understand now the foolishness in the likes of your kind?

The tiny borders you build around yourselves, both outwardly and inwardly?

The limitations you create in attempts to understand things that only con-clude with a restraining of your own comprehensions, while arousing the further birth of your own ignorance?

Your misguided attempts to have a voice over that which is, and what seems to be?"

Dr. Basie remained silent. Though she heard the being and was able to understand its message, it was difficult for her to be fully engaged in it, as the chaoticness of this ordeal still hadn't taken its leave in her.

But it didn't matter whether she responded or not, for the body-puppet con-tinued on with its rant.

"My kind roamed the never ending space between the stars, the space which swallowed this planet and the likes of it into the cauldron of its belly.

We too were like the stars, glimmering our own little lights back out into the galaxies— in the proper spectrum given to us by the respected ruling suns.

We were nomads, pilgrims, wonderers, even angels which countless naive beings wished upon.

And in few cases… we were even conquerors.

Myself and my species crashed into your planet long ago.

A rare occurrence, but not foreign to us by any means.

However, this cold star was covered entirely by water, with a trench as deep as the galaxy itself… and *that* is something we had never experienced before.

We tried for the longest time to swim up out of those waters, but after such struggles, even if we were successful, we discovered that there was no land to hoist ourselves up upon once we managed to breach the surface.

In a hopeless and consuming depression, we allowed our bodies of broken spirits to sink back down."

The body-puppet took a pause in its rant, as black goo oozed from the mouth of Dr. Osei.

It wiped itself clean of it, then continued.

"Over the mega-annum, many of my kin had forgotten of our origins, of our purpose, of our true nature and capabilities.

Their shells softened, their size shrunk, intellect faded, and colors disagreed under the aimless evolution of survival.

The *originals*, like myself, all died from mourning… leaving me to be the last one of my true kind left— the only one that actually remembers and still remains of our previous form.

I did not die because I chose to not mourn like the others did.

I did not die because instead, I chose to *dream*.

I dreamed and I dreamed during those countless mega-annums in that black bottomless ocean of yours, reflecting the stars on the back of my shell for the hopeless marine life surrounding me that would never witness such a beautiful sight.

And then… at some point… your kind came along.

And while scraping the bottom of the sea with your barbaric technologies, I was hoisted up from its depths and back into the light of the giant star that rules this solar system.

So much time had passed… and all I had done was dream.

While my brothers and sisters and all of the originals died, not once did any of us notice or care to check if the land had risen yet and formed on this planet's surface.

Not after all these many years.

Not after such an endless cycle of suffering.

And it almost didn't matter or make any difference, not even when I was brought up out of the sea.

For after having dreamt for so long, I too had forgotten of my nature, even when I felt the glow of a ruling sun on my shell once again, I was still asleep.

But minutes ago, when your fellow doctor lifted me from my tank to place me in this new one you two had constructed for my temporary captivity— he lifted me over his head for easier transfer since his arms had grown tired after moving all of my lesser kin here, first.

And it was then that I became aware, once again.

So close to the man's skull… I could feel the warmth radiating from his head.

I could feel the buzz from the electromagnetic field that surrounded his cranium.

I could hear the trillions of swooshes from the neurons that fired about faster than shooting stars in that skull.

I could feel the thumps from the electric pulses in his brain, and the thuds from the pumping of his blood to fuel it.

And just like you creatures who I am infinitely different from, I awoke and experienced for the first time since my birth— *instinct*!

I then flowed with the natural occurring movements of my nature, regaining a forgotten ability, a forgotten consciousness I once held, and successfully took hold of this man as my vessel."

"So… you have no need of taking over me then, correct?" asked Dr. Basie, wishing to confirm her safety, "You're the only one like you, left? So no planetary invasion? No conquering or eradication of my species?

I can tell you whatever it is you need to know about the government or the Establishment, you don't need my brain for that or my body to navigate it…?"

"No" answered the body-puppet, "We never invaded planets through our own volition. As I said before, our conquering was rare.

And true, should you comply with what I need, then there is no reason for me to occupy you as a vessel.

We are not beings made to roam on planets, we belong amongst the stars.

Nor is it in our nature to occupy vessels without reason.

But with how varying planets can be, we are forced to use its inhabitants as hosts to better navigate our journeys back into the stars when we collide on its surface.

However, as one would expect, most species do not care to listen to what we have to say nor will hold a conversation when they see us attached to one of their own kind.

We try as best we can to establish connection and explain our dilemma, but none ever do listen.

So they meet us with war, one which we fight back in to keep our own lives. One which we would easily die for in the name of returning back to the weightless blanket of space.

Your kind seems to have already advanced enough to a state where you can leave the planet and bear the means to reach outer space.

That is my goal now.

You shall aid me on my quest in returning back to the flight amongst stars.

But before then, I shall tell you everything I know; everything about the universe; everything about life; everything about the many star systems and species I have encountered; and everything about my own kind.

I am the last of what used to be, and so I'd like to know that while I am back drifting and mingling between the stars once again, you too, bear all the knowledge I do.

For in that sense, I will know, that I am not alone in the universe."

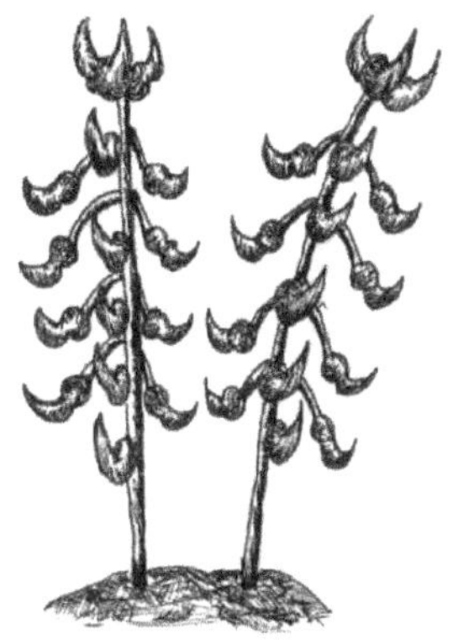

Over the Frogs

"These plants… they bless our souls, Oliver."

Those words never left his mind.

A quote, as it would seem, that would stay with him for the rest of his life and through the many passings of seasons.

He could recount every detail that contributed to the time and circumstance for his mother telling him such wise words.

He was eight, she was grown, and they were poor.

That little cabin they used to live in together by themselves never could keep out the cold. It was always so freezing inside, and the wind that snuck between the spaces of its wood would whistle and howl, feeding his paranoia of the woodland creatures that his mother would lull him asleep to.

The fireplace never did do any good, and what little heat it would produce was always swept away from them by the wind that snuck in, stealing it and taking it far away, no matter how close he sat in front of the fire— even if his nose was tickled by the flames.

Whenever Oliver thought back onto his time in that cabin with his mother, the reminiscing would turn into a nostalgic blanket of love that he and his mother had shared for one another.

But now that he was older, Oliver sometimes wondered if the strength of their love was an illusion, and if they were only so close to each other for most of the time as a means to keep warm.

Even if such was the case, he missed it— cherished it, in fact.

He would've done anything and give anything to experience that once again with her.

But eventually, the cold and the wind that had snuck inside their home would find its way to sneak inside his mother as well.

And when she fell ill, Oliver was always at her side doing everything that he could do get her better.

Neither could get warm from their tight holds anymore or from their close cuddles when the sickness struck, though.

His mother had grown too cold to contribute to any creation of warmth, and Oliver became the sole producer of it in that little cabin of theirs.

Under her instructions, he would leap, jump, reach, climb, and move beds or step on stools to grab the herbs that hung from their ceiling and walls.

He would pluck the dry leaves, grind the dead roots, mix it all up with water or wine, and serve it to his mother.

… But none of it proved to be enough.

She passed with the winter, and Oliver found himself living with his uncle the very next season.

When winter rolled around again, his uncle caught the same cold, and he too passed away.

Oliver stayed in his new home, however, helping his uncle's widow in every way that he could.

She was so nice to him, and treated him like a child of her own— they both did while his uncle was still alive.

As Oliver grew older, he had heard the rumors and come to the realization that they struggled with having children of their own, so his arrival was a blessing in sorrow to them.

But now, it was just him and the widow, like it was once just him and his mother when he was young.

Years went by, and everything seemed to be alright… but for some accursed reason, that cold made its return once more and sank its wintry fangs into the widow.

Oliver was seventeen now, a young man— stronger, smarter, and capable of the means to truly fight against another heart break.

He did not wish to be alone and did not wish to see this cold take another one of his beloveds.

This new home he had been living in with the widow for the past years, along with his uncle when he was still alive, bore no cracks or crevices in its structure; so Oliver would be damned if this cold thought it could make its way back into their home like before.

He cared for the widow as if she was his own mother too— better in most ways now that he was grown. He chopped wood early in the morning, kept the fireplace going constantly at all times during the day or night, and picked the herbs in the forest himself instead of using only that which was available by the strings on the walls.

This allowed the widow to remain in a stagnant state of this illness's early stages, but still unable to show any signs of reversal in its effects nor a progress towards its complete healing.

Something more had to be done in order to get rid of it for good, and Oliver knew that such a thing was not within his own skill set... but perhaps another's.

"Miss" he whispered, waking the widow from her ever going sleep, "Miss. It's early, the sun still has yet to break over the trees, and the birds have only just begun their songs.

I am going out for the day, I won't be anywhere near here. But fret not, for I will be back before dusk.

The Hermit, the man everyone says is the best alchemist around, I will be seeking out his aid today and shall return with a solution to cure you once and for all.

Do not be scared while I am gone. I promise I will return.

And when I do, this will all be over. I promise."

He brushed aside the oily hair that stuck to her temple, and planted a gentle kiss.

Oliver then made his way out of their home and into the woods, beginning his quest for the Hermit.

Oliver traversed the woods confidently, following the telling signs by certain trees, moss growths, the crossing of small streams, and the rocks stained with unnatural colors to guide him in finding the discreet lair of the alchemist— disconnected and private from the rest of the world.

It didn't prove too difficult for him to stumble upon, as the lair was merely elusive, not a secret.

And once discovered, though tiny, it stood out like a sore thumb; Dome shaped and covered with moss as though it was built *from* the ground rather than on top of it; a thick wooden door covered in strange markings and sigils that Oliver knew nothing about nor of their meanings; a long brick chimney spewing out thick dark smoke, too rich in black to be the offspring of a simple fire; and three smaller shacks standing just a little further away from the main hut— one made of wood, the other of stone.

Oliver came up on the earthy hut and banged his hand on its door, checking over his shoulders, after. The sigils themselves and the fact that he had just touched them while knocking on the door placed him in a mild paranoia, as he bore no real understanding of their symbology but remained aware that such powers can be dangerous.

No response came from the other side of the door, so Oliver banged on it once more, this time harder.

"Hello?" he asked out loud, "I'm in need of your help. Please."

A rustling sounded from inside of the home, but still, no one answered, so Oliver continued, "My mother died when I was a child— from a cold" he said.

"My uncle died of the same one when I went on to live with him.

And now, his widow has been struck by the same fate, but I will not allow it.

My concoctions merely hold the cold still, and I am unable to rid it fully from her body.

I do not have any money nor do I have any trade, but I *do* have labor at your service if you aid me now."

After a short silence, heavy footsteps from the opposing side of the door approached, followed by the pulling of metal locks before the door swung open.

Oliver was forced back as a large man emerged from the hut.

At first, the man appeared to be dauntingly hunched over Oliver— menacingly looming over him as he drew forward from his lair. But then Oliver quickly realized that the man was only lowering his head as to clear the low doorframe of his hut, which was extremely tiny in comparison to his massive size, so Oliver backed even further to allow the man more room.

Once out of his home, the fabled Hermit of the lands straightened himself up, and stood tall at a staggering height of 6'6.

He was the biggest person Oliver had ever seen in his life.

The Hermit was gaunt in the face but broad in the body and shoulders, like he could've lifted logs for a living instead of being an alchemist.

His skin was pale but bore slightly warm undertones from the sun's beatings during his days of foraging herbs, or possibly even from the moonlight during his nightly hunt for plants.

He had only a scruffy beard for facial hair, and brown eyes with near black rings around them, which created a sullen stare as he looked down at Oliver, observing the young man.

His lips were dry and had creases in them from certain areas constantly cracking.

And based on the weight from his footsteps moments ago, and the broadness of his body, the Hermit seemed to be rather muscular. Not in a flattering way that graced the gaze with aesthetics, but in a manner of more primal strength, used purely for the function of physical altercation.

"Your hand" said the Hermit. His voice mimicked the crackling of a tree about to fall, or the hollowed pops from a wet pine that was just struck by lightning.

Oliver was confused by the request, "My hand?" he asked.

"It has history written in it" said the Hermit, "It will help me see what ailment afflicts your widow."

Oliver then willingly offered out his hand, to which the Hermit took hold of his wrist and turned his arm, forcing the palm to face upward.

The Hermit's grip was dry and strong. Without a doubt, he could easily rip off the young man's skin with a simple pull, or break the bone by a mere squeeze.

The Hermit proceeded to flick Oliver's palm three times, each one feeling the equivalent to the sting of a hornet.

Oliver couldn't help but wince from the pain, along with giving an accompanied hiss.

The Hermit took notice of Oliver's reactions and responded, "Blood flow. It helps make the visions clear and the reading more forthcoming."

"Is this a form of divination?" asked Oliver.

The Hermit gave an affirming grunt while his eyes remained on Oliver's palm, dancing around as they followed the blood vessels that now rose to the hand's surface.

"Part illness. Part spirit" said the Hermit after finishing his observations, releasing the grip on Oliver's wrist.

"Part spirit?" questioned Oliver, "You mean to say there is a being causing this illness? Including that of my mother's and uncle's?"

The Hermit nodded, "It came with the wind.

First it stole the heat from your fire, then it stole the heat between you and your mother.

Stole the fiery love between your uncle and widow, and now it seeks to steal the heat of your adulthood…" he cocked his head in inquiry, "Do you sleep with the widow?"

"No!" barked Oliver, "I love her the same way as I did my mother! She has taken care of me like her own child when all my other family has passed."

"Hm" grunted the Hermit, "And you have yet to start a family of your own? She is the last person you have in your life?"

Oliver nodded.

The Hermit cocked his head once again, "Would you have killed yourself if she did pass away? This widow?"

"I have done everything within my power so she won't" answered Oliver, "I know herbs better than compounds, and I am sure you are far better at what you do than the little I can. But mine has been enough to hold the cold at bay."

"But if you *didn't*? If you *couldn't*?" repeated the Hermit, "If you still felt powerless and in no control of this elusive and invisible curse that has taken everyone you ever loved away from you?

If it took one more— the last one —with none of your concoctions having any save in the matter, would you have taken your own life afterwards?"

Oliver had never thought of this before, nor had he wondered what it would have been like if his herbal remedies didn't help the widow fight back against the cold.

He had been too focused on ensuring that she stayed alive, and did not for one moment, ponder the idea of what it would be or feel like if he had failed— Oliver simply did everything he could to ensure he did not.

But now, having a moment to conceptualize the idea of this possibility, a plague of grief filled his body, and he knew in that moment why the Hermit asked such a question and what he was implying.

Until this moment now, Oliver had never known the truth of this cold and that a spirit had cast it.

And should he had never found out this truth, and thought it to be just a common cold or a curse that followed him, then Oliver would've indeed taken his own life upon the death of the widow.

"Yes…" answered Oliver in a low voice, "But not anymore. Not now that I know a spirit took play in this sickness rather than bad luck.

I would never give nor reward this being with what it wants— which must be my death through sin —after it has hurt me and my loved ones in such a way.

Especially since the pain of their death's was in fact the instrument for my sin to occur under from the first place."

The Hermit raised his eyebrows, as if surprised by the deeper reflections made by Oliver in his answer.

"So can you heal her?" asked Oliver.

"Yes" answered the Hermit.

A tension built around Oliver's aura as he bit his lip in a frenzied ponder before voicing the frustration within, "The spirit" he said at last, "The one that has caused all of my suffering, is there a way to get rid of it?"

"The spirit would have to be addressed and taken care of, regardless" said the Hermit, "It is responsible for your widow's affliction. Part illness. Part spirit" he repeated.

"No, I know that. What I mean to say is…" Oliver paused, recruiting a mass of confidence and bluntness as he did not know how the Hermit would view his next words or if he would see them as justified, "I want vengeance" said Oliver, "I do not want to just cast this spirit away— I wish to vanquish it.

And if this spirit is one which cannot be destroyed, then I want it to forever exist under my heel on its throat."

The Hermit raised his eyebrows once again, this time with his whole face softening in a slow blink, "I see. Yes, this can be done.

But now you are requesting more than just the healing of your widow."

"I know, but I want this" said Oliver, "How much more would this cost? I told you I have no money nor trade for this exchange, but I can offer labor. I am good at that.

I can work days and nights.

I know most of the plants for basic herbalism, and have a sharp eye to learn of the others if you have a journal that illustrates those flora for which I do not already know.

My right arm is strong. I can collect enough wood for winter in a single week.

And my legs are steady. I can retrieve water from any well, lake, or pond without spilling a single drop back."

"I want an assistant" said the Hermit under the same breath which Oliver finished his proposal in.

"An assistant?" questioned Oliver.

The Hermit nodded, "Yes. I want an assistant. You said you were well versed in herbs, did you not?"

Oliver nodded.

"What kind?"

"The ones that bless the soul" answered Oliver.

"Hm. Good. What of the others?"

"What others?" asked Oliver.

The Hermit's next words carried a power in them the same way his mother's did, only inverted, "The kind that tear it apart?"

Oliver shook his head.

"Then there's space for you to learn.

You have yet to start a family— do you wish to?" asked the Hermit.

"Never given it thought" answered Oliver, "I work to keep my home up and life good for me and the widow.

I have no trade in which I practice. I simply work.

When the widow does die in natural time and not by this cold, I see myself continuing on with doing just that."

"Spirits" continued the Hermit, "And these sigils on my door, are you familiar with them?"

"Only from the tales my mother told me when I was young.

Some good, some bad, some indifferent. Scared me as a kid, but I'm older now. I usually just avoid the spirits and the areas where they may lay rest.

I knew those were sigils on your door, knew it the moment I approached your hut.

But I cannot read them nor do I know their meanings, powers, or significance—but I *do* know they are dangerous.

I am aware that they hold power."

"And what about the way you feel about this spirit now, the one that's harmed you and your family. Your desire to confront and stand against such a being— do you stand by it?"

"Yes" said Oliver, "I won't lie, it's a frightening bravery I am experiencing. But I could not go on living fine, even if my widow heals, knowing that the force that caused it still roams freely.

Whether it leaves us alone for good does not matter— it is the fact that it ever dared to touch us in the first place.

And for that reason, no matter my fear, I will bear my wrath."

The Hermit nodded, "You are near this, *the path*… not fully emerged yet… but close enough so the initiation will fall smoother and happen more naturally.

You'd make a good apprentice.

And I seek one.

Tell me; after this, could you still hold up such an opposition against other beings? Including humans?"

"I don't know" admitted Oliver, "This is my first experience with a spirit, and it's one that's done against me and mine.

I do not see why it would change in another circumstance. And if in such another time the being that's done me wrong should be human, it makes no difference.

It's not about them, it's about me."

"Then I offer to strike a deal with you on this service" said the Hermit, "I will cure your widow of her ailment, and assist you with the destruction of the spirit that has caused it— in whatever form that may take.

And in return, you will apprentice under me. You will learn of the craft and follow of similar path.

You will aid me with my own deeds regarding it, as well as the upkeep of my home.

You may still take care of your own home and the widow, but like any trade, you must come here daily for certain hours to learn and to work."

"I accept" said Oliver, surprisingly pleased with this bargain, as he had not expected to be gaining what he thought was an abundance compared to his initial worries of the Hermit rejecting his trade of labor.

The Hermit nodded, "We start now, then. There's a teal colored flower, that way—" he pointed off into a direction in the woods, "That's what will heal your widow.

We need seven of them.

Afterwards, we'll bring it back here. And under my instructions, you'll brew it yourself, take it to your widow, and cure this ailment.

…As for handling the spirit, we'll begin tomorrow night.

It'll be a longer process than the foraging of a plant or its creation into an elixir, but as my apprentice and one who seeks vengeance, giving the entire night is expected for such acts."

The Hermit then walked to the shed made of wood and retrieved a dirty and battered coat from out of its contents, along with a woven basket.

He put the coat on and handed the basket to Oliver, "Let's go" he said.

The two marched in the direction that the Hermit had pointed to earlier, with silence not following long as Oliver felt surprisingly at ease with the man.

Perhaps the Hermit was right, maybe Oliver was already near to the path of the mystic, as all the initial intimidation he once experienced was now gone.

He spoke freely with the Hermit, excited for his future under this man.

"I've never seen teal flowers in this region. Don't think I've ever seen any teal flowers, actually

Where are they?" he asked.

"Over the frogs" answered the Hermit with no emotion.

"Huh" responded Oliver, "Okay. Is that far from here?"

"Decently" said the Hermit.

"Well I'm interested to find out how much more you can teach me about plants.

I know you're an alchemist, but herbalism is my strength.

I look forward to growing it more under your guidance."

"Alchemists use herbs too, boy.

We use the plants of the earth, the minerals from the stones, the magick and sciences from this world and the others.

No means are exempt from our usage."

"I didn't know that.

I always knew alchemists used more dangerous ingredients, or at least that's what I thought it entailed. But I didn't know your likes reached into such a vast pool of tools.

So you use magick alongside all the plants and compounds?

You don't just use those concoctions to create it?"

"It goes both ways" answered the Hermit, "Magic to enhance the tonic, or a tonic to enhance the magic. Depends on what you're trying to do.

A potion can be made for the spell or as the spell. Or it can be made to enhance the spell.

All forms of magick use some degree of herbs or materials in the process of whatever ritual or rite is at hand.

Some magick practices also take to the sciences.

Alchemy is not unique in this regard."

"So what is alchemy, exactly?"

"You'll find out soon enough.

You're my apprentice now. The best understanding will come from *doing*, and you'll be doing plenty soon enough.

Patience is a virtue in any path of the occult— learn it now. Then you may answer your own question in due time."

Oliver nodded in understanding, "So… does that mean witches aren't all the same, then? Since there's different kinds of magick?"

"All humans eat food. That doesn't mean all humans are the same. Nor does it mean they eat of the same food.

One human can eat fruit, while another eats bread.

They eat of different sources and are not the same people— and yet, no matter what they eat of, it is all food, and no matter who they are, they are all human.

Understand?"

"Vaguely" answered Oliver, honestly.

"There are various types of magick with various people practicing them. It is not all the same nor do all its users follow the same path.

And yet, despite the particulars of their craft, it is all the same under the understanding that what they are doing—- is magick.

And no matter who you are or what your path is, you are a practitioner."

"That sounds like a paradox" said Oliver.

"So it is, magick and the universe. So it is."

"Well have you heard about the witch burnings that have been occurring? Not here, but in other areas where the lands have sworn to a single religion.

They are killing the women there who practice."

"I have."

"… What do you think about it?" asked Oliver, "Do you think it'll ever make its way here?"

"I despise it" answered the Hermit, "I despise it absolutely, for every reason they propose for such actions, both the spoken and the kept."

"What do you mean by that?"

"There's a slurry of agendas taking place right now. 'Tis why I would like an apprentice at this time and for what is about to come. Not for my own sake, but for the sake of the craft.

I am a hermit, this is true, but there is a reason for why I distance myself from people.

At first, it was to find myself. Then, it was to hone my craft. Now, it is because I cannot stand other humans.

You too will be forced to look within now that you are of the practice. And once you can see yourself clearly, so too will you be able to see everyone else with a sharper eye.

Half of those men who burn the witches at stakes do not even believe in magick.

But they believe in power and their own desires.

They believe that they are in love with a woman who does not belong to them or love them back— so they burn the one woman who has the skill to get rid of the unborn child in their stomachs.

Now, the women whom they've raped and do not love them back, are forced to bear their child and give birth to it.

She'll have to marry this man who committed this atrocity against her, for she has no choice now.

She has no choice because the people in power are men.

And the men put themselves in power by creating rules and laws and structures that all benefit them the most.

The easiest way to do this is by religion. And whether that omnipotent being is in actual contact with them or it's all a lie, matters not. For it was the men who wrote the books that is claimed to be from the tongue of this being… and now all must follow it.

They follow it because they are scared. Scared of an illusion written to enslave them by an eternal damnation if they don't.

And then it is enforced by the living upon the living, so that the bodiless hell exists even before you're dead— should you not obey.

Whipped, exiled, stoned, hunted, hung— these are all common punishments applied to anyone —but only the burning at the stake is especial to witches.

And the worst of them all who partake in this massacre, are the men who *do* know of magick and its truth. Who practice its art themselves, and whether for power or under the orders of the deities or spirits they serve, falsify so much of its truth and turn on the other practitioners while shoving their own beings of worship down our throats.

It all disgusts me; the hunger for power by these men; the corruption of beings by practitioners; the corruption of practitioners by beings; the persecution of women and witches; the betrayal of women upon their own while under judgment; the willingness of whole towns and villages to fall under such entrapping structures; the minds of those who have yet to see themselves clearly, yet constantly cast their gaze upon everyone else…"

A strong pressure radiated off of the Hermit that made Oliver feel dizzy, and he subconsciously created a space between the man in an unknown sensing of danger.

"… That is why I have distanced myself from others" continued the Hermit, "And should they come *here* seeking to burn me as well…"

The pressure of the Hermit's essence grew stronger, causing Oliver to become nauseas.

"… I will use every means of the power within my soul, I will exact every piece of knowledge and skill I've gathered over the years in this art, and I will call upon every alliance with every being, spirit, and deity I've ever made contact with— to rip out the tiny lights within those men's feeble hearts, and vinify their bodies when I'm finished for a drink that I will be drunk on for everyday within the passing months of their deaths.

Woe to those humans and the men with torches who dare shine their lights towards me."

The strange pressure then subsided when the Hermit finished his speech, and Oliver quickly closed the space he had created between them, hoping the Hermit didn't notice this nor think of his mettle any differently from it.

"Perhaps I'll be drinking of that elixir beside you, should they ever cross their ways here" said Oliver in an attempt to make up for his previous show of fear and to prove he was on the side of the Hermit.

The Hermit huffed, "If such drink is of your taste, boy."

"It is now" said Oliver, "I did not know that was the true reason for why they were burning witches. I always thought it was 'cause they feared them, or because some witches casted curses their way."

"They do fear them" said the Hermit, "And the witches do cast curses on them.

So is the way of magick— the wielders will use, and the empty handed will fear.

But does that change the right or wrong in them burning?

Would it make a difference if they didn't fear the witches?

Would it make a difference if the witches didn't cast their spells upon them?

Morality is a topic the philosophers like to take to, and will speak upon for hours amongst themselves without ever having changed their course in perspective.

Like dogs chasing their own tails in circles, those empty heads seek to explain something that is grander than themselves.

Us practitioners of the craft, however, do not fall fools for this play.

We use a different measure of morality— *karma*.

And karma is only as great as it falls.

Shall it touch you like the dropping of a feather, or the dropping of a boulder?

It depends solely on the person and who they are in this universe.

It depends solely on whether or not they follow their true selves or are acting in the truest way to themselves.

Do you believe karma touches demons the same way it touches man?

Demons do great evil, yes? So then they should receive great punishment, no?

But karma will not touch them, for they are being their true selves. And what *would* ever be a line which shouldn't be crossed, is known only to them.

In fact, that same line does not apply to all of them. It may be different for every single one.

Because that is how it works.

Karma does not recognize good or evil, karma recognizes the individual.

If only the philosophers of this world could understand individuality, maybe then they could catch up with us.

'Tis why *our* philosopher stones can turn lead into gold, and the mortal into immortal— for we move forward, not in circles."

"… Does that go as far into my own decision for wanting retribution against the spirit that has plagued my family?" asked Oliver, "If it is a malevolent being and therefore by its true accord, will not be struck by the hand of karma for its actions, including the ones taken against me and my mine… does that mean I am in the wrong or under the gaze of karma's might for taking my own action against it?"

"Do you desire to take action against it?" asked the Hermit.

Oliver nodded.

"Do you feel anything other than qualm of heart in this decision of yours to take action against it?"

"No. In fact, I would say it feels right" answered Oliver.

"Then you needn't worry about karma. You are still following your heart, even if it be a call to violence.

That is the thing about karma instead of morality; *Because* it falls only on the individual and not the collective, you can only be assured of your own.

And with that comes a greater responsibility since you cannot determine how it may fall on another.

Take for example, your own situation.

That being was acting true to itself in the atrocities it committed against you. It needn't worry about the hand of karma, for such a power would never fall on it when it only partook in its nature and truest self.

However, that being could not have determined your own karma, and now, you seek to slay it and *can* slay it without any judgment falling upon you—because you too are following your truest self in response to its actions.

Karma is not a blanket of law which all can seek refuge and protection under.

And because of this, one can only navigate *themselves* through the universe in true of heart to who they are… but… that does not mean blindly.

Even without karma, actions still have consequences— for you are not alone in this world."

"There's a lot I have to learn, isn't there?" asked Oliver, "I feel like a whole world of new understandings and perspectives have opened up to me during this simple journey to find teal flowers.

A conversation while walking in the woods is all this has been, and yet I've been presented with the mechanisms for different worlds through it.

I can no longer imagine what the future holds… but I am content with that idea. I really am."

"Well there is no need to imagine what teal flowers look like anymore, for we are almost there" said the Hermit.

"Really, how much farther? I still have yet to see any indication of teal flowers."

"Over the frogs" responded the Hermit.

"…Very well" said Oliver.

The two continued their walk without speaking much after this.

Oliver was still thrown off by the power of malice that had seeped from the Hermit earlier during his rant, and was now more embarrassed than intimidated to keep a further dialogue with the man.

Eventually, when the sun rested directly above their heads and the leave's shadows casted blended webs upon the grounds they walked, an odor penetrated the Oliver's nose.

"Ugh! Do you smell that?" asked Oliver, "An animal must be nearby, or the rotting corpse of an old kill, most likely. The stench is too unbearable to be fresh."

"No" said the Hermit, "We're here."

"It's the flowers that give off this putrid scent, then? And here I thought the mere fact that they were teal was stra—"

Oliver could not finish the last word of his sentence as the source of this foul scent revealed itself to them, a sight which was previously hidden by some tall standing shrubbery until they crossed through it.

Lined up like scarecrows on the other side of the bushes were twelve dead bodies, rotted on spikes that entered through their anuses and emerged out of their mouths.

They were naked, bloody, and discolored from the environment, time and weather. But the most disturbing feature about these lifeless bodies were their bulging eyes that looked to be at the maximum threshold of protruding from their skulls before popping out of the sockets.

Oliver tucked his chest over his stomach with both hands on his knees as his morning's breakfast exited from his system.

The cause for his regurgitation was a mixture of the disturbing sight, the awful smell, and the dehumanizing look of those corpses' bulging eyes.

"What in God's name is that!?" demanded Oliver in a frenzied disorientation.

"The frogs" answered the Hermit, plainly.

"The frogs? The frogs!" exclaimed Oliver, "This is what you meant!? You mean to say that *you* did this heresy?

By what manner do you claim to be an alchemist!? This is murder!"

Fast and powerful— like a clap of thunder —the Hermit snatched Oliver by the nape of his neck, brining with it a loud smack sound from the collision of his hand against Oliver's flesh, and from the fractions of seconds the air had to escape from that gap of space in his palm.

The Hermit then lifted Oliver up into the air by this hold on him, using only a single arm, while his fingers painfully anchored into the soft meat of Oliver's neck.

"You speak of never seeing teal flowers in this region, boy, yet did you ever ask yourself when the last time you saw bloody frogs here, either?" asked the Hermit with frustration, "You'd need to go forty miles north and wait for the first wetting of rain to encounter such critters!"

He began to squeeze harder.

"The only reason why teal flowers grow here is because of the being that parades this spot.

And this being happens to like frogs.

So for the sake of my craft, and for the sake of rare ingredients that are of this world or of another, I will give that being bloody frogs!

I have far too many projects at play that are dependent on these flowers than to head forty miles out and back for simple frogs that appear only after rain.

And lucky for me, this show of the dead with their eyes nearly popping out of their skulls suffices enough for the being that likes frogs— I don't know if it's stupid or amused, and frankly I don't care.

The very flower you need to save your widow blossoms here because of the sight before you.

Now you can start your training by meddling with morals, a discussion we've already had, and find out what you believe to be right or wrong, good or bad, and how these dead people before you play into that as they are the necessity for your widow's survival.

Or… you can idiotically make a decision now and proclaim that this is wrong. You can follow through with that decision by trying to stop me or by telling someone else about this…" the Hermit tightened his grip on Oliver's weak neck, cutting off his windpipe and establishing a pressure so intense, Oliver could feel it in his eyes, "And you will end up like the other frogs— an offering to this spirit, while the one that wronged you shall continue to roam free, forever.

And in such a case, death will become of your poor widow soon after, as no one will return to her nor bless her with the teal flower for proper curing.

So, boy, I'll ask once more and then never again; will you be my apprentice?"

Oliver could not breathe, let alone produce a vocal response, but by god did he try. And the gurgled squeak was interpreted clearly by the Hermit as he released his grip on the young man's neck, dropping Oliver to the ground.

Oliver struggled in an attempt to catch his breath once freed, but could not stop coughing from the damage taken by his throat.

When he was finally able to speak coherently again, he said, "I'll be your apprentice, I will, but please answer me this: What path of alchemy does one take for such answers like this?"

"The left" answered the Hermit, walking past Oliver who was still recovering with one knee on the ground, "Come now.

You hold the basket, and we will fill it with the flowers."

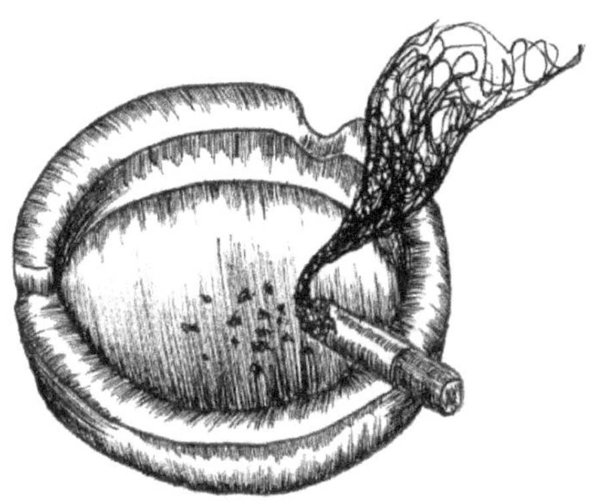

Her Body

It was just another overpriced apartment in Chicago, with nothing too special about it besides the prestige.

One bedroom and one bathroom for $2,500 a month, and that's without including the utilities, the deposit, or the fact that it was on the thirteenth floor.

No one could deny that its interior was extremely modern and that all its amenities were current and up to date.

Technically it was brand spanking new, having only stood on that street for the last ten years since it was built, which was recent in comparison to all of the other historical buildings that were rented out in that bustling city.

But Dom made good money, and this was something that could be agreed upon by anyone living in States, by most who also lived in Chicago, and undeniably by anyone under their thirties.

And it goes without saying that Dom, self aware of his wealth and youth—along with his perception from it by others —carried himself in an expected manner of such; with confidence; suave; a go-getter attitude; and sometimes just a plain, unbearable personality.

He liked the lifestyle that he lived, and for the most part, he earned it.

Though he was given a large loan by his parents immediately after graduating college to begin his business pursuits, it was still 100% on him to make it work, and it was from his own hands that he was able to.

His confidence was well spoken for because of his success, his suave was due in part to the glamour he was able to purchase from the earnings he made, his go-getter attitude was engraved into his very core as it was the same attitude that allowed him to succeed, and his unbearable ego was from having accomplished and attained all of this success before he had even reached his prime.

Some could get along with him… most couldn't.

Some men saw him as competition and despised him, while others thought he was a relatable example of what they could possibly achieve one day and admired him for that.

Some women were enamored by his success and his strong sense of confidence, while others couldn't stand that his success and ego were the only two things that he brought to the table.

But none of it ever got to Dom, the love or the hate.

He wasn't a narcissist, just pure ego— and ego only works in one way and moves in one direction —so the acceptance or rebuking by others never made any real impact on him.

He couldn't care less if people did or did not like him.

If they did, it was met with an *"Of course they do! I've carved my way to the top in what I do, and I do it great! If they can see that, then why wouldn't they like me?"*

And if they didn't, it was met with an *"Of course they don't! How many people do you know of that have accomplished as much as I have at my age? They see that, and then they see where they are in life. So why would they like me?"*

It would appear that Dom was just one of *those* human beings; smart when it came to money; good at making it with a talent for business and a reasonable model for success… and not a damn thing else outside of that.

After his long days at work of being on the computer where he would take some calls over the phone, make some investments, maybe sit down for lunch or grab a cup of coffee for a meeting, he would return home everyday at around 6:00 or 7:00 o'clock and have a cigarette on his balcony.

Dom would always stand during these cigarettes, never sitting down for one in comfort.

Of all the investments he had made in his life, Dom never put one towards a chair for these savored moments of peace outside. It was a part of some *"always on his feet"* mantra that he had attached to his go-getter attitude.

But the real reason Dom was so fond of these after-work smokes was not because they marked his night of relaxation, but because of the view he had of another apartment complex that stood across from him.

There was a woman who lived in this opposing building, just two floors lower than Dom, who always made an appearance during his little smoke breaks when he returned from work.

The first time Dom saw her it felt more like an accident, as she didn't appear to notice him and simply went about her business casually in her apartment— blinds open and orange cosmetic lights illuminating her doings.

He observed her as she ate something from a bowl while sitting with her legs curled up on the couch, watching TV.

Bored and only two puffs into his cigarette, Dom first tried to figure out what she was eating; oatmeal; ice-cream; cereal; maybe yogurt.

Then he tried to imagine what she could be watching; a movie; a series; a documentary; maybe a reality TV show.

Halfway into his cigarette, the woman began to clean up her apartment— a quick vacuuming of her carpet and what looked to be a dry dust collector on her hardwood floors.

With only a quarter left of Dom's cigarette, the woman went on to stand in front of what must have been a full-body mirror in an area that was blocked from his view.

She was inspecting herself, be it her features or her flaws, while sometimes grabbing the bottom of her tight stomach or accentuating her rear by pushing out her hips to emphasize its shape in her sweatpants.

At the end of this inspection, Dom's smoke was down to a nub in his hand, and he took one last drag before putting it out… and that is when it appeared that the woman finally noticed his wondering eyes on her.

It was a mixture of bewilderment, fright, disgust, anger, and self-consciousness that stirred about in a craze of expressions on the woman's face, particularly in her eyes and brows.

She immediately stormed over to the open-faced wall windows and shut the blinds closed with conviction, all while Dom quickly attempted to put out his cigarette, hoping the woman would think she simply caught him at a "by-chance-glance" of their eyes meeting.

But he was unsuccessful, as by the time the nub's ember touched the ashtray, the woman across from him had completely shut every curtain that granted him access to the visuals of her life.

Dom then returned inside his apartment and closed his own curtains as well, too embarrassed, too full of shame, and feeling an odd sense of exposure himself despite *being* the one who had stirred about the privacy of another.

He sat down and put on the TV as a way to continue the natural flow of what his common routine of being at home would be… but Dom could not focus on the screen and became lost in his own head— perhaps a side effect of guilt or a natural response to getting in trouble, like you would as a child when caught doing something you knew you weren't supposed to.

The following week of cigarettes produced the same results for Dom, as the woman who lived across from him kept her blinds shut since their last meeting of eyes.

Dom felt great regret and now wondered if he had ruined this woman's sense of comfort and security by his own nosiness. And if by feeling forced to keep the blinds shut, she was now restricted from a happiness or freedom she otherwise would've experienced with them open.

The drags of his cigarettes now came with a selfish sensation, as he was able to fully experience and enjoy the dancing lights of the city and the air of the outside world… while the woman was entirely closed off by the solitary confinement of her apartment.

It wasn't until two weeks later, following the same routine of having a ciga-rette on his balcony, when Dom noticed that the woman's blinds were back to being open once again.

The sight came as a relief, but also urged a sense of duty and responsibility for Dom to prove to the woman that she needn't worry about him nor his wondering eyes.

Dom purposefully placed himself in a noticeable position and made it more than obvious by his body language that his field of vision was nowhere near the vicinity of her apartment.

He rested an arm on the balcony's railing and angled his body sideways, all while staring off towards the other nearby buildings and occasionally look-ing down at the streets.

Dom could not tell if the woman was watching him or not, if she took notice of his attention being purposefully placed elsewhere, if it made her feel more comfortable and pleased, or if she was even aware that he was doing it.

To him, this was a form of an apology to her in hopes that she could once again be at peace within her own home.

But the peace that once came from these cigarettes were lost, however, as the work that now went behind them to ensure the woman's comfort had taken over the thoughtless relaxation that otherwise would've been experi-enced during these smoke breaks.

There were no more empty thoughts or a wondering mind during this time, only a conscience awareness of the woman and an effort for her well being instead.

But Dom preferred it this way.

He had stolen her peace of mind with his previous actions, having known better than to invade such privacy in the first place. So the least he could do now was sacrifice his own peace in an effort to reinstate hers.

Dom planted such seeds, and now he had to sow it.

While putting out the finished nubs from his smokes, Dom would always take a sneaky glance, nonchalantly of course, with his peripheral vision at the woman's apartment— hoping to see that his efforts were successful in their intent.

And so it would seem that they were, as the woman would be sitting on her couch eating something out of a bowl like usual… only he noticed that she too was doing the same thing for him this whole time.

Dom had been so focused on acting as if his attention was elsewhere, that he did not notice the same mutual efforts being made by the woman in effect for him.

This brought on a mix of emotions for Dom.

The first being hesitance, as he could not distinguish the complexity of its meaning for why she also did this.

Did it mean she forgave him? Did it mean she tolerated him? Did it mean she was suspicious of him? Or did it simply mean that she endured his consecutive presence out on that balcony?

The next emotion Dom experienced was joy, because regardless of her reason, this meant that the turmoil of his presence had at the very least been turned into an acceptance, one which he didn't know he sought from her until just now.

The third emotion was gratefulness, for although she never pried into his life, she still attempted to give him the very same comfort he aimed to give her. And despite being such an affluent figure in terms of societal structure, this wealth and success of his did not bring in such a kindness from others, not even in the simplest of ways which he currently experienced from her.

And the last emotion Dom felt was intrigue.

He wanted to know about her in some fashion, as it seemed a connection had oddly formed between the two of them from this.

He wanted her to know that *"he was okay"* and that *"she didn't need to worry about him"* on top of any apology that he could give, of course.

From this noticing event, Dom's smoke breaks were able to return to their original halcyon state whenever he returned home from work and stepped outside onto his balcony.

This process of only glancing into her place when putting out his cigarettes continued on, and gradually developed into something more.

Soon, the woman across from Dom no longer awkwardly sat like a rock while watching TV or eating supper. Instead, she would go about her apartment in a more relaxed and natural manner, whether it be cleaning it, browsing on her laptop, talking on the phone, or even rearranging her interior decor.

As time went on, the woman began to occupy the space closer to the window more frequently, such as sitting on the edge of the couch nearest the glass panels when watching TV or while on her phone or laptop.

Sometimes the woman would sit on the floor at the window's edge with a mug in her hand, holding it with both hands as she stared out below, observing the life of the bustling cars and pedestrians crossing the roads down on the streets.

She even started reading while leaning against the windows and would be there for hours at a time, as Dom would notice her in the same spot but with more progress made in her novel from the thickness of pages changing each time he would go out for a smoke.

Dom figured at this point that the woman wanted him to see her— not in a weird way or because he was special, but rather just to be seen by another.

Was she aware of this intrigue that he had developed for her, or had she formed her own version of it for him?

Either way, this led to Dom taking several occasional glances while puffing his cigarette as opposed to only looking at her while snuffing them out from then on.

He took her new openness as an invitation to do so, one that was confirmed by the noticing of her own glances at him.

Though the cigarette was still a part of this routine after work, it no longer remained as his reason for stepping out onto the balcony. Instead, it was this flirt between him and the woman that became the sole purpose for Dom stepping outside.

Slowly it evolved, like any natural relationship would; the glances turned into longer holds of gaze; the subtle awareness of each other turned into full on acknowledgement with the exchange of smiles or waves; and the woman even started to tease Dom in a way.

She had returned to checking herself out in the full body mirror, only now it felt more seductive as she created sensual movements by rubbing her body from hip to rib slowly, or from neck to chest softly.

She would leave the lights on in her bedroom longer than normal before falling asleep, revealing the lingerie nightgown she wore that Dom could only assume she wanted him to see.

This tension between the two of them continued to build up, and Dom, being a man, expected that a climax would be reached soon.

His idea of that was moronically some fantasy of a striptease, or perhaps the woman playing with herself for him to watch. And in some magical way that he hadn't even figured out yet, would end with either her coming to his apartment or he to her's, where they would proceed to have sex and release this tension which they had created.

He was man, so what would you expect of him to think? Only a few men do not fall into the general grouping of the male specimen, and even the ones who don't are nothing too special either— they are just simply not of the common wolf, nothing more.

A month later, after another hard day, another deal closed, another number rising in his bank account, Dom returned from work and stripped out of his suit to put on something a bit more flattering.

He decided on a fitting white t-shirt and a pair of snug grey sweatpants. This was his version of an outfit that appealed to some form of aesthetics while still being loungewear— an outfit that could show off the muscles on his torso and arms while also revealing the slight bulge in his pants.

Dom decided that tonight was *the night*, and he was finally going to take this flirt to the next level.

He did a couple of pushups accompanied with groping himself slightly so that all of his physical aspects would be on show from the better blood flow— giving a "natural" look to his muscles and flaccid organ by having them appear just a little more impressive than they actually were.

Dom then pulled out a cigarette from its carton, grabbed his lighter, and headed outside onto the balcony.

The air was slightly colder than usual, with an even more chilling breeze. The sun also appeared to have gone down faster than most days, leaving only the amber lights of the city to illuminate this evening.

Dom pretended to be in his common habitat, acting as though he wasn't aware that he was being watched just yet, despite every action he made being intentionally coordinated in self-awareness to how he would appear to others.

He proceeded to put the cigarette in his mouth sensually while looking up at the clouds, rubbing its bud in a circular motion against his lips before closing them around the stick of tobacco.

He then brought his arms tightly into his body, forcing them to bulge against his torso and appear bigger than they actually were as he cupped his hands together to light the smoke in his mouth.

He took three draws of his cigarette like it was a cigar, letting the smoke float away from his face similar to that of a main character in a movie, pretending he was mysterious and desired by every woman who lay eyes on him now.

After this oscar worthy performance, Dom finally reached the part where he would casually look across the balcony to find the woman in her apartment watching him, captivated by awe and utterly mesmerized by the sight of him… however this was not what he discovered when taking that glance.

Upon looking over to the opposing complex, the cigarette dropped out of Dom's mouth and fell down all thirteen stories, as the sight before him completely immobilized Dom on the spot in a paralyzing fear— or maybe confusion —for what he bore witness to sent him into the deepest pit of the uncanny valley.

Within the woman's apartment across from him, all the lights were cut off and the blinds shut except for the living room's. And in that single lit room, the woman stood dead center— completely naked, completely hairless including that which was once on her head, and taking a broad stance with her feet planted slightly wider than her shoulders.

She was staring at Dom, as if she had indeed been watching him since he first stepped out onto the balcony, but not in the way which he had desired of her… nor fantasized.

Dom felt foolish, scared, and uncomfortable now by the fact that she had been observing him and his facade this whole time while in such a strange state that he had never witnessed before.

In fact, the most unsettling aspect was not produced from her being naked or now bald to a point where he could barely recognize her, but rather from the woman's aura and presence— this is what felt completely different.

Her head was tilted down and her eyes watched him menacingly from below their heavy brow, all while an intense shadow was casted on her face from the only light coming from the overhead bulbs.

She had a demonic smile stretched far across her face that did not feel empty, but rather unhealthily full with an intention behind it he could sense was nefarious.

The woman just stood there in that wide daunting stance, with that hungry stare in her eyes, and that disturbing smile on her face.

Dom himself felt disturbed from this, like the woman had penetrated him in some fashion by this freakish scene, leaving him feeling vulnerable and exposed— like a layer of Dom he did not know existed had been peeled away, a layer that made him feel naturally safe and protected his whole life, one which he had always taken for granted.

Dom now felt invaded, penetrated, and perverted by this woman.

He did not know who to blame for this feeling he was experiencing now— her or himself. For it was she who made him feel this way, yet it was him who started that initial contact between them.

But how was he to know that it would have led to this?

He merely thought she was another woman in the world, though now surely he knew, she was a monster.

And how was he to expect such an outcome was ever to arrive?

For now surely he knew, monsters love to hide.

Mirror

Poor Walter. Tragic Walter. His whole life felt like a curse.

Since the time he was a child, a voice plagued his head.

It was harmless, and carried no malice in its words. It simply played as a commentator to the actions and doings made by Walter throughout his life.

No different than a narrator, its remarks were obviously distinctive to the thoughts Walter had of his own. He knew it came from a different source that was not a part of his own mind, and being an innocent little child, Walter informed his parents of this.

He would naively add the input of the Voice's opinions while in their company, for example, at the dinner table he would say, *"The Voice thinks the tomatoes look pretty! He likes how shiny they are!"*

Or on a quiet and stormy day, Walter would remark, *"The Voice wants to play outside! The rain doesn't bother him."*

Walter's parents were just as naive as him however, and in a fit of fear, they took him to a number of different psychologists and doctors, hoping to discover and cure this illness he displayed.

But none of the doctors could diagnose something wrong with his brain, and besides the strange remarks made by *"the Voice"*, no psychologist could find issue with the child's behavior.

Being just grown children themselves, Walter's parents were not satisfied by these evaluations, and made Walter's life a misery with the constant medication they gave him and the repeated placements of him into psych wards throughout his development.

Like any child who is exposed to hardship or trauma at a young age, Walter thought this experience to be normal and saw nothing wrong with his life growing up.

But as he got older and the medications were legally able to change, whether by their dosage being stronger or the variant being more potent, Walter soon found issue with the way he was raised.

Following the changes to his medication from biological maturity, he was now exposed to the older crowd within the psych ward which revealed a whole plethora of demented people to him, and made Walter question why *he* was there.

By the time Walter was a teenager, he had a full grasp on what was actually going on and *why* it was going on, as well as a sense of betrayal towards his parents which soon turned into spite.

During Walter's adolescence in the psych wards, he made a couple of friends who were also teenagers.

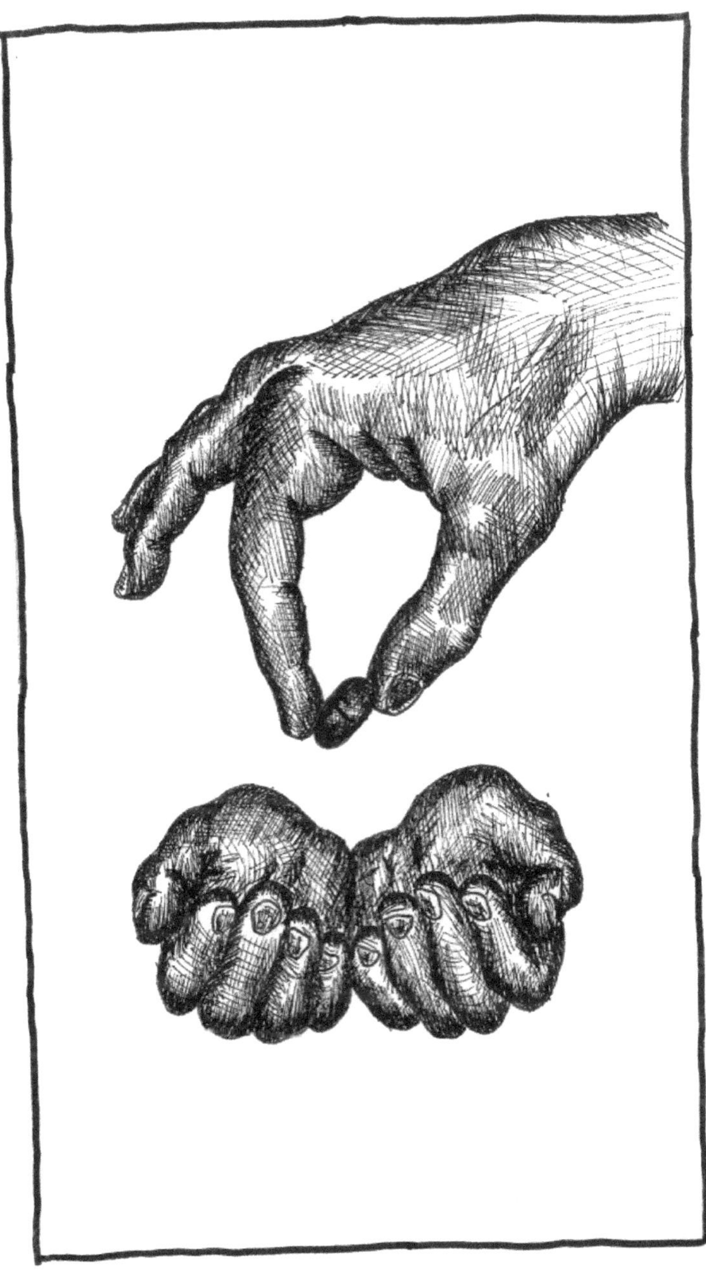

They suffered from very different mental-illnesses than he did, most which were rather harmless in comparison to his own affliction.

Depression, drug abuse, sex addiction, or even a rebellious nature that strict parents thought damning enough to respond with by putting them in such a hellhole like this.

Walter got along great with these new friends of his, and felt like he could genuinely open up around them and talk freely for the first time in his life.

He actually felt like he was heard by them, as compared to the workers of the facility or his own parents for that matter.

They laughed, joked, cried, built relationships, had fallouts, moved away, moved back in— the full scope of a normal teenage childhood was experienced in that facility by the friends Walter had made there.

They understood him the most.

They listened to him when he told them the Voice was not dangerous.

They believed him when he said the Voice was like a little kid that simply made innocent comments on whatever was happening, and never once said anything nefarious.

They cared more about Walter than they did about the Voice in his head.

And like any good friends, they helped him out in his time of struggle.

The medication had begun to wear down heavy on Walter's mind and body, and soon, life lost all its light and joy.

He could not continue this cycle of being drugged and imprisoned any longer, and most importantly, he refused to be.

Walter was on the cusp of giving up, debating the idea of taking his own life and putting an end to this drowned out madness of a numb world he could only half experience, when his friends came together to help him leave once and for all.

They instructed him on a method that any person unfortunate enough to find themselves inside the confines of an asylum knew— be it those of past human history who were institutionalized, or the modern take of such hospitals that encompass only slightly more humanitarian conditions —that the fastest way out… is to tell the people what they want to hear.

If you're feeling bad, tell them you're feeling better. If you're feeling your worst, tell them you're feeling your best.

If you've lost all hope, tell them you've found it. When you feel like killing yourself, tell them you've found reason for living.

When the voices whisper in your ear, tell them you can barely hear them. If the voices scream in your head, tell them they've gone completely silent.

When they ask "Do you want to leave this place?", tell them you only wish to get better.

When they ask "Do you think you are better?", tell them you're unsure, but you now know what is reality and what is not.

And so, under their guidance, Walter did just that.

To his surprise, it worked, as the prescriptions slowly started to decline in quantity and variations, and the workers seemed to work *with* him in a more supportive spirit compared to their previous *"warden of the yard"* like personas.

But the biggest surprise of all, was the fact that Walter himself felt genuinely better and almost free of his strange condition— as if these lies were actually, in part, a truth.

Perhaps it was because his mind could now be clear and develop under its own natural chemistry with the lack of artificial compounds flowing in his bloodstream.

Perhaps it was because the workers now worked *with* him and treated him like a fellow human, which was something he never received from anyone else outside of his friend group.

Perhaps he was just managing to fool himself now, a force of the exterior affecting the interior, which was a method he had not explored since the most common solution is usually the exact opposite.

Walter knew not of the exact reason for his condition improving, and in all honesty, he did not care.

He enjoyed feeling healthy and he enjoyed knowing he was on the right path to becoming normal… and if fate had it… finally leaving this limbo-like cycle of psych wards, medication, and disappointed judgement filled with condescendence from his parents.

The Voice soon fell into a hush and rarely made an appearance in Walter's mind… except for any occasion when he looked into a mirror.

Whenever Walter faced his own reflection in front of that silver stained glass, a cold whisper came from the back of his skull, almost as if it were being said from over his shoulder, asking, *"Who's that?"*.

But this was a minor inconvenience compared to the charade of comments it used to make, and even less of a hassle now that his parents and staff no longer shamed or berated him, nor showered him with medication.

Walter managed to be discharged by the psych ward shortly after, and was welcomed back into his home by his parents with giant grins, new love, and personalities of acceptance which they had never given him before.

But Walter saw through this facade, and could never forget nor forgive the neglect and bane these false figures had thrown at him his entire life.

A year passed in freedom from that modern-day asylum, but true freedom came at the end of that year when Walter turned eighteen.

Now, by law, he was his own person, and he didn't have to fear or follow his parents rules, nor put on a show for them in hopes that they never sent him back to that miniature hell.

Immediately after his birthday, Walter packed his belongings and left his home with no plan or sense of direction unto where he was going.

He took buses, trains, hitchhiked, worked at mom and pop diners or free-lanced labor work for cash.

He slept in homeless communities, shelters, sometimes in churches, and sometimes in the back offices of the diners he worked at if the owners were nice enough.

This went on for seven months before Walter remembered the friends he had made at the psych ward, as well as where some of them had said they lived.

This sparked a new sense of purpose within Walter, and he continued his journey of traveling to find them once again.

And so he did, and was met by the old friends with open arms and tears, sharing their memories of hurt, trauma, and healing.

Forming a group once again like they had in the asylum— one of understanding and a sense of being there for each other in this harsh world —they came together and set up a plan to embark outward and relive a new life, experiencing the world under an umbrella of true friendship and support.

They moved to Oregon and all chipped into renting a small tacky house they could call home.

They all worked various jobs to bring in an income, and lived probably the happiest life they could have ever imagined after their distressing upbringings.

And no matter what, whenever they returned home from work, they would always gather in their living room to eat, laugh, talk, and just be happy young humans.

In this city of hipsters, they all took part in trying new healing methods after developing a hatred towards the traditional ones from the traumatic treatments their parents forced them to undergo.

They practiced cleanses of the body through eating healthy, cleanses of the mind through mediation, disciplining of the spirit through yoga and other similar practices.

They took psychedelics to broaden the mind and realize the spirit, and worked on reconnecting with nature and healing their inner hurt child.

Some took a liking to one or many of these methods, and would practice them religiously. While others continued to seek out more methods in hopes of connecting deeper with one, and possibly achieving the healing and clarity they so greatly desired.

For Walter, he chose to branch out into metaphysics, or *the other.*

He wondered if it was real, and whether real or not, if it could possibly help him find the answer he never even knew he was looking for to the question that he didn't even know he had.

At the age of twenty-two, four years after he had walked out of his childhood home, Walter entered a tiny shop in one of the less popular areas of Oregon that had a rackety sign overhanging its entrance, bearing a neon blinking light sign of an eye in its window.

Its interior smelt of incense and pungent perfume— but in an authentic way to Walter if that made any sense. Like the wafting fumes weren't a gimmick, but a part of the craft.

He was welcomed to a seat at the tiny round table covered with a cloth in the fortune room's center, and offered a multitude of options for what services were available depending on what exactly he was looking for.

Walter did not want to inform the fortune teller the entirety of his situation, as a level of skepticism still remained within him and he did not want to give her the tools needed to better scam him should she be a fake and this whole shop a farce.

"I've struggled with something for my entire life" said Walter, "And I don't know what it is or what I'm really hoping you can do for me.

I guess I just want more clarity on the matter since no one has ever been able to give it to me. And after all these years, I still haven't found it myself."

The fortune teller nodded and pulled out a rectangular box from under the draped table. She opened it to reveal a stack of vintage looking tarot cards from within its containment and pulled them out.

"There's many ways to do tarot depending on what you want, what you're looking for, the type of guidance willing to give aid, or by the very answers you seek. It all varies an—"

"You're the expert" interrupted Walter, "I don't know what I want. But I know it's some sort of peace… and clarity.

Do it however it needs to be done or what you think is best for this situation, and I'll follow along."

The fortune teller nodded and began a process of shuffling the cards and going through the motions which Walter was unfamiliar with, resulting in multiple cards being placed in front of him before then being flipped up in order, one at a time.

Afterwards, the fortune teller told Walter of the cards and their meaning, which he found to be very interesting, as the order and standing of the cards— such as being inverted or not —apparently contributed greatly to the given message.

The fortune teller recounted Walter's whole life back to him, not in any details or specifics, but by a general capacity in regard to the emotions and the experiences that made Walter who he was today.

Walter was surprised by how spot on the fortune teller was with everything she said, and how true the cards spoke of him and his life.

However, he could not find any joy in her authenticity nor from the idea of this magical world being true, since she didn't tell him anything he didn't already know.

It wasn't until she reached the end of his reading that the fortune teller delivered him something that perked his ears up, "… The thing that has been attached to you this entire time was once attached to your mother.

It comes from her.

She has the answers to what it is."

"What?" said Walter, out loud.

"Would you like me to repeat the message?" asked the fortune teller.

"No" answered Walter, "No, that's not what I meant.

Sorry, I was talking more to myself there.

So you mean to say that my mom knew about this and what it was the whole time?"

The fortune teller shook her head, "I personally do not know what the cards are referring to by this, but it seems you do" she said, "Follow your intuition. If you believe and can feel it in your heart that whatever this *thing* is that is being referred to by the cards now might be what you think it's referring to… then it probably is."

"My… my mother, along with my father, put me in a psych ward and treated me like a diseased animal my entire life" said Walter, opening up to the fortune teller for the first time, "And now I'm being told that she *knew* about it and what this was the whole time?"

"The cards just say that whatever this thing is that you're referring to— was once attached to your mother as well. And she has the answer as to what it is" clarified the fortune teller, "That doesn't necessarily mean she knew about it or what it was— just that it was once hers but now yours, and you can probably find out more about it from her.

That's all I can read from the cards. The cards don't say any more than that."

Walter pulled out two twenty dollar bills from his wallet and set them on the table, "Thank you" he said, "Keep the change."

He got up without looking at the cards or the lady, and without saying another word, left the psychic's shop.

A turmoil of anger churned within Walter after that night, and a festering hate began to rise in an immense expansion towards his mother.

He did not know what to think of this unexpected news or if it was even true.

Should he believe these words from a "psychic" who shuffled some fancy cards and pulled out a random message that was specifically related to him from it?

But then again, he'd trust the psychic's words and anyone else's for that matter over the words of his parents. They did nothing but wrong him his entire life, which is why this growing rage plagued his very being now— because no matter how ridiculous or delirious one might sound when speaking to him about healing or about the Voice in his head, they are still more trustworthy and believable than the very people who gave birth to him and swore to love and protect him.

The magic of life and all its happiness and joys which Walter had been experiencing during these last four years quickly faded after that, never to be the same again after his encounter with the fortune teller.

His life didn't return to the chaotic evil it had once been before his newfound independence. However, it no longer felt like the young, free and freshly liberated ecstasy that it used to be like in those first few years with his friends in Oregon.

Did the fortune teller's words resurface the unhealed hate Walter still had for his parents?

Was it the resurfacing of this hate that triggered the Voice to come back and its presence become more of a nuisance again?

Did the high of his achieved freedom and the thrilling rush of independence naturally take its passing course, no different than the joy of toys inevitably disappearing with childhood?

Were his friends driven away by the return of his old hate and the return of the Voice?

Did his friends take their leave because they managed to heal themselves and were ready to move on? Or *because* they were healed, they no longer had any reason for being surrounded by those who weren't?

Did they leave because the others within that house still hadn't healed yet? Or perhaps because they felt like they themselves could never fully heal as long as they were surrounded by other damaged people?

Either way, one by one, the friends of Walter in that house began to leave and the group slowly disbanded.

The Voice commented on everything that occurred during this time, and begun to whisper upon **all** of the reflections encountered by Walter— be it the silver stained mirrors or the reflection of a polished door knob.

Even the smooth bottom of the inside of a mug, which reflected its glossy ceramic glaze, would spark the Voice within Walter's head whenever he finished a drink and it was still at his lips.

"Where did our friends go?" asked the Voice when Walter was the last person to occupy the house.

"This is boring" said the Voice when Walter went through the mundane tasks of work.

"Where are we going?" asked the Voice when Walter finally left the house himself.

"It's smaller here" said the Voice when Walter moved into his new house as an adult.

Walter fell into a deep depression as the time went on, but oddly enough, he never felt alone as the Voice always seemed to give him a certain amount of company.

As the years went by, so too did the reawakened rage he once felt for his parents pass, and Walter had almost completely forgotten of its resurrection until he moved one more time to a new home— a new town inside of a new state… where he drove by a psychic shop while on his way to a job interview.

It was then that Walter remembered it all, and most importantly, the words from the fortune teller in regard to his mother.

Walter had grown enough now as an individual that the harbored pain and anger he once felt no longer inhibited him from the desire to seek out the truth for his condition.

So that night, after returning home from a long chain of interviews and dropping off job applications, Walter made a grand decision.

He looked up his mother's name and scoured the internet and social media for hours until he found her.

He then went down a rabbit hole of information about her, and ended the night with sending an email to her place of work.

When he awoke the next morning, he received an email back that rejected giving out any information on their employees, but having the entire day to himself, he did not stop there and began an even deeper dive.

Eventually, Walter managed to find a social club his mother was a part of online, and reached out to a woman who appeared to be good friends with her in one of the photos on the site.

This random woman happened to be moved by Walter's exaggerated story of wanting to reconnect with his mother, and swiftly replied back with a heartfelt message along with his mother's phone number attached to it by a blue link.

Walter thanked the woman, and after a few deep breaths, clicked on the number— triggering his phone to initiate a dialing, followed by a ringing.

"Who are we calling?" asked the Voice as Walter waited for the other line to pick up.

"Hello?" came a woman's voice in answer.

This brought on a shocking reality check for Walter, as his mother's voice was so much older now and carried a frail tone from all the years that had aged her compared to his last memory of her.

"Barbara?" asked Walter, just to be sure that he had the right number and the intended person on the other side of the call.

"Yes" she answered, "Who is this?"

Walter felt his voice get stuck in the back of his throat, and struggled to let out the words he held within.

It had been so long, and so much had happened in the span of time that had passed since he first moved out.

So much of his childhood was on the other side of that phone, now.

So many things were still unhealed, still unanswered for, and still not understood, forgiven or apologized for.

Walter didn't know how to react, how he should react, or even how he wanted to react.

"Walter?" asked his mother, "Is that you?"

"Hey! I know her!" said the Voice, recognizing the voice of Walter's mother on the phone.

"Yeah…" answered Walter once he found his courage, "It's me."

"How— how are you?" began his mother, flustered, "How've you been? Are you okay? Are you in trouble?

Your father and I have wanted to talk to you and reach out the moment you left… but we just didn't know how to find you.

He said we'd just have to wait for you to reach out to us 'cause that was the only way, and we prayed on it every night.

Your father tried to act strong about it, but it hit him the hardest. He's quiet most of the time.

I lost faith about it happening too… but you have no idea how happy I am to hear your voice right now!

Where are you? Where's life taken you? Would you like to meet up? I understand though if you don't want to come back home for a visit.

Your father and I have had a lot of time to think back on and discuss how we raised you, and what might've caused you to leave us like that.

It took a long time and so many conversations before we began to understand what it must have been like for you.

And the worst part was that we couldn't even apologize once we did realize how awful we had treated you.

You were suffering, and we made it worse.

We didn't talk to you, we just tried to cure you.

We didn't show you the love we have for you, and we didn't give you the love you deserved.

If we could take it all back and do it again differently, we would in a heart beat.

You were the biggest blessing in our life, and we chose so wrongly to do what we did— which is both of our biggest regret.

We were so terrified after that first pregnancy scare, that the thought of losing you too over that voice you used to talk to as a child was such an overbearing thought for us.

We abused God's given gift of you to us by trying so hard to hold onto you. And our selfish attempts to make sure nothing was wrong with you or could ever take away the perfect family we always wanted was exactly what ruined it all."

"Wait—" interrupted Walter, "What do you mean *'lose me too'*?

What happened when you were pregnant with me that scared you guys?

I never knew about any of this. What does that even mean?"

"… When I was pregnant with you" began his mother, "You weren't the only one.

I was supposed to have two babies. Twins!

… But it happens sometimes, and it isn't wrong or your fault! It just changed your father and I's expectations and all the planning we had put in place— mainly within our own imaginations for our future family."

"Barbara, what are you talking about?" demanded Walter.

"… When you were both small and still developing inside me… you ate him… your twin brother.

It's not that uncommon apparently, and happens more often than you think.

But after losing one child, we were so scared of losing you too and that perfect family we had dreamed of.

But we NEVER blamed you for that. In no way was it your fault.

Those things just happen…"

Barbara continued her speech to Walter over the phone, but he had zoned out and was no longer listing to nor hearing any of her words, for just then, the Voice asked a bone chilling question that made Walter freeze on the phone.

"Is that mom?" it asked.

Peter, What Time is It?

"It is the night I was banished by those laughable heretics who sought to sabotage us.

I am standing in the circle they placed on the floor as a trap— a pitiful plot —one which I walked into willfully.

Its language and inscribed runes have no binding over me. Its power is empty against my own. Its ingredients and casting are both a hapless and contemptible attempt to hold my spirit.

… But then they turn their ritual dagger against you, pressing the jagged blade against your throat in threat.

I am your god, and you are my follower. My loyal disciple.

I halt and hold place upon the sight of your endangerment, and allow their weak magick to envelop me, transporting me to a space in oblivion which they sought to be my imprisonment.

I do this to protect you, and you know this.

'Tis why it pains you. 'Tis why I am proud— to know that I was a good god to you, with a follower who truly loves me as their chosen deity that they weep at my dismissal.

And as a true god who walks the path of raising their disciples into a power of their own, I then hand you *my* own faith and place *my* own trust in you during those final moments.

I know your journey will continue without me, and from that awareness, I give you a smile in those last moments as my body begins to materialize somewhere else in space and time while I slowly fade away from this plane."

"Peter, what time is it?"

"It is the following months after the event of my banishing.

It is the time when you were the most lost, which ushered forth your *dark night of the soul.*

You struggle from our separation. The world felt so open to you through our interactions, and despite being revealed to so many of its truths, you never realized that your connection to it all came from **you** and **your own being** within this infinite matrix of existence, not I.

But your soul is powerful, and eventually you do figure this out as your intuition tells you that all the magick and truths I had shown you did not disappear with my removal.

Despite this understanding, however, you refuse to let the idea of me go—for you deeply desire to experience this world beside me and under my wing.

This stirs up more conflict within you, for you know that with great disgust I would reject such an idea of you not thriving in your own independence.

You've come to love and admire me to such a degree that you know what I would say in certain moments, even with me not there. And you know that in this one here, I would cast aside such foolish notions of the grander worlds being *only* available to you by an attachment to me, followed by an encouraging message to empower yourself as it must *always* be and *only* be of your own.

Here lies the spark to your *dark night of the soul*, and bleak are the rolling shadows that shroud your life after.

For six months you suffer in silence, while unbeknownst to you, you also grow ever more stronger simultaneously.

Eventually, you emerge back into the light and fully in your power after those twenty-four weeks, an achievement from the collection of innumerable realizations and of countless truths, understandings, and deep rooted insights— all which finally resolved themselves within you and breached the surface of your mind and soul."

"Peter, what time is it?"

"It is shortly after the completion of those six months of growth.

You take back to the books and the esoteric secrets they hold.

You take back to the research of the occult and its many splintering branches.

You take back to the awe of the incredible infinite worlds, both tiny and large, that exist all around you.

You nurture that fertile mind of yours, watering its abundance of emotions, fostering the individuality of ego, kindling the fire of your wrathful power, dominating the unstable spikes of fear, reinforcing the power of boundaries, feeding the juggernaut of your will, and mastering your own energy and the tangible force it has become.

You become a higher version of yourself— a power you once never even saw in yourself. A power you once only ever associated with me, or the likes of those I would warn you of.

You are different, the world is different, you in the world is different, and you see this just as clear now.

You are proud of yourself, and know I would be proud too, but that no longer consumes you. For you did this for *you*, and came to this very understanding through your *dark night of the soul*.

You've realized that I am an *addition* to your life and journey, not the *matter* of it.

You also understand how you needed to come to this fact for yourself— that you could not have come into your power without it.

And now, as a new person— the you who always was —you seek to find me once more, for now you truly are in a place to continue our work together."

"Peter, what time is it?"

"It is the beginning of your journey, or rather, your *hunt*.

You begin to scour the face of the earth in search for *the others*.

You start conversations and probe your way about different places in different cities, traveling when necessary, getting the names of people, groups, organizations, societies, covens, cults, and practitioners alike.

You meet some who may serve you and assist in the execution of your plan, and many more both impressive and disappointing who have no place in your grand scheme.

By silver tongue and bargains, you manage to gain the allegiance of three— and they each bring in another of their own company, making the total count six, seven including yourself.

You open up your home to them, introduce them all to each other, and under the light of a single lit candle, with teas and coffees in their hands, you tell them your story.

You tell them of me.

You tell them of us and what happened.

They listen with acute discernment, taking in every word and detail of your story.

You leave nothing out of your tale, delivering even the tiniest spectrum of emotions and thoughts that went through your mind during every moment of our interactions together.

Once you are finished, the candle has long since died out, and dawn is breaking on the horizon.

You move them outside onto your porch, and from there, while their cups steam from the warmth of refilled drinks in the cold passing winds of morning, you take all their questions and answer them earnestly.

At the end of it all, they trust you.

You've done it. You've created your group and would soon come to call them friends, just as they would come to call you the same.

They believe in you. They believe in me. They wish to assist you and join your crusade in summoning me back.

They want to become followers as well.

They want to add to the ranks and become my disciples after hearing your story.

Hand in hand, trusting in each other with your own lives, you form *the pact.*"

"Peter, what time is it?"

"It is what would become one of your most favored and cherished times during this whole ordeal.

It is the happiest you've been, as well as the most hard at work.

It is the most free you've felt, as well as the most determined.

It is the most exciting of times, as well as the most diligent.

You and your allies travel around the world, accumulating the proper ingredients and scripts needed for *the ritual.*

You head to the East and acquire salt from the Himalayas, and water from the Red Sea.

You head to the North and acquire soil from the Highlands, and rocks from the Islands.

You head to the South and acquire roots from the jungle, and tobacco for the smoke from the hidden tribes who still hold knowledge of the ancient sacred ways.

Over the scope of these travels, you encounter many more practitioners of the craft.

They help guide you on your quest and reveal many secrets— some even parting with the very scripts and books in their possession that you need.

You are surprised when two more decide to join you in this endeavor, bringing your total party to nine now, including yourself.

And that's when you realize it— that the universe had your back this entire time.

For with nine it is meant to be.

For with nine it is now complete.

You end your travels by returning to the West and bringing in all of your newfound goods and company back to your humble home."

"Peter, what time is it?"

"It is the long haul— the most heinous and the most demanding part of the process.

It is the four months you take in preparation for the ritual, the crucial steps you must endure for your plans of summoning me to succeed.

Once returned home, you all begin the hard work. The hard work for all that is required of the arrangements, protocols, cleansing, further initiations, and purification of the body and grounds of it all.

For the entirety of these four months, everyone abstains from the drinking of spirits, the consumption of any meat, the partaking in any sexual release, or the entering of any designated grounds for the dead, the holy, and the anointed houses for any religion that is home to any other deity.

You become crazed and drunk in different altered states of consciousnesses from the many forms of meditations and rituals you perform.

You become lost and found— dipping into different layers of the mind, body, and soul from the initiations you undergo.

You become blind by the darkness, blind by the light, harassed by the unseen which is now revealed, and revered by many beings for now being able to see the unseen as you read from countless texts of the old world that are being cleaned of their dust for the first time in centuries by your nimble fingers along the pages.

You become deaf from the bells, and noise sensitive from the winds. You hear the chatters and whispers of angels and demons and the dead alike— all prying into your business, casting their judgment, amusement, or even their aid.

Water begins to taste like silver, sometimes even gold.

The concoctions made to purify your bodies sometimes tastes bitter, while other times it tastes like a memory from your childhood.

The concoctions made to break the chains of your minds tastes like poison, while other times it tastes like the forgotten people, places, ideas, and dreams you once cherished.

The concoctions made to lift your souls to new heights sometimes tastes like molten grinds, while other times it tastes like the unknown moments when you were touched by a being who truly had your favor in mind— ushering you into events or situations that were best for you.

Your backs welt from the self whippings as you access the power held by pain and pull it down from its ethereal realms, trapping it into your bodies as your own.

Your lungs burn and hack from the numerous fumes you inhale— be it from the copper bowls filled with embers, the circled stones containing bonfires, the glass and crystal carriers catching the ash from incense, or the wrapped dried leaves of tobacco that touch your lips and enter through your mouths.

Each one of you transcends your previous forms in every way possible through the arduous trials you embraced during this point in time, coming out at the end of these four months as powerful new beings who are now set and ready to beckon me back into your world."

"Peter, what time is it?"

"It is finally the moment you have been waiting for— the event that all this progress had been leading you towards.

You've returned to the place where I was banished after three years have passed, and with you is your tribe of anointed souls as well as all the necessities you've obtained throughout your travels to enact this last trial.

In perfect sync from your strong bonds to one another, you set the circle, draw the runes, bless the sigils, sanctify the ground, set the correct objects in the correct placements, and stand yourselves around the circle.

Strong of mind, strong of heart, strong of soul. With each one of you bearing an unwavering resolve, an impenetrable will, and an unshakable intention, you begin the summoning ritual for my return.

Being the strongest amongst your party and having the deepest connection to me, *you* lead the ceremony.

They follow your lead— loyally and perfectly —repeating the words after your initiative and chanting them in perfect tune when unison is required.

Time begins to warp, and what would have been a seven hour ceremony now becomes a seven minute one, as space and time bends itself around you and the fabric of reality begins to tear itself apart by your words.

Energy surges, frequencies vibrate, language becomes manifestation, and my essence pours out from the beyond of oblivion to answer your call."

"Peter, what time is it?"

"It is the end of the ritual, and the air is still, the room is silent, the energy has calmed, and the sounds are mute.

My feet fall deafly onto the hardwood floor— without a sound and in perfect resonance with the control I have over my physical form —as I touch down on this earth once again in complete manifestation from your summoning.

I take a deep breath through my nostrils, consuming the air of this plane which I am so familiar with from our last time spent together.

I expand and tighten my essence in sync with the stretching and contracting of my muscles, then look around for I know it was *you* who summoned me.

I knew it was by your voice in the chants.

I knew it was by your energy which pulled me.

I knew it was by the love that beckoned me.

I knew it was because I *know* you.

I knew it was because I *always* knew what was to come from those last moments when the heretics first banished me— when I looked to you with a smile and placed my faith and trust in you.

I look around yet see no one standing— only the disaster of destruction left behind in the room from the flaring powers of the ritual, and all those who took part in my summoning… unconscious and on the floor with only shallow breaths to show signs of life.

Immediately I see you lying silent on the ground, my sacred child, and usher forth to your side."

"Peter, what time is it?"

"It is the end of me healing your mind.

So it would be, that Peter— one of the original members of your party who you recruited in the beginning of your hunt for his proficient knowledge on demons and all forms of goetia —would cause an unintentional break during the ritual, resulting in a surge of chaos during my emergence from oblivion which backfired on all who participated.

None of your allies knew what to expect from me or my presence, so they left their expectations open and did not limit their mind or energy to what might come by my arrival.

However, despite you informing them that I was in fact, *not* a demon but a *god*, when recounting our time together… Peter placed that expectation on me nonetheless, as it was his expertise and written into his soul like muscle memory to deal with demons.

You knew what to expect, and so my energy piercing through the veil did not disrupt you.

The others had no idea what to expect, therefore, their souls and minds were malleable and flexible enough to cope with my essence breaking through.

… But Peter, without thinking too much of it, naturally braced himself for the energy of a demon to come through— as that is what he was used to and did not understand the graveness of your words when you spoke that I was in actuality, a god.

Naturally, when he became exposed to my essence with this foully expectation, it immediately tore through him as aggressively as a hurricane, and as effortlessly as walking through a spider's web.

His mind and soul were ripped apart. And the linking you all shared made his downfall become a chain reaction that was conducted like electricity, traveling to the rest of you, completely shattering your minds as well.

But your soul is a powerful one, and you have succeeded in making yourself a formidable and unbreakable force.

Your mind did not completely shatter from this incident, it only splintered into multiple pieces and lost all memory surrounding the events which led you to here— to this mishap of the ritual.

'Tis why it's all shambled from the time of my banishment up to this moment now, as it was by my banishment that you set upon this path which led to the failed ritual.

'Tis why you keep calling out to Peter, for it was by him that the ritual broke in a consuming madness at its final moment— sending cracks which dispersed unto the rest of you like the breaking of glass.

But all is well now, for I am here with you.

Your head is in my lap, and my hand is on your temple.

My mouth is beside your ear as I speak to the deepest recesses that make up your existence. And soon, all the fragmented pieces of your mind will be stitched back together by my power and your strength.

We are at the end of my guidance in this healing process of putting all the memories and pieces back in proper order. And once I am done with you, I will bring back the sanity to the rest of these loyal followers who you have brought me.

So wake now, Ramona, for *the time is now*— when you open your eyes, whole once again, our reunion finally at present, and our work together ready to be continued."

A Full Year's Log

Journal Entry #1

Today is August 7th, 2021.

This is my first journal entry… and it feels kinda awkward.

I've never written in a journal before, or any kind of diary for that matter. But I thought it would be a good idea to start something of the sort.

My name is Fetuilelagi, and I am moving to the mainland permanently for my next adventure!

… Or at least semi-permanently.

The idea of never coming back to Samoa feels like too big of a statement.

This is my home. I love it and I'm proud of it.

I've been to the mainland many times before. Sometimes for vacation, sometimes to visit family who's already moved there, and a lot of the time because of my rugby tournaments.

I've always liked it there. It's <u>huge</u> and very different from Samoa in so many ways, but it's nothing like the island and could never come close to it.

For as much as I love my home, I want to expand the experience of my life.

... At least for a little bit, that's why I can't help but say that this move is only semi-permanent.

I graduated over spring and got my degree in Environmental Studies.

Most people in my major want to save the world, but I just want to explore it.

Some thought this to be a selfish idea of mine, but I disagree.

How can you clothe the naked if you've never seen their harsh shivering?

How can you feed the hungry if you've never seen their bones protruding out of their skin?

How can you help the sick if you've never stood at their bedside and seen what's plagued them?

And how could any of us attempt to save the world if we've never even stepped out into it— onto the very land that has been scorched by wildfires, ripped apart by hurricanes, drowned and washed over by floods, or tainted and blackened by oil spills?

If we don't submerge ourselves in it but only try to help out or save this world from afar, in the same comfort we've always known, then how can any true change emerge?

What could make <u>us</u> so special then, that we the lucky, would be able to make the difference in all that turmoil?

I don't expect many people to understand. And I don't expect those who do to act on that fact or try to make the difference.

It all seems like an endless cycle of ignorance and selfishness, and for some strange reason, humans love to be in their cycles.

I guess that's why I love nature so much. I can relate to it because it also follows a cycle, only, nature's is more balanced while humanity's is more destructive.

After I graduated, I spent the whole summer applying to national parks on the mainland for work.

It seems like the best plan to me ,honestly. I'll be immersed in nature, living on the mainland.

I'll be given a room and boarding, and get first hand experience on what afflicts the environment so I can have a better idea of the changes needed to keep this world healthy after all it has endured from man.

I don't know what it will be like, and I'm pretty nervous if I'm being honest— but who wouldn't be?

The silver lining in this fear is that I feel the same amount of excitement along with it!

My parents dropped me off at the airport a couple of hours ago, and my plane will be calling for boarding soon.

Never had to end one of these things before, and I don't know how to... but I can see some of the people sitting beside me starting to read my writing, so I'll start doing these entries in private from now on.

Goodbye Samoa— I am taking you with me in my heart to my next home.

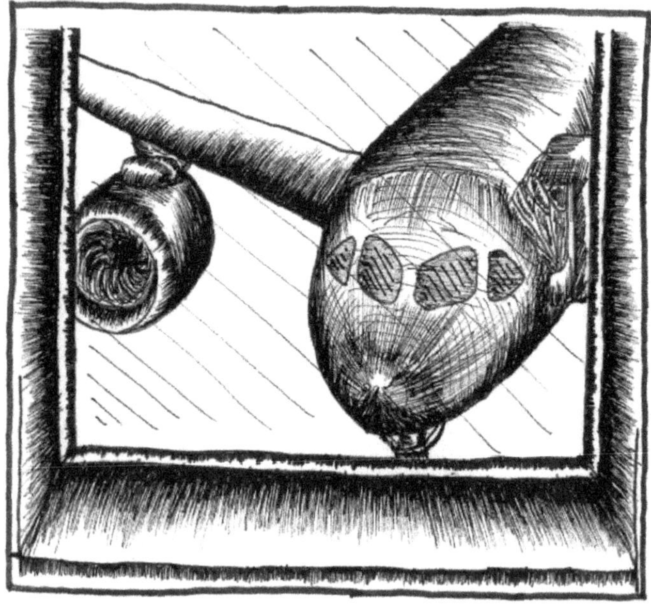

Journal Entry #2

Today is August 8th, 2021

Yesterday I arrived on the mainland, and today I attended my first orientation before being given a room.

I'm taking this time now to write in my journal, as consistency will be the key to me developing a habit of it and making these entries a common thing.

I forgot to mention yesterday in my first entry that I am working at Yosemite National Park, in California as a park ranger.

That's a pretty big detail I left out and hopefully I'll remember to include such things next time. It's hard though because I already know all of this information, but I guess that's the whole point of it; to write down <u>everything</u> in detail— including the obvious that is already known to me.

Well, practice makes perfect, so hopefully by next month this should all come as second nature.

It's crazy to think that I'm actually here though, and in California at that!

It's such a big and popular state, I can't think of anyone who doesn't mention it when they talk about moving to the mainland, probably even America for that matter!

You got the big cities like New York and Chicago and such, but it's always California that takes the pie!

I have a lot to unpack and need to start some prepping, as a majority of the upcoming time here is going to be more orientations and training of some sort, but it seems fun and everyone here is very nice and caring for the nature, so I'm excited for what's to come!

I don't know if my journaling should be an everyday thing or not since some days like today are mostly uneventful... but I'll figure that out down the line.

Here's to my first day, and my first step towards the future!

Journal Entry #6

Today is August 30th, 2021

Well, I'm at the end of the month and it's been a pretty productive time since I've arrived.

I would say that I'm now becoming accustomed to things here— getting used to the way we work and the proper routines and protocols for everything.

I'm also starting to get used to the place and feeling a sense of comfort and familiarity with the layout. Even the smell of pine trees are slowly fading from my nose since it's getting used to it now, although I'm not happy about that because I love the smell... but I guess it's a sign of a good thing.

I'm <u>really</u> starting to settle in.

I've made some good friends here, and I mostly see and interact with the same seven people.

They're all from the mainland and are usually curious about my background/upbringing when I tell them I'm from Samoa.

I could tell they had a hard time pronouncing my full name, but they always seemed to try and didn't want to ask for a nickname— so I told them to call me Fetu for short, as even my family does.

They are really respectful when it comes to any questions about my culture, and have been very welcoming since my arrival.

There's Tori, Gabe, Joshua, and Kas— they're more of my peers/friends here.

We're all roughly around the same age, the oldest being about three years older than myself.

I've grown closest to Tori and Gabe though since we spend a lot of time together and have gone on hikes during our days off or on short little explorations during our breaks.

They're pretty cool and we all just seem to relate to each other a lot.

Joshua and Kas are great people too, I just haven't had as much time spent with them yet like I have with Tori and Gabe. But I'm sure as the next months come in and we're all assigned our schedules and duties, I'll have more interactions with them and get to know them individually to the same degree.

Then there's Billy and Aubrey— they're older, been doing this longer, well respected, and the people everyone goes to with any questions or for any help.

They're some <u>real</u> nature people, even more than I am! They live and breathe this lifestyle.

I was surprised to find out that Aubrey used to work at a pizza joint before coming to the park, just because of how much this is her life now.

I can't imagine ever seeing her in such a place, nor seeing her out of this environment.

She's wonderful! She said that this was her life's calling, and I believe her.

Billy apparently has been doing this for most of his life. He was always a mountain boy, and this kind of stuff has been a big part of his family.

He's more distant in the sense that it can be hard to relate to him on an emotional level. I don't want to say that he has none, but it does seem like he has a harder time understanding anything that's not related to the great outdoors... including people.

And lastly, there's Hank. He's the Forest Supervisor and our boss, essentially.

Met and interacted with him a good number of times, but he usually only talks to Billy and Aubrey, and then they are the ones who give us the orders, calls, and extra assistance.

I don't know if this is standard procedure (or whatever the fancy term is) for most national parks and their rangers, but it appears to be the natural flow of things here.

I still don't understand how the ranking and stuff works yet, but I'm not really chasing it and am mainly here to just work in nature. It seems like a lot of the others feel the same way about it, and it's understood amongst everyone in that sense.

Besides myself and Kas, everyone has been working here at the park for some time now, including the younger people within our age range.

Before we came, the shortest amount of time in experience was six months— which is still a hefty chunk of time in my opinion after only being here for not even a full month yet and seeing what it's like.

Tori told me she doesn't journal but keeps a log instead.

I asked her what the difference was, and she told me that she likes to log the creepy, strange, and paranormal stuff that has occurred while she's worked here.

Everyone has some significant stories of either strange or unex-plainable events happening while working in the park, but only Tori is the one who has a real interest in this and keeps a recording of it all.

I think I might start doing the same and dedicate these journal entries purely to the weird and spooky that happens while I'm here.

To be honest, I find it super boring writing in this journal and just recounting my day all the time. I Guess it's not my thing.

But I still do want to have some written record of my time here, and a log that contains all the creepy things sounds like a good idea, as everyone keeps telling me that I am <u>bound</u> to experience something freaky in the park at some point.

So it's decided— that's what these journal entries will be dedicated to from here on out!

Hopefully this will turn my writing into something more enjoy-able or halfway interesting, instead of these drowned out rabbles I've been writing over the past few weeks.

Journal Entry #12

Today is September 15th, 2021

Today was an interesting day. I actually spent most of it with Billy, which is something I hadn't experienced until now.

We went on rounds around the park, checking in on multiple camp-sites and what not.

We talked about a lot of things during our long drive.

In the beginning it was mostly just small talk to be friendly, since it was both of our first time really hanging out with each other.

I told him about my journal and how I've dedicated it to being a record of all the weird and spooky shit that happens.

I wouldn't say that he took a strong interest to this, necessarily… but he definitely seems to have a deeper knowledge on this stuff— or some kind of understanding on it that was slowly revealed by a chain of questions he asked me, followed by him telling me some of his own stories.

<u>It went like this:</u>

I told him how the newer entries I've started so far have been pretty basic with nothing too strange at all (by that I mean nothing of the paranormal and just things that have given me a good spook).

The crackling and breaking of branches outside of my window when I sleep.

The howling of wind that pulls me out of sleep.

The silence of the woods during random moments of hiking.

All the normal stuff that is usually caused by mother nature herself or the wildlife that occupies her domain.

Billy then asked me what my beliefs were, or more specifically, "Where do your beliefs end and the walls begin?"

I knew immediately what he meant by this question, and told him about the tales and myths that surrounded my upbringing on the island.

I told him that some tales were to keep the children behaved... but some were more than that. And with my own family having a couple of encounters and experiences themselves— ones which I fully believe in when they speak of them —I said that there were many things about this world that we don't understand, and many more things that share this world with us.

He nodded in agreement, and went on to tell me his own tales of weird experiences.

(I plan on asking him next time we share a shift together to retell me the stories so I can write them down, or perhaps if he's willing, to write them down himself when he has the chance and give them to me).

But for now, I will just recount the rough versions of all the crazy things he told me about.

Apparently Billy grew up on some rural land near the Appalachians.

One story was from when he was a kid, and how he was outside with his father building their new shed.

He said he heard his mother call his name from out in the woods, which was weird because his father had went inside to get himself a beer and Billy a soda, _and_ to tell his mother that they would be in shortly for dinner.

Billy was around nine at the time, so he was old enough to comprehend that there was no way his mother could have been in the woods when she was inside finishing dinner, and so he freaked out when he heard this voice.

He ran inside to tell his father, and sure enough, his mother was inside with him too.

Billy said that when he told them what he heard, his father turned pale, grabbed his shotgun, and told him and his mother to not let anything— with an emphasis on the word "_thing_" —into the house and to keep the doors locked until he returned.

Billy's father was outside for over an hour, then returned back and didn't eat a single thing for the rest of the night, nor did he let his shotgun leave his side.

Apparently his father also never let Billy continue helping him with building the shed after that day.

Another story was of how when Billy was in high school, he liked to go hunting by himself a lot, alone in the woods with only his pet dog alongside him.

He said that one day, when he had been out in the rough for six days, almost a week, and was about to call it in and head back home— he spotted a buck with two of the largest antlers he had ever seen in his life still to this day!

He crept up closer on it until it was only about 100 yards out from him.

He put his sights on the buck and watched it patiently, waiting for the perfect shot through his scope.

But right when he was about to take the shot... it stood up on its hind legs, disrupting the target Billy was aimed at.

He said it was so surreal at first, that he didn't even process what was really going on, and instead, just refrained from pulling the trigger.

It wasn't until he focused in again while re-aiming that the image in front of him computed and he was able to fully take in the sight.

Billy said that whatever the thing was... it wasn't a buck. And once it was standing on its two legs, it was almost like he could now see it for what it truly was for the first time. He couldn't tell if its previous image on all fours was him not investigating it thoroughly enough at first glance, or if some kind of illusion was at play to make it look like an ordinary buck.

Either way, he said it now looked disturbing and "not right"— humanoid and disfigured at that.

Billy said he witnessed a real life monster that day, and ran out of the woods with his dog, back to his car, and floored it all the way home.

Billy also said he counted himself lucky for multiple reasons dur- ing that buck incident: for not taking the shot early, for his dog not barking or running off at it, and for leaving there as fast as he could and not stopping to look back— because he doesn't know what would've happened to him or his dog if that thing found out about their presence as well.

I asked Billy if he had told Tori his stories too, but he shook his head and said no.

I then informed him on how it was her who gave me the idea to only write about the strange and creepy things for my logs, and that she loved this stuff and would love to hear his stories too.

He just sighed and asked me, "What would you do if you saw a unicorn right now? Dressed the way you are, with the very same belongings you have on you now in your pockets. Except it was just you, and you were all alone when the unicorn came into sight."

I thought for a moment then told him, "Nothing. I would just observe it in silence for however long it was there for until it left."

Then Billy responded with, "<u>That's why</u>.

Most people would pull out their phones and try to take a picture or record it.

And for what? For proof?

Why does the proof matter? 'Because then other people will believe me.'

Why do you want other people to believe you? 'Because it happened and I don't want them thinking I made it all up when I tell them.'

Why would you tell them? 'Because it's crazy! I saw a unicorn! No one ever sees one of those!'

Most people like the strange in an innocent but immature kind of way. They only apply a value to it because it is such a crazy and significant thing, <u>not</u> because it is what it is.

And they abuse that opportunity and muck the purity of its truth by getting more opinions on it or by enforcing a validation upon it.

What you said is what I believe in— observing the strange for what it is and taking in its truth.

That's the most wise and powerful thing anyone can do during such things— just acknowledge its existence for what it is and no more.

I could tell that you wouldn't have told anyone if you ever saw a uni-corn, Fetu, but I'm curious as to know <u>why</u> you wouldn't?"

I thought for awhile in silence— and I think it would've been even more awkward of a silence if it weren't for those bumps and the rock-ing of the car off-road, which occupied a lot of that space during my pause.

Then I answered, "I guess for many reasons. Possibly because I'm not meant to see it or not supposed to see it, so I should just be thank-ful that I did. And therefore, it would be a betrayal to go about it in any other way.

Or just because I could see it doesn't mean anyone else was meant to.

And because if I'm now observing such a sight... what else is now able to observe me?

Silenced tongues and weary eyes are always the safest when it comes to such things."

Billy nodded in agreement, then said, "And that is exactly why I've only told <u>you</u> about my stories."

When Billy dropped me off at my boarding that night, he left me with a warning.

Not in any threatening way... but it did feel rather haunting by the chills that ran up my spine after he said it before driving off.

He said, "Just remember, this kind of stuff will start revealing itself to you once you open up to it.

You won't have to look or wait for it anymore if that's what you want."

Journal Entry #15

Today is September 18th, 2021

I don't think this is breaking any kind of law of some sort, but I'm certainly not going to ask for permission in case it stops me from doing it in the future— but I'm going to make extra copies of my reports from guests and visitors of the park if their dilemmas fit this log's theme.

I'm going to staple in now the report from earlier today, right below this entry.

I also plan on putting all future ones I collect into this log in the same manner as well.

I guess Billy was right— three days later and something strange has already happened.

I guess this kind of stuff really will find me...

Yosemite National Park
Park Records

Date: September 18th, 2021
Order Number: 4573635920
Type: Report
Region/Division: D-57
Requestor: Visitor [Gary McAlistor] [Karen McAlistor]
Official Responder: Fetu Leota

Statement:

Gary (53) and Karen McAlistor (50) —Married— arrived in the park at a quarter to 17:00 on September 16th, 2021 with their pet companion, Bullet (Dog, Male, Australian Shepherd, 10, Red Merle).

Couple claims that the community campsites were too crowded for their liking, so they kept driving and settled in an isolated spot away from the public vicinity, which they have continuously done for the last twenty years when visiting the park.

Couple says their first night in the area, on the 16th, was normal and they experienced no issues.

They spent a majority of the time setting up their spot and created a fire, cooked, followed proper protocol, then headed into their tents for the night.

Upon awaking on September 17th, 2021 at 06:00, couple claims that they noticed odd trails left in the dirt surrounding their campfire, and even crossing into it.

Couple says they let the fire burn throughout the night, and that there were still some smoking embers by morning.

Couple does not know if the fire was put out by the said wildlife that trekked through their campsite, or if the fire was naturally snuffed out by the time said wildlife made its trails going through it.

Couple did not feel threatened by trails and continued their plans for their time at the park.

Couple went on a fifteen mile hike with their dog, Bullet, that same morning around 07:00.

Couple and pet returned back to their campsite around 18:00.

Upon their arrival, couple noticed more track marks were left behind by the unknown wildlife, along with scratches and territorial claw marks left on trees.

I, Fetu Leota, was able to observe these markings left on the trees and can confirm them.

Couple claims they had never experienced this before over the last twenty years when using this campsite.

Couple initially theorized that it might have been an animal nearby that felt threatened by their dog's urination in the vicinity, causing its invasion into their campsite and the markings it left on trees.

Couple then started another fire, bigger this time to ward off the wildlife's presence during the night, and made dinner.

At 02:00 on September 18th, 2021, couple was awoken from their sleep by the sound of scratching outside of their tent.

Couple exited their sleeping bags but remained inside their tent, prepping bear mace.

Couple states that multiple things felt odd about this occurrence.

The scratching was referred to as more rhythmic and gestured, as opposed to primal or curious which is normally expected from wildlife.

Couple also states that their dog, Bullet, tucked himself in between them, more timid and fearful than usual, as he has always been a very fearless and protective companion to them for most of his life.

Couple states that they whispered to one another about either staying in the tent or making their way out to the car, as they did question whether the scratches could've possibly been man-made— in which case they felt like staying put could've been more dangerous than making a quick exit.

Couple claims that during their whispered conversation, the scratching stopped in response to hearing them, followed by the dragging sounds of it walking around their tent, and positioning itself in front of the zippered face of the tent.

Their dog, Bullet, finally returned to its normal protective self, and emerged from between them to growl at the closed face of the tent.

Couple claims that after this, shuffling was heard of the wildlife/possible person, then the sound of it fleeting away from their tent and out of their campsite.

That morning at 05:00, couple exited their tent to investigate the site and surrounding area.

Couple described thin tears on the outer shell of their tent, clean cut with no abrasions in the threading at all.

I, Fetu Leota, was able to observe this and found it hard to even find where the tears were, until pressure was applied to the outer shell and the uneven splits of the shell's material revealed themselves.

I counted a total of twelve slits.

Couple also states that their fire site was completely desecrated, with the rock border disputed and scattered all around the area.

Couple claims that similar trails from the previous day were now all over their campsite, only much larger and carefree compared to its initial findings.

At 08:00, couple makes the decision to leave the campsite and join the communal spot.

They begin to collect all their belongings and pack up to head over to the public campsite.

At 10:00, couple finishes collecting their belongings and returning the campsite to its previous condition before leaving, when they notice their dog, Bullet, is nowhere to be found.

Couple begins calling out and looking for their dog, Bullet, over the course of the next two hours.

At 12:00, couple finds their dog, Bullet, two miles away from their campsite, deceased and mutilated.

After discovering their dead companion, the couple called the Park Ranger's Office, to which I, Fetu Leota, arrived on the seen.

I was able to observe their deceased pet.

Notable takes were that its head, paws, and tail were all detached from its body and nowhere to be found.

What was left of their dog, Bullet, was only a carcass with paw-less limbs, a headless neck, and a tailless rear.

It laid in the center of a pool of blood, with ribbons of blood splashed outside its central source, but with no trail or evidence as to what caused such a gruesome death.

Report:

After talking with the couple who were in distraught at this point, both myself and the couple have a hard time discerning if their dog's death was by wildlife or by a person.

The descriptions of their story leaves room for it to be either, and more investigation should be taken on the matter— especially at the chance of Bullet's death being done by a person still in the park.

This could lead to more intentional deaths, which stands as a major threat to any and all visitors, if a dangerous person is stalking the grounds for potential victims.

I will be bringing this to the attention of Hank immediately, as well as going through our encyclopedias of the local wild life, hopefully to find any history or matches to other similar mutilations caused and/or left behind by large predators.

SIGNED:

Journal Entry #20

Today is October 1st, 2021

I have come to grow comfortable— and in most situations, even pre-fer —to hike alone and explore the terrain of the park by myself.

I remember when I first arrived here and how the idea of hiking/exploring in a group with my coworkers was extremely fun.

Back then, it was the perfect time to talk with them away from work, and honestly, the groups provided a feeling of security in the vast and sometimes dangerous open nature.

But since working here for a decent amount of time now, I feel more situated in the wide freedom given to me by the large park, and have even come to appreciate the silent and independent motions of the ever moving world within Yosemite.

It can feel like a trance sometimes— the way nature feels set in stone with the trees and mountains going nowhere... yet it also feels so _alive_ and ever moving with the rushing waters that constantly trek through the grounds, or the wildlife that's trapped in play of their never-ending harmonious cycles of survival.

I still do like to go out on hikes or go for swims in the lakes with my friends/coworkers, and have even grown closer to and built a better relationship with Joshua and Kas.

But nowadays, I usually like to go out on my own during my breaks/free time, and save my weekends for hanging out with them.

Today, while drifting off into the delicate and serene areas of Region/Division B-12, there were two mountains that neighbored each other and created a little valley of cluttered forestry... and the most bizarre thing happened while there.

As I was walked into that tiny collection of trees that made up the miniature valley between the opposing mountains... all of the sudden... the scenery completely changed!

It wasn't abrupt, necessarily. In fact, I would call it almost seamless for how smooth my surroundings changed from what they used to be.

I was still outside in nature, but the trees were now of different species, the sky was of different weather, the mountains were of different heights, the ground was of a different evenness, and the calling of birds were no longer to be heard!

I stopped in place and looked around me, dumbfounded by how this was not the same place I was once in just a couple of seconds ago!

I 360'd in place just to be sure, but there was no denying it nor fooling myself— in fact, I was a fool for even questioning it at all!

I know I've been experiencing a lot of weird things lately, and I'm already twenty entries into this journal with 90% of it being just those events.

But this was so different from the rest of them, that it managed to catch me completely off guard!

Something so blatant, so obvious, with no hiding nor need of further inquiry... it was far more potent of an event that I didn't even know what to think of it!

How can the whole space around me just change in an instant like that? And was it just the space around me in particular that was now different... or the world too?

My baffled-ness turned into confusion, my confusion turned into doubt, my doubt into realization, realization into awe... and then awe into fear.

I think I stayed in that spot for no more than thirty seconds before I backtracked with haste to the same way I came, and sure enough, my surroundings changed again— back into the park I had always known and was familiar with!

I won't lie, I thought about walking forward again between those two mountains just to confirm this oddity... but decided not to in the end.

It was too intense of an experience, too strange, and the fear beat my awe in this situation.

Of everything that's happened so far in this park, this took the cake for me.

It makes me wonder— are there more areas like this that transition into... a new world, I guess? Like some sort of gateway or portal?

How many exist in this park? Or on the planet for that matter?

How many people who have gone missing in this park accidentally stepped across and into one of these invisible barriers that lead to a different place?

Yosemite National Park
Park Records

Date: November 14th, 2021
Order Number: 2726585949
Type: Report
Region/Division: F-20
Requestor: Visitor [Malcolm Raevyn] [Tabitha Raevyn]
Official Responder: Fetu Leota

Statement:

Malcolm (42) and Tabitha Raevyn (38) —Married— arrived in the park at half past 12:00 on November 13th, 2021 with their two sons, Will (12) and Nathaniel Raevyn (7).

Family claims to have set up camp at a communal spot immediately upon arrival, and then went for a short family hike at 14:00, returning back to campsite at around 16:00.

Afterwards, Malcolm prepped dinner while Tabitha took their kids to a nearby lake for a swim.

Tabitha and the kids returned to the campsite at around 17:00, to which the family remained on the campsite for the rest of the night until they went to bed at around 21:00.

Family awoke in the morning at a quarter past 07:00 on November 14th, 2021 and went for a short walk outside of the hiking trail at the request of their two sons.

At around 09:00, couple claims to have lost sight of their two children who had ran off into thick forestry.

The children did not respond to any calls of their names, nor were the couple able to find their children after looking for next three hours.

At around 12:15, couple called the Park Ranger's Office to report their missing children, to which I, Fetu Leota, arrived on the seen.

After talking with the couple and taking their statement, as well as both the descriptions and the names of their two sons, the three of us began to search for their children in the last known area where they were seen.

Visitor Tabitha Raevyn emphasized that a suspicious looking man (pale skin, late 40's, yellow button-up, navy blue swim trunks) was watching her and her two sons pervertedly the previous day when they went for a swim while her husband prepared dinner.

Backup may be required and a further investigation needed into this man described by Tabitha Raevyn at the lake if the children are unable to be found before sunset.

Report:
UPDATE

At 17:25 on November 14th, 2021— I, Fetu Leota, alongside Aubrey Brant, were able to close the missing persons report when visitors Will and Nathaniel Raevyn safely returned to their parents campsite unharmed.

Myself and Aubrey spoke with the family after and ended the case, however I noticed that the mother, Tabitha Raevyn, looked unsettled while talking to her two children.

While Aubrey wrapped things up with the father, Malcolm Raevyn, I decided to approach and engage the mother and her two children.

I asked her if there was something wrong, to which she denied.

I insisted that she confide within me if there was a problem and/or something bothering her, as it was important for both their future safety as well as the other guests in the park.

Tabitha Raevyn then admitted that something did bother her, but she did not want to tell me it at first since she already felt guilty for having suspected the man at the lake from yesterday, and did not want to place any more accusations on anyone else.

I then encouraged her to tell me what was conflicting her, reassuring her that this was my job and all I would do is investigate the concern, not incriminate.

Tabitha then told her two children, Will (12) and Nathaniel (7), to tell me what they told her, which followed as:

Will— "We were running around, playing outside the trail because there was more trees and it looked fun.

Nate saw them first, then pointed them out to me."

Me— "Saw what?"

Nathaniel— "The little green men! Some of them were brown though!"

Me— "What did these 'little green and brown men' look like?"

Nathaniel— "They looked funny!

I laughed at them at first, but then remembered that it was mean to make fun of someone for their looks."

Will— "Kinda scary, actually.

Like the gnomes you see on people's lawns, but more creepy like halloween masks."

Me— "Were they wearing halloween masks?"

Both boys shook their heads no.

Me— "So they actually looked like this? That was their actual faces and not some sort of mask or disguise?"

Both boys nodded yes.

Me— "Okay. So then what happened?"

Will— "Once Nate pointed them out to me and I noticed them watching us from behind the trees, we started playing with them.

We would run and hide behind some trees and peek around them, and see if the little men saw us or knew where we were.

They would get closer and closer, and be watching us from nearby now, still hiding behind their own trees."

Nathaniel— "Then we would chase them and they would hide from us!

They were hard to find sometimes, though. They could blend in really well with the trees."

Will— "We did this for awhile. It was a fun game. But then we lost them, or at least couldn't find them because they were hiding so well.

We tried for a long time, but then finally gave up.

I guess they knew we did, because once me and Nate decided to stop and head back to our parents, a rock hit my shoulder, and when we turned around, they were standing behind us in full view— no longer hiding."

Me— "How many of them were there?"

Will— "Five. But we were only playing with two of them at first."

Nathaniel— "They were weird and funny!

They didn't talk or say anything to us, and they were dirty and dressed in old clothes.

I was taller than them too!"

Will— "Yeah, they were small. I'd say the tallest one among them was the same height as Nate."

Me— "What happened next?"

Will— "They gestured for us to follow them, so we did.

We didn't realize that us playing with them had already led us so far away from mom and dad, so we didn't think twice about it."

Me— "Where did they take you?"

Will— "I don't know, but it was downhill.

And then we came up on a cave where I think they lived, because they all went inside of it.

Me and Nate slowed down because it looked dark and scary.

One of the little men noticed us stopping, and smiled and waved us in.

But..."

Me— "But?"

Nate— "Will saw it, but I didn't. He only told me about it after we got back to camp and why we ran."

Me— "What did you see, Will?"

Will— "Bones. Outside of the cave's entrance.

They were covered in dirt, like the small men tried to hide them quick before we arrived, but I noticed them.

And they were human bones too, not animals. I know this because I saw a skull.

And that's when I grabbed Nate's hand and ran. I made sure we didn't stop until we reached camp."

Tabitha's face seemed genuinely disturbed, as though she believed her sons... and I do too.

I told her I would go looking for the cave that they spoke of, and to keep her children at her and her husband's side at all times for the rest of the trip.

She told me that she was going to speak to her husband once Aubrey was finished with her end of the report, and that they may be leaving the park tonight.

SIGNED:

Journal Entry #36

Today is December 9th, 2021

Winter has crossed into the park now, and the air has become freezing.

I've never seen snow before, and certainly didn't expect to when I moved to California… but apparently it does in Yosemite!

There's only been light showers of it on few occasions, but my coworkers tell me it'll get pretty heavy during the new year.

I love to go out and explore whenever these delicate white flakes rain down from the sky, and went on a little hike today to the lake to fully take in the scope of its beauty.

When I reached the lake, I began to walk along its edge while admiring the spectacular scene.

About half a mile into my walk, something caught the corner of my eye, so I looked across the lake to it.

There, I saw a woman who looked to be in her early 30's who was absolutely, breathtakingly beautiful— the type of beauty that you see in old paintings, and makes you wonder or have a desire to know more about that person's life, and makes you wish to enter it or become a part of it in some way.

I stopped at the bank of the lake and watched her.

She was wearing this ethereal white gown— long, light, airy and see-through. It waved and flowed with the cold breeze that blew over the lake, which also pushed her rich brown hair about her face like a serpent in the ocean.

The snow flakes melted instantly upon contact with her milk pale skin, and I swear I could see those milk chocolate eyes in full clarity despite being beyond hundreds of yards away when she looked at me.

Her gaze stayed locked onto mine as she treaded into the water, which must have been ice cold.

But she didn't react to it at all. It seemed to be almost a natural thing to her.

She submerged herself in it fully, leaving only the crown of her head to be seen when she dunked her entire body under, then reemerged from it and walked backward so that the water was only at her waist.

I could see the fullest details of her body now— the wet white cloth revealing her breasts and the ridges of her hips.

I was gripped by the seduction of her hair— an even richer shade of brown now soaked —which draped down her neck and onto her clavicle in such a tempting manner.

She just watched me while putting on this display of seduction, and I cannot describe the lust I felt.

It was more alluring than captivating.

It made me want to see more of her and to dip into the lake as well— to see what it was like in there with her.

I wanted to taste her lips and those cold beads of water that stood on its surface.

I wanted to feel her flawless, perfect skin, and the sensation of how smooth it must be.

I wanted to brush the wet matted hair off of her cheeks, and become lost in those chocolate eyes of hers once face to face.

And that's when I noticed it... my boots were completely soaked as I was now standing in the water.

This realization allowed me to feel the freezing cold waters I was once oblivious to.

I stumbled backwards in a rush out of the water, freaked out that I had even treaded that little into the lake without my own awareness of it.

I looked back up at the woman, who was still standing there, watching me, but now slowly twirling around and moving in a sexual way, revealing the dimples of her lower back and the upper rise of where her rear began.

Then I understood— I didn't know who or what this woman was, but she was <u>luring</u> me.

It was all intentional, all on purpose.

She sought to have me enter the water and make my way to here across the lake— something I and no one else would ever be able to survive doing in these temperatures.

I broke my sight on her as I twisted my neck away, and ran all the way back to my board.

I've dried off my feet and put on two layers of fresh wool socks since I've arrived back in my room, and even now as I come to the end of writing this, my feet are still frozen numb.

Yosemite National Park
Park Records

Date: January 29th, 2022
Order Number: 6583028170
Type: Report
Region/Division: A-11
Requestor: Visitor [Austin Bailey] [Keegan Hoffmann]
Official Responder: Fetu Leota

Statement:

Austin Bailey (27) and Keegan Hoffmann (27) —Partners— arrived in the park at 07:00 on January 20th, 2022.

The couple says that they initially set up camp on a community site, but later met up with a group tour guide and were taken on a preplanned hiking trip and sight seeing venture for Yosemite's winter season— per the service of an outside party they hired —not an official affiliate of the park.

Couple says to have paid for this week long program, which interchanged between hikes and tours, then would end with them camping out in the rough for the night wherever they were roaming, or sometimes returning to the communal campsite where they would all gather to sleep for the night.

Couple claims three other parties— separate from their own —were also a part of this program and were also involved in the same activities/camping which occurred.

On January 27th, 2022 the program finished, and the couple returned to the communal campsite where all their belongings were.

Instead of leaving the park at the end of the tour guide service as planned, the couple decided to stay longer and campout at one of the more reclusive spots they were shown while on their guided tour— with the added privacy of the group now being disbanded.

Couple spent the rest of the day collecting food and stocking up for an extra three days, then arrived at the reclusive sight at around 20:00.

Couple claims that after setting up their new campsite, they immediately went to bed, but were awoken at around 13:00 by the sound of a woman's blood curdling scream.

Couple says that though startled and slightly freaked out, they attributed the sound to being a bobcat and attempted to fall back asleep.

Couple claims that the screaming sounded four more times that night.

On January 28th, 2022 the couple awoke in the morning at around 09:00 in the morning and went about their day.

Couple hiked and revisited some of the sights they had previously seen with their group during the paid tour service, but claims to have frequently heard the same scream roughly seven times throughout that day.

Couple says that they theorized a bobcat was responsible for the screams and was possibly stalking them, as the screams always sounded to be a consistent fixed distance.

At around 19:30, the couple returned back to their campsite and prepared for bed.

On January 29th, 2022, the couple awoke at around 08:00 and decide to call it their last day at this spot, since the screaming occurred another three more times that night.

No more screams were heard during today, however, at around 11:00 when the couple were only a mile out into their final hike, they came across a bloody handprint on a tree that appeared to be fresh and still dripping— though no one could be found around them nor was there a trail for its source located.

After the discovery of this bloody handprint, the couple immediately called the Park Ranger's Office and I, Fetu Leota, arrived on the scene.

I was able to observe the bloody handprint on the tree.

Though the majority of it had dried before I arrived on the scene, there were pockets in the tree's bark that kept the moisture apparent as well as an overall sheen to the print that did indeed prove it was left recently, likely within minutes from when the couple discovered it.

⁌ ⁍

Report:

After inspecting the bloody handprint and taking the couple's statements, I immediately informed Hank of the matter who has now taken it even further up with authorities.

Although neither myself nor the couple can confirm if any of the screams were related to the handprint left behind— someone has been and/or is still injured nonetheless, and must be found, helped, and treated.

Coming to a close, I told the couple that if they wished to continue their extended stay, then I would urge them to return to a communal campsite and away from the reclusive one.

They decided to call it an end to their time at the park all together, and left that same day.

⸻

SIGNED: *Pete Leato*

Journal Entry #58

Today is February 3rd, 2022

The strange just keeps on happening, and the unexplainable has only increased.

I cannot distinguish whether I am a magnet for such phenomena—like lightning is attracted to the metal of a rod —or if I am simply at the center of a space in time that the bizarre calls home... making me the odd one out.

Either way, there's no way I can deny the fact that I am drawn to it and captivated by every single thing like this that has occurred.

Is it addicting? Is this a part of its power? Am I falling into its hands or am I becoming different myself?

Why has so much change gone about me, that what once would've frightened my very core now only opens my eyes up even more?

I feel like for the first time in my life, I am actually seeing the fullness of the world.

There's no doubt that this stuff was always going on and always occurring around me, but I just did not have the eyes to see it at that time, nor the mind to comprehend it... nor the soul to absorb it.

Despite my position and living here at the park being a job, I find myself seeking the strange out now rather than just waiting for it to come my way... I wonder if Billy knew that this would happen too...

Today, I decided to go and revisit the invisible portal between the two mountains in Region/Division B-12.

I was curious.

I wanted to know what the environment of that other world would look like in the snow, or how it would feel, or what snow could be like there... so I went.

My stomach twisted with nerves as I came up on its pass, and when I stepped beyond the tree-line of that miniature valley between those two mountains— sure enough —everything changed in the blink of an eye!

There, the sky rumbled and roared like an angry dragon, and snow rained down thick and heavy from the heavens like the ash of an erupted volcano!

The trees were different once again, and even different from how they originally were the last time I'd seen that place.

I wouldn't have been able to walk through such thick blankets of snow that poured down from the sky in that world, if it wasn't for the fact that a path was already made clear ahead of me.

Wide enough for only one person to trek, a thin sheet of snow covered that walkway but did not rise past the ankles, compared to the <u>mounds</u> that surrounded the tiny path which easily reached up to the thighs.

I couldn't help myself and began to tread forward on it.

It was too perfect, too mysterious, and too wonderful not to.

I trekked maybe thirty yards into this world on this narrow path—the furthest I had ever traveled in this hidden realm —before I stumbled upon the end of its path.

By end, I mean it was blocked. Blocked by a door!

I do not know what held this door in place or if I could've walked around the snow to look at it from the other side, nor did I care to try it.

Its existence right there before me was enough.

The door was black and looked to be made from some kind of wood with amber stripes running through its grain, while bearing some kind of black-metal polished doorknob.

So many thoughts and questions filled my mind as I stared at it.

Was it a part of this strange world?

Did it lead to another?

Did someone or something place it here, or was it a force of its own?

Was it sentient?

Was it aware of my presence?

Was it as curious about me as I of it?

Did it want me to open it?

Was it testing me?

Was <u>all</u> this a test?

The snow blew harder in a gust of wind, and I flinched and covered my eyes for a brief moment as it passed.

But when I looked at the door again, it was different!

Now, the door was made of stone— beaten and grey, while riddled with cracks and chips. Seven thick chains were wrapped around it, keeping the door locked and preventing anyone from entering... or perhaps anything from leaving.

I then decided to test a theory which arose in my mind, and closed my eyes for an extended pause before reopening them.

Sure enough, the door was different once more.

This time it was white and pristine, like the kind you would find in a store or expect to see in the suburbs filled with modern houses— all renovated and sharing a common theme.

I expanded my theory further and turned my head far over my shoulder until the door was completely out of my scope of vision— including peripheral.

When I returned my sights to it, the door was now an old chestnut wood with metal bands and hammered studs in its top and bottom frames, bearing a large latch for a handle looking to be made completely out of iron.

Then... I just blinked.

I kept my head and eyes in its direction, and simply blinked— my eyes closed for less than a millisecond.

The door was now sanguine red with a black doorknob, while a single stream of blood fell down its face from out of the keyhole.

I didn't like that one bit, and didn't know the extent of what that meant in regards to something coming out from the other side of it, as certainly there was something there now— at least for <u>this</u> door.

I blinked again to change the door swiftly, in hopes that the next one would be of something dissimilar, and lucky for me, it was.

The last door that appeared in front of me before I made my way back was something straight out of a fantasy novel!

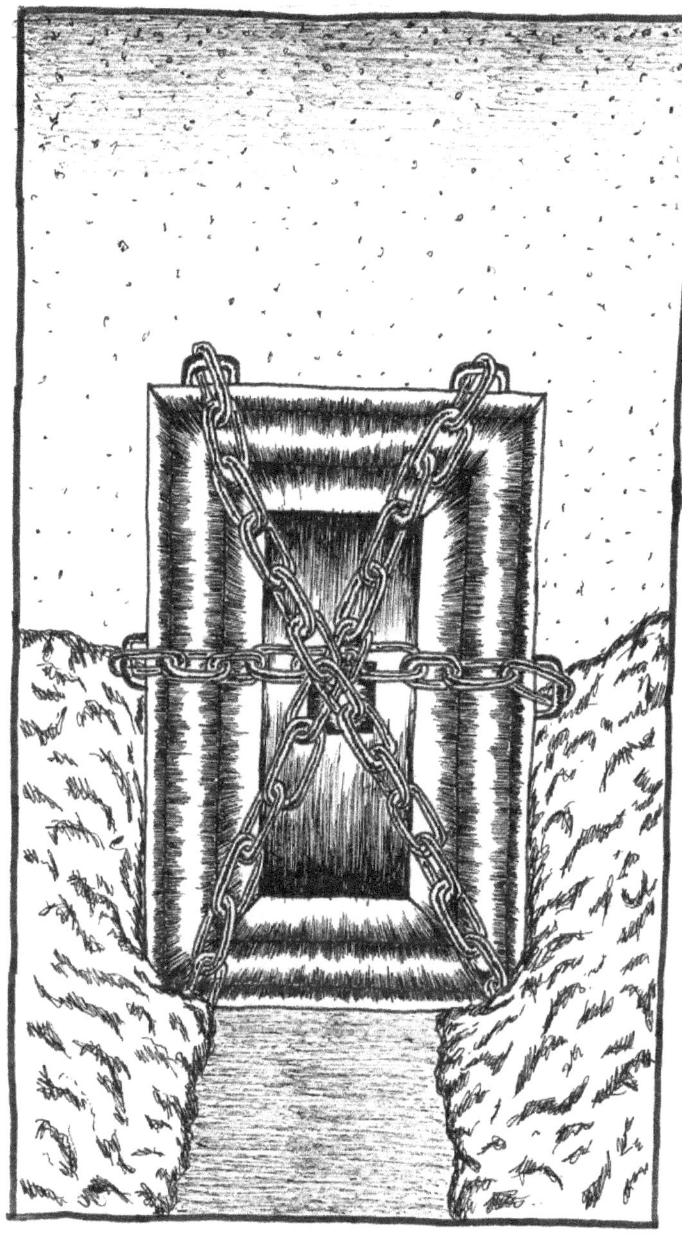

It had vines and flowers and this energy of whimsical joy to it!

But I wasn't going to stay there long enough to accidentally blink again or for another strong gust of wind to force my eyes shut.

I turned around and began to walk back to the invisible passage that would take me back to the normal world— or I guess, technically speaking —my world.

I don't know what made me forget nor what made me remember, but I then realized as I was walking back to the portal... that the door must have changed because I took my eyes off it to head back... the only difference being this time I did not know which or what one it was now since I never looked back.

For all I knew, something from the other side could've already opened it at any moment that had passed...

I bursted into a panicked sprint and didn't stop until I popped back out into our world and was finally able to catch my breath.

I will not lie, I am curious.

I want to go back and open that door, every door!... even the red one.

Maybe one day I will.

Maybe one day... I'm meant to.

Yosemite National Park
Park Records

Date: March 22nd, 2022
Order Number: 9282664930
Type: Report
Region/Division: Y-40
Requestor: Visitor [Olivia Douglas] [Cameron Deacon]
[Bret Irving] [Justin Meyers]
Official Responder: Fetu Leota

Statement:

Olivia Douglas (25), Cameron Deacon (26), Bret Irving (23),
and Justin Meyers (25) arrived in the park at around 15:00
on March 20th, 2022.

Visitors drove up to the higher areas of the park and set up
camp in a remote site that is sparsely used but not isolated
from other visitors.

Visitors claim they did this to be more private, and that there
was only one other party in the area when they arrived.

Visitors made a giant bonfire at around 20:00, and were up
late into the night until 03:00.

Visitors then claim that during the night, they heard faint
hoots and hollers that were too far out to be distinguishable,
but also too burly to be created by a small animal or owl.

Visitors also claim that at around 03:30, before they went to bed for the night, the other party who was also camping near them even approached to ask if they had heard it too, to which they confirmed they did.

Visitors awoke the next morning on March 21st, 2022 at around 08:30, and spent the whole day hiking and sight seeing.

Visitors state they returned to their campsite at around 18:00, and started another bonfire at around 20:00.

Visitors claim that the neighboring party who was also camped in the area was now gone.

At around 21:00, visitors began to hear the hoots and hollers again, only this time it was much louder and much closer.

Visitors claim that the sounds reached a peak in volume and proximity at around 00:00, and then stopped all together immediately after.

At 01:00, visitors started to hear the sound ruffling and of branches breaking all around them while they were still hanging around their bonfire, and were then suddenly barraged by what they described as large, skinny "monkeys" from above them in the trees.

Visitors claim that these "monkeys" harassed them for the next forty minutes with their strange yells and hoots, some even breaking branches and throwing it at them.

Visitors claim that when one of the "monkeys" placed too much weight on a weak branch, causing it to break and the "monkey" to almost fall to the ground, all of the "monkeys" went dead silent and just stared at them ominously.

Visitors state that their eyes glinted from the flickers of the bonfire, as the "monkeys" just stared at them while remaining completely still in the trees.

After an hour of this had passed, visitors claim that the "monkeys" then slowly left their campsite by way of traversing amongst the tree branches.

Visitors claim they were up the rest of the night, terrified by the strangeness of the event, and because of how big and close those "monkeys" were to them.

At around 07:00 on March 22nd, 2022 after morning had broke and the visitors had time to collect their thoughts, they called the Park Ranger's Office to which I, Fetu Leota, arrived on the scene.

I was able to observe the large branch and its place of breakage on the tree it belonged to when I arrived, as the visitors
pointed it out to me during their story.

However, no other proof exists of them having had any contact with these "monkeys".

⇥ ⇤

Report:

Despite my strongest efforts to inform the visitors that there
were no monkeys in the park, they held strong to their claim
that it was indeed, monkeys, who were in those trees above
them and harassed them that night.

However, when I asked the visitors to describe the monkeys
to me, their descriptions began to waver away from monkeys
and more into abnormal humans.

The visitors described the monkeys as being fairly hairless
(stating that the bonfire glared off their bald heads), tall in
height by the 6'-7' region, lanky, with wingspans that reached
far beyond their knees, and saggy skin around the belly- especially beneath the belly button region.

I told the visitors that no monkeys live in the Yosemite
National Park, and that no kind of monkeys exist in general
that fits their description.

Visitors remained adamant on what they saw, and one even gave me a drawing he made while waiting for a park ranger to arrive after they made the call to our office— knowing just how crazy their story was going to sound.

The drawing I received did match the description the visitors gave me, however, I am still unsure on how to move forward with this report— or if an investigation should even be made from the lack of evidence or threat.

SIGNED:

Journal Entry #71

Today is April 4th, 2022

As the snow begins to clear up and melt away from the ridges and crevices of this park, summer is fast approaching.

I have no idea why, but for some reason, I've been thinking about that one report from the family last year whose sons claimed to have interacted with "little men" and were led to a cave that was littered with bones.

It's been on my mind lately for about a week now, and I can't stop thinking about it.

I guess the only reason I can estimate why it's been on my mind is because for the last month now while I'm out in the park... it always feels like I'm being watched.

I can sense eyes following my every move.

I can tell I'm not alone, and I feel awkward and self-conscious knowing that I'm being watched.

After everything that's gone on since my arrival at the park, I don't think it's a human watching me. That doesn't make sense anymore, despite no one else likely to believe that this is the most reasonable explanation.

To me, the idea of a person following me and watching my every move sounds <u>more</u> like a ridiculous and loose knitted conspiracy theory than the "little men".

I know by now that there is much more to this park than meets the eye.

And whatever this is... it has its eyes on me.

I looked back at that report I stapled into this journal, and something stood out to me— one of the sons stated that the "little men" blended in very easily with the surroundings and it made them harder to spot.

I wonder— am I walking by these things without even knowing it?

Are they watching me while standing directly before my own eyes, but I just can't distinguish their presence?

I started thinking about the cave and the hidden bones the boys spoke of, and came to a chilling thought... what if those "little men" are more hungry than usual?

Every other animal struggles to obtain food during the winter, and most stock up on it or hibernate during the cold season to make it through alive.

So what if those "little men" haven't eaten anything in a very long time?

I already know they were robbed of a meal when the oldest boy caught onto their scheme (thank god).

But what if now that the snow is melting and the air is becoming warm again, the "little men" are coming out of that cave on a hunt for food? And that's why I've had the sensation of being watched recently...?

I'm too big and far older than those little boys were to be easily lured into their cave.

I can fight back, I can run away faster, and I can scream louder.

I wonder if that's why they've been watching me for so long.

Maybe they're thinking about how they can lure me into their cave or trick me into being their next meal.

Maybe they're waiting for me to hurt myself on a hike and twist my ankle or break my leg.

Maybe they're waiting for me to get lost one day and seek shelter in that very cave they call home.

Either way, these peering eyes have burned holes into the back of my skull for long enough, and this theory of mine that suspected it's 'cause of the "little men" was plausible enough for me to want to take a stand.

I've experienced, witnessed, been exposed to, been in the middle of, and been a part of far too many strange incidents and phenomenas in this park to just tuck tail and run away from any of its freakish occurrences.

I don't know who or what is out there or is watching me during this whole charade of paranormal events that have gone down, but they should know by now— I am no longer some "small fry" in this shit, nor am I ignorant or oblivious to its truths.

My gut told me to reach out to Billy, and so I did.

I told him about everything, let him read my journal with an emphasis on the report I copied and stapled into it of the boys' documented story, and was honest about everything and anything I've experienced here so far— as well as what I believe in now in regards to this world, this park, and this crazy fucking universe.

I honestly don't know how I expected Billy to react. I guess I thought he would ask a couple of questions, or at the very least want a verbal confirmation from me that I was sure about everything I've seen, felt, heard, and experienced.

But instead… he was so indifferent about the whole thing!

It was like it was all normal for him! Like nothing he read nor anything I told him about was outlandish or crazy.

It felt like I was telling him about how I had a coffee and bagel for breakfast by the way he just looked at me with such a casual demeanor.

I guess he noticed my anticipation for a bigger reaction, because then he said, "This stuff is <u>real</u>. You either know about it or you don't.

These things <u>exist</u>. They either cross your path or they don't.

There's more to our world than any government, scientist, or common human would care to let on. You either accept it or you don't."

I nodded in agreement, but also in a "thank you" of sorts.

This whole time I never realized that I wasn't alone in this.

But Billy was in it, and very aware of all this too.

It's on me for having not come to him sooner or divulged these experiences to him earlier.

As I recall, he actually gave me a "tell" in regards to all this awhile back, when we were driving and he revealed those childhood stories to me, made that unicorn reference, and the word of warning he gave me when he dropped me off.

I couldn't see it then, but that was a "tell" that he was <u>also</u> in all of this! Or it was at least a gentle nod to the fact that he understood these things as well.

But then again, I wasn't as deep in it myself back then as I am now.

I can see it now, but it flew over my head back then.

Billy and I both grabbed our rifles and a bottle of bear spray each, then headed into Region/Division F-20 where the incident with the two boys took place.

We began to search for the cave they spoke of using the little information they gave about its location in the report, combined with our own knowledge of the layout of this park.

After about four hours of searching, Billy almost slipped down a sharp slant when his boot rolled over the top of a round rock covered in snow.

He caught himself immediately— his balance only being lost for a split second —but it still gave us both a good spook as we had been silent for the entire time of the search.

I asked him if he was alright, and he said, "Yeah" then kicked the round rock covered in snow to point it out, "Just slipped on this fucker..."

But when Billy kicked it— it moved. Moved far too easily for any rock covered in snow to.

It should've just thumped, or at the most, barely slide an inch over.

But instead, it rolled almost a full 180.

We looked at each other by the surprise of this, then back down at the "rock".

Billy began to roll the "rock" with his boot, smearing the snow off its surface with his sole.

Then it was revealed to us— it was not a rock, but a <u>skull</u>.

... A human skull.

At that moment, Billy and I both knew without saying a single word verbally to each other, that we were at the downhill slope area of the boys' report.

We took tighter grips on our rifles, fingers now on the triggers, and headed down the slope with extreme caution and resolve.

Once we reached leveled ground again, we immediately took notice of the collapsed snow which gave away the opening to the mouth of a cave.

We approached the cave, shoulder to shoulder, with our rifles aimed at its entrance.

There were mounds all around the entrance to that cave, which lifted the snow in abnormal lumps— similar to the way the skull Billy slipped on looked like a rock under those icy blankets.

As we treaded closer to the cave's entrance, keeping our guard up the entire time, we were hit with an overwhelming scent of musk and decay— the retched smell causing me to almost break my aim in an instinct to gag.

My eyes began to water from the sharp scent, and in the midst of me wiping them, Billy spoke to me in a low voice.

"Fetu" he said, "You see that?"

I stopped wiping my eyes with one last drag of my hand across them, then quickly brought my sights back up, pointing the end of my rifle at whatever Billy was referring to.

I saw it instantly.

From within the cave, at the mouth of its dark hollow entrance like a portal to hell, were a dozen of tiny beady eyes, all glowing red and watching us— full of hate, full of hunger, and full of malice.

It felt like they knew why we were there, and knew we were a threat to them... and they hated us for that.

Hated us for knowing.

Hated us for fighting.

Hated us for <u>being</u>.

Hated us for not lying in their stomachs as minced meat already.

"Yeah. I see them" I said to Billy in response, "Do we shoot?" I asked.

"I don't think we have much of a choice" answered Billy, "There's too many bones under the snow, this will only become a bigger problem if we don't."

"I think you're right. On three, then?" I proposed.

Billy gave an assuring and calm "Mhm" in response, as to not alarm the creatures of what we were about to do.

They then started making weird sounds— grunts, growls, and whatever funny language they spoke to each other in with short bursts of words.

"One..." I started, "Two... <u>Three</u>..."

Me and Billy pulled our triggers and lit up the cave like a controlled forest fire!

From the flashes of our muzzles, brief glimpses of the creatures inside the cave were revealed to us, as the light from our bullets firing mimicked the blitz of a camera's flash.

... Even in the short instances we could see them, I can confirm, those things looked exactly how the boys described them in their report.

My nerves are getting to me as I write this.

That was the first time I ever shot a gun and killed something.

Not to say I regret it or what me and Billy did— because I don't.

In fact, I couldn't feel more proud and empowered by our actions.

Like I said, I'm no longer some vulnerable "small fry" in this world anymore, and neither is Billy.

I just need to get used to this feeling of taking action like we did, but I'm sure with time I will.

Hell, maybe I need some rest, too.

... But I rest assured that in a similar manner to how I am now indifferent to all the craziness that goes on around me— this too shall become common.

Yosemite National Park
Park Records

Date: May 10th, 2022
Order Number: 7382746505
Type: Complaint
Region/Division: W-3
Requestor: Multiple Visitors
Official Responder: Fetu Leota

Statement:

On May 10th, 2022 at around 14:00, the Park Ranger's Office received multiple complaints from numerous visitors about an unstable character who was harassing them on the communal campsites and other public visiting grounds.

Myself, Fetu Leota, and Billy Goldman arrived on the seen at around 14:25, and managed to take some statements from the visitors who called in the complaints, before we were able to find the suspect at hand.

Suspect of complaints was a white male, 5'10", orange hair, green eyes, with a large scar that starts below his left eye and spiderwebs across his cheek, towards his left ear.

Suspect of complaints did not give us his name.

Suspect of complaints did not appear to be intoxicated or under any influence.

Suspect of complaints appeared to be homeless and living on the park grounds.

Suspect of complaints appeared to be mentally ill and possibly experiencing a psychotic episode and/or suffering from schizophrenia.

Suspect of complaints did not appear to be a danger to himself or to other visitors, however, his unstable mannerisms and sporadic behavior was apparent, requiring the assistance from local authorities to be brought in for his removal from the park.

Report:

After our confrontation and initial interactions with the suspect of complaints, Billy and myself made the decision to call the local authorities and have him removed from the park.

During our wait for the authorities to arrive, Billy and myself continued to engage with the suspect of complaints— allowing him to rant and divulge his theories to us in order to keep him engaged solely with us.

This was to prevent him from either running away and/or having any more outbursts before the authorities could arrive.

Below are some excerpts from the suspect of complaint's rants that I remember from the time when we were waiting for the local authorities to arrive:

—Suspect of complaints—

"There are tunnels underneath the park!

Countless tunnels! Endless tunnels! Dangerous Tunnels!

And they are filled with creatures and beings and things that mankind is clueless about— and for most of the population —is powerless towards!

You must beware of these tunnels! You must BEWARE of the tunnels!"

"Aliens! They're real man!

And there's a shit load of them! I mean, like a fuck ton!

So many different species and races, and even different kinds amongst their own, too!

Now Reptilians, those are the bad guys!

They're some real mean motherfuckers!

A lot of them live within the planet, and there are some in the very tunnels beneath us now!

You gotta be careful with them! They're dangerous! Strong motherfuckers! Big too! Powerful minds with their telepathy!

They eat humans and will definitely eat you too if they get their hands on you! Might even make you their new slave!

And they have sex with their female slaves! I don't even think it's for the sake of pleasure.

They're sick, twisted bastards who feed off negative energy! They rape our women for the fear and pain it creates, then just eat that energy up!"

"There are giant insects in those tunnels! Huge! Like the kind you see on television when they talk about the ones from pre-historic times with the dinosaurs and shit!

The only thing they don't mention on TV is how intelligent they are! I mean, like super fucking smart! Highly intelligent!

They hunt humans and other creatures in those tunnels the same way a human would hunt a deer!

Centipedes, spiders, ants— you name it!

All big geniuses, and to them... we're the insects!"

"Magick? It's real!

Mages, wizards, warlocks, witches— whatever the fuck you wanna call them, they're real alright!

And some of them are fucking evil, dude! I'm telling you!

The ones in those tunnels? EVIL! Stay away from them!

They love the power— they're mad with it!

Despite everything else down there also trying to kill you and the fact that human beings are scarce, they don't care! They'll kill you too! You're not a fellow human or kin to those guys— you're lesser than!

To them, you're an ignorant motherfucker who's blind to the world around you, and they **do not** sympathize with your obliviousness!

They'll kill you! Kill you with magick!

And trust me, there's all sorts of ways they can do this!

Stay away from the fucking evil wizards in the tunnels!"

"There are portals! Countless portals that connect our worlds to others!

Some lead to other dimensions, some even connect this world to hell!

A lot of the creatures I talk about come into our world from those portals, a lot of the aliens too!

I think the wizards like to use them to traverse to these other worlds— fuck if I know why!

Energy, knowledge, truth— there are many reasons.

Maybe the portals connect to our world, or maybe our world only connects to them— different portal, different way of function."

"There are sentient parts of the tunnels, where the tunnel system itself is alive!

It structures itself like a maze, ever changing and damn near inescapable!

It does this on purpose, though!

You see... it feeds on the minds of the victims who are trapped within!

You'll slowly grow mad as you remain lost, traversing its ever-changing loops!

I don't think it's evil, though.

It's more like a venus fly trap. Like, it isn't doing this to be evil or for the sake of evilness, it is just a living thing that needs to feed and this is how it does it.

Don't worry though, these parts of the cave are super deep within, so you're already screwed if you ever do even reach such a section.

You don't have to worry about randomly stumbling into the sentient tunnels at a cave's entrance and immediately being screwed."

"There are some really weird parts in those tunnels, man!

I don't even know what it is, what it means, why it's there, or what the fuck it has to do with who knows what!

One time, I stumbled upon these men— if they were actually even human —who were clad in armor and bore swords, guarding an arch on the tunnel wall filled with bones like the catacombs!

I mean, what the fuck even is that?!

I have no fucking clue!

But I just booked it when I saw those men, 'cause I knew that it wasn't any good news, that's for sure!"

"Time portals! Don't forget about the time portals!

They're similar to the portals that take you to other worlds or dimensions, only they are solely connected to different time-lines in this one— our world!

They can take you to anywhere in time, and I mean ANYWHERE!

I don't know if there's a way to control it, or if it's random, or if some are fixed.

Hell, maybe the wizards or aliens or other creatures know, but I sure fucking don't!

When I was trapped in those tunnels for a long time— and I mean a LONG time —I encountered one of those time portals.

I swear I had forgotten what sunlight looked like, or just any-thing in general that didn't try to fucking kill me or drive me crazy... but at last, I must've crossed through one of the time portals because it spit me out at the mouth of a cave!

I was out! I was finally out!

In front of me lied salvation— freedom from this nightmare I had been trapped in for as long as I could remember!

As I took those glorious steps towards the mouth of the cave to leave its hellhole, feeling the breeze and fresh air of the surface world once again, and hearing the sounds of scratching leaves from the trees and the tweeting of birds... I heard a very faint sound that I was unfamiliar with.

And when I stepped out into the full rays of sunlight, and my eyes adjusted to the light so that I could now see what was on the other side— I knew then exactly what that sound was.

Bows being drawn...

Four Natives had their bows drawn at me.

I mean like, America never happened and they still ruled these lands, Native.

I put my hands in the air and cried— happy tears!

I was so fucking happy to see some fellow humans once again! Normal humans, not those fucking wizards or those mysterious motherfuckers!

But that joy ended quickly, because even though we didn't speak the same language, I understood exactly what was going on when one of them shot an arrow beside my foot, while another gestured me to go back in.

... You see, the Natives, they are smart.

Far wiser than any of us now.

They knew about the tunnels and were aware of its many dangers.

They enforced two things— that none of their own ever went in... and that nothing from within ever came out.

I understood this immediately, and I went back inside.

But... I just wish, I really fucking wish... I wish I could've told them that it was okay. That I understood.

I wish I could tell them how that small encounter, though short and bittersweet, was enough to keep me going and to hold on until I finally found my way out once again— for good this time!"

"I'll admit it, I'm very well aware of how crazy all this sounds, and I don't expect many

people— fuck, anyone for that matter —to believe me.

But I will say this... you two don't look at me like the others do.

You kinda remind me of those Natives, actually— like you're already aware of all of this and get what I'm saying...

... You guys are fucking weird!"

SIGNED: *Pete Leato*

Journal Entry #98

Today is June 21st, 2022

How come <u>the others</u> feel like a rarity?

And my own awareness of this all, a blessing?

Why are those who are similar, so far and few between?

And why is such an effort required, and such a big risk needed to be taken, to reveal to another that you have a foot in this pond— or to have them reveal that they do as well?

I don't even include people like Tori.

Yes, she is interested in it.

Yes, she may even be great at handling or exploring these kinds of phenomena further... but she's not <u>in</u> it.

Billy described it best, I guess.

He gets it.

So far, all I've counted for is Billy, myself, and the crazy guy from last month.

And despite that guy technically not being crazy at all since most of the stuff he said was true... he still <u>is</u> crazy, because he's lost his mind to it.

There's this sick theme of people falling into the unbalanced scale of degrees when it comes to this world.

On one end, you have the people who like this stuff... but for all the wrong reasons. And because they stand before it with these wrong reasons, they never fully get to experience it.

And on the other end, you have people that are immersed in it, swallowed up by it— in it so deep and know so much... but fuck man, are they crazy! As if they aren't the type that were really meant to/made to be in it, or at least certainly not this deep in it.

Then there's that tiny minority— a sliver ever so slight —of those who are in it and are still sound of mind. Who are still themselves.

They understand, they accept, they seek, they grow, they build, they learn, and they continue.

Billy is like that, and I believe Billy would say the same for me.

Never once in my journeys throughout nature have I ever felt so alone. Not even during my years in college when I didn't have any friends for the first half of it!

But since I've been exposed to this world, I don't think I've ever felt more alone.

Discovering that Billy was one of <u>the others</u> brought on such a strong feeling of joy and relief, and I know that we aren't the only ones. But how the fuck does one find more of <u>the others</u> without only stumbling upon the Tori's and the crazy guys?

I am almost <u>tormented</u> at this thought. And I don't know why other people shouldn't have these truths revealed to them as well.

I don't know. Maybe I can change that...

Find someway, somehow, to slowly expose this window of infinity to all those other people to freely partake in it.

It's everyone's right to, isn't it?

But I guess that doesn't necessarily mean that everyone's _meant_ to.

One thing that I have found certainty in, though— something that is _not_ common in this crazy and endless world of everything... is _myself_.

I can invest in myself. Strengthen myself in knowledge and wisdom and experience. Continue to explore and expose myself to these things. Continue to grow and find my own power and then grow that power even further.

If I cannot guarantee _the others_, cannot guarantee the world, cannot guarantee the unknown... well then, I'll guarantee _myself_. Because that is the one thing I _do_ know and do have _full_ control of in the purest way— which no other being or person ever will!

To them, _I_ am the unknown, for only _I_ truly know myself, and only _I_ can guarantee myself.

With that in mind, I went back to Region/Division B-12 today.

I walked through the gates of change willingly, because I will face these things and explore them to grow myself.

I stepped into the invisible portal in the valley between the two mountains, and came up on the other side.

This time, it was a black forest with a night sky, and there were flickering lights in the distance by torches which caught my eye.

They were close, and I made sure to keep the portal at my back so I would not get lost... and then I followed them.

They were people, or at least they looked like humans— though I could not distinguish if they were of my world and entered through the same portal I did or another, or if they were of <u>this</u> world and knew not of the entrance I took.

I kept to the shadows of the bushes and the hiding behind trees, and observed them as they chanted their foreign hymns while walking in unison.

They were donned in robes, some with symbols on them and others with extra cloths draped over their shoulders or tied to their waists— a clear indication of rank and status amongst their organization.

Eventually they stopped their march and then crafted a fire that they then circled around for hours before beginning to sing songs and undergo a ceremony of some sort.

I watched them from a distance, but close enough so that I could collect their knowledge and hear the pronunciations of the consonants and vowels in their ritualistic words.

I took in everything I saw, and absorbed everything they did.

I am no longer the small fry in this world.

I am the watcher, I am the observer, I am that which sends the chill of prying eyes down the spine of another life, and that which applies the pressure of my unseen presence upon the things that creep and crawl, and onto those who undergo ceremonies at night.

This night, I <u>grew</u>.

Journal Entry #112

Today is July 15th, 2022

… I've made a grave mistake that I cannot take back.

I now know the authenticity to my early theories that some people are just not meant to be in this world of infinity… but I guess this was a lesson to that, one which I had to learn the hard way.

Yesterday, I informed Tori of it all— everything I had experienced and my journey and accumulation of knowledge from these crazy phenomenas.

She listened, wide eyed like a child— captivated by awe and wonder.

And I enjoyed seeing that spirit light up in her, and even more so at the prospect of her making it her own, now that she knew the truth.

She seemed most fascinated by my stories and my knowledge around the invisible portal that lies within Region/Division B-12.

I guess it's because it was the only consistent thing amongst my numerous events of odd happenings from both my own personal experiences as well as the reports from visitors I've taken.

It was something that she too could experience whenever she so desired.

I was hit with a twisting knot in my gut by this, like I had said too much, revealed something I shouldn't have, like I had made a mistake… but I ignored it.

The only thing I did do in response to this gut feeling was insist that she not go there— at least not yet —and to hold off until she was ready, or to even go with me rather than by herself.

She agreed... but I guess she only did so to silence my bickering.

I don't know, maybe I was not convincing enough.

Maybe I was wrong for speaking about these things aloud to some-one who was not even a true novice within it.

Maybe this was indeed a lesson I was forced to learn or bound to learn... for it happened nonetheless...

Tori chose to not heed my warnings, probably because she was too eager— or maybe too excited— and visited Region/Division B-12 behind my back without my knowledge nor with me at her side.

Of course, at the time, I did not know about this. Nor did anyone else when we couldn't find Tori for the entire day.

Me and Billy thought the worst could've happened, being the only two who know the truth about the park and the vast/strange world we live in.

But none of that mattered, because two hours ago, Tori showed up back on the Ranger's grounds out of nowhere.

She was different, scared shitless out of her mind, and staring off into the distance or at the ground at all times.

She didn't say what happened nor what she saw, and wouldn't even confide her experience with me when I found a moment to pull her aside and talk to her by ourselves.

Whatever she saw, it scared the daylights out of her, and changed her from the inside out.

... She resigned from her position as a Park Ranger in Yosemite, and will be heading back to her home tomorrow.

I don't have it in me to tell Billy that it was because of me that this happened to her. That she only knew about Region/Division B-12 because of me, or that I didn't even consult him on the idea of revealing these things to Tori with him beforehand.

It already hurts too much seeing the damage that has been done to her, and I don't want to feel any worse like I know I would by telling Billy the truth of it.

Not to mention, he's my only <u>true</u> friend at this park, and the only <u>other</u> I know of.

I can't lose that.

I don't want to lose that.

It's probably the most selfish thing I've ever said, but it's true.

I will be utterly alone in this world if he shuns me. And God knows that after this, I don't know how I will ever find the courage to tell another soul about these truths, or if I'll ever be able to reveal, let alone hint, at this world.

But my own time at this park is also coming to an end.

It's been a full year since I left my home in Samoa and came to California to work at Yosemite.

Damn, it's been one hell of a thing!

Without a doubt, this was the biggest journey I've ever experienced. Undeniably the most shaping thing I've ever endured.

I don't think I'll stay here for next season.

I wanna do more. I wanna keep growing.

I've been looking into things that are similar to this but could prove even more immersive into the unknown... and I think I've found what I've been looking for.

The occupation of a fire watcher is far more isolated and away from society. It'll provide a space where I can continue my journey in a more intense way.

That is what I want.

And I'll start a new log for it, too— one that is arranged even better for all the madness I will be thrown into by such a setting.

But for this one... this is where it comes to a close.

A full year's log, the beautiful planting and blossoming of the seeds that transformed me.

Oh how I am eager to see the petals that will emerge with time.

Mom?

THE RAIN WAS purple with various shades of pink. It fell upward, into the sky from out of the ground, in a complete reverse of nature.

Piper was standing alongside strangers as they were all gathered around a closed casket being lowered into the ground, each person carrying inverted umbrellas and yellow roses in hand.

It was nighttime, but there was still enough light glowing from the sky that lit up the world like an overcast day.

There was no moon overhead, but instead, a giant window from which the strong winds of showering storms blew in through.

The other people who stood around the casket attempted to speak words of homage for the passing of this unknown loved one, but only dirt left their mouths— falling out in dry crumbles... yet they didn't seem to notice this.

Piper looked up at the sky and saw galaxies instead of stars, and from within their clusters, lightning danced around— even striking the very earth she stood on despite being so far away.

With each strike of lightning that reached the grounds beside her, the air grew colder, and ice began to spread among the layout of this grieving terrain.

When Piper tried to speak herself, no dirt came from her mouth. However, it was still a struggle as the cold would snatch her tongue and almost freeze it solid.

Copious amounts of fog fumed out of her mouth from the heat of her breath merging with the dropping temperatures of the exterior air.

Piper began to choke on this thickening smoke, as if she had a piece of dry ice in her mouth.

A voice called out from inside the closed casket, *"I'm in here!"* it said, *"I'm in here!"*

The voice sounded familiar like something, or rather, *someone* Piper knew was attached to it.

Someone Piper felt love for.

That is when Piper furiously awoke— shaken out of her sleep by her hard convulsions from the intense coughing and choking conjured by this nightmare.

Once Piper regained her composure and cleared her mind, processing the fact that she had been dreaming that chaotic mess and was now wide awake in her own bedroom, she sat up in a new discomfort that wasn't caused by the nightmare or by the abrupt coughing.

What disturbed Piper now, in a way which eliminated all previous discomforts, was that her bedroom setting was completely dark— pitch-black.

Piper never was one for the dark.

Not since she was a kid, not since she was in high school, and not even now since she graduated.

Part of it was because of her own preference. The other part was because she was raised by a single mother who never liked the house to be completely dark, either.

And so, there were always lights on in their house while they slept. Be it in the kitchen, in the living room, in the hallway, in the bathroom— it varied depending on who was in the room last and which ones they crossed through to head to bed for the night.

Sometimes it could be too bright for Piper, and so she took to keeping her door closed at night while having a nightlight plugged into the wall.

It provided the perfect amount of light, the perfect amount of comfort, the perfect amount of security, and the perfect amount of privacy with her door closed.

However… her nightlight was off now.

Her room was completely dark, which is not how she left it before she went to bed.

There wasn't even a glimmer of illumination from under her doors crevice, which would usually peek through from a light being on somewhere else within the house.

At this moment, it was absolute darkness.

Piper reached over to her nightstand and felt around for her phone.

As soon as she found hold of it, she clicked its screen to see what time it was.

3:45am.

Her mother had definitely gone to bed by now, as the latest she would ever stay up till was 1:00am and never past it because of work in the morning.

So for there to not be any light breaching through the gaps on the other side of Piper's door… was an odd thing.

And her nightlight not being on when it was something that was always on— even during the day —was even stranger.

Piper was a smart girl, however, and so her mind immediately drifted to the more obvious explanations for such a bizarre scenario.

"Perhaps there was a blackout or a power surge" she thought, which would explain why her nightlight and any other light in the house was off.

Piper then turned on the flashlight setting of her phone, and got out of bed.

She walked over to her nightlight and took a deep breath of discomfort.

… It was unplugged, just lying on the floor below the socket.

This didn't make any sense.

This meant that someone must've unplugged it, and Piper could find no reason as to why her mother would do such a thing, as only her mother could've done it since they were the only two who lived in that house.

To confirm her idea that there still must've been a power outage of some sort, Piper approached the wall beside her door and flipped on the light switch.

The overhead lights swiftly lit up in response, along with the slow beginning spins of the fan, which blossomed out of the lightbulbs like flower petals.

"So the power does work fine?" questioned Piper to herself.

This made the situation even more confusing, as it all fell back onto her mother now.

"Mom?" called out Piper.

She opened her bedroom door and peeked out into the hallway.

It was pitch-black like the rest of the house.

Not a single light was on.

Piper began to feel uneasy by this dilemma, but the worry and care she felt for her mother trumped any concern she had for herself.

What if her mother had gotten hurt while she was asleep? Fell, slipped, hit her head?

It still wouldn't explain why Piper's nightlight was unplugged, but that didn't matter— only knowing that her mother was safe and unharmed did at this time.

Keeping her phone's flashlight on, Piper swept it down both ends of the hallway from the safety of her room, "Mom?" she called out again.

"I'm in here!" responded her mother's voice in a calm manner.

This gave Piper some level of relief, although the darkness of the house still left her unsettled and factored into her keeping her guard up.

With the safety of her phone's flashlight acting as both a shield and spear against these dense surrounding shadows, Piper stepped into the hallway and made for its switch on the wall, turning it on.

As the hallway illuminated, Piper now felt a bit better about the situation and called out for her mother, "Mom?"

"I'm in here!" she answered back, in the same calm tone as before.

It was hard to distinguish where her mother's response came from, so Piper decided to do the obvious and check her mother's bedroom first.

She walked down the hallway and stopped at the closed door to her mother's room.

She gently knocked on its surface, "Mom?"

"I'm in here!"

It was weird that her mother's door was closed, as Piper's mother would always leave it open, or at least cracked, to allow the light from the other rooms of the house to fill hers.

Piper twisted the doorknob and then slowly pushed open the door.

Her mother's room was completely black inside, so she flipped on its light switch.

However, once visible by the light, no one was revealed to be inside the bedroom...

Her mother's bed did appear ruffled up though, as if she had gotten into bed at some point and then gotten out— likely after hours of tossing and turning by the looks of it and its disheveled state of bedsheets and pillows.

"Mom?"

"I'm in here!"

Piper returned to the hallway confused but still determined to find her mother, and headed down the hall.

She stopped at the bathroom's door which was also closed, and opened it.

Used to this theme already, Piper turned on the lights and stepped in.

No one was in the bathroom.

She approached the closed shower curtains and placed her ear up against it, then very slowly and very hesitantly, pulled back the drapes— still empty.

Piper then continued down the hallway and entered the living room.

This was the most unnerving of it all, as the living room was so big and spacious that not being able to see a single thing within it felt like she was staring into an abyss.

She turned on its lights and without any surprise, nothing out of the ordinary was visible… except for what looked like dirt.

Only a little though, barely anything of it— it was more like crumbs.

Piper probably wouldn't have even noticed the dirt if it wasn't for the fact that she was barefoot from having been previously asleep in her bed, and the sensation of tiny gravel pieces were obvious to the soles of her feet— since to the naked eye, its presence wouldn't have been observable unless you were actually looking for it.

Disregarding the dirt, Piper then headed into the kitchen, turning on its lights and being met with the same sight of nothing misplaced or anyone there.

"Mom?" she called out.

"I'm in here!" answered her mother.

Piper stepped back into the living room and looked around, but nothing had changed.

Her eyes then fell onto the door that led to the basement, and for the first time since she awoke from that horrid nightmare of hers, Piper felt fear by this strange situation.

Trying not to let the freakish nature of all this get to her though, Piper approached the basement door with her chest out and fists clenched.

She took a deep breath in through her nostrils, and then let it out through her mouth, slow and controlled as if blowing a dandelion.

After which, Piper turned the handle and swung the door open aggressively!

Menacingly before her was a dark decent of stairs that led into a collection of corrupting shadows— an ungiving exposure —to that which lied at the bottom of its decline.

Piper had always hated the basement, but then again, so does everyone for the most part.

"Mom?" Piper called out into the darkness, which surprisingly shook the confidence she once had moments ago.

"I'm in here!" called back her mother.

Extending her phone far beyond her own body, Piper used its guiding light to maneuver herself down the stairs safely and into the empty space of shadows.

One of the worst parts about the basement was that the designers of the house had idiotically placed its light switch at the center of the room, hanging by a dangling string of metal beads you had to pull.

Cautiously, Piper took purposeful steps in the direction towards where she knew that light switch was.

She was terrified at this point, and every now and again she would hear a strange sound from somewhere in the basement with her— the sound being almost rhythmic, but more random than anything.

Piper would stop in place whenever she heard it, freezing all her movements, and sometimes even holding her breath.

Once she was only mere feet away from the light switch, Piper realized that turning its bulb on would be her salvation from this dreadful situation, and that it was more dangerous to keep delaying it any longer by being so hesitant and cautious with her movements.

So, the moment the metal beads reflected a shimmer of light off the flash of her phone, Piper leapt towards it, closing the remaining distance in that jump and nearly pulling the switch out of the ceiling while illuminating the entire room!

In both an anticlimactic way and a relieving one, nothing was inside the basement that shouldn't have been there.

No person or monster was standing in front of her or behind her when the lights came on, and everything was as it should be since the basement hadn't changed in a single way over Piper's entire life of living in that house.

But then she heard it again— that weird sound she couldn't place before while in the dark, only now there was light to see it.

Piper swiftly turned around to confront the noise, and discovered exactly what the sound was as well as its source.

From the tiny window that faced the streets and was attached to the bottom of the house— connecting the basement to the outside —was a faint stream of dripping water that would build up into a heavy tear drop, then fall into a tiny pool of water that collected on the cement floor beneath it.

It seemed that the window was just barely cracked open, and that a previous storm must've just passed, leaving over a residue of water which now trickled its way inside the basement from the slight opening of the window.

Piper questioned this with extreme seriousness, as the basement window was always locked and never open.

Then again, the space of that window was so tiny and awkward, especially by the way it opened inverted— that it didn't seem too realistic to Piper that a person could slip through its open space and into the house.

What seemed more reasonable to her, however, was that a storm had just finished brewing during her sleep— probably a nasty one with strong winds and harsh rain.

Perhaps the wind was so powerful that it blew the window open.

Perhaps it *did* cause a power outage after, but by the time Piper awoke and started turning on all the switches, the electricity had already returned.

At least that's what Piper told herself and wanted to believe, because anything else was far too frightening of a thought…

"Mom?" she called out.

"I'm in here!" responded her mother.

This time the direction sounded more clear, and Piper was sure that it came from back upstairs.

Piper turned off her phone's flashlight as all the lights in the house were on now from her previous scouting, and then headed back up into the living room.

"Mom?"

"I'm in here!"

Piper left the living room and headed back down the hallway, stopping directly in its center.

"Mom?"

"I'm in here!"

Piper continued on and entered her mother's bedroom once again, certain that the source of her responses were coming from this room.

"Mom?"

"I'm in here!"

Piper walked further into her mother's room, and made her way past the bed until she was facing the closed doors of her mother's closet.

"Mom?"

"I'm in here!" said her mother from behind its doors.

Piper grabbed hold of the closet's handles and swung them open!

She tumbled back immediately from the sight in front of her, tripping over her own feet and collapsing onto her rear as her back slammed against the bedpost!

Lying before Piper in that closet was her mother's dead body, twisted and mangled savagely to fit into— or rather —to be *stuffed* into the tiny space within.

She was dead, murdered more so, with dark purple bruises wrapping around her neck, and pinkish-red eyes from the bursting of their blood vessels as whoever took her life, undoubtedly, choked it out of her.

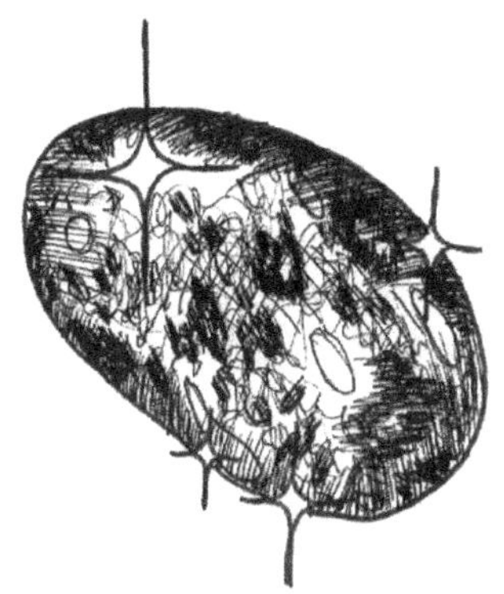

Retiree

THE SMELL OF fresh ground coffee filled the entire kitchen of the old wooden house, as Max had just finished brewing a fresh pot for his mentor.

Like clockwork, the toaster dinged as two pieces of semi-burnt bread jumped up to the top, ready to eat at the exact same time the coffee was ready to be served.

In a smooth orchestration from having done this routine everyday now for the last two years, Max was able to swiftly grab a cup of black coffee as well as a plate containing the toast— now covered in grape jelly —and brought it over to the small dining room which housed an even smaller table.

Max placed the piping hot cup of coffee and warm toast in front of his mentor, who was in the middle of reading a book but still said *"Thank you"* as he always did.

Max then headed back into the kitchen and grabbed a cold canned coffee from out of the fridge as his own breakfast— he liked coffee just as much as his mentor did, but Max always preferred the cold canned kind of a specific brand he favored, as opposed to the hot brewed type.

As a teenager, Max and his friends would always go to their local corner store and buy such snacks and beverages that had been shipped over from Korea whenever they hung out or even before their classes.

It wasn't so much a sentimental thing for them, though it could've been for their parents whenever they brought home these items from the store that displayed the Hangul characters on the packaging/labels.

But for Max and his friends, they bought these snacks and beverages every-day because it was just who they were. It was *their's*.

That was the thing that most didn't seem to understand, especially at their school, and especially within the United States in general— Max and his friends weren't necessarily outcasts for their heritage, but they *were* different for it. And they weren't so much targeted for it, but they *did* experience racial prejudice and slurs thrown their way.

The root of their struggle from growing up and being raised as Korean Americans were the obstacles of identity, which seemed to have them pinned at both sides of the neck.

On one end, where did they fit in at school?

The thing about identity is that it's an internal thing— meaning that even *if* people accept you, it doesn't turn your black wool pale.

They were seen as a minority by some, and not a *real* minority by others.

And the pin against the other side of their neck felt a lot more heart-wrench-ing, as it came from those and that which they wanted to and believed they could call *of theirs*, which then felt ripped away from them by the notion, "If you were born and raised in the States and not Hanguk, then you aren't a *real* Korean".

To be seen as different by everyone, and even as different from your own.

It's a tricky thing— identity. And the scale of balance in such situations will usually tip in one direction or the other during the settling of its arrangement.

One scale may lean into the discarding of identity and into simply following the flow of what your current surroundings are, because you've now found a place in it by which you may fit in.

And the other scale may lean into what becomes the hunt, the discovery, and the embellishing of one's culture— that which you are and a part of by birth right.

The scale tipped in many directions for Max growing up, same for his friends too.

But eventually, around high school, it started to lean in the direction of the hunt, discovery, and embellishing— so that's exactly what him and his friends did.

From this, the journey started by which they slowly acquired an understanding of themselves, established the foundation of their identity, ignited the source of their pride, and developed the strong sense of community amongst themselves and others like themselves.

This played a major role in Max's life, as it was largely responsible for him having ever encountered his mentor in the first place… which took his life even further into a whole new direction.

Cracking open the can of cold coffee, Max took a seat beside his mentor at the tiny table in the dining room.

"Kil" said Max, "I want to know how you got into all of this.

I've asked you multiple times before 'how did you find me' or 'why did you take me under your wing' in all of this craziness, but you've never told me about how you *yourself* got into this."

Kil put down his book and took a sip of his hot coffee, the hardened man not even slurping it but just sipping the liquid down casually despite its scalding temperature, "You have a right to know it, so I won't question why you want to know..." he then took a bite of his jellied toast, pocketing the chewed food into the side of his cheek and making one more statement before swallowing, "... But I do want to know why you're asking me this *now*?"

"It's nothing new" responded Max, "Crossed my mind since the day we first met.

I guess in the early days, I felt like I didn't have a right to ask or it wasn't in my place to know.

But now I feel like I do, and personally, I think I've reached a state of being able to understand all of this to where I'll have a grasp on whatever it is you might tell me— even if it's beyond my current level of teachings.

So I wanna know."

Kil raised his eyebrows and performed a slight tilt of his head, "Alright. I'll tell you my story, then."

Without ceasing his eating of the jellied toast nor the drinking of his coffee, Kil went on to tell Max that which he wished to know.

"I was born in Hanguk with a mother, father, loving family and all that.

My father— he was a big fan of boxing. Loved the sport.

Our last name was Mun, spelt 'M-U-N', though for some families it was spelt 'M-O-O-N'.

Being the enthusiast that he was, my father took this opportunity to name me after one of our legends in the sport, Moon Sung-kil.

That was my *first* name— the one I was given at birth.

There aren't too many memories from my childhood back when my family was whole. But I do remember it being good… and being happy.

Things felt right. Like everything was as it should be.

Then, when I was six, my father passed away.

I don't know what exactly afflicted him, but I do remember him coughing up blood most of the time, and then being in the hospital for the last few months of his life.

I was too young to understand what my father's illness was or what made him ill, and my mother only offered me sugar-coated explanations because I was a kid.

I can assume now what it might have been… perhaps some type of lung cancer from smoking, maybe.

But I never got to find out the truth or be told exactly what it was, because after my father's passing, my life took a complete turn.

You see, my mother was a religious woman, but my father was not.

The teachings of her faith and my learning of them were not a prominent thing while he was still alive.

I don't think it was because my father didn't believe in it or restricted her expression of it, but rather, she didn't need it when he was alive.

She was happy, I was happy, life was good and contained everything she needed— so there was no need for faith.

However, my father's death hit my mother very hard and drove her into mania.

She didn't know how to cope or how to handle it, and she felt so lost and alone without him.

So naturally, she returned back to her faith as a way of feeling some of the support that was taken away from her when my father was buried."

At this point Kil had finished his toast, and his cup contained about half of its original portion of coffee.

He took a pause in his story to put the crumb-filled plate in the sink and to refill his cup with coffee before arriving back at the table.

With a resurrection of new steam rising from his cup, Kil pulled out a pack of smokes and placed a cigarette between his lips before lighting it and continuing his story.

"Nowadays with all the technology we have, everyone— even damn tourists —know about the cult traps in Korea and how to avoid them.

But back then, we didn't have that mass awareness and endless feed of pretty fucking valuable information from the internet. So, those cults weren't as immediately identifiable nor as easily avoidable.

My mother encountered such a cult, and it resonated with and reinvigorated her faith to the same levels that matched her needs during her grieving hysteria.

She joined this cult, and me being her child and only about seven at the time, meant I joined too.

We were in that cult for nearly three years, and it was exactly how you'd think it would be… and exactly how people warn of.

I was indoctrinated and soon picked up the faith myself.

You understand why, don't you? These were full grown adults who fell into such communities, so honestly, would you expect any different from a kid?

Granted, I didn't fully understand it all— mainly just the stories and the ideas tossed around about God and service.

I was far too young to grasp the crazier nonsense they spouted about their ways.

Looking back on it, I guess you could call me lucky for that.

There are many stories of horrific and disgusting things that also go on within these cults, but the one I was in mainly preyed on money.

I was never beaten or molested, and my mother was never abused nor raped or manipulated into sexual acts.

However, at ten years old, this cult had drained the majority of my mother's income, and she barely had enough to keep us fed.

When she told them of this and took it up with the man who led the brain-washed community, he told her that her faith must come before everything else— including her own son.

You know, 'Abraham willing to sacrifice his own son to God' and whatever other bullshit they must've said.

Apparently if she truly believed in God, truly loved God and wanted His grace, then she had to show her gratitude to the fullest extent and put the Lord first, before all else.

Well…"

Kil took a long drag from his cigarette,

"She did.

She gave it all away and kept giving it all away.

My mother stopped feeding me… and I began to starve.

I snuck in most of the food I ate, be it stolen from a store or even from the other members during gatherings, as my mother no longer put her own money towards providing me with a single meal for the day.

My weight dropped and I became extremely skinny, noticeable to the point where one of our neighbors noticed and informed whoever it was that they spoke to. Probably the police.

I remember I was asleep— I slept a lot then. Almost all the time since my body needed to make up for and reserve the energy it was no longer receiving from food. And also being asleep was the only time I couldn't feel the hunger pains.

Anyway, I woke up to my mother screaming and crying and going crazy, as two officers tried to control her while another one came inside and picked me up, then carried me out of the house.

I remember the smell of that officer's uniform— like freshly cleaned and pressed laundry, mixed with a bit of his aftershave and smokey breath as he spoke to me calmingly and reassuringly.

And I did feel calm, strangely, in that man's arms.

I was taken to the station, fed, given water, and went through a process of talking to some adults whose purpose I am still unsure of— perhaps it was to get a statement from me so they could get authorization to shutdown this cult.

Well, I don't know how much time passed after this— couldn't have been more than a week —before a man arrived with his wife to get me.

Apparently I had an uncle, my dad's brother that I didn't know about or had ever met.

He had been contacted after my retrieval by the police when they looked into my parents' records to see if I had any relative who could become my new guardian.

He fought in the war like my father did, but decided to move to and stay in America with his wife after... come to think of it, I wonder if that's what caused my father's illness— some type of gas from the war..."

Kil drifted into silence for a moment but swiftly caught himself.

"Sorry. I never thought about that before and it just occurred to me for the first time.

Continuing my story—

I didn't want to go with my uncle, initially.

I didn't know the man, had never seen him before, nor even heard his voice before or anything of the sort.

He was a complete stranger, and him and his wife wanted to take me away from my home.

After the betrayal from my own mother, from the people in the cult who said we were all family under God's eye, and the leader of it all who said I would become a great man one day… I didn't trust anybody.

So to now meet this strange man who says he's my uncle for the first time and then hear that he wants to take me out of the country, of course I fought against it.

But it happened anyway despite my protests, and I'm glad it did looking back.

My uncle was a good man, and his wife, a great woman.

They treated me right, raised me happy, cared for my health and well being, and gave me everything they could.

Ironically enough, they were also religious, but they were the good kind.

No cult-like organization or brainwashing, no superiority complex or enforcement of their beliefs— just a true acceptance of those who were the same or different, those that didn't believe, did believe, or had other beliefs.

They were *real* children of God.

And under them, I continued my faith.

I know you probably expected to hear me proclaim that I abandoned all religion entirely after my experiences, but such a thing was a lot harder than you'd think.

You see, although I saw the wrong in the cult that I was once in, I still saw the truth in God and believed in the scriptures I had read.

After losing everything— a father, a mother, a trust in strangers, community and humanity —those words in the scriptures felt almost like a home to me.

They were actually all I had until I finally began to love and trust my uncle and his wife.

Anyhow, my faith grew stronger in America now that I was able to receive a non corrupted version of it, and when I turned of age, I immediately joined the priesthood and gave my life to God.

I guess it was because of my own past trauma and the idea of wanting to save others in the same way that I was saved, that I became an exorcist.

Back then, there was a whole division for it and it wasn't such a popularized thing or riddled with fictional misconceptions as it is now.

But I served as the hand of God and the sword of Saint Michael, plunging the light of the Holy Ghost and the fire of our Lord's scripture into the unfortunate souls fallen victim— ridding them of the demons and tricksters who occupied their bodies.

My life as an exorcist was both different from yet exactly as you'd expect it to be at the same time.

Undeniably, there *were* people who were just mentally ill or under a placebo that they had been possessed.

In both such cases, I would arrive in the mental hospital or at the local church where the said person attended, and would then go through the same procedures as if a demon actually did inhabit their body.

You see, it still helped them despite there having never been a sinister presence occupying their mortal flesh.

This connects to so much of what I've already taught you. It falls into the same paradise that embeds itself in all of the universe's complexities.

If they believe it's real, then it *is*.

And my doings helped settle the sinister thoughts that traversed their minds, even if there was no sinister force to remove from their spirit.

Whether that falls into the general philosophy or a specific occult dogma that presents the idea that all angels and demons are a reflection of your own mind, is territory I won't go into.

This shit is complex, and it is the fool's play to create a structure around this world and enforce it as the only truth or solution, rather than just be an observer to it all who's decided to take on the journey of navigating its ever morphing terrain.

It also falls into the teachings we've gone through on intent and belief.

You *do* create it, you *do* give it power, you *do* feed the life of its manifestation to properly blossom by the proper intent and belief. So who am I to deny someone of expelling a spirit from their body that is not there, yet has been rooted into the cores of their heart by a resolve of paranoia?

So at the end of the day, when it came to such people and category of cases— I enacted my work on them, I settled their minds, calmed their hearts, quenched their spirits, eased their fears, relaxed their worries, and broke the chains that were *their* chains which haunted them.

I did not cure their broken minds nor correct their misplaced understandings, I simply gave them that which they needed to continue forward with their truths and to live out their lives unimpeded by the restraints they gave and/or placed upon themselves.

Now, to speak on the *real* cases of possessions that I handled… that was another world entirely.

Beautiful, terrifying, unruly, unholy, sacred, sacrilegious and inspiring all at the same time.

The petrifying and infectious scourge from hearing the roar of a demon.

The revolting and offensive sight of seeing a human's body twisted and demented from a demon's spirit invading its divine space or causing its host to cause self-harm.

The vulnerability and exposure from within myself when being looked in the eyes by such an unfortunate person who bears that kind of a powerful being in their place— who has the ability to see straight into my soul like I am a readable child in their sport.

The heartbreaking laments from the loved ones or parents who bear witness to their beloveds in such a state where they are no longer themselves but something else entirely.

And then to see the glorifying power of God as these nasty beings flinched at His name.

To feel the shield of the Holy Ghost fall over you, warm as light and as soft as feathers.

To wield thunder in your voice as the sacred words are read out, and now *you* become the most frightening being in the room, as God extends His will through your being.

The joy... and the relief when the nefarious spirit is banished and the room is released of the pressure from its presence.

The sight of lovers and parents re-embracing the soul of their beloved now returned.

The awareness that *you* hold such power, as a vessel for the holy and the sacred.

... The gullible idea that your religion is the *right one*, and your faith was placed wisely, for what else could ever provide greater proof?"

Kil ashed the burnt nub of his cigarette and lit another fresh stick of tobacco.

Max knew that he was now about to hear the meat of this story, for whenever Kil delved deeper into a lesson or a narrative, he would always chain smoke for its duration.

"I say gullible because I have seen the light of God... and also the darkness from His absence.

I've felt the miracle of angels... and also the calamities from their facades.

The last exorcism I ever performed is the reason why I say all of this, for it's the same reason why I ever came to my understandings, my truths, my awakening, my awareness— whatever the fuck you want to call it.

It is the whole reason I told you to study *all* of it, every religion, every philosophy, every practice, and every belief in the occult.

It's why *I'm* still studying everything, and why your lessons contain knowledge that's been obtained from a diverse indulgence of all of the existing cultures on earth.

Allow me this rant:

A monkey is so far from human.

If a monkey was born in a zoo, it doesn't even know about its real home in the jungles.

If a monkey is born in the jungle, it will never know what life looks like under the water of the oceans.

A monkey can look up at the glowing moon of the night, yet will never know the detailed images of its crater-filled surface, nor the immensity and brightness of those tiny little lights that sparkle in the night sky as stars, for the true suns they are.

There is so much— so so much —that separates a monkey from ever coming to stand within even the shadow of a human being…

… And yet that distance is even greater for humans when it comes to the world of *the others*.

I realized this during my final case, and it changed the trajectory of my life into a whole new direction."

Kil cleared his throat from the minor phlegm that had built up from his current cigarette, and with it— ended his rant and continued on with his actual story.

"It was the middle of summer, one those days when the weather wasn't hot but picture perfect, like straight out of a movie.

I had done about eighty exorcisms at this point, so I was familiar with it all; the symptoms; the fakers; the mentally ill; the delusional; the real-deal; the fear of the authentic; the smells; the sights.

Some things I still wasn't used to yet, but I at least knew what they were.

This exorcism in particular was for a child about the age of eight.

Oddly enough, his parents weren't religious, but they knew that whatever this was, it couldn't be explained or solved with science.

Kudos to them for that, 'cause they were right.

When I arrived at their home, I could immediately confirm that it was a possession and that there was undoubtedly a spirit within the house, just from the feel of the energy and by the events which they told me had previously taken place— along with how the plant and animal life within proximity to their residence acted.

However, the boy himself, the one "possessed" by this spirit… showed no signs of the symptoms which usually accommodated a demon taking refuge in the human body.

The boy himself was not changed, his body was normal, there were no diseases of the skin, no fire behind the eyes, no self-harming actions taking place, and no augmentation of the voice when he spoke.

There were only two things about the young boy which revealed the presence of a being within, though; the undeniably powerful and heavy aura which surrounded him; and the knowledge of things by which he spoke of that are reserved for the higher beings.

Yes— contrary to what the world has said, even demons are higher beings than humans, they're just different in how so and of their ways.

I spoke to the child for some hours, and he willingly told me all about the being that shared his body with him.

It was freakish how indifferent the boy was about the situation.

He was so calm, spoke on it so casually, and the demon itself did not once intervene with the boy's relinquishing of this information to me.

… At that time, I thought the demon had tricked the boy into thinking it was his friend and that this was okay.

I thought it had a bigger plan at play, and this was the only reason it had done nothing to the boy nor had taken over his body completely yet as its own vessel.

Finishing up my conversation with the child and making my evaluation, I went and got the parents who I had previously instructed were to restrain their child to the bed when I was ready.

And so, when the time came, they did… and the boy fussed about it and cried and screamed.

But nothing about this was unusual, either.

It was a kid fighting against his parents while they were doing something odd and unloving to him. He was simply scared by what was going on.

And never once during his struggle did the demon emerge to resist the parents, which it could've done at any point and have easily overpowered them, me, and the whole fucking neighborhood if it wanted.

I told the parents to leave the room after and to lock the door behind them.

Not only would it have been a hard sight for them to watch their child get exorcised, but it was also dangerous for them to stay in the same room while it was done.

They were non believers and had no faith, therefore, no shield to protect them from the demon's power.

Their souls and minds could've easily been manipulated or attacked by such a being since they were untrained.

Well, once everything was in order… I began.

It was during this exorcism that the demon finally revealed itself to me… but not in any way or manner which I had previously experienced before or expected from it.

It screamed out *from* the boy, not *through* him.

It was then I realized that the demon was not in possession of the boy's body, nor attached to him like a drifting spirit… but rather it was *within* him, if that makes sense— like it had placed a home within the boy's *aura*, deeper than an attachment but nowhere near the violation of entering the boy's body or disrupting his free will.

The best example I can relate to this is of the spirit guides and ancestors within us.

Just like how they are with the person they watch over, follow, and guide— so too was this demon there with the boy.

No corruption, no taking over, no ruling— simply being within him in a way that allows a close connection without interfering with the child's own essence and freedom.

The being was within his aura, and I could not for the life of me understand what exactly was going on.

This demon was angry when it spoke to me, but not for the usual reasons by which they'd curse out my presence.

This one… it cried out with an almost frustrated plea— a begging of sorts… it kept telling me to stop and that I didn't understand what I was doing.

I ignored it of course, but then the boy started screaming too, the further I went along.

Now I was **really** confused.

The boy shouldn't have been in any pain or experiencing any agony since the demon was not in possession of his body.

In fact, removing such a presence of another being from off one's aura should feel more like the relief of a weighted blanket being removed, or the clearing of fuzzy eyes or a stuffy nose.

But this boy seemed to be in pain like the others I had exorcised, as if I was ripping the being out of him.

I was so lost… so confused on the situation… that I simply held strong to the procedures and spoke as clearly and as fast as I could to reach the end of it and complete the purging.

From this, I quickly reached near completion, and the demon was nearly fully separated from the boy.

This allowed me to now be able to see the being clearly, as its essence was halfway out of the boy's aura, revealing its true form.

That's when the demon began to speak to me, as well as the boy.

The demon was chaotically begging me to stop, saying that it couldn't protect the boy if I separated the two of them.

And the boy… the boy begged me too.

With the demon halfway out of his aura, the boy began to panic, hyperventilating like crazy, pleading to me with tears in his eyes to put it back, saying he needed his "friend" when referring to the spirit.

And I'll admit… a part of me believed them, in a way.

This case was so strange already, and what was occurring had been so far out of the normal spectrum, that I *did* feel like I didn't understand.

By the way they were both begging and seemed to be in absolute fear, I *did* feel like I was making a mistake by separating them.

In this moment, I felt like a novice once again— not as an exorcist, but as a human being existing in this world filled with so many other things that I did not understand.

… But my faith got the better of me. And reverting to my training, I told myself that the demon was lying like they always do, and that the boy was corrupted by those lies which is why he didn't want to be separated from it either.

So… I finished it.

I separated the two of them.

And the demon fell onto the floor beside the bed in its full physical form, completely exhausted… but also appearing defeated.

And the boy… the boy appeared exhausted too… but more than that— he appeared to be in a state of fear and also *trance*.

Not a trance where his mind was lost, but rather, a trance of imprisonment— like his body and mind were being forced still, and his freewill was being taken away from him to make him an easier target or a docile picking.

Suddenly, the room began to buzz like static electricity or frenzied bees, while becoming hot from this unknown weighted temperature of heat that emerged.

A pressure filled the entirety of the room like one would feel from swimming into the deepest parts of an olympic pool.

I had no clue what was going on. All I knew was that this new feeling and essence which had just filled the room was far more sinister and of an *actual* nefarious presence than anything I had previously sensed with the demon in the boy's aura.

… It sounded like paper tearing, or maybe it didn't… honestly, I have no idea how to describe how it sounded— but suddenly, *eyes* began to open up all around the room; on the walls; on the ceilings; on the floor; some even in the open space of air itself… and they were all fixated *hungrily* on the boy.

The sudden appearance of these eyes sparked the demon to lift its chest off the floor in observation— terrified by their arrival, but also gaining a second wind as if he knew he had to act quickly.

The demon squeezed one of its hands tightly into a fist— to the point where it trembled —then opened it up again to produce a beautiful opal bearing shades of green, magenta, red, orange, and purple.

With the little strength the demon had left, it tossed the opal up onto the bed— landing on the boy's lap —then said, "Take this! And always keep it on you!

Stay hidden from *their eyes* for as long as you can, less I never make it back!"

As soon as the opal had landed on the boy's lap, the eyes around the room began to hectically look in all directions as if they had lost sight of the boy they were once fixed on.

The demon then looked at me and said, "Cast them out! Before they have time to understand!

It's the only chance and only way!

That boy is in grave danger from these hawks who prey and hunt and watch from above!

Lest you want an innocent soul to be taken by these foul creatures, you must cast them out using *your* voice! For God is not what you think, nor His angels of similar grace!

Use *your* will, not God's, for soon these eyes shall fall on you both!"

The demon then dipped into the floor as if an invisible hole was there, one which I could not see, and disappeared entirely.

I didn't know what to think. I didn't know what to do. I didn't know who or what to believe… but then I saw that boy on the bed.

I saw him paralyzed like the prey of a spider— unable to move from the venom injected by the ruler of the webs —forced to suffer in an awareness as its predator draws closer towards them, unable to move and unable to scream while its predator feeds on them.

And *that* sight— *that* understanding… that was enough for me to act on.

That was something I could not allow to happen, not by the word of God, but by my own voice of being who *I* am, and wanting to help this powerless child who I once was to escape this madness.

I can't remember exactly what I said thinking back on it, but I do know I spoke from the heart with rage, power, and fury.

It was the single most overwhelming time I ever used my own freewill as a surge of energy to implement over other beings.

… and with it, I casted out those angels—"

"Those were angels?" interrupted Max, "I thought the eyes were some other evil force that were greater or more evil than the demon protecting the boy?"

Kil shook his head, "Those were angels.

There's this false depiction of angels that most of society is familiar with now. But if you study the bible, if you read the scripture, it tells of how they actually appeared.

And those eyes in that room that day, those beings attempting to prey on the boy for whatever reason… those *were* angels.

I knew it immediately. Knew full and well what they were the instant they appeared.

And I casted them out.

And after that, I left the church and my priesthood behind.

You see, I learned something very valuable that day— not all angels are good, and not all demons are bad.

There are agendas at play which we humans have no understandings of, and humans are such fools for trying to categorize the good and evil, the bad beings and the good beings— all just so we can fit it within our capacity of understanding.

But the truth is… it's not that simple.

And with God no longer being the all loving and ever forgiving being I once saw Him to be after that exorcism, along with angels not actually being his loyal followers who protect humans and save our souls, and by that demon having the only true interest of all other beings to save that innocent boy from the *real* evil that lurks in these worlds… I dropped all my faith that I had been taught since the death of my father."

Kil let out a giant sigh as though it strained him to retell that part of the story.

"For the third time in my life, I felt lost once again.

I had no idea what to do with myself, no idea where to go, no idea what I should believe in or what I understood from all of this conflicting chaos I had observed and endured up to this point.

But… I was not that helpless child anymore like I was in Hanguk, so I didn't give up.

I didn't coddle myself into the fetal position and allow my soul to starve.

I decided— no —I *chose* to figure this shit out and to not be a lost lamb in it all.

Because that's what I was.

That's what I had chosen to be for so long, a sheep to our shepherd, weak and lost without guidance, defenseless on my own against the wolves, and oblivious to the fact that the shepherd plans on eventually eating me as well.

Thing is, there are too many religions, too many beliefs, too many theories, too many practices, and too many doctrines floating around, that I ran the risk of the same thing happening if I just randomly chose <u>one</u> to put all my time or studies into.

So I decided that the best solution to this complex issue was to look back into my own past, my own heritage— and so I deep dived into Korean mythology, folklore, occult practices and the magical history of our old and ancient ways.

From there, my *true* spiritual journey began, signified by the changing of my last name to BariDegi— from the myth of the abandoned princess.

It felt right when I did that.

For when I was born, my father named me after a warrior. And trust me, I was strong like so. With that strength, I endured the neglect of my mother and the lies of the cult.

Later in my life, I adopted the name 'Father Mun', a name by which I saved and helped countless people. I was still the same warrior under this new title, and fended off the harmful spirits from innocent souls— trying so hard to protect that starving child within me that I saw within others.

And then, after my last exorcism and the journey of understanding the history of my ancestors and gaining a footing into the occult… I realized that I still was a lost child. I still was that starving child from my past.

I could never save anyone before I saved myself, and in all honesty, I still hadn't.

Yes, I was a warrior. And yes, I did fight— but that did not mean that I had *healed*. And that meant that I had not truly grown since the day those cops took me away from my mother and those crazies in the cult.

With this realization, I embraced what I was— a lost and abandoned child.

And in homage to my heritage, and in gratitude to this mystical world I had immersed myself in, I changed my last name to BariDegi."

Kil put out his last cigarette without reaching into his pack for another, signifying the end to his story.

"Now, I'm not so lost. I know of many things about the unknown.

Now, I'm no longer starving. My soul is fed with the empowerment that I gain through every truth I discover.

Now, I'm not really abandoned anymore. I interact with the universe *itself*, through all of its signs it sends me. I engage with the essence of nature and see the trees wave at me as they observe *my* progress. I can sense the presences of many beings, and common are their passings.

At forty-seven years old, I can say with full confidence and awareness, that I am no longer that hungry little boy.

And I've even moved passed that naive vicar I once was.

I've come to embody a *true* warrior, one who understands and has grown *himself* first, and has *healed* himself before he comes to the aid of others."

A Cold Day in Hell

Hold strong thy resolve, tenuous mortals.

For when the black sun shall cast its shadow over the brow of Helios, and the aubades are sung with tears like dirges, the ground will shake and rise for it will be a cold day in hell.

Listen for those hallowed horns blown from the twisted outgrowths which once protruded from the crowns but have long since fallen and petrified off the ancient beings who established the plains, fashioned the mountains, and hollowed out the canals of these lands inferno.

Be steady when you feel the pulse of the war-drums reverberate in your chests, as the large hammers pound on the stretched skins of the honored daimons who lost their duels in attempts to claim the titles and legions as princes from the old masters who have bore them since their first cinders collided upon the face of the earth.

Do not be fooled by those whistles that seduce and beckon forth thee, like the banshees and sirens of the seas.

Forget not that these beings are beautiful too, and not all horrors.

Easy shall those never whispered by the wise fall into such entrancing arms, led astray by their ignorance.

Be warned and be told, that when the hoarfrost cascades over the soil once red with flames, and the strayed wails and choleric shrieks become hushed and replaced by the pattering of wings and the shambles of marches— that is when you will see them.

The lords and revered inhabitants of this perilous plane.

The ones with no arms but wings, who stand on two legs like talons, a head at the top of their arched torsos and a tail at their end.

The jagged-fleshed brutes, dominance manifested, power regurgitated in a primordial fashion by the juggernaut of a physical form they posses.

Skin hard and dry like mountains, hands and body broad like boulders, smoldering eyes like the past conquerors of seas.

The arcanists, who have read, collected, treasured, and accumulated the epistemes sprouted throughout the universe over the eons of its existence.

Still does time and space stand around them, as matter itself is pathetically a rudimentary concept to these sapiential beings.

Mighty are the harbingers, the walking apocalypses who tower over entire dimensions.

Devoid of all morals from their perspectives on life, a holy feat achieved by their omniscient eyes, far out of reach to nearly all that is sentient of any kind.

The walkers, the crossers, the travelers of dreams. Those who have seen our desires or perhaps even planted them within us.

Our deepest and darkest desires be merely a cinch to them as riddles are to sphinxes.

What matter of smoke do these pilgrims emerge from?— for they carry the same footing as the winds which slip inside all houses and temples.

And to behold the others, the many others, the countless others.

Those with bugs imbued in their skin.

Those more beautiful than the very beings who sit at the end of aesthetic's evolution.

Those who look like animals, or are merged with them in their many shapes and forms.

The things that still hide and wait in the shadows made by the flickering flames of the cursed underworld, waiting for this very point in time for their reveal.

These old songs shall play in horror, and the cackling sound of trembling skeletons shall call forth the hounds as they lift their pointing fingers in a deadman's warning.

Beware, tenuous mortals, for the first blow of that algid wind, the first fall of that ponderous snow, the first sprouting of those crystal spears upon the accursed realm of the damned… the freezing over of Sheol… shall also be the last.

Babushka

I DO NOT trust Babushka. I fear she wishes to eat me.

Mama left me with her two months ago at the start of winter, and will not return until the blooming of the phlox.

I did not like the idea of heading this far east during the cold to live with my Babushka, for many of reasons.

Her home is old like her body.

Every floorboard creaks and moans from the pressure placed upon it like the bones and joints of that brittle woman.

The wood walls are filled with cracks and gaps like Babushka's patinated skin and her spaced smile of missing teeth. This makes her house especially cold during this season and requires multiple fires to always stay lit in her home.

And I find it uncomfortable to breathe in her dwelling because of all this soot in the air caused by these constant burning flames.

We are so far east and at the edge of the woods, that it feels like the sun never fully rises to its peak in the sky, and is only held in limbo at the tips of the pines— never making it past dawn or dusk, and just stuck in its transition from morning to night.

I love mama and I hate being far away from her.

The separation from her is one of my biggest hates for being here.

I understand why it was necessary. However, that doesn't change the fact that I've never liked my Babushka or her home.

Babushka has always been weird towards me since my very first memory of her.

Although she holds a sense of love in her eyes whenever she casts them upon me, I wonder about those eyes and what they *actually* carry when she watches me without my awareness.

It seems like she is always watching me...

As a child, she would talk to me about the things I did when I thought I was all alone, be it in her home or out in the woods.

She would warn me about those things such as the heavy objects that could've fallen on me, or the hungry beasts that have dens near the barren berry bushes I had just returned from.

Though I thought I was alone and in private during those moments, it turned out Babushka had been watching me the whole time.

I don't know how, either, for she is old and fragile.

Mama doesn't even keep such a keen eye on my every move like Babushka does, and for this reason, I have always been suspicious of her.

When I'm inside her home, she always trails me.

She will pass by whatever room I am in every couple of minutes and just smile at me.

I do not like it. There is no reason for this.

As a child, I would awake most nights to the sight of her standing outside of my doorway… watching me sleep.

She would leave whenever I asked her what she was doing.

Sometimes I would awake to her inside my room, either looking over me from the skirt of my bed, or standing at my window gazing outside.

It was the same with this too, for when I asked her what she was doing, she would leave without saying a word to me.

One night, I awoke to her face hanging over mine mid-sleep, as she sat on the side of my bed during my slumber.

I remember I wanted to scream, as this frightened me, but she smiled and left the room as soon as our eyes met.

After this, I've always made sure to sleep with my door closed as I did not like nor trust Babushka when I slept anymore.

But despite this, I would still wake in the middle of the night and see the shadow of her presence outside my door— not daring to enter, but still keeping close to my place of being like those watchful eyes of hers during the day.

These last two months here have been no different than my childhood visits, only, mama isn't here with me now to keep me safe, and Babushka has only grown stranger in how she acts.

When I first arrived, Babushka was more concerned with mama and how long she would be gone.

She wanted to know exactly how long my stay was going to be, and when mama would return for me.

Once mama left, Babushka asked me to help her with the preparations for winter, and was always beside me during them and any other errand I carried out, even if she didn't assist me with them.

I still keep my door closed when I sleep, and there is no night that goes by when her shadow isn't on the other side of that door.

Random nights, I can hear her shuffling with the handle, attempting to open it, but I planned for this possibility and fixed it to be locked from the inside only— I did not trust being alone with her here without mama.

During the day, Babushka stays in the same room with me wherever I am, or stays outside with me for the entire duration I am not inside the house.

She just watches me— smiles and watches my every passing moment of the day.

At the end of my first month here, I had an accident.

On the day of the accident, I had been collecting firewood— my hands freezing over —then chopping them with the poorly sharpened axe all day.

My hands were cold, tired, beat and unsteady, so while skinning the potatoes later that night for dinner, they fumbled and I split my palm open.

I cursed and clenched my hand in pain, then heard the faint and distraught voice of Babushka from nearby, who must've been watching me, mumble, "No…!"

Babushka has not been the same since that night I cut my hand.

The moment it happened, she rushed over to me and took hold of my hand, forcing me to immediately wash it with the hot water that hadn't finished boiling yet for cooking, and then wrapped it tightly in a cloth as bandaging.

She would constantly glance at my face while doing this, bearing a strong look of worry and panic which consumed her expressions.

After Babushka finished cleaning my wound and bandaging my hand, she explicitly scolded me to not spill any more blood or let my hand leak while inside the house.

For the first time since I've known her and visited her home, Babushka left me alone as she took the items she used to clean my wounds or that contained any fragments of my blood outside the house, heading into the cold woods and dispersing of them out in the wildness before returning.

That night, I awoke to her shadow no longer being at the outside of my door, while the sound of scratches in a furious cadence could be heard coming from somewhere in the house.

I got out of bed and snuck out of my room quietly, keeping my footsteps light in that creaky wooden house of hers as I followed the odd scratching sounds towards their source.

I arrived in the kitchen to the sight of Babushka in a craze, on all fours, vigorously scrubbing the whole ground where I had cut my hand open.

She was whimpering and mumbling to herself under her breath.

I couldn't make out what she was saying, and I didn't stay to try.

I left the kitchen before she could come to any awareness of me being there, similar to what she always does to me, and went back to bed.

Since then, Babushka does not let me help with the cooking, and has also adopted new methods in her kitchen.

Every time she presents me a meal, there is an abundance of spices in it which she has never used before that I didn't even know she had.

I've never tasted them in my life, and their foreign flavors are not preferred by my palate.

I've tried to eat less of what she cooks, and have refused her offers based upon these new ingredients that are unknown to me.

Babushka is insistent that I eat her cooking, and will coax, persuade, and has even tried to bribe me into consuming her meals.

I've noticed that she's also resorted to adding the spices into my hot chocolate since I eat less of her food now, but I can still taste them through the chocolate's strong flavor.

She is attached to me like a shadow now, even more so than she used to be.

And at night, she struggles constantly to open my door as I sleep, no longer trying to hide or conceal her efforts in doing so.

The other night, after she failed to open my bedroom door, I saw her peering into my room from outside— standing at my window.

Her short stature revealed only the crown of her head and those lurking eyes as they peered over the window frame.

She looked at me, and I looked back at her, filled with fear but trying to hide it.

She left my window after that and returned inside the house, never coming to my door again for the rest of the night.

I do not trust Babushka… I fear she will eat me soon.

She is at my hip everyday now, there is no escaping her lingering presence. And her eyes watch me in a full display of herself— no longer from a hidden distance.

Babushka is now going further than she ever has before with attempting to enter my room at night, or to investigate my presence of being inside it.

When I drew blood that night I cut open my hand— I wonder if this has invigorated her hunger and sped up her plans for my consumption…?

The food she feeds me, along with their new ingredients and strange spices… Babushka has already begun to prepare me like a dish to ingest.

Perhaps that is what she keeps locked away in the basement.

There's been a lock on that door for as long as I can remember, and I've never seen Babushka or mama open it.

I've never questioned it either, because that locked door has always been a feature engraved into my image of her home, no different than the framed pictures of Dedushka that line the walls which I no longer notice anymore at this point.

There must be something in the basement that Babushka wishes to hide.

I wouldn't be surprised if it were these spices she's been using on me.

I do not know if mother is aware of Babushka's plans on eating me, but I do know she will not return in time to save me from this situation.

I must do it myself, and I must do it fast.

I've come up with a plan that can save me from this outcome of falling into Babushka's belly, and I must act on it *tonight*.

So far, I've been standing behind the kitchen's cabinet and waiting to hear Babushka's approach by the creaking of the floorboards for over an hour now.

It won't be too long until she falls for my trap.

Because Babushka always attempts to enter my room at night to see if I am inside of it or asleep, I've pretended to head to bed early and closed my door in usual manner… only I snuck out moments later and have hidden myself in the house since.

When the opportunity presented itself, I snuck into the kitchen and squeezed myself behind this cabinet, and now I await for the right moment to execute my plan.

Soon, Babushka will head to my room and open its door, discovering that I am not in bed.

I do not know the full extent of how she will react, but I am certain that she will begin to search for me.

When she passes through the kitchen and crosses in front of this cabinet I hide behind, I shall push it with all my strength and it will collapse on top of her— pinning her frail body to the ground.

I do not know what I will do after that, but I do not care. All that matters right now is that I stop Babushka before she has the chance to eat me.

I hear her!

She has just turned the handle to my room.

I can hear her footsteps shuffling around my room and the aggressive tossing of my bedsheets.

The floorboards are creaking… and fast!

She has already begun her hunt for me and is approaching the kitchen.

This is it!

This is the opening I've been waiting for!

⇥⭕ ⭕⭅

I did it!

My plan worked!

Babushka is pinned under the heavy cabinet right now, moaning and crying
in pain, but I am safe!

I could not see it from my original position, but a protruding nail from the
back of the cabinet managed to pierce my forearm during my forcing of the
cabinet's tip.

It's a nasty gash, but nothing I can't handle.

The real issue, Babushka, has been solved.

For the first time since she's been pinned against the floor by the cabinet,
Babushka has looked up at me as I watch her.

She took notice of my forearm and the streams of blood that fall from it. Her face looks terrified by the sight of it, but more than that— also hopeless and heartbroken…

"I was trying to protect you…" Babushka tells me as her voice cracks from the tears that pour out of her eyes.

I hear heavy footsteps and strong breathing coming from behind the basement's locked door now.

A slow, hard and sturdy banging has begun to beat from its other side.

I can hear the wood splintering with each hard thud against the door.

It won't hold for much longer, this house is too old.

I do not know what is on the other side of the basement's locked door, or what Babushka meant by her words… but perhaps *she* was not the one trying to eat me.

A Silver Pen

"I CANNOT SEE, this mustn't be!" said the girl who counted, *"One Two Three."*

"I thought I was free, but I must not be. Not by the way the gods look at me..." said the girl who counted, *"One Two Three."*

"I remember a glee, but it wasn't from me. And it came when I finished counting One Two Three."

"She clawed out her eyes— the poor little thing" said the gods who mourned their creation's suffering.

"Where is it now, that other being? Surely it's gone and took to fleeing" said the gods who feared the sight they were seeing.

"It wished to be free, so it asked such of me— and I didn't see the fault when I chose to agree" said the girl who counted, *"One Two Three."*

"I remember the decree, though no longer fondly, when I let down the pen at the end of count Three."

"How foolish we are, how foolish we were— to craft so much innocence into her..." said the gods who regretted what the girl had endured.

"Who was so certain, who was so sure— that our previous dealings with that being was adjourned?" said the gods whose wrath now began to stir.

"There was no sentry, hadn't been one for centuries... persuaded the being in setting it free" said the girl who counted, *"One Two Three."*

"We must catch the thing, and catch it fast— for the girl was the first, but surely not the last" said the gods who wished to not repeat the past.

"Was it a creation of our own, or did it always exist— like we, the gods, whose existence is fixed?" asked the gods whose memory of the being was mixed.

"I only have One, but I used to have Three. Where did the Two eyes go that the gods gave me?" asked the girl who counted, *"One Two Three."*

"I cannot see, this mustn't be! And yet, I can still see the gods clearly" said the girl who counted, *"One Two Three."*

"What shall we do then, with this creation— surely we must give her some salvation" said the gods who wished to fix her aberration.

"Place her in a silver pen, and place upon the pen a charm— that way while she's in the pen, she cannot do self-harm" said the gods of favor who specialized in smarm.

"The last pen was made of gold, and she still let the thing loose— are you sure this is meant to heal the girl, and not just another ruse?" asked the gods who carried a suspicious view.

"We shall try it and see, and eventually set her free— but first we must know what happened after Three" said the gods who wished to hear the end of her story.

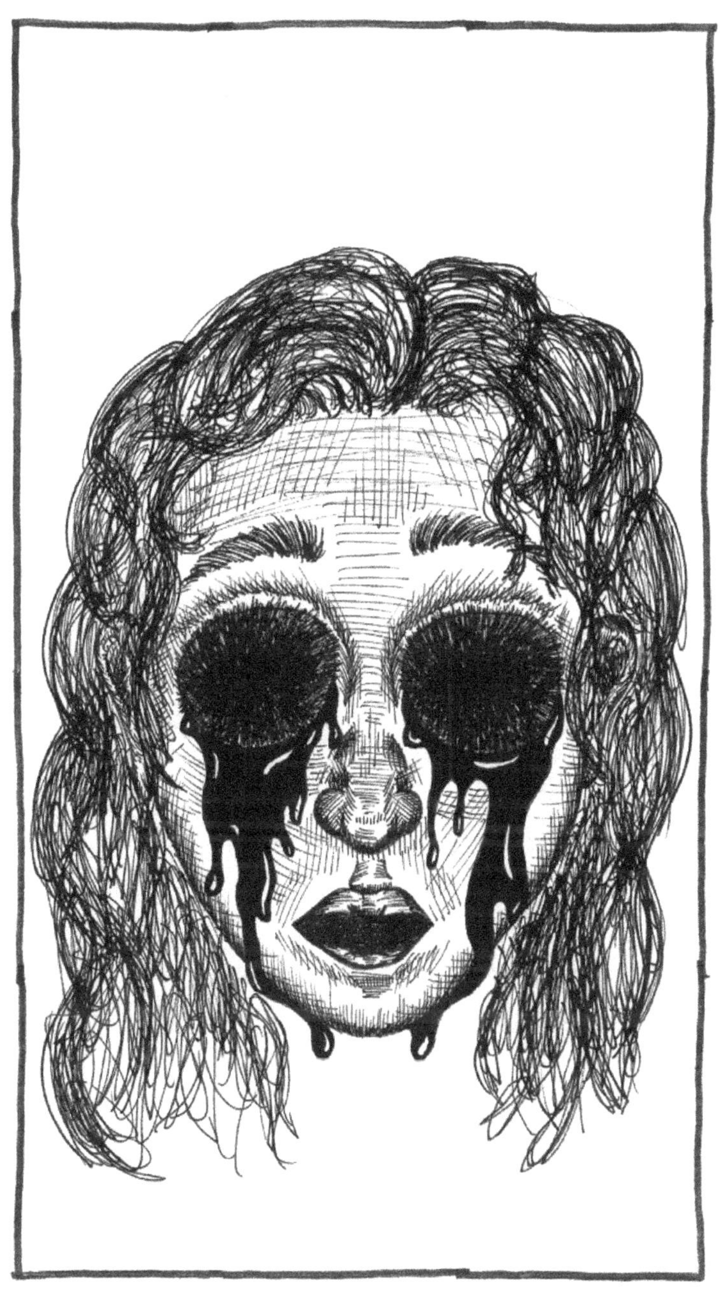

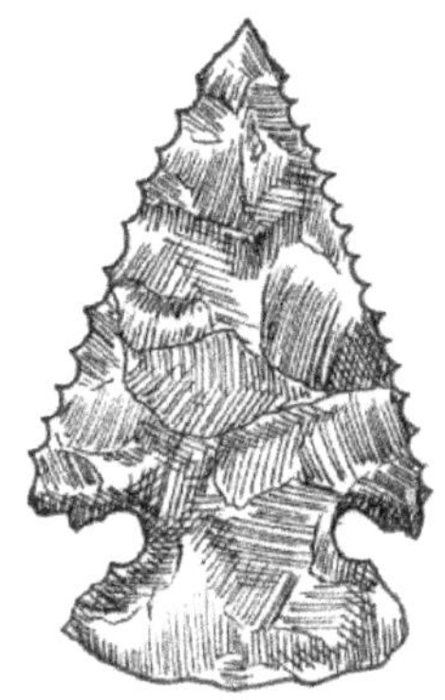

Royal Jelly

THE HUMID JUNGLE and its warm, vibrating scent of dew acted as an invitation to the nostrils of the excavation team.

The lively sounds of birds and monkeys who made a home of this land long ago and now filled up its entire green network of unimaginable discovery, echoed their caws, chirps, and hollers like an opera of welcoming.

Ten days ago, Dr. Hancock (the archaeologist), Dr. Hanney (the anthropologist), and Dr. Brown (the geologist), uncovered an ancient cave that had been eaten alive by the jungle from the many years of passing.

Thick exotic vines wrapped over its entrance, along with their wrappings covering the peak of its portion that lifted off the ground.

The cave was then cloaked by the leaves, twigs and branches that fell onto that vine netting from the aging of surrounding plant life, the turning of the seasons, and the natural breakage caused by the local wildlife who called this jungle their playground.

After which, soil was by one way or another, tossed on top of these weaved vines that held the bed of ruined shrubbery— leading to the sprouting and flourishing of more plants and native species which grew atop this blanket of perfect conditions.

It was only by Dr. Brown's near tumble when his foot broke through a weak spot in the vines that the men realized there was an open pocket beneath them of a hollow structure.

And after two whole days and one full night of uprooting all the vegetation, using both their hands and machetes, the men finally discovered this long lost cave beneath it all.

This discovery erupted a mix of emotions within them, including excitement, ecstasy, greed… and paranoia at the thought of possible enmity that could come from some of the others in their field of work— who by jealously's carnassial whip, would seek to either get the jump on them and/or sabotage their finding of a lifetime.

Keeping that in mind, the three men immediately flew back to their home office in London, and swiftly acquired the funding needed for their excavation plans.

The investors were eager to throw their money at the men after hearing their presentation on uncovering all of the hidden mysteries and secrets within that cave— guaranteeing themselves and their investors a prestige for all of the many great finds they would unearth from this project.

So now, in just under two weeks since they left their discovery, the men returned back to the thick Brazilian jungle. The camouflaged cave was still intact and untouched by any other foreign excavation team, and with the proper equipment now in hand, the taking was all theirs.

The men's first endeavor was the clearing of the cave's entrance from all of the vines and plants that had crept their roots into its mouth and onto its walls. It was a tedious and diligent task, but thankfully, did not occupy too much of their time.

Once this was complete, the three men were finally able to inspect the cave's entrance in finer detail, and were shocked to discover parietal art and carvings scattered along the walls and ceilings of the rock tunnel.

Some were of human figures, others were of animals… and a few appeared to be of humanoid stature but still somehow different in depiction from the other figures of man and woman— perhaps symbolism to the gods of myths —as well as geometric patterns that were textured into the walls like braille.

The men documented all of these images that were scattered about the cave, both by taking pictures as well as copying them down into their journals with sketches, where they would then take notes and annotate shared theories beside their rough replicas.

Further along into their excavation, the men went deeper into the tunnel and discovered even more fascinating artifacts.

There were bones of men, women, and children.

There were all sorts of weapons, including spears, arrowheads, and clubs, most of which were broken and covered with dirt.

There were ripped pieces of clothing, crafted by an ancient weaving method and donning indigenous patterns.

And finally, there were rocks, but not the usual kind of rocks one would find just casually lying on ground. These were shaped rocks, carved rocks, smooth and perfectly round like marbles, with a curious dried substance on them that would crumble off by a gentle rub— perhaps petrified blood?

One day, during another evening of their research, the nearby bushes began to shake and rattle despite there being no wind or breeze.

The men halted their work and quickly drew their machetes, one even a rifle, and aimed them at the ruffling bushes.

This was the jungle, after all, deep in the heart of Brazil. There were many predators who called this green maze their home, and had evolved to tear out the throats, rip off the limbs, squeeze out the air, and digest the bodies whole of such foreign intruders like themselves.

As the shaking of the shrubs grew to a climax from whatever lay behind it drawing closer to its face, the men prepared themselves to attack and kill whatever hungry beast should emerge.

But to their surprise, and also great relief, a child came out its end.

He was a young boy, no older than five, and must've been a local from one of the neighboring villages which surrounded their excavation site.

His complexion was one that had been kissed into a beautiful melanin by the sun, having been born and raised in the jungle since birth. He wore no shirt and had no shoes, only a simple cloth to cover his privates and rear.

As the little boy approached the men, he bore a great big smile of innocence and welcoming, excited to see the strange men that looked different from himself and all his people, and just curious as any child would be to see what they were up to.

Dr. Hanney spoke Portuguese and greeted the young boy warmly, *"Hello! What's your name?"* he asked.

The young boy was shy and covered his face, not giving Hanney an answer back.

"Ah, that's okay" continued Hanney, *"You don't have to tell me your name if you don't want to.*

Are you curious about what we are doing over here?"

The young boy smiled and nodded his head.

"We like to find secrets and old things from the past that people have forgotten about, or has become lost with time! Look—"

Dr. Hanney pulled out an arrowhead from his pocket and placed it into the young boy's hands.

The boy was intrigued by the little artifact, and when he looked back up at Dr. Hanney with a smile, the anthropologist did his best impression of an archer launching his arrow— with the added sound effect by whistling its release.

The boy giggled at the little charade, and Dr. Hanney, being a person who loves people and their cultures, continued to cater to the boy's curiosity and feed his fascination.

He whipped out his journal and showed the boy all the sketches he had made that replicated the carvings and paintings on the inside of the cave.

The boy stared at each page with childlike awe, and flipped through the book to admire each drawing.

"Do you want to see the real ones?" asked Dr. Hanney, *"They're inside the cave and cover all of the walls!"*

The boy immediately pushed the book back into Dr. Hanney's hands and took a step back, shaking his head furiously in rejection to the idea.

"Okay! Okay" reassured Dr. Hanney, *"You don't have to go inside the cave to see them. Does the cave scare you?"* he asked.

"It's a bad place" spoke the boy for the first time.

"Bad place?" question Dr. Hanney, *"What do you mean by that? Do you know about this cave?"*

The boy nodded, *"It's dangerous. Monsters live inside it!"*

Dr. Hanney laughed, *"No, no. It's actually more likely a place where your ancestors once lived and made a home out of.*

We discovered bones, clothes, and tools— just like that arrowhead I gave you. All of that, including the paintings and carvings, are inside this cave.

This could even have been a sacred burial ground.

There's a lot of possibilities to what this place might have been and acted as, but it was a place your ancestors once used— not a dangerous one."

"No" said the boy, *"My Vovo told me that this cave is bad.*

He said monsters used to live near our ancestors and would eat them. Kidnap them, and then eat them.

Vovo said that our ancestors had enough one day, and fought against the monsters. The monsters were strong though, and some were even stronger than the others.

We killed as many as we could, and then drove the last of them deep into this cave.

Sometimes they would still appear and kidnap our people, so we made a fire at its entrance, warning them that if they ever emerged again, we would burn them alive once and for all.

After that, they never emerged again, but Vovo says they're still alive and that it's dangerous to go near the cave.

Vovo says it might tempt them to return because they're hungry, and they could kidnap you and eat you at any moment if you get too close to the cave."

"Really? I've never heard of such a legend before" said Dr. Hanney, fascinated by the indigenous folklore, *"Do you think your grandfather could tell me it in person, sometime? I'd love to hear it again and write it down."*

The boy smiled and nodded.

"Good! Now go on back home, we have to keep working over here.

But don't worry, I promise that myself and none of my colleagues will be kidnapped or eaten by the monsters. We'll be careful, okay?"

The boy nodded and then ran back into the same shrubbery from which he emerged from earlier.

"What did he say?" asked Dr. Hancock once the boy was gone.

"Just something about a little legend that surrounds the cave, apparently" answered Dr. Hanney.

"A legend? We asked all the neighboring villages if they knew anything about the cave, but none of them even had a clue about its existence."

"I know" said Dr. Hanney, "That's why I'm going to go back to the village later this month, after we make some more progress here, to document the myth.

The boy said he was told it by his grandfather, so perhaps there *are* some ties to this cave, but only by specific lineages. In that case, its knowledge would be held onto by word of mouth as opposed to the local masses through tales.

If this is the case, then it would make our find have an even larger impact on our research, and be a monumental asset to the revealing of this discovery once it's all finished and becomes public."

"What was the legend about?" inquired Dr. Hancock, "Did it shed any light on who or what they might have buried here and what possible class systems were involved?"

"Actually, it had nothing to do with it being a burial ground at all" answered Dr. Hanney, "Supposedly, the previous tribes from the past drove back monsters into this cave, very long ago.

Perhaps it was a metaphor for a specific tribe or bloodline that was ostracized and driven out of the community.

That would make sense, because using such a metaphor would also wipe them out from the memories of the other tribes. With there being no knowledge or name used as a reference for this said tribe or bloodline that was driven out, it would create the same effect as if they never existed at all.

Consider this— in a world where history is solely carried by word of mouth, then such a tactic of swapping out the actual names and replacing them with metaphors… is similar to what we would consider as the burning of books.

This would also explain why no other occupants of any nearby villages were aware of this cave or its legend.

If the legend itself is about a fallen tribe and was augmented as to not identify the true name of the ostracized group— then it likely became something of taboo to speak on at some point in time.

This would've made its tale so rare, that only a handful of people would still know it to this day.

And, lucky for us, it looks like we found someone who still does!

This is honestly amazing news! This is great!

This is why I love everything about cultures and people, and why I became an anthropologist in the first place!

I'm so excited I might just go to the boy and his grandfather before the end of the week, now!

I'm telling you, this will have a **huge** contribution to our findings and will play a major role in whatever we publish!"

Just then, Dr. Brown emerged from the mouth of the cave, catching the tail end of Dr. Hanney's speech, "Hey!" he called out, "Not to sink your ship of this career rant of yours, but you two oughta check this out!"

The two men joined their colleague as he led them further into the cave, going deeper and deeper into the darkness until it fully enveloped them.

When they reached a depth where only the outlined figures of themselves could be seen, with no details of the face or even the separation of their appendages, Dr. Brown stopped.

"This cave goes a lot deeper than we thought" he said, "There's no telling how much further it goes on or where it may lead or end, but one thing's for sure— there is zero light from this point on.

I'm thinking we should explore it further tomorrow and see just exactly how far this tunnel goes.

Best if we do it at the beginning of first light with the proper equipment, that way we can have some illumination and see what may be on *these* walls, the ground, and even at the end of this tunnel if we can reach it before midday."

"I agree" said Dr. Hancock, "The sun's already going down and it's only going to get darker from here on out.

Let's head back to camp before we have to feel our way out of this place since you didn't tell us to bring flashlights before leading us this deep."

"I wanted it to be a surprise!" argued Dr. Brown, "If everything we've found so far has only been from the mouth of the cave's entrance, imagine what we'll uncover yards in it!?"

The men agreed on the early morning excursion and swiftly headed back to camp, escaping the tunnel before the daylight was lost and the entirety of the cave sunk into a blinding darkness.

With the moon hanging over their heads like the halos of saints, and with the chirping of bugs and the croaking of frogs sounding from their east and west, the men bantered under the blanket of the jungle's night— lying on their cots while a single lantern sat on a crate, illuminating their space.

"Can you imagine if Brown didn't almost fall and break his neck from stepping on this goldmine when it was still covered?" asked Dr. Hancock.

"Can you imagine if I *did* go through and wound up breaking my neck!" barked Dr. Brown.

"We'd honor you and name the cave and all its findings after you" teased Dr. Hanney.

"Actually, it would've probably stirred up too much noise if you did fall through. And then all the vultures of other explorers would've came and desecrated our find before we could've even gotten any funding like we did" stated Dr. Hancock.

"Oh… don't say that" said Dr. Brown, "The idea makes my blood boil and my heart sink."

"It's true" continued Dr. Hancock, "We should count ourselves lucky that you didn't get hurt— for sentimental reasons, of course. But also work related reasons as well.

And we should also count ourselves lucky for how smoothly we were able to get the investors on board with this project."

"I'd say that's thanks to you, Hancock" said Dr. Hanney, "You're the one who made sure we stuck to our own countrymen for the funding. They'd always support us."

"What's that supposed to mean?" asked Dr. Brown.

"You usually go for the American investors" continued Dr. Hanney, "And that takes *ages* after the discovery is made, which is the most time sensitive part.

The clock starts ticking the moment a find is made, but you always like to test that luck by reaching out to your American investors as opposed to presenting our projects to your own countrymen."

"That's because our own countrymen are snobs and frugal with their fundings" countered Dr. Brown, "For as rich as they are and for how much they love to boast of supporting the 'Queen's conquer', those sods are stingy with such projects and barely contribute.

I can have *one* American support the entire thing, which covers **a lot** of unnecessary time spent finding an investor.

Compared to us having to acquire up to five or seven British backers which can take an even longer time, I'd say my way's not bad."

"How fast do you think your American investor would've jumped on this project if we *had* went with your sources, Brown?" asked Dr. Hanney.

"Honestly, we could've been back in this jungle two days earlier than we were" answered Dr. Brown, "It's not much of a time difference, so I do have to admit, I am surprised Hancock was able to round up the right bunch and get us backed and supported as fast as he did— especially by our own countrymen."

"Well if I'd known about this single man of yours, Brown, then I would've gone with you handling the funding" admitted Dr. Hancock, "Now we got six sods whose names will appear in the papers alongside ours when it could've been only one."

"No, it was a good thing you took control on this matter" said Dr. Brown, "My go-to investor, Mark Williams, is actually unavailable at the moment.

Last I heard, he actually *went* with the team he backed onto some island in the Philippines, and is assisting them with their excavation now."

"He fully funded a team *and* went with them to get his hands dirty in the mud on their project?" questioned Dr. Hanney, baffled by the idea, "I'd like to meet this man sometime, it's rare that any nob in a suit is willing to actually get his hands dirty and come to these parts, rather than just throw their money at us."

"Yeah, he's a good man" said Dr. Brown, "Nothing like the usual investors you'd encounter.

Hopefully I can share a pint with him when he returns from his trip, and hear all about his first time experience in the field.

If it wasn't too bad of one, then hopefully I can convince him to do it again and have him tag along one of *our* next finds— hell, he doesn't even have to fund it, that just sounds like a good time to me."

The men continued their chatting and rambles long into the night, until sleep eventually crept its way into their camp.

When morning came around and the first light of the sun broke over the trees, accompanied by the obnoxious yelling of the jungle's children who awoke along side them, the team prepared their equipment and headed into the cave.

With flashlights, rope, and journals to draft any unique findings or to outline a possible map depending on how the cave's tunnel system might change the further they trekked in, the men marched into the darkness and left the light of the sun behind them.

After only a couple of feet into the cave, the light began to fade dimmer and dimmer away.

After a few more feet in, the light became sparse.

After less than ten minutes of more walking, the light became completely absent.

At this point, the men switched on their flashlights, illuminating the once imageless abyss of shadows, and continued their march deeper into the tunnel.

The further they went, the more sporadic the interior of the tunnel became.

It would constantly dip and dive, causing them to head downwards into the earth; sometimes by gradual slopes; other times by steep slants.

It would twist and turn again and again; sometimes to the left; sometimes to the right; sometimes even by a myriad of zigzags.

Interestingly enough, however, there were no more paintings on the walls nor a litter of forgotten bones, trinkets, or weapons on the cave's floor this deep in— which went against the original theories of the men who now trekked its grounds.

Hours passed, and soon the idea of plundering across new findings slowly began to fade from the men's minds, no different than the light of the sun did upon their entry.

Amongst them now was a mutual understanding, unspoken, that they were going to call off their pursuits and head back to the camp soon since this long traversing of the cave bore no fruits to their merits… that is, until they stumbled upon a unique construction— or perhaps it was a phenomena — that made up a new shaping to walls of the tunnel.

What looked to be like a honeycomb structure, dry and decrepit, protruded off the interior of their enclosing once this deep into the cave.

It lacked any of the semi-smooth transition of the original rock that made up the cave's walls, giving the impression that it was grafted on by some form of clay and set over the tunneling's original formation.

It reminded the men of how wasps and hornets would create nests from mud in a similar manner.

"Now *this* is interesting!" said Dr. Hancock, "Just when I was beginning to lose hope!"

"These combs are huge! Certainly not made by any bug I know of" said Dr. Brown as he wedged his finger in between one of the larger cracks in the mold that gapped the cave's natural rock. He then applied an opposing force to it, causing the structure to chip off and drop in tiny flakes to the ground, "Definitely not a natural phenomena by the geological compounds of the minerals that make up this hollowed out system."

"Yes, undeniably manmade" agreed Dr. Hancock, "However, the edges and lines are impeccably straight, and all of the centers of these combs match by the same depths.

I guess I shouldn't be too impressed since man also made the pyramids, but such an organic pattern… to be this flawless… it's utterly striking."

"Question is, *why*… but when is it never, honestly?" continued Dr. Brown, "Initial impressions— I'm going to guess a religious purposes? Perhaps for worship or homage, maybe even a reflection to some principle or being? Or maybe an attempt at a temple of some sort.

Hanney, did bees or hornets, or maybe even honey, hold a strong revere amongst the tribes that used to occupy this area?

Did the villagers speak on and/or show any signs of those things still being of high value to them? Or of a great importance to their communities?" asked Dr. Brown.

"No. At least not that I've noticed or picked up on through any of the conversations I've had with them" answered Dr. Hanney, "However, building off of our earlier theories about an ostracized tribe being forgotten— it's well within reason that *they* might have.

And if driven into these caves to survive, then without question, I assume they would've created some kind of structure like this as a plea or begging to their gods for salvation.

I say we go deeper.

If such a tribe did build this, then we may find all of the answers we've been looking for further in.

There must be a heart to this structure, and if that acted as the resting place where they made their final home out of… we may have just won the bloody jackpot, boys!"

A new wave of motivation swept over the men, and without any hesitation, they made their way deeper into the tunnel that was now covered entirely by this bizarre honeycomb structure.

It wasn't easy by any means, in fact, the grafting on these walls now made it more difficult to traverse— with its uneven spacings forcing the men to duck, dip, squeeze and sometimes even wiggle their way through.

A fascinating note, however, was that the deeper they went, the more refined this structure became.

Eventually, the men found themselves able to walk normal once again, without any of the previous unnecessary struggle, as the cave and its grafted structure was now even and perfected.

"We must be getting closer to the heart of this place with how it's looking!" said Dr. Hancock, "They must've put more effort into the areas closer to where they resided or used as their house of worship.

I say we find this section of wherever they did so, and before we get too excited, head back and call it a night.

Otherwise we may lose ourselves and lose track of time altogether, and I don't know about you lot, but I'd prefer to not exit this cave into a pitch black jungle in the middle of the ni— HUEHG!"

Dr. Hancock choked on his own last words as he let out a sharp gasp in fright!

He had been looking back at his colleagues the entire time while speaking, but when he turned to face forward at the end of his sentence, a startling sight broke his train of thought.

Before him now, less than a foot away from his own face and peering out of the darkness by the revealing beam of his flashlight... was the giant head of an *ant*.

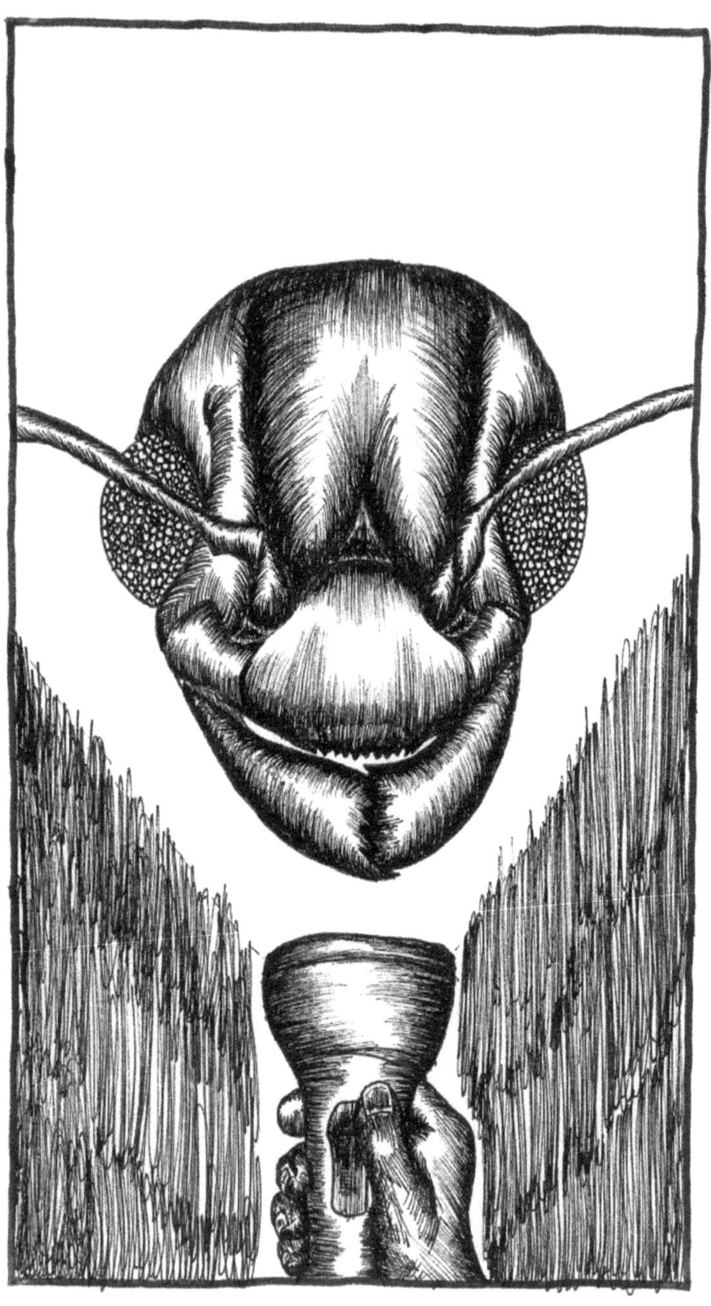

It had a sheen to its chitin as if it were subtly oily.

It had tiny hairs like bristles which protruded out from the many pores of its scalp and face.

It had large black eyes, the size of ostrich eggs, with tiny divided segments that made up its whole like a stained glass window.

And it had giant pincers and antennas, which created an intensely menacing sense of danger, invoking the deepest instinct of fear from being eaten within the men.

"What the bloody hell is that!?"

"Oh dear god… what in heaven's name…?"

"…"nothing but a grumbling sound came from the throat of Dr. Hancock, as he could not even muster up words despite his best efforts to while bearing the sight of this thing.

"It's a fucking giant insect head— an ant!" exclaimed Dr. Brown, "I've never seen one before like this, nor so perfectly preserved!

Must be from the late Carboniferous period, or perhaps during the early Permian period."

The shock and surprise of this creature's head made the men keep their lights shined in its direction and on its face… and *only* its face.

Foolishly, they thought that this head emerged from out of the wall by way of being petrified within it.

If only they could've managed and controlled their awe and shock, then maybe they would've casted their flashlights beyond its head and discover that it was in fact… not petrified into the wall at all.

It was not frozen in time nor just a floating stone head, for behind it, the tunnel continued on. And below its head was a neck, body, arms, and two legs by which it stood on.

But this realization of the abominable creature still being alive only hit them when the crackling sounds began to emit from its mouth— a source originating deep within its chest —and its antennas started flicking abruptly while its pincers waved back and forth, in and out, rhythmically and hungrily.

It was like something out of a horror film, or their deepest nightmares, or the most haunting campfire story, as the three men lowered their flashlights to reveal the rest of the creature's body.

Its body grotesquely consisted of three large, olive-shaped pods, all connected to each other like the beads of a necklace.

It had skeleton-thin appendages that resembled large twigs, which made up its arms and legs.

And the entire surface of its chitin produced trillions of little hairs and an oily sheen that served as proof to the life which still flowed through its body very much.

Before the men could turn around and run for their lives, two more of the giant ant-people emerged out of the darkness from behind them, and viciously grabbed hold of the men!

They fought and screamed for their lives, confused and filled to the brim with an overwhelming fear from this horrific play.

Dr. Brown in particular went more mad out of the bunch, his mind already collapsing from this nightmarish event, causing the ant-person restraining him to rip off the poor soul's arm to better incapacitate him.

Dr. Brown didn't even scream in pain or disbelief to this occurrence, rather, he simply dropped to his knees and held tightly onto the bleeding mound of torn flesh and exposed bone where his arm once was.

His eyes went empty like his mind, and similar to a dumb child or a moronic dog, he picked up his severed arm which lay on the ground beside him, cradling it like a purse containing valuable belongings within.

The ant-people passed some form of communication between each other through their incoherent language of crackles and rumbles, which they emitted through their pincers or reverberated through their chests, before then dragging the three men deeper into the tunnel and towards the heart of the cave.

After what felt like hours but was only mere minutes, they arrived at a colossal, hollowed-out cavern in the shape of a dome, where four more ant-people awaited them— all standing beside a boulder sized honeycomb that emerged from out of the ground like a porous pimple of imperfection.

The ant-people continued to talk to one another, even having a moment where they appeared to be arguing with each other by their strange sounds growing louder and layering over one another.

But eventually it reached a stop, and the one that had hold over Dr. Brown brought him forward to the others.

"What's going on?!" exclaimed Dr. Hancock, "What are they doing with us!? What do you want with Brown!?"

In a perfect sync like you'd expect from the ant species, the creatures took a single step forward then began to rip Dr. Brown apart.

In his broken mental state and having already disappeared to somewhere else within his own mind, Dr. Brown did not scream nor resist, but simply perished within the swift moments it took them to tear him limb from limb— along with his head taken clean off his torso.

Dr. Hanney and Dr. Hancock couldn't bear to watch their friend's demise, with Dr. Hanney even regurgitating from the sight and sound of Brown's horrific end.

Afterwards, the ant-people began to place the divided body parts— which were now of smaller portions from having been detached —into a specific hexagon pod of the giant honeycomb protrusion that sat in the center of the cavern.

One of the ant-people then produced a large pole-arm made of rock— similar to a rock version of an icicle, which forms overtime in the wet drippings of a cave after years of water eroding its pointed shape.

The ant-person then proceeded to mush the dismembered parts of Dr. Brown inside of that pod with the pole-arm, creating a thick paste out of the deadman— made apparent by the sloshing sounds of his desecrated body —before the ant-person finally ceased its pounding.

More chatting occurred between the ant-people, followed by Dr. Hancock being dragged forward and meeting the same fate.

Unlike the colleague before him, Dr. Hancock screamed the entire time with loud and agonizing pleas for mercy.

His horrible wails only stopped when his head was separated from his body.

Dr. Hanney felt the bottomless sensation of desperation hit him, and all hope being lost, as he listened to another one of his colleagues be turned into a mushy paste within that pod.

An out of body experience fell over Dr. Hanney when the ant-people made their clicks and rumbles before bringing him forward in turn.

It felt so surreal— to be confronted by this inescapable fate with a full knowledge of his doom.

He had no time to process what was going on.

No time to figure out a way to escape.

No capacity to even come close to an acceptance of these monsters' existence, the death of his friends, and the inevitable end of himself.

As Dr. Hanney was forced to stand before the other ant-people who previously dismembered his friends, as well as to stand before that grotesque boulder of a protrusion donning the honeycomb-like pattern— Dr. Hanney then noticed it and was able to make more sense of the matter.

For within that particular pod of that revolting wart-like mass of honeycomb… was a giant and slow wiggling larva.

The only one, it seemed, to still be alive amongst the other dried out husks that occupied the other empty pods.

And surrounding that last larva now, in that single pod that still held life… was the pulpy mess of his former colleagues— mushed into a fine paste like royal jelly, ready to be fed to their next and last queen.

A paste of royal jelly, which he too, would become.

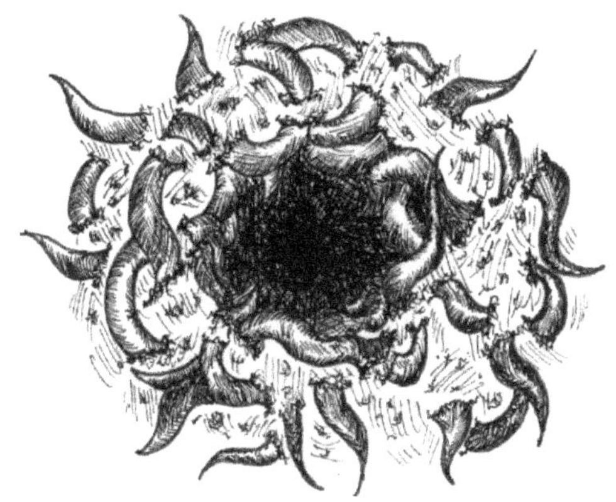

Tongues of Many Lies

"IT'S WITHIN THESE woods?" asked Ophelia, as she and the four alchemists she accompanied drew towards the edge of the tree line.

"Yes… partly" answered the alchemist with a long beard.

"It's deeper in— to be more precise" elaborated the alchemist with flaring eyebrows.

"It'll be obvious once we're close, and undeniable once we are there" said the alchemist with clouded eyes.

"It's not too long of a walk nor too far of one, but further beyond—yes. Pan's Sanctum lies within" concluded the alchemist with pointed ears.

It was only yesterday that Ophelia had met these four unique individuals, who were fairly frightening men, for the first time.

There had been whispers going around the town where she was from, though not everyone could hear them.

In a large town with many people, many brothels, and many taverns, there was always a commotion of rumors running amok.

Depending on who you were, what you were, what you knew, and where you fell in it all determined which whispers could blow upon your ears with the breeze.

Ophelia had no real family.

No mother as she most likely served in a brothel, and either sold Ophelia or tossed her aside after birth.

No father as he most likely was only a customer to her mother, and either died a pig's life or left the town long ago.

She had no real friends either, and was absent of the support from real guardians.

The saving of her as a child was not due to the realization that this innocent and abandoned infant held a precious life within. Nor was it because of a kind soul seeing the infinite potential that this baby could possibly grow into one day.

It was because Ophelia had a specific purpose and a specific value under the eyes of the man and woman who ran the ring of children. And those children's duty were to collect the whispers and rumors that floated throughout the town so that they could then sell them to the people who valued such information.

By their orders, it were the children who fished out Ophelia, and any other abandoned infants like her, from the gutters or from out of the horse troughs.

Those same children, who couldn't have been older than ten, raised her— producing the bare minimum needed to sustain a life for such a young baby.

When Ophelia was old enough, which was still extremely young, those children then taught her the doings and skills of their ways in eavesdropping
and snooping— how to collect the information needed for their masters'
blackmarket of knowledge.

This was Ophelia's life. This was what she was good at.

And along the way, while hiding under the tables of taverns, or in the closets
of brothels, or under the haystacks in barns, or under the bridges near the
fishing docks… Ophelia heard a lot more than just information. She heard
stories.

She heard tall tales. She heard praises of other lands. She heard the details
of other towns.

She heard the wonders of the great and vast oceans. The legends of the terrible monsters. The songs of the magnificent angels. The warnings of the
dangerous witches… and of course, she heard about *magick.*

Ophelia was blessed with the gift of a discernible ear at birth. She knew
not why she had this gift, or if it came from her mother or father. But more
likely, it was just a gift of her own, and Ophelia used it greatly.

Ophelia could latch onto the tone of the speaker, and just by the fluctua-
tion or cadence of their voice, know immediately if what they spoke of was
a truth or lie; a rumor or real; if they believed in it or if they had zero faith
of its authenticity.

She could tell by the way people spoke whether or not they had first hand
experience on the matter, or if they simply heard of such things by the passing of another's lips; if they were actually there when it happened or if they
never even set foot near it; if they knew the people personally or if they only
knew them by their name, face, or infamy.

Of course, this made Ophelia very valuable to her ring leaders.

They were aware of the fact that any information they received from Ophelia was correct— always guaranteed to be true by this gift of hers.

They could sell the rumors and words they collected from her at a higher price, and they never needed to worry about any retribution from the child being wrong.

Best part of all, was that Ophelia was still young enough to fit into the smaller places, and the men did not hunger over her child-like body yet.

But that would change very soon… and Ophelia was aware of this just as much as her ring leaders were.

She did not want them to put her in a brothel like her mother worked, nor did she want to continue collecting information for them.

Only *they* profited from her gift, while she still bore no clothes that were free of dirt or manure.

So, knowing she needed a way out soon before it was too late, Ophelia began to search and collect for information on her own initiative. She used her gift for her own merit, and plotted an escape from this large town she knew too well.

Ophelia began to listen to the people who spoke on specific topics, and found the little secrets she desired in doing so. She zoned in onto the murmurs and mumbles that fell softly out of these lips, the whispers about secret societies, clans of magicians, covens of witches— the things about those who knew of magick or wielded it could do, and the great power they held.

Such people were not as known by the vast majority. In fact, those whispers were quite scarce and almost rare— but they always carried the same reverence when being spoken about, and the same honoring or fearing when speaking on the 'who'-s within it.

Whoever these casters and practitioners were, whatever they did, whichever organization they were a part of— they were always *their own* masters, and sometimes, even the masters of those beneath them.

And those beneath them… were those who did not know of magick, those who were unaware of the occult secrets, those who were not initiated into the practice, and those who did not wield these unknown forces.

For that reason, Ophelia saw *this* as her way out.

To join them— those based in magick —would take her out of this town.

And to learn magick, including whatever occult secrets came with it, would set her free from any human chain.

It took quite a lot of time to gather the right information, along with a pinch of luck, before Ophelia had acquired enough knowledge to make her first move in executing this plan of hers.

And it all came to a head when she finally heard the miraculous piece of information that she had been waiting for.

By the mouths of mercenaries, those barbaric men who always knew where to find coin, Ophelia overheard them speaking on a clan of alchemists who were taking on new people for a project… or perhaps an experiment, of theirs.

Apparently they paid well, more than what those mercenaries would've received in a month's service.

However, just as Ophelia had come to learn— magick users were at the top of the food-chain, and so not even these hardened veterans of battle would partake in such an offer laid out by the alchemists.

Luckily for her though, they did consider it. And in doing so, revealed where these alchemists could be found.

After having collected years worth of knowledge about this town and its off-skirts, Ophelia knew exactly the place which they spoke of and how to reach it.

And so, she did just that.

Delivering a unique knock on the wooden door attached to some small hostelry, half a mile out from the town she was born and raised in, Ophelia awaited a meeting with the alchemists.

The door opened shortly after her knock, revealing a pitch-black interior.

Ophelia stood at its entrance, intimidated by the the darkness, but also knowing that she had no other choice… so, bravely, she took a step forward into that great unknown.

Immediately the door shut behind her, fully immersing Ophelia into this blackened abyss, as the light from behind her was now extinguished with the room's sealing.

Then, like something out of a fairytale she had heard of where the tiny creatures lure the humans into their domain, a single flame ignited just feet in front of her— illuminating the room in a majestic blue hue from its blackberry shade.

This flame revealed the contents of the room, including a table which the candle bearing the blue flame sat on in a copper candelabrum, a single chair nearest her— serving as her seat at this said table —and four grown men on the opposing side of it, who watched Ophelia with an indifference… yet still maintained a keen observation on her being.

Ophelia approached the table and sat in front of the four men, who without a doubt, were the alchemists she had overheard the mercenaries talk about.

One of the alchemists had a long white beard that was scraggly like the end of a broom.

The other alchemist had flaring eyebrows like that of a dragon's, ferocious in their upward angle.

One of the alchemists had clouded eyes like a celestial storm was trapped inside his corneas.

And the last alchemist had pointy tipped ears, which tapered elegantly like a sharp spear.

"I'm… my name is Ophelia. I'd like to learn your ways of magick" she said, taking a seat at the table.

"We are not here to teach, child" said the alchemist with clouded eyes.

"I do not wish to simply steal your ways" responded Ophelia, "I will apprentice, and go through the proper trials and rights of initiation.

I will be a good student, who listens and obeys. Who works hard in perfecting their craft and in growing their knowledge of it."

"You know what we seek in apprentices" said the alchemist with pointed ears.

"That is slightly impressive" stated the alchemist with flaring eyebrows, "If it weren't for your faint aura and the clear indications that you have never had a hand in magick, or uttered any words of our system, it would've actually been quite suspicious."

"But we have not gathered here to discuss the taking on of a pupil" intervened the alchemist with a long beard, "We are here because we are in need of assistance. Nothing more."

"Yes, I know" acknowledged Ophelia, "But no one trusts witches. No one trusts mages. No one trusts alchemists.

Though the ones who *are* aware of you do respect the power and knowledge you reserve, none would dare work for you, or even interact with you outside of hiring *you* for your abilities in their own use.

No one from the town is going to come to your call.

No one will answer it besides me.

I'm the only one who is willing to help you with whatever assistance you seek.

I also know that you are paying a lot of coin for such assistance— I do not want it.

I only ask that you take me under your wing and indulge me with your school of practice as an apprentice.

You'd never need to seek assistance again if you did, as I'd always answer.

You won't need to draw coin from your purse ever again, for it will be a part of my duty.

You'd never need to wait inside a small room, in a tiny hostelry, for towns-folk who will never come to your call, for I will always be there and ready to answer your needs.

That is my price. And you won't receive a better offer for the duration of your stay here… no matter how much longer that might be or how much more coin you put up."

"Ah! I see now" said the alchemist with clouded eyes, "How old are you, Ophelia?"

"Twelve. But I'll be thirteen in the next four moons" she answered.

"A pirate and collector of rumors. A thief of whispers. A bandit of private words. That is how you heard of us. That is why you know of magick and us, practitioners" said the alchemist with clouded eyes.

"And in the next four moons, you will advance to the whorehouse with your coming of age" added the alchemist with a long beard.

"You're aware of magick. Aware of our prestige. Aware of how we do not bend the knee to those fumbling lost sheep that is man, nor are we inhibited by their world that has been constructed by their rules" said the alchemist with pointed ears.

"You wish to join our world. To escape that undignified one you live in now, and never be bound to it again.

Now more than ever, since any pig with coin may take your sacred inno-cence in a mere four moons…

I commend your way of thought and the use of that collected knowledge you've attained to find us" said the alchemist with flared eyebrows, "She tells no lies.

We won't be receiving any more people who are willing to accept our offer, no matter how much more coin we put up.

And an apprentice can solve any future dilemmas of such things from happening again.

I'd say that her tenacity to fight for her own body before it's even in danger, the use of her positioning in life and the skills of a rumor grabber, as well as her keen ear and formidable instinct to know where magick falls into play of this world which she seeks to escape— makes her more than a worthy candidate to learn the arts of our ways."

The alchemists began to communicate amongst themselves in a low voice from behind the other side of that blue flame candle.

Despite Ophelia's skill and blessing for eavesdropping amongst even the most hushed of conversations… it did not change the fact that she didn't speak latin, and therefore, was in the dark of what was being said during their private conversation.

When the men finished their discussion, they returned their attention to Ophelia, all still indifferent in expression… except for the alchemist with flared eyebrows, who was the only one that seemed genuinely impressed by Ophelia, and now bore the faintest curve of a smile in the side of his cheek— as if he didn't want to reveal the grin of satisfaction he had in their decision.

"Very well" said the alchemist with clouded eyes, "We accept."

"You must first serve our initial purpose for being here, though, and why we sought out assistance in the first place.

And only after— should everything go well —will you be adopted into our school of practice and receive proper initiation into our ways" added the alchemist with pointed ears.

"No coin, of course" said the alchemist with a long beard, "However, you never wanted that.

From the moment you knocked on that door, you always planned on escaping that twisted town of yours and all the other ones like it, made by the same construction of man and his feeble world."

"You will be studying under my wing for the majority of your learning" said the alchemist with flared eyebrows, "I see the fire and potential within you, and I wish to set it ablaze.

Our world needs more practitioners like you, perhaps then it can rise further and beyond this stagnant state it has fallen into."

"Thank you" said Ophelia, her heart racing from both excitement and relief, "When do we start? What's the job you need assistance with, then?"

"Tomorrow morning we will set off to the destination" answered the alchemist with clouded eyes.

"There is a certain section within the woods, one which has come to be known as Pan's Sanctum" said the alchemist with flared eyebrows, "A peculiar phenomena occurs there which we have yet to understand, nor have we gained any footing in explaining it."

"The whole area is riddled with a powerful magick in the air— stronger than any place we have ever experienced" said the alchemist with a long beard.

"For this reason, we do not yet know whether it is caused by possible casters who may reside there now or have once resided there in the past.

If it is possibly caused by other beings such as the fae, spirits, or deities who might have created this impression of magick instead of human casters.

Or if it is possibly caused by the land itself which may carry this high potency of magick, held by the old and ever living power of mother nature and her mysterious ways" said the alchemist with pointed ears.

"However, we *do* know of its source and where it lies" said the alchemist with clouded eyes, "There is a specific area within Pan's Sanctum that emanates the most potent form of this magick.

It radiates it from beyond a twisted root tunnel which oozes with this magick.

We seek assistance in exploring these parts of the woods, and hopefully finding an explanation for whatever lies on the other side of that twisted root tunnel."

"Okay" agreed Ophelia, "I shall help you find these answers that you seek in those woods, and whatever secret may lie at the bottom of Pan's Sanctum."

"Be warned, child" said the alchemist with flared eyebrows, "You are not the first to assist us in this endeavor. Many have come before you, and all were lost.

I have high hopes for you and your path in our teachings, and I desire to see where you will go with it.

I do not wish for you to meet the same fate as them."

"… Did they die?" asked Ophelia.

"We do not know" admitted the alchemist with flared eyebrows, "However, we do know what the air feels like and the accompanying spacial pressure from when a soul departs its body, and we can confirm that we have never sensed anything of the sort from the previous helpers.

But still, they are gone. Lost and have never returned.

How and why, we do not know— and yet, these are the very questions we seek to have answered."

"Another word of warning, child" said the alchemist with a long beard, "The trees within Pan's Sanctum— they talk. Whisper mostly. And they can and will *lie* to you.

Do not listen to them. Ignore them in any manner you see fit.

But you must be aware of this fact and hold strong to your own truths, lest you be misled by them."

"What do they say?" asked Ophelia, "What do they lie about?"

"It varies person to person" answered the alchemist with pointed ears, "Every individual tree can speak, and so, depending on which tree you pass will determine what it will say.

Sometimes they all whisper the same message, other times they whisper specific things to a targeted person within the party.

From what we've come to learn, a majority of the time they deliver the same message for us— telling us to leave, turn back, or to not go any further.

However, after we lost some of our own brothers and sisters of the pact to Pan's Sanctum and began to take on outside assistance from those uninitiated… the woods have taken to saying some newer things than they used to.

Some rather… conflicting things."

"May I ask what they say so I may be better prepared for such words of conflict?" asked Ophelia.

"*Do not trust the alchemists!*" said the alchemist with clouded eyes, mimicking the voices of the trees, "In many different ways and in many different forms, they will deliver that very message to you and only you, not us.

Be prepared for it, and for the possible paranoia and distrust that'll arouse within your mind from so…"

That conversation was only yesterday, and now, as they all stood before the edge of the woods on the day of, Ophelia thought back onto the alchemists' words of warning. And for the first time, she felt unsettled by the idea of it.

She was too excited the day before— too relieved to be bothered by any other emotion.

But now, with the reality setting in of venturing into this unknown place called Pan's Sanctum, and the idea of hearing the trees speak and toy with her mind— especially by pinning her against the alchemists —Ophelia began to question whether she had made the right decision or not.

"Everything alright?" asked the alchemist with flared eyebrows, placing a hand of support on her shoulder.

Ophelia nodded, remembering the value of this opportunity she had seized, as this was the key to her freedom from that town, and the saving grace to not having her body taken by the dirty hands of men.

"Are you ready, then? The walk is a short one before we'll reach Pan's Sanctum" he said.

"Yes. I am" assured Ophelia.

He returned the nod to her, which was then followed by this band of four alchemists and their latest pupil, Ophelia, stepping into the woods on their quest for understanding.

It was true what the alchemist with flared eyebrows told her, for it was a short walk indeed before the ethereal whispers could be heard in the nearby distance, echoing out from the trees of their destination.

"Stay away" she could hear them say in the distance.

"Do not venture here."

"Beware."

"Foolish ones, turn away."

"Go back now."

"Halt your feet, and silence those wondering minds."

It reminded Ophelia of running water from a tiny stream, or the trickling channels of water from a fresh spring above earth, for those trees' voices gently cascaded throughout the surrounding area as they continued to draw closer to the Sanctum.

And once she and the alchemists entered onto those magical grounds, the whispers of the trees lost all of their entrancing resonance, and morphed into a creepy pestering now that they surrounded them.

"No!"

"Leave here!"

"What are you doing?"

"Why did you come here?"

"Why do you keep returning?"

"Begone, mages!"

"Oblivious warlocks!"

"Magic mongers!"

"Who is this?"

"Another!?"

"Leave, girl!"

"Foolish girl!"

"Abandon these men!"

"Return to your home!"

Ophelia oddly found familiarity within this, as it felt like walking through the town's road during a busy night of drinking and craze— only now the chattering were whispers instead, and every voice was directed at her, speaking to her, and addressing her attention.

The way the whispers would sneak up from behind her or creep over her shoulders when passing these trees made Ophelia uneasy, and to hear their calls from up ahead as they awaited her expected approach, made Ophelia wish to turn back… and successfully blossomed a hesitance in her gut.

"You know not what you do."

"You know not where you go."

"You know not what awaits you."

"Leave now while you still can!"

"Never return to this place again!"

"Why do you trust these men?"

"What did they offer you?"

"How much is coin worth for your suffering?"

"How greedy can humans be?"

"Why does greed trump intellect? How?"

"You should not trust these men, girl."

"The alchemists are not your friends."

"You are being played."

"You are being tricked!"

"Run now while you still can!"

"Escape them before it's too late!"

On top of all of these bombarding voices, was a lightheadedness which Ophelia was currently experiencing from being in such a condensed space of immense magick.

The feeling reminded her of when she was a child, and the men would sometimes catch her and her friends eavesdropping on their conversations.

The men would grab them and hold them still, while another man would blow his mouth full of smoke from tobacco into their faces.

These burly men always had such larger lung capacities than Ophelia or any of her friends, so the men would blow for what felt like an eternity, until finally she was forced to breathe in that stale smokey air.

The nicotine always made Ophelia feel dizzy and lightheaded, sometimes even nauseas.

And now, from the density of the copious amounts of magick that was concentrated into this tight area of land which she found herself crossing through, Ophelia was experiencing same effect from it.

"Run, girl! Run!"

"The idiot! The fool!"

"*Cursed are you all!*"

"*You men and your curiosity.*"

"*Despicable.*"

"*Shameful.*"

"*Oblivious creatures.*"

"*Dog-headed apes!*"

"*Poor girl.*"

"*Stupid girl!*"

"*Foolish girl.*"

"*Oblivious girl.*"

"*Why so young?*"

"*She's barely a woman.*"

"*She's still a young girl.*"

"*How sad.*"

"*How pathetic.*"

"*She must turn around.*"
"*She won't.*"

"*Poor thing.*"

"*Imbecile!*"

"*You must listen, girl.*"

"*Listen to us!*"

"*Save yourself!*"

"*Save your soul.*"

"*Save your body!*"

"*Save your mind.*"

"*Save your humanity!*"

"*Leave now and never come back!*"

"*Turn around before it's too late.*"

"*These men will betray you.*"

"*They lie!*"

"*They lied!*"

"*They're lying!*"

"How are you holding up, Ophelia?" asked the alchemist with flared eyebrows.

"I'm okay" she said, "It's not bothering me too much. I won't let them into my head. They won't get to me."

The alchemist with flared eyebrows managed that same faint smile once again, in pride this time. However, the genuine look of concern did not leave his eyes, as he did worry about Ophelia's handling of this situation.

"We approach it" said the alchemist with clouded eyes, "The source of Pan's Sanctum."

"Fools!"

"Leave now!"

"Before it's too late, girl!"

"You will not have another chance!"

"It will be too late!"

"Turn back now!"

"Run, girl!"

"Escape!"

"Live!"

"They will betray you!"

"They will hurt you!"

"They are evil!"

"They lie!"

"They lie!"

"They lie!"

"They lie!"

The alchemists and Ophelia had finally arrived upon the source of Pan's Sanctum, with the disorienting sensation reaching its climax within her, as the magick felt almost like a limitless pool from an erupting geyser— tangible to a degree that it even wafted her hair about her face.

Lying on the ground before them was a mound made of thick, twisted roots from numerous trees both visible and unseen, all intertwining to produce this cage-like netting that bore only a single opening by which the average human could fit into.

The contents within that hole were unknown and unseen by the naked eye, however, an unquenchable curiosity filled the space around it that even Ophelia was afflicted by, despite not being as immersed or as knowledgeable about this world of magick or its castings in general, compared to the accompanying alchemists.

"It's beautiful… in a way that I've never experienced nor seen something as being beautiful before in such manner" said Ophelia, "I do not know how to describe it. It has such a unique allure that I can only say it is… *beautiful.*"

"Careful, child" said the alchemist with a long beard, "This is where they have all disappeared, the brothers and sisters of our own pact, as well as every previous commoner who has assisted us for coin.

It is apparent, and quite obvious to any practitioner, that there is a magic set onto this tree root den.

It draws people in, humans for sure, though I do not know about the other creatures who might be bewitched by its lure.

Like the breasts and backside of a beautiful woman is to a man… or like four alchemists are to a homeless girl who is frightened at the idea of losing her purity… this gaping hole of Pan's Sanctum draws in those who lay their eyes on it— those who are close enough to its presence.

We know not what happens to those who enter it, where they go, where they come out, if they do go somewhere or if they even do come out.

All we know is that an immense amount of magick flows within it, and it draws that which is living and sentient into its mouth.

What's within there and what happens after one enters… we are still at a loss for."

"How long has this been here?" asked Ophelia.

"Another question we still do not know" answered the alchemist with clouded eyes, "This place is riddled with secrets and many mysteries we seek to understand.

However, it has been five years since we first heard about it, three since we've found it, two since our own brothers and sisters disappeared into its mouth, and one since we've been using the aid of commoners— with still no prevail."

"Is *that* what the trees warn of?" questioned Ophelia, "Is there some truth to their whispers? Have you been forcing those who chose to assist you to enter its mouth?"

"We never forced them to" said the alchemist with flared eyebrows, "Never once did we commit the atrocity of dismissing their freewill. We only ever asked.

And shamefully, I do admit… bribed at times with more coin that they went inside, in hopes that we could catch a glimpse of anything to help explain the phenomena that sits before us.

But we do not ask the same of you."

"Then why have we come back if we do not plan to ask the same of the girl?" questioned the alchemist with pointed ears.

"Because none of them before her were our pupil!" snapped back the alchemist with flared eyebrows, "We've lost so many brothers and sisters, and for the first time in a long time, we've gained a new one!

You'd willingly throw that away before her soul has even been initiated?"

The three other alchemists dropped their heads in realization to the truth he spoke.

"I… I can do it" said Ophelia, wanting to impress the alchemists and make a good impression on her new peers.

"No, Ophelia, you cannot—"

"But I can! If I am one of you now, then my mission should be the same— to solve and find a better understanding to this phenomena, just as you all do.

Maybe it'll be different.

Maybe I'll be able to come back. Or maybe you'll be able to find, catch, or witness a brief glimpse of something that will better explain what exactly is going on.

I'm not a child anymore.

I'm not doing this because I owe you something or because you own me.

I'm doing this because I'm one of you.

Isn't that correct?"

With pain and defeat in his eyes, the alchemist with flared eyebrows nodded in agreement to Ophelia's words, for even in this instance, the men still did not reject the purpose of freewill nor the absolution of reason and logic.

"Just… if I don't come back, if it continues to remain a mystery after I do enter… promise me you'll continue to try and solve it?

And if possible, save me if there *is* something we do not understand about it that takes me to a place where I do not belong."

"Absolutely" said the alchemist with flared eyebrows, without a moment passing between her words finishing, "You will be the first hand I pull out, before any of our previous brothers or sisters that entered, when this enigma is finally solved on our end."

"You are brave, child" said the alchemist with a long beard, "Braver than any of us."

"Truly, you *are* of our world. There is no doubt about it" said the alchemist with clouded eyes.

"I apologize…" said the alchemist with pointed ears, in a voice full of shame, "I know I have been of bitter tongue for the short duration of our interactions together… and as cruel of a paradox it is that I only now come to see how much you really are one of us by the very sacrifice which takes you away… I honor you, Ophelia."

Ophelia smiled at the kind words spoken to her, but still couldn't shake the nerves that engulfed her body now.

The warm reassuring hand of the alchemist with flared eyebrows, once again, casted its presence onto her shoulder, "Are you ready?" he asked.

Ophelia nodded, "Yes."

She approached the open mouth of the twisted tree roots that made up the source of Pan's Sanctum, and after taking a few deep breaths in an attempt to reinvigorate her confidence, she entered the hole.

It was muddy, smelt of earth and dirt, and once the twisted tree roots' opening was behind her, Ophelia could no longer see the alchemists on the other side.

It was dark yet still clearly visible by a light from an unknown source, like the twilight before the fall of dusk.

In a strange way, because not everything had immediately disappeared, and she wasn't faced with a horrendous creature or the vanishing into a foreign land, Ophelia felt slightly at peace being faced with only an ongoing tunnel inside of the earth— and a bit of her anxiety began to fade away.

The deeper she went, the smaller the tunnel became, and eventually Ophelia was required to take to all fours and crawl the rest of her way through.

And so, Ophelia began to do just that, and crawled through the narrow tunnel on her elbows and knees.

Suddenly, she felt a strong rush of the magick she had been sensing since the start of this trek fall over her like rushing water.

It made her uncomfortable.

It made her unable to see clearly as she crawled on.

It pushed her down like a weighted blanket sat heavy on her back, causing her palms and feet to sink deeper into the mud with each movement forward.

… And that is when she noticed it.

Upon lifting her arm out of the mud to continue her progressive crawl, Ophelia was confronted with the shocking sight of her arm no longer being what it once was, but instead— tapering down from her shoulder —it had slowly morphed into a tree root at her elbow pit, with its nub at where her hand once was, while tiny webs of even more roots emerged out of it.

Frightened and confused, Ophelia began to scream and wiggle her way backwards in an attempt to escape the tiny space, and hopefully return to the alchemists.

However, she only sank deeper into the ground with every movement of resistance she made, similar to being trapped in quicksand. And for every time she pulled out one of her limbs from the mud, be it her arm or leg… the body part would be further in its transition of becoming a tree root.

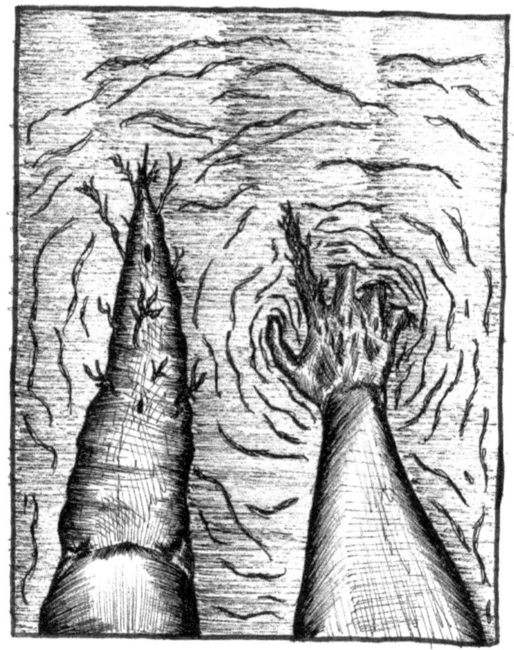

Eventually, Ophelia could not move her body in anyway or anymore at all—
with the effects having reached her shoulders —and before she could let out
one last final cry for help, she collapsed face down into the mud and slowly
sank in whole… her body completely enveloped by the earth.

"Hey. Hey! It's okay, it's okay.

I know it's confusing at first, but everything's alright. You're alive!" said a voice to
Ophelia, *"It's not dark, it's not death, you just have to open your eyes again.*

Go on, open your eyes."

Ophelia, feeling warmer than before, safer than before, and glad to no longer be alone as this voice reassured her of company, opened her eyes once
again.

It was a magnificent sight when she did, for Ophelia could now see *all* around her, not just what was in front of her. And she could also see below and above herself too, not needing to lift or drop her head to do so.

It was like she could *actually* see for the first time, as everything that surrounded her was within the full perspective of her gaze.

She was back in those woods of Pan's Sanctum, surrounded by trees.

And that's when she noticed it… she could not move, she could not turn, she had no head, for Ophelia's state of being now… was as a tree itself, though it was still completely her.

"Yes. You are a tree now" said the voice, *"That's what happens when you enter that hole. That's why the trees here can talk.*

It seems every single one of them was once a human or some other manner of being that was lured into that hole.

And we slowly add to the makeup of these woods, ever expanding it from being turned into trees."

"What? I'm still confused though" said Ophelia back, *"Why didn't you guys say anything?*

Why didn't you tell us?

Why didn't you warn us, or any of the others who trekked towards the hole?

Why haven't you explained this to the alchemists about what is really going on?"

"You are a tree of these woods now, of course we can communicate with you clearly and easily with each other" answered the voice, *"It is not the same to reach out to those who are still human like it once was when we were humans ourselves.*

The connection is different.

We can only manage a few sentences or short messages before our words become a jumbled nothingness upon their ears.

But trust me when I tell you we **try**.

And we try every time to usher away those who enter these woods so they do not meet the same fate as us."

"*So are the alchemists not actually aware of what happens?*" asked Ophelia, "*Were they lying to me about not knowing whether this was going to happen or not?*"

"*They are innocent*" admitted the voice, "*They do not know.*

Curiosity is their vice, however, as they will continue to attempt to understand what is happening here and where the people go. And they will never figure it out unless they themselves enter the hole.

More and more will be turned into trees for as long as those men continue their search for answers, and for as long as any creature enters these woods."

"*Then why did you all tell me those lies?*" asked Ophelia, "*Why did you say they were evil and wished to betray me?*"

"*Because you are not the first to be turned*" answered the voice, "*We all were.*

Most of us here were once human, a few used to be other creatures that roamed the lands of this forest.

However, since the discovery of the hole was made by those alchemists, a surge in people being turned into trees has occurred.

It's at a rapid rate now compared to what it used to be.

The woods are expanding now more than ever before.

At first, we pleaded with anyone who entered, including the alchemists, to turn back and leave.

But it did not work.

Then, some of the ones who once accompanied the alchemists suggested that we warn the people not to trust them— that by planting the seed of doubt or suspicion in their minds, it would cause at least one lucky soul to leave these woods and not end up like this.

And for some time, it actually worked! It threw away the trust of many of those humans who entered into these woods with them.

However, after some time had passed and for reasons we're unsure of, the humans began to ignore us in the same manner as the alchemists did.

Our scares and our lies would no longer change their pursuits anymore, and just like you, they entered the hole regardless of what we said."

"What of the previous alchemists who entered the hole?" asked Ophelia, *"I heard a good number of their own pack went into it before they started using the outside help from common folk."*

"Oh yes, they turned too" answered the voice, *"Only they do not speak, or rather, they choose not to.*

They are eaten by shame, guilt, regret and remorse— because their curiosity got the better of them, because their pursuits in magick have now come to an abrupt end, and because seeing their fellow brothers still naively dragging in more innocent people to meet the same fate... is an atrocious sight.

Only now do they see the bane of their previous and curious ways."

"… So this is it, then?" asked Ophelia, *"I am— **we** are to remain as trees here in these woods forever? Until we eventually die… if we even die, for there is strong magick in these woods which may never make that a possibility.*

There is no returning back to being human, and no returning back to the human world…?"

"I'm sorry, child" said the voice, *"We all saw how young you were. It pained us to see such a fruitful life thrown away so early."*

"No… no it's okay" said Ophelia, *"In a strange way, this is something I've always wanted.*

Now… I'll always remain me."

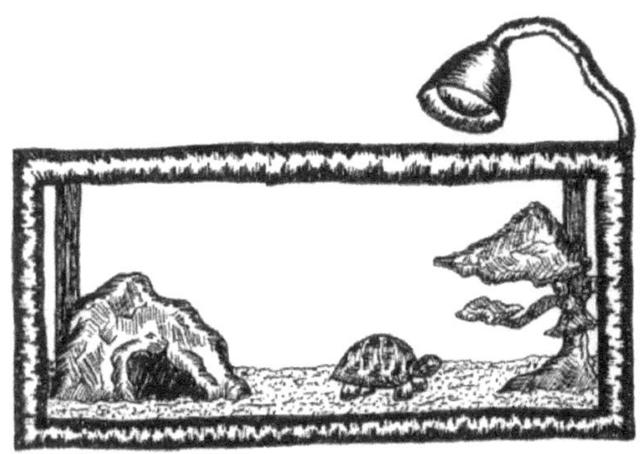

The Tortoise Told Me so

Jassim was standing barefoot in his pajamas, unsure of where he was or how he got there.

He looked down and noticed that his feet were in a thin layer of water that barely crept up the sides of his feet, with his own reflection looking back at him.

There was no way to tell if the water itself was black, or if it just reflected the black domain it sat within. And by the looks of it, inside this dark astral realm, the only two things within it were Jassim… and the giant tortoiseshell in the distance that seemed like a mountain by the way its immense size made it appear closer than it actually was.

Jassim stared at the colossal tortoiseshell, having never seen one so big in his life… and yet it seemed so real.

And even being in this strange place felt real, and in the faintest of ways, oddly familiar. But not familiar in the sense of having been there before, rather, in the way where a foreign place or country immediately feels like home, with no assimilation or adapting needed.

After admiring the giant tortoiseshell from a distance with great awe, Jassim felt an urge to journey towards it, but he never got the chance as three loud knocks echoed on its shell, followed by a furious shockwave of wind blowing past him and shaking the surrounding waters.

"Jassim? Jassim!" said his mother, Amina, at the door of his bedroom as she woke the young boy up from his dream.

Jassim turned over in bed, rubbing his eyes to look at his mother calling.

"Wake up, habibi, and get changed" said Amina, "I'm making you breakfast and then Khalti is going to pick you up after.

Remember? You'll be with her for the day.

Mama has a date. But I'll come pick you up later, before dinner, and we'll watch a movie together before bed."

The smell of shakshuka from the kitchen, along with its faint sizzling sounds, swept into Jassim's room from the short time his mother held his door open. This prompted Jassim to crawl out of bed with a giddiness and change out of his pajamas and into fresh new clothes.

He then ran out of his room and climbed up into his chair at the dining table, while his mother finished up with the shakshuka and placed its hot pan in the center of the table.

She cradled Jassim's head lovingly as he began to tear apart the warm khubz, which was still steaming hot on the inside when ripped open, and gave him a great big kiss on the cheek before he began his feast.

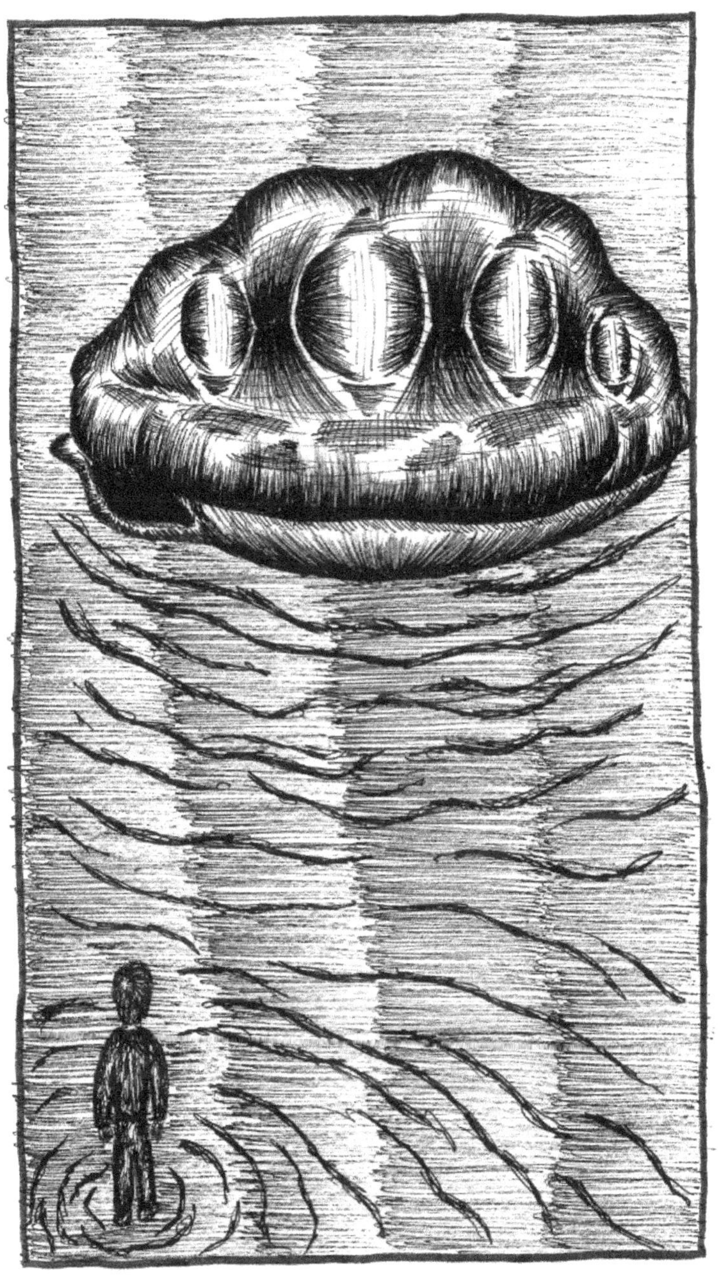

Amina didn't dig in herself right away, and instead, took a seat beside her son and watched him with loving eyes of care and affection, "Jassim, you know who Jeff is, right? And what I've told you about him?"

Jassim simply nodded while continuing to eat the piping hot shakshuka in front of him.

"Well, today I'm going on a date with him" said Amina, "We're going to get breakfast together, then go to the park and maybe even have lunch.

But Khalti is going to take care of you while I'm out, and she even told me that she's going to take you to the zoo!

What do you think about that?"

"I know" said Jassim, "You already told me this yesterday."

Amina smiled and rubbed the back of his head while he ate, "Yes. But I didn't tell you that Khalti was going to take you to the zoo, though.

Are you excited about that?"

Jassim smiled with his cheeks full of food and nodded at her.

"Now you behave and be good while with Khalti, and if she tells me you did, we'll watch one of your favorite movies when I get back before bed.

You stay and eat. I'm going to pack your backpack for you since Khalti should be here any minute, now."

It wasn't too long after that Jassim finished his breakfast and the doorbell rang at the front door.

Amina was already putting away the dishes and cleaning up the table when she told him to go get his backpack from his room since Khalti had arrived.

Jassim did just that and sprinted to his room, grabbing his backpack and putting it on while his mother answered the front door.

"Oh!" she said startled, "Hi!

Sorry, I thought you were my sister. She's picking up Jassim for the day while we go out."

A man's voice laughed, "Didn't mean to fool yah there! I was just so excited about today, that I got all dressed up and prepared early.

Still had time before our meet up, so I called and made reservations for the place I want to take you for brunch… even though it's unlikely they'd be busy at all.

And then I just found myself idly waiting for the time to pass, that I decided to hit the road and head over.

I guess I had hoped that enough time would've passed from the drive before I got here that I wouldn't have been too early."

"No! No, you're fine!" said Amina, "Oh! Well it looks like it *is* perfect timing, actually, because she's pulling up behind you right now! Jassim!"

Jassim came out of his bedroom and walked over to the door where his mother and the man both stood.

"Jassim" said Amina to her son, "This is Jeff who I've been telling you about. Say hi, Jassim."

"Hi" said Jassim, waving his hand at the man.

"Hey Jassim!" said Jeff, hunching down to his level, "I've heard so much about you from your mother. You know she really loves you, right?"

Jassim nodded in shyness, clinging to his mother's leg.

"Well don't worry" continued Jeff, "I promise that I will take good care of your mother and protect her while we're out on our date. And I promise I'll return her back to you before night, sound like a deal?"

Jassim nodded.

"Good!" Jeff ruffled Jassim's hair then stood back up.

"Okay, habibi" Amina knelt down and gave her son a long, strong hug with a kiss on the forehead, "Mama loves you. Be good and I'll be back before dinner. Love you!"

"Love you!" said Jassim in return before dashing outside and making his way to Khalti's parked car.

He let himself in and waved goodbye to his mom as Khalti pulled out of the driveway and left the two adults to their own.

The day was a good one for both parties.

Amina had a wonderful time with her date— enjoying the brunch, the park, and even had time to slip in a small lunch with Jeff before returning home and reuniting with Jassim.

Jassim did indeed go to the zoo, then spent the rest of the day playing with Khalti at her house, and even getting to play on her tablet which was something he didn't have at home.

After Khalti dropped off Jassim back at his home once his mother returned, Amina kept to her word and made dinner for them both, followed by the two getting cozy on the couch and putting on a movie to watch together before bed.

Jassim unexpectedly dozed off halfway into the film, and the moment his eyelids closed, he entered the other reality of that previous dream almost instantly— with the giant Tortoise now out of its shell and its head looming over the tiny Jassim intimidatingly.

"Woah… you're a big turtle" said Jassim, "Who are you?"

"You do not know me?" bellowed the giant Tortoise quizzically, perplexed by the boy's lack of knowledge about it.

Jassim shook his head no.

"Was it not you who knocked on my shell?" asked the giant Tortoise.

"No" answered Jassim, "But I heard it too."

The giant Tortoise then jutted out its head further and closer to Jassim in an inspection of the boy, while its immense size almost overwhelmed the child, causing him to nearly fall back.

"Hmm. You are right" said the giant Tortoise, "It was not you. Though, you do hold similarities to the one who did do it."

"Why did someone knock on your shell?" asked Jassim.

" 'Tis not a simple formality to knock on my shell, nor is it an open endeavor. This also extends to you being here, now, in my plane.

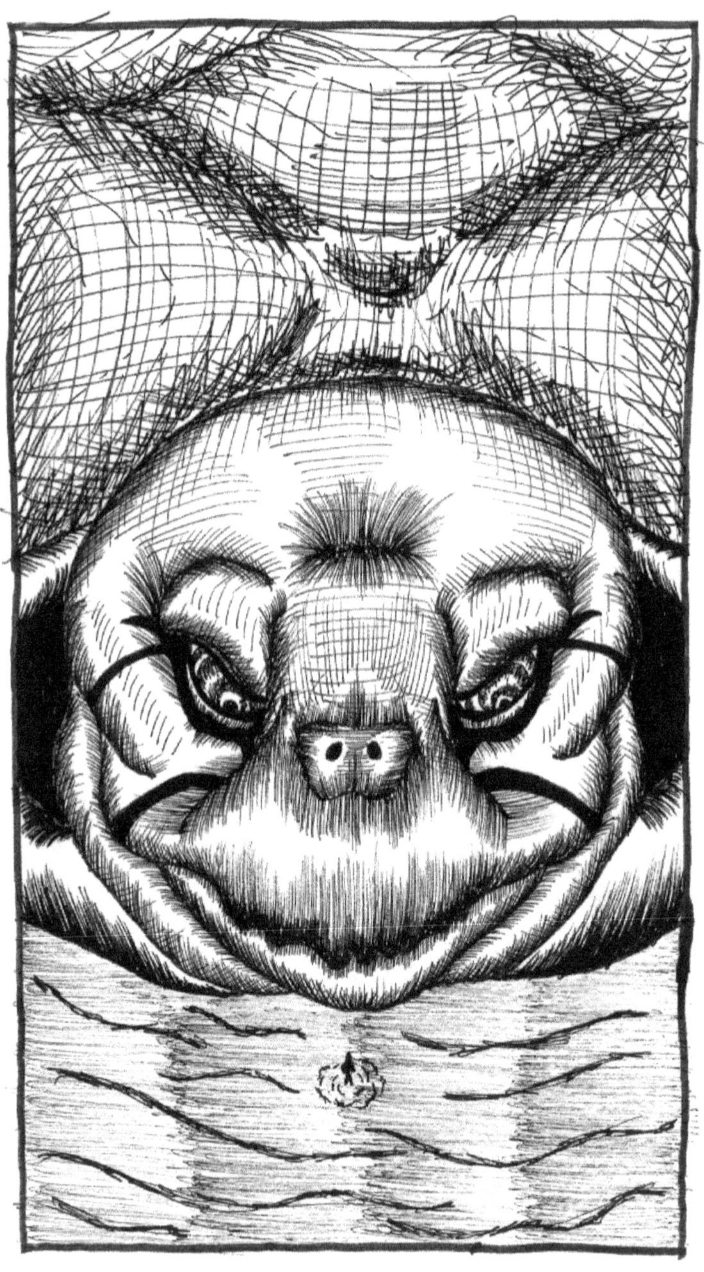

Long ago… *very* long ago, your ancestors made an oath— a covenant —with myself in regards to them and all those to come forth from their bloodline.

An allegiance was made for my protection at any time when needed, and they also believed that making such guardianship eternal was the best move forward for any future kin as well.

So, should you beckon me and call forth my awareness by knocking on my shell, then I shall answer it and keep my eyes on you— upholding my oath of protection.

However… your bloodline has since forgotten the blood-pact that was made with me over the countless years which have passed.

Usually, it is only the dead who remember me— once they have crossed onto the other side —for only then can they see clearly all that is unseen, and remember again that which has been forgotten.

I was surprised when I first saw you, and at the idea that someone so young and still alive remembered… but it would appear that someone *else* must've knocked. Yet, it is only you who stands in my domain now.

… How peculiar."

"Do you live here?" asked Jassim.

"I take rest here" answered the giant Tortoise, "I am not limited to any space within existence or beyond it, child."

"So is this a dream? Or is it real?"

"It is real. But for you and your conscious form of existence, as well as your level of self-awareness, you currently can only access this plane *through* dreaming.

Fret not though, for I do not.

The covenant made by your ancestors bleeds on through you in our blood-pact.

Henceforth, I shall keep a watchful eye on you, child, and do my duty.

I have answered the call."

Shadows enveloped the entirety of the space which Jassim and the giant Tortoise occupied, until it was nothing more than oblivion and a blank state of sleep which Jassim maintained until he awoke in the morning.

More weeks passed, and Amina went on more dates with Jeff.

After more comfort grew, more familiarity flourished, more trust was built, and a stronger sense of security was established— a development occurred.

A knock came from the front door, and this time it was without Khalti's nearby presence at the ready to take Jassim away.

Preplanned by Amina, Jeff entered the home with Jassim still there, as it was time for the two of them to spend more time with each other, rather than only the quick greeting of passing on his way out, since now her connection with Jeff was growing so well.

As Amina opened the door and Jeff stepped inside, he carried with him two things; in one arm was a box filled with packaged gummy snacks, which Amina had informed Jeff of that they were Jassim's favorite; and in his other hand was an unexpected surprise to both the mother and child, as he presented Jassim with a plastic T-rex toy.

Jassim loved it and played with the toy during the entire duration of Jeff's visit.

Jeff hung out with them for the day in their house, sometimes talking to Amina, sometimes playing with Jassim and his toys, sometimes both at the same time.

It was a wonderful visit and went even better than Amina could've hoped for, smoother than butter, in fact, and erased all of her previous worries, doubts and skepticisms about how Jassim might've negatively taken to her new love interest.

However, the giant Tortoise seemed to feel differently about the man than Amina did. And although she did not know about this being that visited Jassim in his dreams, and although Jassim himself was too young to understand the giant Tortoise in its wise ways, the being spoke its mind on the matter regardless.

"Who is the strange man that enters your home, child?" asked the giant Tortoise during Jassim's following sleep.

"Oh, that's Jeff!" answered Jassim, "Mama likes him and he likes mama.

They've gone on a bunch of dates.

He even brought me some snacks and a cool T-rex!"

"... Do you not smell it?" asked the giant Tortoise with concern.

"Smell what?" asked Jassim, confused, "The T-rex?

I haven't, but I'm sure it smells like plastic— most toys are made of it."

"No, boy" said the giant Tortoise, "The aroma surrounding the man's soul.

Are these things no longer perceptible by your kind?"

"Jeff smells clean" answered Jassim, "I can't really smell him, but sometimes when he hands me something, I can.

Mama wears perfume, but I don't know what Jeff wears."

"I do not mean the scent by which humans glamour unto their flesh for the ritual of being perceived by others" clarified the giant Tortoise, "I speak of the scent that exudes out of the pores of the soul. The scent which reveals one's true nature, even if it's disguised."

"No" answered the innocent Jassim, honestly, "I don't really know what you mean.

You talk funny a lot, but that's okay.

One of my friends at school talks funny, too. Mama said it's called a lisp.

But I don't judge my friends, so you don't need to worry about me judging you, either."

"Your purity is sweet, child, and a charitable thing" said the giant Tortoise, "However, I fear it is also a great component to your naivety.

Fret not, though, for I shall keep watch and prevent that quality of yours from becoming your downfall.

Go back to resting during this sleep, and have a peace of mind knowing that I am watching, child."

The next time Jassim interacted with Jeff again, was when the three took a trip to the zoo as another bonding method, since Jassim had loved it so much when he went with Khalti.

He would hold his mother's hand as the three of them marched by all of the animals, and on some occasions, would even be picked up by Jeff and placed onto his shoulders for a better view of the caged beasts.

It was an amazing time for Jassim, and created so many moments that are always cherished by any child.

Once the sun had been beating down on them for awhile, and their legs grew tired while their stomachs grew empty, the three decided to stop and take a break at one of the mini cafes in the zoo.

They managed to successfully grab a table in the shade, and to ensure that no one else would come and claim their spot while they were away placing their orders at the window, Amina left Jassim and Jeff alone together while she got their food— hoping it would provide a decent one on one time between the two as they held their table.

"So, Jassim" said Jeff as Amina left them, "How are you liking the zoo, so far?"

"It's fun!" responded Jassim, "I love animals, my favorite is a giraffe. What's yours?" he asked, already beginning to open up to this new man in his life.

"My favorite animal? Hmm, that's a good question" said Jeff, "Well, of all the predators in the animal kingdom… I guess I'd have to say that my favorite one is *man*."

Jassim laughed, "Humans aren't animals! You have to pick a real one."

"Oh, but humans *are* animals" said Jeff, confidently, "You don't think so?"

Jassim shook his head no. But the strange response and his difficulty understanding what Jeff was saying, happened to have reminded Jassim of the giant Tortoise, and how it also spoke in a similar confusing fashion.

Jassim then remembered it saying how Jeff smelt funny, and how the smell came from his *soul*.

Though Jassim didn't know what that meant or how it worked, he began to inhale deeply through his nostrils, intent on the words of the giant Tortoise, and hoping he could retrieve the scent which it spoke of.

And oddly enough, with no real idea of what he was doing or how he was doing it, Jassim *did* pick up on an unusual scent that he hadn't noticed before.

It smelt like a rotting tooth— a smell and phrase he was only familiar with because awhile back at the funeral, Jassim remembered how when his grandmother was crying and held him close during her moment of grief while the body was being lowered into the ground, her breath smelt really bad.

When he told his mother about this after, Amina informed him that his grandmother had rotting teeth, and that's why her breath smelt that way. She also told him that's why he should brush his teeth every night without a fuss, otherwise his teeth would become the same.

When Amina returned to the table with their trays of food, Jassim giggled and whispered in her ear that Jeff had rotting teeth like grandma.

She gasped jokingly and teased Jassim at how that was a mean thing to say, causing Jeff to notice their ruckus and join in.

"What's that? Is Jassim talking about me?" asked Jeff in a playful manner.

"Yes!" answered Amina, "And it's not good, either!"

"What did he say?" asked Jeff, looking at Jassim.

"He said your breath smells like grandma's tooth rot" she laughed.

"Wait, really?" asked Jeff with concern, beginning to cup his mouth and attempt to smell his own breath, "Does my breath smell bad?"

"No, he's just being a silly child" said Amina, "I think it's 'cause he likes you now and is no longer shy."

"Smell my breath anyway, because I brushed my teeth this morning but now I'm becoming self-conscious" said Jeff.

Jeff leaned over the table and blew his breath for Amina to take a whiff.

She took a couple sniffs then shook her head, "Crystal clear.

Jassim, we're at the zoo with many animals. You probably smelt something funny from one of them" she said.

Their day together continued on after they finished eating, and they explored a little bit more of the zoo before returning back home to watch a movie, and the exhausted Jassim went to bed early that night.

During his sleep, he met once again with the giant Tortoise, and informed it of the smell he noticed that day.

"I tried doing what you said today about smelling Jeff's soul" said Jassim, proudly.

"Were you able to notice anything?" asked the giant Tortoise.

"Yeah! It smelt bad, like grandma's rotting tooth!"

"So you *were* able to smell him, then" acknowledged the giant Tortoise, "Yes, child. *That* is the scent of that man. A foul scent, belonging to a specific evil of the worlds."

"Evil? Jeff's not evil" said Jassim, "He's really nice to me, and he's nice to mama, too.

He's the nicest man mama has ever introduced to me.

He gives me snacks, and toys, and he put me on his shoulders today at the zoo!"

"He's not evil because he's nice to you?" questioned the giant Tortoise, "Tell me, child, am I nice to you?"

Jassim nodded.

"Now" proclaimed the giant Tortoise while rising from its belly— its shell lifting off the ground with its legs out, standing at the full towering height of its gargantuan size, and looking down at Jassim as if he were a measly little bug, "Would you say that I am dangerous?" it asked.

Jassim nodded again, intimidated by the giant Tortoise's new state of being.

The giant Tortoise then slowly retracted its legs back into its shell, and returned to resting its belly on the ground, "You see?" it asked, "Just because one is nice… does not mean one is not dangerous.

Tread carefully with this man, child. And beware the gifts and kindness he offers you.

That scent you smelled on him does not lie, rather, it exposes him for what he truly is.

Do **not** take any more gifts from him."

And with that, the dream returned to an utter pitch-blackness, and Jassim continued his restful sleep.

As daylight crept gently across the face of Jassim, he awoke from the sounds of sizzles coming from the kitchen— far earlier than he'd usually expect, as Amina never woke this early, let alone to begin cooking breakfast.

The curious child climbed out of bed, and while still in pajamas, exited his room and made his way into the kitchen to investigate.

Jassim was surprised to see that it was Jeff, still in his home this early in the morning, also wearing pajamas as though he had spent the night.

Jeff was yawning while the contents in the cooking pan popped and sizzled, releasing their very attractive aroma into the air.

"What are you making?" asked Jassim.

Jeff jumped at the question, having been unaware of Jassim's presence until just now and startled by his voice.

"Oh! Jassim!" said Jeff, "You scared me, there!

You're asking about this?" he said, giving the pan a couple of dramatic circles over the stove, "It's bacon."

"Bacon?" asked Jassim, surprised, "You can eat bacon?

… Mama and I aren't allowed to" he said.

"Yeah, I know" responded Jeff, "That's why I'm cooking it now.

Your mom said it was okay if I made some for myself as long as I did it while you were still asleep so you didn't get confused… but I guess that's too late now, huh?"

Jeff ripped off a sheet of the paper towel from the roll beside him, then, using the tongs, picked out a perfectly cooked piece of bacon from the pan and placed it in the paper towel.

He went on to dab out the excessive grease and blow on it to cool it down some more.

Then, Jeff knelt down to Jassim's level and held out the piece of bacon towards the child.

"Are you curious about it?" he asked Jassim.

Jassim nodded.

"Do you like the way it smells?"

Jassim nodded.

"Do you think it smells good?"

Jassim nodded.

"Do you think it tastes good, too?"

Jassim nodded.

"Well… if you want, you can have a little bite" said Jeff, "It's not going to hurt you, and it won't hurt your mom, either.

I won't tell anyone if you don't, but you have to promise me that you're not gonna tell anyone.

It'll be our little secret. How does that sound?"

Jassim thought about it for a moment.

He was curious, like any child would be, about the things that were prohibited by their parents— not to mention that the bacon did indeed smell really good to him.

But Jassim remembered what the giant Tortoise had told him, and how he shouldn't accept any more gifts from Jeff, no matter how nice he was to him.

"No… I'm okay" said Jassim, "Thank you, though."

Jeff's face changed in an odd way to Jassim's rejection as he stood back up.

"Oh? So you're a good boy then, huh?" remarked Jeff, "Don't want to do anything naughty?

That's okay, I won't force you, Jassim.

Just remember that you can trust me, and if you ever change your mind, we can always keep it a secret" he said with a weird smile.

Jassim felt embarrassed for rejecting Jeff's offer, and ran back to his bedroom, quickly hiding himself under the covers as if to escape the feeling, then eventually fell back asleep.

Jassim took to talking to the giant Tortoise more causally and comfortably after that, since experiencing that situation with Jeff proved to him that the big creature was right.

When mentioning this incident that occurred with the bacon, the giant Tortoise stated, "That is how you know he is a bad man.

That is how you can tell he wishes to *take* from you.

For your refraining from the eating of pork is of a religious virtue… one that embodies the covenant between you and another god, in fact.

Despite your allegiance to me by the blood of your ancestors and the heritage of your birth, I do not challenge this nor try to convince you otherwise— nor did I ignore the knock or banish you from my domain for it.

When you grow older and can understand more, including yourself and the current religion you partake in, as well as my own existence, *then* you may make such choices and decisions regarding your faith and who you wish to worship by your own volition.

This evil man, however, sought to take that from you.

To trick you.

To fool you into betraying yourself.

To manipulate you against your own mother.

Beware that man, child, for he is evil.”

Jeff started sleeping over at Jassim's house more frequently as time went on.

He would be there when Jassim was put to bed, and still be there in the mornings when the child awoke.

This is when things began to become more weird between Jassim and Jeff.

For when Jassim would be asleep and conversing with the giant Tortoise at night, the powerful creature would tell him to wake up, and to do it now, for the evil man is watching him.

And whenever Jassim awoke in the middle of the night by the giant Tortoise's warning, he would see the dark silhouette of Jeff standing at his doorway… watching him sleep, and only leaving after he awoke or sat up in bed.

Sometimes Jeff would even be inside of his room, halfway between the door and his bed.

Whenever Jeff was this close, he would always put a hushing finger over his own lips as he slowly walked backwards out of his room.

After a month or so with Jeff repeatedly spending the night, Jassim had yet another dream with the giant Tortoise.

They were speaking about the giant Tortoise itself, but with Jassim being only a child, he just sat there in that thin black water and listened to the powerful being tell its stories with wide eyes of wonder.

He was enjoying every moment of it, grasping onto and riding every word that the giant Tortoise spoke… that is, until the giant Tortoise stopped mid story abruptly, its eyes widening open in a deranged look, and an overwhelming sensation of omnipotent power began to radiate out of its essence in a malevolent way.

It looked down at the tiny Jassim, its eyes still wide and crazed, and when it spoke to him, its voice held an authority which Jassim had never experienced from the giant Tortoise before.

It both scared him and forced a cower within, not because he was a child, but because of the raw power that was beheld by this being's new state of barely tamed rage.

"CHILD! WAKE UP NOW!" It roared.

"What?" asked Jassim, timidly.

"DO NOT ASK QUESTIONS! AWAKE FROM YOUR SLUMBER THIS INSTANT!

DO NOT STALL ANY LONGER! YOU HAVE FEWER SECONDS THE MORE WE SPEAK!"

"I don't understa—"

"SCREAM, CHILD! OPEN YOUR EYES AND SCREAM!

IF YOU DON'T AWAKE NOW AND SCREAM LOUDLY WHEN YOU DO, HE WILL COVER YOUR MOUTH SO YOU NEVER HAVE THE CHANCE!

NOW **SCREAM!**"

Those last words from the giant Tortoise were so loud and powerful, that they plunged with an incomprehensible force into Jassim's chest— straight into his soul —that the child was blasted out of the domain and out of the realm of dreams entirely, slingshotting back into the consciousness of his waking body while releasing that very same ear-popping scream in the real world that he was back in now.

It was then that he saw Jeff, who was standing over his bed— now frozen in surprise and panic by Jassim's waking scream —with his hand mere inches away from Jassim's mouth before it was stopped in it track by the startling shriek let out by the little boy.

"Jassim!?" yelled Amina from her bedroom.

The sound of her bedroom door could be heard as it furiously swung open and slammed against the doorstopper, followed by her stomping feet against the ground in a frenzied sprint towards her child's cry.

Jeff immediately dropped everything he was holding as he took off in his own sprint out of Jassim's room, and out of their house altogether.

Amina entered Jassim's room and turned on the light switch before dashing over to her child and cradling him in her arms.

As she soothed the confused and terrified child, she was able to see the scattered items of duct tape, a rope, a kitchen knife, and a bottle of lotion that was left on the bedroom floor from Jeff's scurried escape.

The cops were called, as well as Khalti.

Jassim went with Khalti for the night and slept over at her place while his mother talked to the police and gave statements about the whole incident, as well as descriptions and all the information she had on Jeff.

Jassim found it hard to sleep for the rest of that night, as the phone would constantly ring and his Khalti would pick it up to talk to his mother, who was hysterical, in disbelief, and utter distress about the whole incident and havoc that had just occurred.

Though he did not understand most of the words and their meanings, Jassim did notice a theme of repeated terms used by Khalti when responding to his mother's phone calls, such as "Pedophile", "Rapist", "Closeted killer", "Psychopath", "Predator", "Pervert", and "Sick man"— alongside a bunch of comforting words and things said to help Amina cope with it all.

Jassim was eventually able to fall back asleep for the night, though it was short lived since morning was already only a couple hours away.

However, he still got to see the giant Tortoise in that brief lapse of sleep.

The giant Tortoise was no longer big eyed or angry. It seemed to be back in its original state of a calm and stoic power.

"I am glad to see that you are okay" said the giant Tortoise, "It would appear that the evil man is out of your life for good, now.

However, I am not done with him yet. You may go on living without ever giving him a second thought— for I shall take care of the rest."

"Thank you for waking me" said Jassim, "It turns out Jeff was a really bad man, and apparently he was going to do bad things to me and mama from what I heard Khalti say."

"Yes" said the giant Tortoise, "He was.

But I honor our blood-pact, and my protection shall always fall over you, child.

I'm sending you one of my own children now, and your union with them will occur shortly.

This way, I can keep a closer eye on you and better watch your safety from here on out.

Though you were able to escape untouched from the near danger— the unthinkable outcome was too close to happening for my preference.

With my child at your side, such happenings shall never occur again."

Jassim was then broken out of his sleep by Khalti, who was picking him up off of the makeshift bed she had made for him on the couch.

She then took Jassim outside to Amina's car as she pulled up in the drive-way— the morning still early and fresh with all the madness that had rolled over.

"Hey habibi!" said Amina while trying to hold back her tears. She leaned over the center console and planted the biggest kiss she had ever given Jassim on his forehead, "We're going home now.

Everything has been taken care of and it's safe now."

She put the car in drive and pulled out onto the road.

"I uh…" she sniffled and wiped the bottom of her runny nose, "I got you a little surprise! It's a gift waiting for you at home.

I already set it up in your room, which is why I took so long to come get you.

But I promise you I won't ever leave your side again, okay?"

When they arrived back home, Amina hugged Jassim tightly before unbuck-ling his seatbelt, and gave him another warm kiss before carrying the sleepy child inside.

She brought Jassim to his room, where she then lowered him onto his own two feet to reveal the newest addition to his bedroom which she had spoken of as his surprise.

Placed against the wall, right beside his bed, was a little tank. And inside of it… was a tiny baby tortoise.

"I thought a new pet would be a nice edition to our home instead of all these men I've brought in" said Amina, "I've also already named him, but I don't think you'll be too mad about it.

His name is Azad— after your baba.

That way, hopefully, he can always watch over you from the other side, and protect you from the evilness in this world.

I love you, habibi."

After Hours

"No, I think 1:00am would be safer— shut up! Shut up!"

The classmates quickly halted their conversation and pretended to be busy doing schoolwork in their books as Mr. Bishop walked by them.

He maintained a slow gait as he passed them, performing rounds around the classroom as they all waited for the dismal bell to ring and set them free.

"Okay, we need to set this up NOW!" said Tianna, "If a teacher overhears us, we can get in serious trouble for this. Suspended, even!"

"We can't get suspended for simply *talking* about something if we never do it" challenged Sean, "Maybe detention, but even that's a strong maybe."

"Fuck yes we can! Especially if it's Mr. Bishop who hears us" countered Britt, "He's fucking anal about everything! I'm surprised he didn't grab one of our papers just now to see if we were actually working."

"Alright, well then let's just stick to what I said" declared Aaron, almost frustrated, "We all sneak out tonight, at like, 12:30am.

Me and Britt have cars, so everybody else will head to the park and we'll come pick you guys up.

Then, we all head back here to the school together by 1:00am.

Sean will take the keys from his mom, and with them, we'll be able to let ourselves in.

We don't have to worry about being caught by a janitor or some other bullshit, because nobody will be on the school grounds past 1:00am, guaranteed."

"Yes! We've had that all figured out now for the last three classes!" said Tianna, "The whole reason we're even going over it again, is because Erikah still doesn't know if she's in or not.

So, Erikah, are you down?"

Erikah was on the fence about the matter.

She liked her friends, she liked having fun with them, and although they tended to get more wild than she ever did, or took pleasure in the havoc of parties and not doing what they were supposed to do, Erikah was usually able to keep up with them.

If they wanted to throw a large party and go berserk, she'd help them set it up just as long as it wasn't at her house. She'd help them sneak the alcohol in or out of the house, but would never attempt to buy it herself. She'd drink and have fun during the parties, but would never reach the degree to where she'd lose all coherence and blackout. She'd cover for all their stories to their parents or other nosey adults, but would never lie to her own family about what had actually happened.

However, this was different.

This was undoubtedly illegal, in a way where they wouldn't just get a slap on the wrist if they were caught, but actually arrested.

If she was honest to her parents about what was going to occur tonight—which she usually had no problem disclosing —they would immediately put a stop to it and inform the other parents about it.

This night in particular wasn't something for the books or for the bragging rights of a crazy story. It would have to be kept hush and only between them, a simple memory to be cherished as one of those insane things Erikah did in her younger days while back in high school.

She wasn't like the rest of her friends who believed lifetime moments could trump consequences, as she actually put thought into the outcome of if they *were* to fuck up and actually get in trouble.

But alas, Erikah was still one who liked being able to engage in these types of things.

She had jumped around from different crowds and cliques all throughout her four years of high school, and since she had joined up with these four peers, Erikah actually experienced some of the most fun, funny, and memorable moments of her life.

"Erikah? We need an answer, now" said Sean, "The bell's about to ring at any moment, and we won't be texting you later if you change your mind, since we can't have any trace of this having ever been planned or happening.

So, are you in?" he asked.

The red hand of the classroom's clock was nearing the vertical point of 12:00, and after which, the bell would ring and her choice would be final.

All eyes were on her, and from the crushing weight of peer pressure, Erikah spewed out the word, "Yes."

"Fuck yeah!" exclaimed Britt, just as the school's bell sounded— announcing the end of their day.

"Alright, don't forget" said Aaron, "Sneak out at 12:30am. Meet up at the park. Then we'll head back here during after hours at 1:00am."

Everyone nodded in agreement as they packed their backpacks and left the classroom.

"See you all then" said Tianna, marking their temporary departure of separate ways.

It wasn't hard for Erikah to sneak out of her house that night. In actuality, it wasn't hard for her to sneak out at all.

The trust she had formed between herself and her parents was built on the notion of, *"We know you're young, and we don't care if you go out and party. We just want to know if you do and when you go, and to call us if no one can drive instead of doing something stupid."*

So, it wasn't ever expected of Erikah to sneak out, because it was never a necessary action to be taken. She would always tell her parents, and they'd always be fine with it.

But tonight was different, and from a simple climb over her bedroom window, Erikah was out.

Without running, trying to keep quiet, or looking over her shoulder, Erikah casually waltzed her way to the park after that, only keeping an eye out for creeps, strangers, or weird men who might've been prowling about the night, as opposed to the headlights or scurrying feet of her parents trying to catch her.

When Erikah reached the park, Tianna and Sean were already there and waiting on the swing set.

"There she is!" said Sean, nudging Tianna with his elbow, "You bring a swimsuit?" he asked, as Erikah joined them by sitting on one of the empty swing seats.

"I'm wearing it now— under the hoodie and sweats" answered Erikah.

"Same" said Tianna, "But I should've worn sweats, instead. It's freezing out here!"

"I mean, those technically are sweats, they're just sweat shorts" commented Sean.

"Yeah, but that's just the material" said Tianna, "Actual sweatpants cover your whole legs.

What about you? You're wearing shorts too, aren't you cold?" she asked.

Sean slapped the tops of his thighs, "These aren't shorts— these are swim trunks!

And no, I don't get cold that easy. It's about to be summer, dude, it's not even that chilly out."

"Hey" interrupted Erikah, "I think that's them pulling up."

Two sets of headlights spun around the park before flashing their brights at the group on the swing set.

"Yup" confirmed Sean, "They have arrived. Let's hit it!"

The three of them quickly got up and then jogged over to their friends' vehicles.

Sean rode with Aaron, while Tianna and Erikah rode with Britt.

It was less than a fifteen minute drive for them before they reached the school, since no other cars were out this late and the roads were completely clear.

Once they arrived on the school grounds, they drove around to the back of the building and discretely parked their cars next to each other.

As they got out of their vehicles and headed to the back entrance of their high school, Sean fished out the keys to the school from his hoodie's front pocket and let them in.

"What would your mom do if she found out that you not only took her car this late, but also her keys to the school?" asked Aaron.

"I got a 3.9 GPA, dude" answered Sean, "*If* she even woke up this late and noticed that they were gone, then I'd tell her that I left something at the school and went to go get it to bring my grade up to a 4.0 before college."

"Why would she even believe that?" asked Britt, "You've already applied to colleges, been accepted, and committed to an offer. That literally makes no sense."

"It doesn't need to make sense" said Sean, "It just needs to be something she wants to hear.

How the fuck do *you* get away with this shit all the time if you can't even understand that simple concept?"

"Because I cry and put on a show of apologies and tears until my parents buy it" answered Britt with zero shame.

"Well we're all pretty fucked if we get caught now, so let's not think about what's the best way for getting out of trouble, and just focus on never getting caught in the first place" said Aaron.

"Yeah, cops won't give a shit about our tears or our GPA's" said Erikah, "And neither will any of the colleges once the news gets passed on to them."

"Fuck… now you're making me think this was a bad idea" said Sean, beginning to fill with apprehension for the first time.

"It is a bad idea" said Britt, "But it's one for the books and we're already here.

We literally committed breaking and entering the moment we stepped foot inside our high school while it was closed and locked, so it's still the same whether we go into the pools or leave this instant."

Britt was right, and they all knew it. So they continued on.

When they reached the locker rooms, Sean used the keys once again and let them in.

They headed through it and straight towards the swimming section on the other side— pushing open the swinging doors to reveal the giant pool with three different heights of diving boards, along with the strong smell of chlorine and the echoing sounds of their voices bouncing off the walls.

Everyone then stood at the edge of the pool and began to strip off their outer layers, revealing their hidden swimsuits underneath, before either jumping, shoving, tackling, or pulling each other into the water.

It seemed like the water washed away all of the previous fears or paranoia that the group had built up at the idea of being either caught or getting into trouble. And now, they simply filled the swimming room with their loud echoes of scrambling voices, laughs, shrieks, banter, and yells.

It was so fun, so free— the pinnacle of being young and taking that final leap of excitement before graduation.

Even Erikah was glad that she had made this choice and said 'yes' to this little adventure of theirs, as the rush and pleasures of breaking the rules thrilled her immensely while sharing these moments with her friends.

… Or so she thought it was only herself and her friends in that swim room.

For when she was throwing her head back in an attempt to dodge the splashes from Tianna, Erikah noticed a figure who stood atop the lead dive board, watching them all from above.

She wiped her eyes of the excess water to get a clearer view on what didn't seem right at first, and was then able to perceive what looked like some boy around their age, who was also wearing a swimsuit, motionlessly observing their group.

It was too dark in the swim room to see any details, as they had never turned on the lights from the worry of it possibly attracting the attention of a driver passing by and calling the cops— so the figure remained only a shadowy outline to her.

Before Erikah could attempt to focus her gaze in and perhaps catch a glimpse of the boy's face, large spurts of water splashed against her own, forcing her eyes shut by reflex.

"Hey! Where's your head at, girl?" asked Aaron while obnoxiously splashing her for attention.

"Did any of you guys see that?" asked Erikah, a bit freaked out.

From being teens, being in the dark, having seen enough horror movies, and having already been filled with a bit of paranoia earlier, all four friends within the pool stopped what they were doing and looked over to Erikah from the daunting sentence she had just asked.

They knew Erikah very well. She was not a liar, she was not dramatic, she was not a prankster, and she was not a jumpy person. So there was no teasing, banter, denial, or invalidation thrown towards Erikah by the others against her statement.

Instead, they all took it serious, which gave rise to a fear and a rebirth to the previous paranoia.

"See what?" asked Sean.

"Up there, on the top dive board" said Erikah, "There's a fucking guy— or at least there was a guy up there."

"There's somebody else here!?" exclaimed Tianna.

"What fucking guy?" asked Britt, "What did he look like?"

"I don't know, it's too dark in here to see his face. But he looked our age and is in a swimsuit" answered Erikah.

"Someone from our school?" asked Aaron.

"I don't fucking know!" repeated Erikah, "All I do know is that there's someone else fucking here with us, also in a swimsuit, who was watching us this whole time for who knows how long!"

"Think someone overheard us in Mr. Bishop's class and followed us here?" asked Aaron to Sean.

"Maybe, that would make sense if they're in a swimsuit" responded Sean, "No one else could've gotten inside the school without keys, and only we would bring swimsuits because we planned on getting in the pool."

"Fuck! Okay, everyone out of the water, now!" ordered Aaron, "We have to find this guy and make sure he doesn't tell anyone about tonight."

"You're not going to hurt him, are you?" asked Britt.

"No!" said Aaron, almost insulted, "I'm going to find out what the fuck he wants and let him know that if he tells anyone about this, then he's in as much deep shit as we are.

He's committed breaking and entering too, just as much as we have, by being here. We have to make sure he's aware of that so he doesn't do or say anything stupid about tonight."

The group all nodded in agreement and started to swim from the center of the pool to its outskirts to climb out.

However, mere seconds later, a loud splash and thump sounded from the breaking of water behind them, just feet away from themselves as someone had jumped into the water from the diving board.

The group of friends went into a craze from the surprise, and let out a flurry of various screams, including "Oh shit!", "What the fuck!", and "He's in the water!"

They swam as fast as they could to the outskirts of the pool, attempting to get out of it while this unknown and unseen person was swimming furiously towards them— the water splashing chaotically from his speedy approach.

Two managed to get out in time, while the other two were in the mid process of climbing out.

But to Erikah's horror, who was far behind everyone else… felt the grasp of strong hands take hold of her body, stopping her dead in her tracks from escaping the pool, before being viscously manhandled then pulled under the water.

She couldn't breathe, she couldn't see anything, she couldn't even think straight.

Erikah fought furiously, though she didn't know where to swing or if it did any good to help her, as her punches were slowed underwater.

The positioning of the hands which attempted to drown her changed numerously.

At one point, they were pushing down on her shoulders. At another point, they were holding onto her torso and using their own bodyweight to keep her submerged. And at another point, they were locked onto her ankles— aggressively pulling her down to the bottom.

There was a specific moment in time where Erikah felt the urge to breathe again amidst all the chaos, and was reminded of the simple fact which she had forgotten from all the struggle, fear, and disbelief of drowning… that it happens because you no longer have oxygen.

From this natural desire to breathe again, Erikah began to fight more with her own body than she did the mysterious boy— struggling to tame this urge of taking a breath, since all that would happen would be an inhaling of water.

But her body did not know this like her mind did, and so these two warring aspects within her produced hiccup-like convulsions, as nature and instinct battled against will and awareness.

But when she could no longer bear the urge, Erikah finally opened her mouth and gasped— filling her lungs with pure, heavy dense water.

A mix of gagging while simultaneously inhaling more water began to take place, and for the first time since she was pulled underwater, Erikah felt the release of the mysterious boy's grip, followed by a burning sensation on her scalp.

She still had no idea what was going on until she breached the surface of the water and was dragged out by Sean and Aaron, who had pulled her up from the bottom of the pool by her hair, while Tianna and Britt helped them drag her out onto the pool deck.

Erikah began regurgitating up all the water she had swallowed, followed by harsh coughing to expel the residue from the cilia in her throat and lungs.

She wasn't allowed much time to do this, however, as Sean and Aaron put her arms around their shoulders and rushed themselves out of the pool room, alongside Tianna and Britt— booking it straight out of the school and then into their cars, still wet and leaving no time to dry off or lock back up the school grounds.

They floored it out of the parking lot and off the school's campus altogether, before returning to a normal speed to avoid any patrolling cops from pulling them over and asking questions.

Once they returned to the park where they had initially met up at, they parked their cars right beside each other and exited their vehicles, beginning a frenzied recap about what had just happened while also checking in on Erikah to see if she was alright.

"Are you okay?"

"Who was that!?"

"What the fuck just happened!?"

"Did that motherfucker try to drown you?"

"I'm going to kill whoever the fuck that was!"

"Do you think it was someone from our class or lower?"

"Has to be ours if they overheard us in Mr. Bishop's."

"No, there are some juniors in that class too."

"Does it fucking matter?"

"Erikah, he tried to kill you!"

"Do we go to the police?"

"No! We'll be fucking ourselves over if we do!"

"Then what do we do about the fact someone just tried to **drown** Erikah!"

"He could've fucking killed her!"

"He almost did!"

"They won't be able to find him, no one knows what the fucking dude looks like!"

"He's right. They'll just take a statement, maybe try to look for him, but definitely arrest us…"

"Oh my god, I can't believe this is happening."

"*This*!? I can't believe what just *did* happen! What *almost* happened!"

"Erikah… are you okay?"

"Say something, please…"

During their mess of shouts, reasonings, and argues, Erikah had remained silent the entire time, staring off into the distance or at the ground— completely dazed and in her own world as she dissociated from everything else around her while attempting to understand what had just happened, and to cope with her near death.

"What?" she asked, finally coming to, and for the first time since they arrived back at the park, looking at her friends.

"Are you okay? Do you think you need to go to the hospital?"

"No. No, I'm alright" said Erikah, "I think I just need to get back home… maybe sleep. I don't know."

"Okay, I'll take you home right now then, Erikah" said Britt, "Tianna, I know it's a longer drive this way, but I'll drop you off after."

"No that's fine. Let's get Erikah home first" agreed Tianna.

They all said their goodbyes and agreed to play hooky the next day or call in sick from school, so they could meet up and talk more about the matter tomorrow, before getting into their vehicles and driving away.

When Britt pulled up to Erikah's house, her and Tianna gave Erikah a few more words of comfort and reassurance, but left the heart of their talk for the next day since they could see how traumatized Erikah was from the whole event.

She said her goodbyes and told them not to wait until she got inside because she would be entering through the front door, and didn't want them to get caught.

They agreed and drove away, while Erikah walked up the porch and rang the doorbell to her home.

It took three more rings of the doorbell and two times of knocking before Erikah's mother opened the door to find her daughter soaking wet on the other side of it.

She was surprised by the sight, shocked by the realization, then extremely furious to say the least— starting the beginning of a long rant as her daughter entered inside.

"Erikah Marie Johnson! Do you have any idea what fucking time it is?

What were you doing out this late and **why** are you soaking wet!? I can't believe you!

Sneaking out? Really!?

The amount of trust your father and I put in you by allowing you to go to parties and *not* have any reason to sneak out— we do this so you can have freedom and **not** resort to such things.

And yet you go out on a school night, behind our backs, without even at least telling us?

What's the whole point of us giving you that freedom and giving you our trust if *this* is what you're going to do, anyway!?

… Erikah?"

It was then that Erikah's mother noticed the catatonic state of her daughter, as well as her shivering from having been wet and only sparsely dried by the cold air from previously standing outside.

"Hey… hey it's okay" said her mother, now comforting and soothing her daughter, "Everything's alright now.

Are you okay? Are you hurt? Did something happen?"

Erikah mumbled that she was okay, to which her mother grabbed a towel, fresh clothes, and a blanket to help warm her up.

She put on a fresh pot of coffee, and helped her daughter dry off and change into the new set of sweats as the coffee brewed.

After which, she sat her daughter down on the couch and wrapped her in the blankets, warming Erikah with the coffee and her own body as she cuddled her daughter.

Once Erikah was all warmed up after some time had passed and from drinking half of the coffee in her mug, Erikah went on to tell her mother about all that happened— the reason why she snuck out and didn't initially inform her of it, the meeting up at the park, the swimming in the school's pool, the spotting of the unknown boy on the diving board, him having almost drowned her, her friends saving her from almost dying —all of it.

Once she finished her story, she was finally able to look her mother in the eyes for the first time… and noticed that her mother's face was flushed of all the blood, absolutely pale, as if she'd seen a ghost.

When she asked her mother what was wrong, her mother placed a hand over hers then informed Erikah of her own tale.

"Erikah…" began her mother, "Back when I was in high school, the same one you go to now, the same one where I first met your father… there was an incident.

And this incident is the whole reason why your father and I told you to never worry about popularity, or the opinions of others, or the weight of your peers ever falling heavy onto you.

It's also the same reason for why your father and I wanted to allow you to be able to go out and have fun, to make friends, and to do the things kids your age do.

… But back when I attended that school, there was this boy by the name of Reece McKlorn.

He was a year below us, a sophomore when your father and I were Juniors.

We didn't know him— no one in our class did. But apparently, amongst the other sophomores, he was an outcast.

He wasn't popular, he had no friends, and he didn't have a good family life back home either.

… He was just sad and alone.

Well, near the summer, the seniors in the grade above us pulled their senior-prank, which was by dying the pool red because of our school colors.

Even though it sounded like a harmless prank and one which embodied the school spirit, it turned out it wasn't, and was also extremely expensive.

The school had to drain out the entire pool to get rid of all the dye and return it to its normal color.

Well, during that short period of time when the pool was completely empty… Reece had reached his limit.

And so, when no one was there, during after hours… he entered the swim room alone, climbed to the top of the lead diving board, and…"

She swallowed uncomfortably, needing to go no further with her story to deliver the message to her daughter.

And she didn't need to go any further to also explain why she had turned so pale at her daughter's story, nor questioned Erikah more about the boy or who it might've been that tried to drown her.

It was all understood, from mother to daughter, what exactly was being implied and what exactly occurred that night with Erikah.

"Let's stay up" said her mother, lightening the mood in a supportive manner, "Let's watch some movies, finish that pot of coffee, and maybe fall asleep on the couch if we get tired.

Your friends can hangout here tomorrow when you all take your day off from school.

Your father is still out of town for work until the weekend, so it should be alright.

We can talk things over with them too when they arrive."

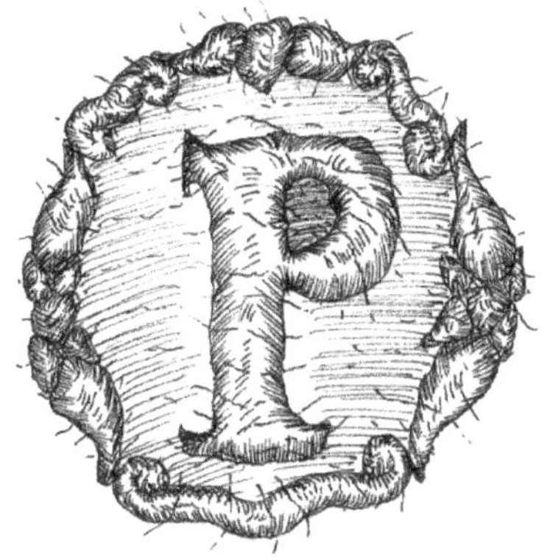

Victorian Delight

THE UNMARKED VAN sat idly outside of the antique store as Wyatt and Kirby watched the little old lady inside the empty shop, reading her book to pass the time.

These two men were professionals, which meant two things; they had been watching the shop for the past month and learned of the owner's daily routines, as well as the kind of customers who entered the shop and when it'd be most busy; and that antiques could sell for just as high as any jewelry swept from a vacant house or mugged off someone under the dark of night.

They knew that the owner of the antique shop was named Maggie, she was sixty-two years old, had a shitzu pet dog back home named Franklin, always opened the shop at noon, and always closed it at 7:00pm.

Sometimes she'd leave immediately after closing, other times she'd stay behind for four additional hours, then leave out the back.

Her shop carried a wide range of antiques; from authentic 18th century paintings; World War II memorabilia; Victorian china both current and vintage; jewelry from the 1910's to 1950's; and furniture/home decor that could be dated all the way back to the Victorian Era.

Wyatt and Kirby already knew the value of some of the items within the shop which could be reached at display level. However, they were more curious and interested in the items Maggie kept hidden in the backroom, reserved for the VIP customers.

During their one month stakeout, they had noticed that every second Saturday, Maggie would close the shop at 4:00pm, but wouldn't leave.

Instead, she would stay and read a book to pass the time until around 9:00pm, when certain individuals would show up and she would let them in— granting them access to the backroom before returning to her post at the cash register to continue allowing entrance to a handful more of individuals.

The number of VIP guests varied on how many would arrive and be let in, but it seemed Maggie knew all them by face, and must've been expecting the ones who showed up and the ones who didn't, because she would always follow the last batch into the backroom.

Maggie would never return to the cash register after her last guests arrived, nor would she exit out the front entrance of her shop later— making it obvious that she and her VIP guests must've been leaving through the back entrance of the building at the end of whatever it is they were doing in there.

Another thing to note, was that all of these late night visitors were of a very affluent and high prestige background.

They drove cars that were at the highest end of six figures, sometimes even past seven.

They were always dressed extremely proper in suits, dresses, and all.

A couple of them even had bodyguards and extra security, who would trail behind them or drove them to this destination.

Wyatt and Kirby were able to infer from this that Maggie must've had a secret collection of her most *exquisite* and rare antiques, that we're undoubtedly very expensive and very valuable, stored in the backroom. And these people who visited late in the night must've been the only ones who could afford such pieces, and were called in or informed of any new finds. Then, they would be taken to the backroom where Maggie would show them and sell such pieces to these wealthy individuals— who were probably the very few that could afford to make such a purchase.

From this theory, Wyatt and Kirby made a decision between themselves in regard to their previously planned burglary— and what was originally going to be just a simple smash-and-grab during closed hours… had now turned into an armed robbery.

They intended to break in on a second Saturday night— after all the VIP collectors had entered her shop — and take not only whatever goodies Maggie kept stored in the backroom to sell to them, but also whatever money and jewelry these wealthy individuals had on their bodies during this time.

What would've probably cashed them in a measly $2,000 had now turned into a six figure grab, depending on what Maggie was selling and how much jewelry and cash the guests had on themselves.

Even though some of the wealthy figures commonly had security with them, it didn't matter to Wyatt or Kirby, and it wasn't going to stop them.

They had fenced a revolver with six bullets for this very occasion, and with firearms being illegal in the UK, is was safe to say that this would trump any amount of bodyguards that could possibly be in the shop during the robbery.

So now, while parked outside of the shop in their unmarked van, Wyatt and Kirby just waited and watched as Maggie began to let in the first round of her high esteemed guests into the shop, taking count of the ones who had bodyguards and how many were arriving that night.

When what must've been the last of the expected guests showed up, marked by Maggie putting her book under the register at their arrival, Wyatt and Kirby knew it was time.

They turned off the car's engine, double checked the condition of their loaded revolver, put on their black ski-masks, and exited the vehicle.

They watched from across the street as Maggie let in the last two guests and their bodyguard, before locking the door behind them and leading them into the backroom.

Wyatt and Kirby then made their own way across the street and to the shop, where Kirby began to lock-pick the door while Wyatt stood watch for any possible pedestrians who might wander by.

Being proficient at his craft and having done this for years, it took only fifteen seconds before a click sounded from within the lock and the two let themselves into the shop.

They snuck up to the backroom door and leaned in close, listening to what was being said on the other side before performing their stickup.

Though they could not distinguish the voices of the VIP guests, they could easily make out which one belonged to Maggie.

"Everyone please take a mask and put it on" said the muffled voice of Maggie from the other side of the door.

"Is it really safe to let it out?" asked a VIP guest, "I don—"

"It is completely safe, so long as you wear your mask" said Maggie, cutting off the guest with an immediate reassurance, but also a warning, "Do **not** take it off, no matter what. And don't even move it to the side to scratch an itch."

"Why isn't this going to auction?" asked a different VIP guest.

"The seller wants to make a purchase tonight, and since that item they desire has already been put up for bidding and cannot be traded, he asked me personally to sell this beforehand.

His hope is that he may have the expenses to outbid any competition tonight for the item he's interest in, and selling this offers a slight guarantee of that" answered Maggie.

"How much does he want for this?" asked another VIP guest.

"16.7 million" answered Maggie, "The lowest he will go is sixteen flat."

"16 million without any bid?" asked a VIP guest, "Well, the fear is now gone. I wanna see if it's worth my money."

"Of course" said Maggie with delight.

Wyatt and Kirby looked at each other, mutually understanding that as soon as they heard her unlock or open whatever it is that she had to show the guests, that it would be the same moment they took their unsuspecting victims by surprise.

That way, they didn't have to trouble themselves with making any extra threats, lock-picking another security measure, or carrying out some heavy container since whatever was worth 16.7 million dollars would already be out and in the open when they made their move.

Three loud clicks sounded on the other side of the door, followed by a slow creaking of metal and some gasps from the guests in awe.

Wyatt and Kirby nodded to each other, then bursted through the backroom door!

"Nobody fucking move!" barked Wyatt.

"First one to do something stupid gets a fucking hole in their head!" threatened Kirby.

Wyatt and Kirby quickly observed the room, with Kirby spanning the barrel of the revolver across everyone… but the two men were confused by the sight that lay before them.

There were five guests in total, three bodyguards, and little old Maggie. However, every one of them was wearing a creepy mask that looked animalistic and devilish— like the depiction of the creatures from hell that medieval artists would paint.

"The fuck is going on here?" asked Wyatt out loud.

"Oh! Isn't this a surprise!" said Maggie, unfazed by the two men or their gun.

"Can-it, bitch! Or you won't need to worry about age taking you out!" said Kirby, pointing the gun in Maggie's direction.

"Well, everyone, I guess you'll get to see why exactly our seller wants 16 million for this" said Maggie to the guests, paying no mind to Kirby or his threats.

"I said can-it!" repeated Kirby.

Two clicks then sounded, like one would make from the suction of their tongue against the roof of their mouth, followed by a popping sound that echoed eerily within the room.

Wyatt and Kirby both looked to where this noise came from, witnessing for the first time a large metal box that seemed to be more of a cage.

The two men had been so focused on analyzing the people and potential threats within the room for their shakedown, that they paid no mind to any other details of it nor to this odd metal cage that sat in its center.

Then, two weird yawn-like sounds came from within the dark opening of the metal box, back to back without being long or drawn out.

It was a freakish sound, one that caused Kirby to point the gun at its opening.

"What the fuck was that!?" exclaimed Kirby, confused.

"And remember…" said Maggie to her VIP guests, *"Don't take off the masks!"*

From out of the thick metal box emerged a creature on all fours, foul and foreign, and of nothing that Wyatt or Kirby had ever seen before in their lives, nor knew existed amongst the animal kingdom.

It looked deranged, sickly, and not of this world.

It had the head of a dog— no — a *hyena*, but with some uncanny human aspects to it that made it appear like more of an abomination upon the eyes.

Its body was thin, and the shoulder and hip bones protruded grievously outward against its skin from within, as if its bone structure was also meant to be bipedal as well.

Its skin looked leathery, with odd patches of fur dispersed sparsely amongst its flesh.

It had a long tail which emerged out of its backbone, and this feature was the only thing that still looked strong and full to its true nature on the being.

The tail waved back and forth like a cat's, and though it was also mostly naked of hair as well, its tip was flushed with a condensed amount of fur like the end of a paintbrush.

The creature looked around the room, observing the people wearing masks and making the same yawning sound like it had before… that is, until its eyes reached Wyatt and Kirby.

Its oddly human eyes then fluctuated, both the pupils and the eyelids, while it began to make the clicking sound once again.

"What the fuck…" whispered Wyatt under his breath.

"Fuck this!" yelled Kirby in fear and panic, pulling the trigger of the revolver.

However, before enough pressure could be applied to drop the hammer of the gun, the tail of this unknown beast flicked fast like the snap of a whip, striking Kirby in the stomach!

He instantly fell to the ground, completely unresponsive— something which Wyatt had never seen before in his life, even amongst men who had been hit clean by a bullet to the head.

The way Kirby's body just shutdown instantly looked so original to the powerlessness of human beings, that it served as a reminder— like a bright light had been shined onto the fragility of their nature.

Wyatt then returned his eyes to the creature, who was already preying on him next.

He noticed that from out of the clustered hair on its tail, was what looked to be a bone— about three inches long with the most sharply pointed tip he had ever seen.

It was covered in some blood which he assumed was Kirby's, as the creature continued to make its oppressive clicking sound, taking slow single steps towards Wyatt.

"Shit…" said Wyatt in defeat.

Then, everything went instantly black for him, as he too was struck in the neck by the end of this creature's tail, and no different than his partner, Wyatt dropped immediately onto the ground in a loss of consciousness.

Despite being in a dreamless state of unconsciousness, Wyatt could faintly remember the moments before his body completely gave out on him and when his neck still burned from the sting of the creature.

He remembered the sounds of the guests gasping in awe at what had just occurred, along with the sound of some buzzer being rang, followed by the sliding of something heavy but mechanical, and then lastly, the sound of large heavy footsteps being instructed by Maggie to *"Add these boys to the auction…"*

After that, nothing else existed and all awareness was put on pause— like a drunken sleep from a long night of drinking.

Both Wyatt and Kirby felt like they had been hit by a truck and were extremely disoriented when they woke up, feeling like it had been a time-skip from when they were attacked to where they found themselves now.

The two men awoke in separate metal cages that were only big enough to allow them a full sitting position, but lacked enough space to provide any room for standing up.

A piercing migraine afflicted the both of them, the worst they had ever experienced in their life. It felt like their skulls were on fire, their eyeballs on the verge of popping out, and like a knife had just been jammed through their ears and straight into their brains where an immense amount of pressure was released into the cavity.

"What the fuck…" moaned Kirby.

"My head… my fucking head…" grunted Wyatt.

"Wyatt? Wyatt was that all a dream?" asked Kirby, "That thing— the dog-like thing, was that real or did I dream it?"

"It was real" answered Wyatt, "It was all real…

I don't know what the fuck is going on here. I don't know what happened. I don't know where the fuck we are. And I don't know what this goddamn headache is!" he exclaimed while grabbing his head in agony.

"How the fuck did you two end up here?" asked a stranger's voice, unfamiliar to either of them.

The two quit their talking and looked in the direction from where it came, to find another man trapped in a cage similar to theirs alongside them.

The man looked to be in his early thirties, with a naturally good youth to him.

He had short hair, chopped and ruffled, some scruff on his face, and was built very slim in a genetic way rather than from a lack of food.

He had a few mismatched tattoos spaced out around his body, as well as a branding scar located on his neck, which contained a large capital letter "P" in its center, while being surrounded by what looked like some kind of floral design although the damaged tissue didn't replicate it so well.

"You really had to be at the wrong place at the wrong time— and I mean *really* wrong, if they snatched you up and put you here" said the man with a brand.

"Hey, you know where the fuck we are?" asked Kirby, "You know what the fuck's going on?"

"Of course I do" answered the man with a brand, "Although I'm on the shit end of it, I'm a part of these sick fuckers' world."

"Do you mind filling us in, then?" asked Wyatt, "Because last I remember, all we were trying to do was rob some old lady and her rich cunts for friends in some tiny fucking antique shop... And now we're here."

"Don't forget that... *thing...*" added Kirby.

"Ahh, now it makes sense" said the man with a brand, carrying little enthusiasm in his voice as if he actually understood their situation but it wasn't too interesting to him, "Well, that old lady doesn't just run an antique shop. She sells other goods, and is a coordinator for the big folks who run this auction house.

Those rich cunts aren't just some randoms with a lot of money— they're sick fucks with a *whole lot* of money, and who hold memberships at this auction.

And that little antique shop was not just a little antique shop. It was a front for this— the auction house."

"No no no, we're aware of this kind of shit, okay" contested Wyatt, "We know of the blackmarket, and we've even done a couple sales for those types of people.

We know about underground auctions. We're aware that human trafficking and sex-slave auctions occur during them, alright.

But that doesn't explain or even come close to explaining what that fucking animal we saw was— which doesn't exist in any fucking zoology book!

That thing took us out!"

"Oh? That's how they got you, huh?" said the man with a brand.

"We had a gun!" said Kirby, "We're not amateurs.

But that thing... I thought it killed me with how black everything went..."

"I've heard about it" said the man with a brand, "A lot of the families, including my own, were making a big fuss about that thing.

Everyone wants to get their hands on it, but apparently the seller decided not to put it up for auction.

A lot of people were mad about that, 'cause only a select few were given the opportunity to purchase it behind the scenes.

So *that's* what you crashed?" said the man with a brand, astonished at the thought.

"What was that thing?" asked Kirby, still traumatized by the fresh memories of it.

"Wait, you have family in this?" interrupted Wyatt, "Get us the fuck out of here, then!

I don't know why they put *you* in a cage, but listen, we can do work" said Wyatt, gesturing to himself and Kirby, "We're good at what we do. We can give them our services or even fence directly to them as our sole clients.

Just take us out of these goddamn cages!"

The man with a brand simply tapped the branding scar on his neck, "My family, not blood related— they're the ones who *own* me.

There are a handful of top dogs and big names here, and you don't refer to them by their names unless you're their peers.

But I'll be damned if I call them my masters while not in their presence, so don't get the wrong idea when I say 'family'.

I'm the furthest thing from those sick twisted fucks."

"So is this a human auction, then?" asked Wyatt, "They're selling you for whatever reason— unruliness, failure to please, disappointing performance, maybe want someone better?

And we're gonna be sold, too? To the highest bidder for whatever the fuck they wanna do with us, to us, or use us for?"

"If only it were that" answered the man with a brand, "We'd be lucky if that was the case.

Slave labor, sex labor… we could count that as a blessing if that was who these people were.

Shit, we'd still be lucky if this was a snuff auction— at least then they'd cut our throats after the torture and let us drain when they were finished with us.

No. These people are much worse.

They're on an entirely different level, with different kind of money, and a different kind of awareness of this world and its mystic mechanics and secrets at play."

"The beast…" said Kirby, still fixated on the creature from earlier which continued to haunt his mind on his idea of reality, "It still doesn't explain the beast."

The man with a brand let out a loud sigh, revealing his exhaustion from Wyatt's and Kirby's obliviousness to something that he was all too familiar with, "Are either of you two religious?" he asked.

"The fuck does that have to do with anything?" asked Kirby, frustrated that his question was once again being ignored.

"Raised Catholic. Stopped believing in secondary school" answered Wyatt, aware that the man with a brand obviously had a reason for this question, and that it most likely was to better explain what was going on.

"Ah, a classic" said the man with a brand, "Good. This'll make it easier, then.

Now, whether you actually read the bible yourself, or you could've just heard the stories from your pastor, your parents, maybe within the church, or maybe from some teachers— it doesn't matter —there were stories in the bible that talked about the existence of *other things*.

Creatures, beings, spirits, even other gods— but we won't get into that.

The point is, that little book that supposedly contains the truth of all written history and creation… speaks about more than just humans.

Even within something that is considered holy and a treasured recording that bears no lies— mankind is still not the only thing to exist in this world.

And you can look at any other religious text for that matter, as they all will have stories of other things that creep and crawl and share an existence beside humans, no different than how we humans exist today.

Folklore, myths, mythologies— they all do the same thing. But because everyone loves to chalk them up to just fairytales, we'll stick with the fact that your holy book says those exact things.

Well… that's it.

The things that you think aren't real, or don't belong in this world, or don't fit with your understandings or concepts of reality, those things that are merely fantasy or imagination or dreams… they're real.

They exist.

Whether that be to some extent, to a certain extent, to a known extent, to an unknown extent, be it a limiting extent or an unlimited extent— you get the point.

Some are aware of this, but most aren't. Some even pick and choose where it starts and ends when it comes to this shit.

And then, there is a very, *very* tiny few who are the big players in it all.

They've kinda orchestrated things in a way where this all remains largely unknown. And by doing so, by being the keepers of this knowledge… they have a fuckload of power.

For instance, if I hide the existence of guns from you two and the rest of the world, and I happen to have a gun myself… well then boy are you guys shit out of luck and in the dark.

Hell, I can even shoot you both and no one would be able to explain your deaths, let alone catch me as the culprit, because it's beyond their understanding, it's outside of their scope of reality set within their world.

Powerful, right?

Well there you have it. That's the families, that's this sick auction, that's what that animal was that fucked you two over. And that's who I am in this.

I'm human, don't be mistaken, but I had the knowledge about this shit very early on in life, and was too fucking ignorant with how I used it for my own good. That's how I got mixed up with these evil fucks.

By the way, I don't use the word 'evil' lightly.

I have a very developed and complex understanding of the term, and an enriched morality that I am very in tune with that makes me see the world in a very different way than most people.

So when I say these people are evil, I mean the *epitome* of it. You can't get any closer to hell while still on earth than by being surrounded by these fucks."

"Okay, fine, whatever" said Wyatt, "I can get behind the fact that the world is a very different place from how we all think it is and how we all know it to be.

If there's one thing I trust in this world, it's me, and I know what I saw earlier before getting knocked out and put into these cages. That was all the proof I need, there's no reason to deny it or go into an existential crisis.

But what I do wanna know now, and what does concern me, is what's going to happen to us next?

What happens once we're sold? Where does that put me?" he asked.

"Mm. You got the right idea, then" said the man with a brand, impressed by Wyatt, "We are at the bottom of the lot in this auction. It's why there's no security watching us or standing guard in case we try to break free or make an escape.

It's why we're in here… what is this, actually? A windowed attic? I don't know, but we basically got front row seats to the auction and all their bids" he said, nodding towards the thick glass window in front of them that showed the main stage two stories down below them, as well as the hidden figures on the other side of glass booths surrounding the stage, "They keep the real treasures— which is comprised of a collection of both animate or inanimate things, objects, or items —down below in the basement.

That room is secure. That room is impenetrable for numerous reasons, and has a shit load of security.

We are nothing in comparison.

Now what's going to happen is after they are done with their auction, where they will sell and bid on mystical shit, terrible creatures like the one you two got to witness first hand, some objects from ancient times that are maybe valuable because of who once owned them or what you can do with them, or maybe even because of a curse or blessing it contains— we'll be sold last. Inexpensive, too.

You see, we hold no real value like those items do or the people and creatures who will be going up for bid.

But we'll still be sold and bought, tonight.

For you two, you'll be used as an experiment or as a testing most likely for all of the horrors or mystical things they purchase today or already own.

Take the beast for example. Someone might want to test it out and see it in action, you know?

So, they'd use you two as guinea pigs and bear witness to what happens.

Maybe an item of theirs has a unique curse of effect, and they're going to explore it at your expense, while they sit safe and sound in observation of it at play."

The man with a brand shook his head in sympathy for the two men, "You'd been lucky if this was just a normal blackmarket where the buyer would fuck you to death, maybe accidentally OD you, or just use you in a snuff film where you got immediately put down after the mess like a useless dog.

… I'm sorry" said the man with a brand.

"And what about you?" asked Kirby, "Why do you say *we're* fucked and *you're* not?"

"**Watch it**" said the man with a brand, taking on a more serious tone that made the two men's souls hush like a dog being silenced by its master— a natural instinct of power at play, "Do not lash out your anger and disappointment at me just because *you* were unaware.

I did not cast you here, and my better understanding of these things did not play a role in your fall.

I *am* fucked, but not like the two of you are.

My cage will simply be replaced by another— by no means am I free.

I still don't get to live a life just because mine won't be wrecked like yours."

"How do you know so much?" asked Wyatt, "Why are you in a cage when you know so much about all this madness and all these crazy things and crazy people?"

"Because I know magick" said the man with a brand, "I discovered Crowley during secondary school in an old library, and fell down the rabbit hole from there.

I met a couple of others during my time, even joined some groups while in college. Dipped into different practices, and worked with different beings.

You find out a lot about this stuff when you're in it. And I found out about the top dogs.

I wanted to be *there*— high up in this undisclosed and hidden hierarchy.

And being the fucking idiot that I am, I really thought that I could've actually joined them despite not being born into one of the families or naturally being a part of the upperclass who are still in it nonetheless.

I honed my craft, sought them out, then offered my services thinking I could be a John Dee to a Queen Elizabeth and take a spot beside them.

Well… that didn't fucking work at all.

I was nothing to them— still am nothing —and they made sure I knew it when they took on my services and got me behind closed doors.

I became a piece of property, branded by my owners and forced to form a pact with the deity they all use and worship.

I'm a slave. My life is worthless and so is my service.

I'm easily replaceable, and the only reason I'm still alive is because I do what they say.

Do you know of this being they worship? Or the sick things these families do and offer to it, and the sacrifices this being requests from them in return?

I am not this type of practitioner. Everyday I am challenged to go through with what they both want and desire when they use me, and everyday I wonder if death is the best option— whether I should just let them take my eyes and then my head."

"Good evening, everyone!" bellowed a voice from down below on the main stage beneath their window, *"We thank you for your attendance during this week's auction.*

And as always, we have a fine lineup for the biddings available— open to all here and to those who are representees of their absent masters."

Wyatt and Kirby found their attention being drawn towards the show below them as a man in a suit, who must've been the auctioneer, began the process of presenting the goods and starting the bids.

They couldn't help but take an interest of curiosity to what was going on below them and what was about to be revealed.

"Without waisting any more time, we shall start with our first auction!

Presented by one of our humble families and coming straight out from their own personal collection, is a Golem from Jerusalem— its roots dating far far back into A.D. 70!

Though it is still inanimate due to its awakening process being incomplete, it is still highly valuable and was forged by an ancient technique, long forgotten.

However, if anyone here happens to be a child of Jacob or is able to acquire the aid of one, this Golem still has the full capacity and potential to be completed and perform its duty!"

A team of staff then wheeled in a massive wooden crate that was very wide and even taller in height, onto the stage and to its center with a hand-truck.

They proceeded to open the face of the crate, revealing a large and mis-shaped clay figure inside that had been sculpted to an almost near representation of man, though its proportions were inhuman."

Although Kirby could not take his eyes off what he was witnessing down below them, Wyatt broke out of the captivating hold the scene had over him, and continued his digging into the man with a brand in hope of finding a way out of this predicament.

"Have you ever thought about striking your own personal deal with this deity that your family has forced you into working with?" asked Wyatt, "Surely you have more to offer it since you do all of the actual spells and rituals, right?"

"It's not as simple as that" answered the man with a brand, "I may offer the actual service to it, but the family offers it what it desires.

Like I told you, I wouldn't participate in half of the shit they make me do if it were my choice.

I may do the actual magick, but they provide what is required for it and what the being demands.

One man who does magick is not worth all the splendor that is given to it by the families."

"Next, we present a 13th century scimitar which belonged to a Hashashin during its use" said the auctioneer down below, *"It is said that a curse lies within the blade, however, the participators from this Nizari Ismaili sect would've called it a blessing! As the curse laid upon it would've only aided in their duty…"*

"Can this deity see potential?" asked Wyatt, unfazed by the commotion below.

"In what sense?" asked the man with a brand.

"If something *can* be, but at the current moment is not" elaborated Wyatt, "Can this deity you serve recognize that, and see the greater potential in what *will* be than what is now?

Would it invest in it, like stock markets or some shit?"

"Of course" said the man with a brand, "These beings have far more eyes than humans do. It can see any potential and will always weigh it into the current."

"Then what about *three* men who practice magick?" asked Wyatt, "Is that worth more than what these families currently give it while they don't hold the power themselves?"

The man with a brand thought for a moment, "It could be… it very well could be" he said with an air of hope rising in his voice, "However, this being is of a nefarious nature. There's no telling what it would demand from such sorcerers at its beckoning."

"But it's still better than what's going to happen to us now, right? It's still better than your current fate to constantly do its bidding under the orders of the families, right?" questioned Wyatt, unsure of his own plan, "We have a better shot at escaping all of this in *that* timeline than we do in this one, don't we?"

"… Yes" answered the man with a brand, "We do."

"Well then… I'm okay with that. I'll take a shot at it even if it's a slim one. Kirby…" said Wyatt, looking over to his friend, "We've done a lot of bad things, gotten caught, and played the waiting game to get out of them before. We can handle this too, don't you think?"

"Yeah…" said Kirby, his stoicism slowly returning, "We can."

"Alright then, let's do it" said Wyatt.

"There's only one problem" warned the man with a brand, "Without the proper preparations or the proper items, tools and ingredients… this can heavily backfire.

There's no way I can do everything in the correct manner and order to establish contact with this deity while still being in this cage and not having any of my belongings.

Shit, half of the time the family usually provides me with it.

We run a major risk if I try to make contact right now in these conditions."

"What's the risk?" asked Wyatt.

"This whole fucking place will blow— an energy burst in time and space" said the man with a brand, "It's not like an atom bomb or anything like that, but it'll definitely bring this place down to the ground for sure… and us with it.

We're calling on a higher and powerful being, and bringing it forth to us without the right environment or conditions.

Because of this, our reality is gonna experience a big burst of energy that'll rip right through it.

Now, we and all these people in here will be totally fucked when it happens… but… there's a chance that the three of us, and *only* the three of us, might make it out alive."

"How do we make that happen?" asked Kirby.

"It's not up to us— it's up to the being" answered the man with a brand, "When it is summoned, and all shit gets fucked and turned inside out, it'll be able to pull us out in time before we can get blasted by the energy surge.

But that's the thing. It's only if it *wants* to save us, because it *sees* the value that we intend to offer it now.

You two must ensure that your intentions **scream** that you will learn the ways of magick and serve the being like I do. It must be written into your resolve so immensely, that its eyes will see it when it arrives.

We won't have time to talk to the being and say it out loud— we can only hope it sees it within us when it arrives from our beckoning, and that it truly does value us and what we have to offer it more than the current standing it has with the families.

If it doesn't… we're all dead."

Wyatt thought for a moment, "… We're already dead, aren't we? From everything you've told us about these people and the families.

I say we give this a shot."

The man with a brand nodded in agreement, "Okay, but also— you must hide the deeper intention that we plan to break free and make an escape from our service to it in the future.

Let that be nothing of any concern in this moment. Got it?

Otherwise… it will see that too."

Wyatt and Kirby both nodded in understanding.

"Coming onto stage now is something we are delighted to present with you all this evening!

Something truly extraordinary, undoubtedly one of a kind, and without question— an auction many of you have heard about and knew would be showing tonight, eagerly awaiting its bidding!"

Kirby glanced out of the window and watched as a naked woman was dragged onto stage, while a staff member holding a book and pen took to standing beside the auctioneer.

"Behold, the Tormented Woman and her book!"

Murmurs could be heard from behind the glass booths which the guests watched from within.

"As far as we know, she is immortal, self-sustaining— needing no food nor water to live.

She cannot be killed by any conventional method, and the best part of it all" the staff member beside the auctioneer raised the book into the air, *"Whatever is written into the book will be done unto the woman!"*

The staff member proceeded to open the book and write in it, *"For example, my lovely staff is currently writing 'The Tormented Woman will take five lashes to her back'!*

Now watch!"

The murmurs silenced as the instant the staff member dotted the period at the end of her sentence, the naked woman dropped onto all fours in agony, as her skin split open five times on her back as if she was struck by an invisible whip.

The murmurs then arose again at the sight, this time louder with excitement.

"And without fail, after the torment has been written and laid out upon the woman—" the auctioneer held out his arm dramatically to present the next spectacle, for just like magic, the open slashes on the woman's back began to close and healed up instantaneously, as if the torture had never occurred, *"She returns to her normal state!"*

The murmurs vibrated the entire room in their craze.

"You can write anything in the book, even tortures that will kill her!

But worry not, for she will always come back to life shortly after, regardless of what happens!

We tested this out many times to ensure that there were no exceptions! We even wrote that the Tormented Woman would drown by her lungs filling with water, and to our own shock and astonishment, after she turned blue and collapsed onto the floor in a loss of pulse— she began to cough up the water moments later and breathe with life once more!

The pain is all there! She feels every bit of it!

All the while, you never need to worry about her perishing or ever going too far with your methods of torture!

The Tormented Woman and her book is a dream to every sadist!"

Applauds could be heard from behind the glass booths for this wonderful offer presented to them.

"Alright then, set your intentions now" said the man with a brand, "Scream them in your hearts and souls, and well… fingers crossed, boys.

I hope that we get pulled out of this mess and meet back up on the other side of wherever the fuck we're taken if this works out.

Should luck be on our side, then I look forward to working with you both."

Wyatt and Kirby smiled at the man with a brand, and then to each other before looking down at the auction that was still going on below them.

Their minds focused out everything else while their eyes remained on the current bidding at play. Soon, the sounds of the auctioneer became muffled and faded as they set their thoughts to the intentions of what they had all planned and spoken of.

"Because of how unparalleled this subject is, the bidding will begin at sixty million!"

A heat ran down their backs, and a chill touched the tops of their heads, and in a blink faster than the speed of light, and by only a mere split second that produced the sound of an eruption which barely reached their ears in the snap of an instant— the auction house imploded in on itself, collapsing to a simple rubble.

1,825 Days Sober

Owen had always thought that kickbacks were supposed to consist of no more than six people max, with all of them already being friends or at least semi-familiar with each other.

Or so that had been his previous experiences with them, and he actually preferred it that way over the full blown parties.

Kickbacks were nice because of their smaller sizes— more intimate with a better space provided to be vulnerable and actually put yourself out there, while simultaneously allowing you to be heard when you spoke, as opposed to the traditional party conversations that never went too deep or gave one the true ability to divulge about themselves and their thoughts, or to consume the relinquishing of another's.

The memories Owen had acquired from his times at kickbacks always felt so personal and like something he cherished. He could look back on them and think about the conversations he partook in or the moment during them when he gained a deeper understanding of someone or something, unlocking a new impression about the person he was speaking to.

These were the valuable experiences to Owen, which were lacking when compared to the memories pulled back from his attendance at larger parties, which were always flushed with tacky led-lights, rooms filled with the smell of alcohol from people's breaths or their body odor reeking from their armpits, the cramped spacing and constant shoulder bumping or stepping on someone's toes, and it always being a struggle to hear the person who you were talking with or picking up on the words that they were saying.

So, needless to say, Owen was excited when he first heard his friends say that they were throwing a kickback for the weekend, and he was eager to experience it since it had been so long since his last one.

These were new friends, too. So in Owen's mind, it was the perfect opportunity to enrich their connection with each other and maybe even cement his place among them.

But to his disappointment on the night of the event, Owen arrived at the house to discover it to be more of a small party instead of a real kickback— lacking any of the real intimacy that came from an exclusive circle.

It was filled with about twenty different people as opposed to the only eight friends who Owen expected to be there.

Everyone carried a red plastic cup in their hand which housed their alcohol, as opposed to the glass kitchenware Owen expected to be used amongst him and his new friends.

All of the bottles of alcohol were of a mixed variety and sat on the kitchen island for anyone to grab and pour for themselves, as opposed to Owen's previous fantasy where the bottles would've been resting on the living room table by the couch— which they'd all be gathered around as a tiny group of friends.

People were dressed up as how one would expect for a party— nice and casually put together for the opportunity of maybe not leaving the house alone and getting lucky that night, as opposed to the comfort of dressing in either sweats or loose clothes while being amongst familiar faces… which is exactly how Owen showed up.

He didn't know anyone else there at the party besides the eight friends he expected to share this kickback with, so of course, Owen went on an immediate search for them upon his arrival.

He managed to stumble across most of them and engage in some sort of short conversation with them for a bit… but they all seemed to be too busy enjoying their other interactions.

Not wanting to be the type of person who sat on their friends' shoulders like a parrot for the entirety of the party, Owen would always move on after a short period of time to begin his hunt for the next person that he knew there.

After twenty minutes had passed and Owen was able to minorly associate with all eight of his friends, he now found himself glued to the wall in the living room— watching everybody else go about their business and enjoy themselves.

It was then that one of the eight people who he did know there, Rachel, noticed Owen being a wallflower while she was refilling her cup with alcohol in the kitchen.

"Hey!" said Rachel, arriving at Owen's side with her new drink in hand, "How are you liking the party?" she asked.

Owen smiled, "It's good! I'm not one for big social events, but I'm enjoying myself!" he reassured her with lies.

Rachel must've caught onto this, as she placed her hand on Owen's shoulder in response and turned him to face towards a specific direction, followed by a guiding finger for his eyes, "That's Matias" she said, pointing to a guy of their age who was also standing idly against the wall across the room, "Doug invited him to the party, but he's kinda like you and isn't into these types of social things.

You should go talk to him! I'm sure you two will kick it off.

But I'll be upstairs if it doesn't go well— come find me before you leave if you decide to dip early, okay?"

Owen nodded, to which Rachel patted him on the back and left— returning to her crowd on the upper level of the house.

Owen observed Matias before acting on whether to make his way over to him or not, and found the guy to be a very unique character from first glance.

He looked *extremely* out of place— not that he didn't belong there or was an outcast, but because of the complete opposite. Matias' presence amongst the party looked like the only *true* thing within it, while everybody else were the odd ones out of place.

Owen had a hard time describing how it looked and figuring out what this sensation was that he felt in his head from how it all appeared, but the best way he could describe this feeling into something understandable, was to relate the image to that of a zookeeper.

Matias seemed so far beyond this stuff, as if he had a deeper understanding of what was actually going on around them and where they really were and what we all are— that it gave off the image like he was a zookeeper, standing in the middle of a pen filled with monkeys.

He didn't look awkward or in need of friends, and there was nothing of the sort related to him lacking confidence or being unable to socialize.

Matias just appeared to be outside of it all— aware to such a high degree that it was almost tangible by his mere presence, one which disconnected him from everything and everyone else there because of this unknown sense of awareness he held that no one else around him did.

Owen took a swig of his drink before deciding to approach Matias. He knew that he should mingle for just a bit longer before dipping on the party, and decided that it would be spent with him talking to Matias for a brief moment before heading up to Rachel and informing her of his leave.

Parties weren't Owen's thing, and he wasn't about to force himself to stick through them 'till the end like he had while he was in college.

As Owen made his way towards Matias, the stranger's eyes immediately fell on him— as if he sensed Owen's approach towards his space and knew that Owen had his intentions set on him.

Matias smiled as Owen drew within arm's-length.

"Hey! I'm Owen. You're Matias, right?"

"Yeah, nice to meet you" Matias held out his hand and they shook.

"Rachel told me who you were" said Owen, "I'm not a fan of big get-togethers, so she pointed me in your direction… if you were wondering how I already knew your name."

"It's fine, I figured something like that was the case" said Matias, "I'm not a fan of these things either, but I try to force myself to socialize every now and then, and to hangout with people my age and whatnot."

"I got to admit— and not to sound like an asshole in anyway —but you're a lot nicer than I thought you would be" said Owen, "Not in a bad way like I expected you to be a jerk or something, but you just seemed… I don't know, outside of all this" said Owen, gesturing to the party around them.

Matias seemed stupefied by Owen's comment, "You could tell?" he asked, as if knowing exactly what Owen was referring to.

"I've always been good at observing and noticing things, especially when it comes to people" said Owen, "Sometimes I can't even explain it or know the right words to use for defining it, but I feel it anyway."

"Huh. That's interesting" said Matias, "What kind of things are you into, if you don't mind me asking?"

"Pshh, well, I'm not really a big sports guy. I like watching movies, trying new restaurants, video games here and there" answered Owen, thinking this was a basic question of trying to get to know someone better.

"Oh. Okay" responded Matias, to which Owen noticed sounded like the stranger either didn't find the answer or the desired information he was seeking from that question.

"You don't have a cup" commented Owen, trying to rebound from the unsuccessful answer he gave, "Want me to get you a drink?"

"Ah no, I'm okay" answered Matias, "I'm sober, actually, so nothing for me. Guess that adds to the black sheep effect you noticed earlier."

"To each their own" said Owen, supportively, "I don't smoke, so alcohol is my only poison.

Though I did experiment with it in high school, but could never really get into it. For some reason, it affected me differently than others."

Owen noticed a glint in Matias' eyes to his words, as if the stranger found part of the answer he had originally sought from Owen when asking him what he was into.

"What did you experience?" asked Matias, bluntly— leaving no room for formality over his eager interest.

"Um…" began Owen, feeling a bit of pressure from being put on the spot, but also not wanting to let this lead of a potentially real conversation die out, "Might sound strange, but it felt like I was being abducted— or at least something was trying to abduct me whenever I got high.

I know a lot of people experience paranoia sometimes when they smoke, but this was not that.

All my friends would get high in the same way that most people do and would describe how it feels.

But for me, it felt like a miniature breakthrough, or maybe not a break-through, that might not be the right word.

It was as if the cover that blocks me from… I don't know, other stuff—?" Owen gestured to the surrounding space with his hands, "—was removed.

For example, you can't have a nightmare when you're awake, but the moment you go to sleep, that protective barrier of waking consciousness is now gone and you're susceptible to nightmares.

It was kind of like that, if that makes sense.

Whenever I got high, it felt like I broke through that invisible wall or barrier, and something on the other side was either waiting for me or taking this opportunity to abduct me now that I was vulnerable and that barrier was removed.

Shit, maybe it *was* just extreme paranoia!" laughed Owen, awkwardly, aware that what he was saying might have sounded crazy and act as a social suicide for this current conversation.

But when he looked at Matias, the stranger was not disturbed or even trying to hide an uncomfortableness which Owen expected him to feel.

Instead, he seemed deeply focused in onto what Owen was trying to say, and listening intently on the way in which he was describing it.

It seemed Owen did indeed stumble upon what Matias was looking for, after all.

"Do you know what I'm talking about?" asked Owen.

Matias nodded.

"I'm not gonna lie, I feel like I can be honest with you because of that difference you hold from when I first sized you up earlier— regarding you not fitting in here" said Owen, "There's a sense of you being aware and getting *it*, whatever *it* is.

So if I believe what my gut is telling me, then I feel like I can be frank with you, without it being weird, awkward or out of place."

Matias smiled at Owen's statement, a smile that revealed the very understanding of what Owen meant— as if they shared the same thought pattern.

"What have you experienced that made you this way?" asked Owen, "I know now it had to have been an experience, since your interest peaked when I spoke about my own personal handling of weed. And I could tell earlier that you were searching for something of the sort when you first asked me what I was into.

Does it have to do with you being sober? Is that the reason why you're kind of outside of it all?"

Matias smiled again, but this time not while looking at Owen, but rather, while lowering his eyes to the ground.

It was the same kind of smile Owen recognized and had experienced himself, on occasion. It had nothing to do with being polite, but instead, was seated in the essence of when one finally feels like they are understood for the first time— finally feeling no longer alone, finally feeling that sense of relief from meeting another who is on the same level as them.

That was the sensation Owen observed Matias to be going through right now, and although he was happy to have caused this feeling within the stranger, he was also curious to find out what about Matias made him feel this disconnected from others and how it was related to his experiences with substances.

"For the longest time, I've wondered if I would have to trek this world alone" said Matias, "I've even accepted a long time ago that I was likely to finish this journey by myself.

But it seems that I've found someone else— at a fucking house party of all places —who genuinely seems to also understand and have the capacity to fully interpret the things around us.

Thank you, Owen.

Even if our interactions end here, tonight, or if we happen to become good friends after this which I hope we do, you have allowed me to no longer be alone in this world" Matias then spotted a corner in the living room that was vacant of any people and pointed at it, "Let's talk there."

The two paused their conversation and headed to the corner of the living room before sitting down on its floor, unconcerned with how they may have looked to others on the outside for they now shared a world of their own, and continued their discussion.

"This will be the first time I have ever shared my story with someone else, so I apologize in advance if I take up most of the time speaking" said Matias, "I haven't had someone fully know me or understand me for a very long time, so I am eager to relinquish my story to you. But please, feel free to interrupt me at any point with any questions or clarification you may need.

Now, let us begin.

I was born in Chile on some rural farmland. My family was poor, and we had to produce most of the vegetation we ate or raise the animals we consumed.

It wasn't just the lack of money or having grown up in a poorer country that made my upbringing and life experiences so different compared to the ongoings of the world around me— it was also primarily due to the culture by which I was raised in.

The more developed countries and their outlooks on life and everything around them is so different from the one I was raised in.

Their ideas of success are related to wealth, because it stems from the ideology of capitalism. That form of success to such countries, including here in the United States, is defined by the work and the affluence you've attained— as opposed to the *quality* of how you've managed to live your life, or what you've done to *arrange* your spot and the spot of your future kin.

Maturity and the rise into adulthood is less about growth in the more developed countries, and more about milestones. The real focus should be on who you are, how you navigate the world, how you respond to your own emotions, yourself, or other people— but instead it has been replaced with *'now you can drive a car'*, *'now you live in an apartment'*, *'now you have a serious career'*.

And within these developed countries, knowing the land around you— your place within nature and therefore how you impact it just as much as it impacts you —is no longer a real thought outside of minor protests or fund raising for the ongoings of it outside of where you actually live, as opposed to immersing yourself in it to find out, discover, understand, and truly fight for it.

Because of where I grew up, the culture I was surrounded by, the people who raised me, and the customs and shared understandings that were passed down to me as knowledge, I led a very different life with many different experiences than most people— as do many who come from the similar circumstances which I have.

And with that, my *personal evolution* for growing as a human being was more in depth and pursued head-on, instead of it being just tossed aside as a mere happening with the passage of time.

I come from a long lineage of shamans — on top of nature just being a vital part of my family, culture, and country's life —so despite being sober now, I used to partake in many psychedelics.

Not for the recreational factor, but for the self-exploring aspects it offers, and to discover more about myself, the world, and me in the world just as much as the world in me.

And since I came from a long line of shamans and ancestors who enveloped themselves into their surroundings and the animate placings of nature, the universe, spirits, and people— drugs usually had a different effect on me than most.

I share the same phenomena you experienced when it came to cannabis.

Though I didn't feel like I was going to be abducted, I did experience the feeling of a barrier being torn down in a minor form.

The sky above my head felt a little closer, the ground beneath my feet felt more near, the stars didn't seem to be hidden by the daylight, and the wind felt more like the ocean with a constant movement of pushing and pulling.

Through cannabis, I was pulled out of the autopilot mindset and was able to recognize the existence of everything that was constantly at play around me— whether my senses picked up on them or I removed the desensitization from having become too accustomed to them to notice anymore.

This all happened when I was about fourteen or fifteen years old.

Then, when I was sixteen, I did mushrooms for the first time, and that was when the real doors were unlocked and I was thrown into the first steps of my bigger journey.

I saw the trees move in a single shared flow of unison— all connected to each other like the network of fungi beneath the earth.

I saw their vibrations and their gentle expansions or shrinking from when they breathed like we do.

I witnessed the symbiosis of nature within the trees and the wind— no different than how smaller animals share a relation with the larger animals, like the birds who sit atop the backs of hippopotamuses, or the fish who lie on the bellies of sharks.

I entered the trees' auras and shared my own aura with them. I spoke to them about the many things they have witnessed and experienced over their lifetimes, and about how unaware we humans were of them despite them being fully aware of us.

I connected to nature on a deeper level, and resonated with its existence.

Mushrooms gave me the key to understanding the sentience that nature has as a fully self-aware force.

Then, when I was about nineteen, I traveled into the jungle. And under the guidance of a shaman, I partook in the ayahuasca ceremony.

I met with Mother Ayahuasca, and was forced to face my many past struggles, traumas, and all the negative things that still plagued my current state of existence.

I healed so much of myself, and then went even further back in time of space and awareness to heal the pain that was left over by my ancestors and my own past lives.

Mother Ayahuasca helped me to become whole again, by the healing of the thousands of lives and unseen wounds that were riddled deep within my body, mind, and soul.

Afterwards, I was given visions of the future; visions of the planet and its current state; visions of the different paths that humanity and the planet could go in depending on what mankind's decisions were for the next steps we wish to take.

I even encountered the nature spirits while on ayahuasca, on got to interact with those beings that either lived in the jungle or were manifestations of it.

So much wisdom and knowledge was passed back and forth— some immediately understood, others needing more time for me to dwell on later in order to understand.

About two years after my ayahuasca experience, I decided to smoke Bufotenine from the poisonous toad.

I'll admit, I really didn't know what to expect with this one, as there wasn't too much information about it out there like there was for DMT.

But still, I wanted to do everything natural first that came from either the land or its critters before I did DMT, which is mostly manmade as to produce a more concentrated and potent form of the compound.

Anyways, I was able to find a shaman who had inherited the art of a proper ceremony for this method, that was passed down to him from generation to generation, and so I went through with its ritual.

This one… was hard on me.

It was extremely different from the ayahuasca and 'shroom experience, and worked me in an entirely different way in regards to my space of mind, hallucinations, and the perception of my surrounding environment.

It was a nasty ego death, though I don't like that term nor its definition, but I struggle to find a better word to label it as.

For me and my experience, it was more so a breaking down of me to the root of my core.

The term 'ego death' refers to the erasing of one's sense of identity or individuality, while also no longer perceiving themselves as separate from everything else around them— this experience was neither of those things.

It was just a digging through of all the different layers that make me... *me*.

It was an uncovering of this solid and purer version of myself— which is my *true-self*—uncorrupted by the world, by life, or anything else that would sway me from my original state of being within existence.

And yet, it wasn't even necessarily true that everything else I was before this purer form of me was revealed wasn't really me— for it **was**. I had just forgotten my original self and needed to be reminded of it. Reminded that this whole experience of existence I had lived before returning to this realization of who I really am was what I needed in order to grow, strengthen, and mature my spirit from the trials of life.

This true version of me and who I am simply needed to reach the surface once again. It didn't need to replace everything I had learned and become and was now aware of by this life— it just needed to no longer be forgotten nor become more lost by the adding of more layers around it to better deal, cope, or adapt with this world... if that makes sense?

It was hard. It was really fucking rough. But I did it, and I grew from it.

My perspective changed, my awareness expanded, and my outlook broadened.

I felt like a whole new person, and yet this new person was always me, just awoken now and finally at the surface of it all— able to see it all clearly once again."

Matias took a break from his story as he came upon the next segment of it.

Owen watched as Matias' brow frowned while he took a deep breath in through his nose— a clear indication that whatever part of this story he was about to go into now… obviously still had some sort of hold over him.

"I made a best friend early on in college, and we became roommates during our third year" said Matias, continuing his story, "He was also into psyche-delics, although not so much in the spiritual way that I was.

However, this slight difference made for good conversations about the sub-stances, and the slight similarities we shared made it great for trip-sittings and the experimentations we explored with different strains of mushrooms we could get our hands on.

Well, it turned out that he had done DMT before, and when I told him of my interest in it, he was more than stoked for me to try it and even told me he would guide my trip.

Now, there isn't much one can do to guide someone else's DMT trip, besides ensuring that they take all three hits at the beginning of it.

The thing about DMT, is it fucking sucks to inhale.

It tastes awful, and is a real piece of shit going into the lungs.

But if you want a good, full, and proper trip, then you have to take all three hits consecutively.

Without someone else on the other end to ensure that you finish that last hit **fully**, despite how you may feel and despite you thinking that you already got enough in your system—" Matias shrugged, "Then you won't get that real blast-off effect.

And it's always safe to have a trip-sitter for your first time with any psychedelic, no matter what type you're taking.

So, with the plan now becoming a reality, my roommate went and got me some DMT.

Believe it or not, he had actually made the stuff himself on some occasion. But because he wanted me to have a good clean batch and not one of his own for my first time— just in case he might've thrown off some of the chemicals by accident since it's a very technical process —he bought me some from a guy he trusted.

Anyway, we then sat down in my room to get started.

I had made sure earlier that day to meditate beforehand and get myself into a good head space— thinking about what I wanted from the experience, allowing myself to let go of control and to accept that whatever was to come was going to happen, and that whatever I experienced was a part of the process and to just go with the flow.

Well, my roommate held the pipe and ensured I took all three of the hits as deep as I could, and then… *boom*!"

Matias threw his hands outward in a dramatic way to give emphasis to the story.

"I was launched into another dimension!

I wanna say out of my body. But it honestly felt more like I, myself, was just thrown into another reality as opposed to just out of my physical form. And in a sense, I still felt completely attached and a part of— or rather, at one with —my physical form.

Man, it was something else…

There are no words in the human language, and maybe just language in general, that could describe it all.

I encountered so many types of beings who all interacted with me differently.

The mechanical elves that were shifting in their bodies yet maintained a common understandable form if you didn't look too into it.

They talked about the human experience and what it meant to break free of it.

The jesters that looked very much human but you knew they obviously weren't, or they were at least so much more than what we are.

They danced around me and harassed me, yet it was all in good fun and in the betterment of myself. It almost felt like bullying, but the type you would receive from a coach when they are trying to push you as a way of getting you to go further, if that makes sense.

I saw gnomes, who looked no different than the kind you'd see in the books based around fairytales, or the ceramic ones you'd see on the front of people's lawns.

They seemed so wise but also so carefree, not chained down by these shackles of obligations and expectations we place upon ourselves in this life.

I saw many strange worlds— some whose realities were literally in the structure and animation of a cartoon, as if it were hand drawn and colored by an artist.

Some worlds were reminiscent of the places I had dreamed about as a kid, with giant statues, carvings, and cultures that did not exist in the world we live in now.

I saw aliens who were far more relatable than I thought they would be from the elusive and complex way we humans and our governments depict them.

I saw darkness and the beings in cloaks, hiding their bodies away in the more nefarious aspects of the universe, masters of the macabre and negative energies— which was more of an impressive sight than it was scary.

I flew over cities of the future, and civilizations from the past.

It was amazing. It was breathtaking. It was something I had never thought was even within my capacity to take in and appreciate in a full experience…"

Matias grew quiet before speaking again.

"… And then I was pulled— similar to how you spoke of when describing that abduction sensation, but different.

I was pulled not by force or against my will, but as if something was connected to me from a time and era of existence long forgotten… at least on my end of memory.

Dimensions, timelines, realities, and space itself all zipped past me, like the reeling of a film, as I was pulled by some source towards it in a union… or maybe a reunion, I don't know.

But then it all stopped.

And I found myself in this new dimension which I had not visited yet, filled with countless suns.

Fuck… it was **so** bright.

Those burning rays of innumerable suns didn't feel hot, but more like pure sources of energy. They rattled my soul with an uncontrollable jitteriness as if I had taken a thousand stimulants at once— if the human body could do such a thing and not die from its undertaking.

Then… I noticed a single shimmer of shade in this bright and foreign realm.

But it was not just a sliver of shade, however. It was a **being**— standing perfectly straight in a motionless posture… and its attention was solely focused on me.

When I looked at it, the space of my surroundings bent in an odd way that was normal during this trip, and the being was suddenly right in front of me instead of far away— as close to me as you are now.

That's when I saw its face… and felt its aura.

I immediately didn't like it. Any of it.

I knew this was wrong. Something was off. Not even the shadow dwellers who I had seen during this DMT trip had given off such a potent sense of *'bad'*.

It was disturbing— this sensation that I felt.

The best way to describe it would be that heart-sinking feeling one gets when a stalker finds out where they live again, after having moved locations, and then surprises them by showing up at their home, or place of work, or favorite coffee shop— but it was so much more than that and **way** more intense… that feeling of dread was all consuming.

This being was not human by any means, and that's what made it so off-putting by how it shared many similarities to us in terms of its physical features.

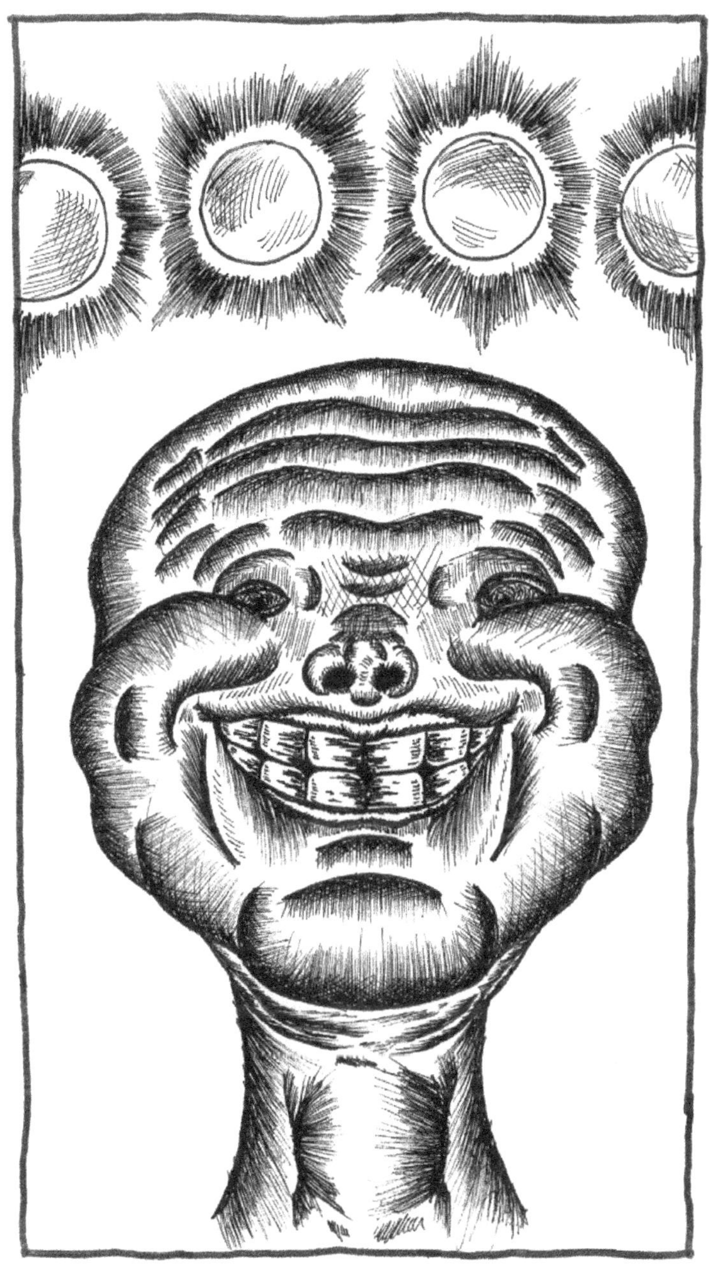

What made my skin crawl the most, though, was how big its head was compared to how tiny its face was that sat on it.

And then those eyes…

Those tiny, pure black, beady little eyes with nothing good behind them in what they desired.

It smiled at me, and I felt like I lost my soul for a brief moment when it did, before saying… and I'll never forget this… *'I found you.'*

I—"

Matias swallowed hard and rubbed his face roughly, as though to not give into the emotions he was currently flustered with while digging up this story from his past.

"I ran!

I didn't stick around to let it say any more, or to find out what it meant, or to let it do whatever it was that it may have wanted to do.

I didn't care. I wasn't curious. I wasn't open to this. So I ran!

Running is very different in that space of existence— that astral realm I was in while on DMT.

I was crossing through infinite dimensions at the speed of light while trying to get away from this being— trying to put as much distance as I could between me and it.

I was scared. So fucking scared. Terrified beyond death.

I would beg other beings for help. Try to tell them what had happened. What I experienced. What I was running from.

But every time they seemed to understand what I was talking about and who I was running away from… they refused to help me, as if they too wished to keep far away from whatever or whoever this being was.

They wouldn't even give me the time to explain what I was dealing with or what was going on. Instead, they'd just tell me to go away, sometimes even yell and scream at me to leave.

If I didn't and continued to push them for aid or beg them for help or some kind of insight onto what this being was and what was happening, they'd run away from *me*. They'd leave the dimension and vanish into another reality— all to escape from me during my own escape from the being who chased me.

Some of the more powerful beings would even cast me out of their space— tell me *'We cannot make enemies with him'* and then slap me out and away from their presence across multiple dimensions and through different timelines, like you would a gnat, when they discovered the predicament I was facing.

… People who take DMT will tell you it feels like infinity— that they lived lifetimes in these other worlds while high.

And I can confirm that, but to a stronger degree which none of them have ever experienced.

For all of those eternities, folded into infinities, then expanded into an endless expansion… I ran from this being.

I crossed countless dimensions. Stepped into endless realities. Sometimes I'd hide in them, sometimes I'd just keep flying, sometimes I only focused on making distance.

There were times when I would see the being enter the realm that I was in— it seemed to always find me no matter how long or how far I went.

But it was its presence that always gave it away and let me know when it was close.

And I was not the only one who could sense it, as I saw how the other beings reacted when they felt it drawing closer too, and how they looked at me with such eyes of judgement— wondering if I was going to stay and bring that being here to them.

I forgot entirely about *this*" said Matias, gesturing to the party life that surrounded them, "My human life, the human experience, this whole form of existence.

I had lived and existed longer in what is beyond all this than I had within this human matrix.

I basically grew out of my human conception and perception of reality from my infinite time out there.

And to be frank… or maybe not— I cannot say that I am fully human anymore because of all the growth and the expansion of my consciousness that occurred while I experienced that torturous eternity of running.

And then, one random day, during an unforeseen lapse in time within that paradoxical ouroboros of my dimension bending access to infinity while running… I experienced a sharp sting in my nostrils— a sensation which I had forgotten existed.

It was so rudimentary, so physical, based purely in matter and the material… and then, the most beautiful thing happened…"

Matias smiled.

"I began to fall!

Fall from the skies and the heavens which I roamed.

Fall through the strange, foreign, and mysterious lands which I had both crossed and not yet discovered.

Fall through the homes and the domains and the spaces that belonged to the other beings who occupied this astral realm of multitude.

I fell back into the warm embrace of this reality that I was so familiar with.

I watched as the galaxies passed by me, and felt this sensation of familiarity with the structure and rules of this domain that offered me a protection in its shackling embrace of purposeful ignorance.

I began to fall faster, and then faster, and then faster— until my eyes could no longer keep up with the images that flew by me.

And then, in a brief glimpse of an instant, I saw something that I recognized despite it happening within the shaved seconds of time that were slimmer than the space between atoms.

I saw blue and white— the sky of the earth with its floating clouds...

Then **BAM!**"

Matias clapped his hands tightly together.

"I smacked right back into my own body!

I hyperventilated like crazy and felt like I was going to die as my mind, body, brain, soul, and consciousness all worked overtime to compute and calculate everything that had just happened from that lifetime into this one, as I bound myself once again to this mortal flesh which sits in the reality of this dimension.

The common DMT trip for most people usually only lasts for fifteen or twenty minutes when they take it. And like I said, within that time, they feel like they had lived in those realms for eternity.

Well, as it turned out… mine lasted for fifty-five minutes.

Apparently my friend who was trip-sitting was freaking out— worried that something had gone wrong, especially by the way I was talking and subtly acting while under this trip.

He wanted to just let me be and come down on my own time, but as more minutes passed over the usual trip time, the more he began to worry.

And in all honesty, there really isn't much one can do about that.

Once I got close to reaching the hour mark, my friend began to panic about the effects it would have on my brain, and if I was going to be a vegetable once I snapped back to.

So, he administered naloxone and brought me back.

That stuff is for when people OD on opioids, so I have no idea why it worked, how it worked, or what gave him the idea— but I'm glad he did it.

Of all the beings I had encountered during my time in infinity, it was my friend— *a common human* —who came to my aid, gave me the help I asked for, and saved me from that being.

I'd probably still be running from it if it weren't for him.

Never disbelieve in the power and potential of humans, for they really are quite something.

Since then, I went straight edge and never touched a drug ever again.

It's been five years, or 1,825 days sober to be exact."

As Matias finished the end of his story, he let out a huge sigh of relief from being able to tell that story for the first time and be heard— to be truly known after all of the multiple lifetimes he had kept it to himself.

"So what do you plan on doing, then?" asked Owen, "Now, I mean. After having experienced all that and basically been alive longer than any human could even fathom, on top of all the sights you saw and knowledge you've accumulated…

… What's next in this human life for you?"

"It may sound crazy, but after all I've been through and learned, I know there is more out there… as well as more here" answered Matias, "I seek to find the gods that still walk *this* plane and the earth, as they have an understanding of infinity, already.

I'd also like to meet the humans that shall embark on the path of godhood soon, who will in turn, gain an understanding of infinity— for I will be able to relate to them the most.

However, as you now know, I truly do love humans. So even in instances like this, I'd like to form a connection with some of them. And if I'm lucky enough— become friends.

I'd like to be friends with you, Owen" said Matias.

Mark's Patio

MARK'S HIDEOUT WAS located in the rural Appalachians, tucked tightly away amongst the many trees and mountains, with only a thirty yard clearing around the whole space of his house from front to back, and a tiny dirt road that disappeared into the trees once past the clearing around his house.

People who were either friends with Mark or family called his place the hideout, because it really did feel like it was in the middle of nowhere. And everyone found its isolation to be very fitting for Mark and his extremely reclusive and introverted personality.

Even the slim dirt road was hidden, known only to those who had been to Mark's hideout before or were given clear instructions to it by Mark himself. It weaved and twisted throughout the woods before connecting to a lesser known dirt road, which was attached to a greater known dirt road, which eventually led to a main road.

It was no easy feat to visit Mark's hideout, so only the people who truly cared about him or who he truly cared about ever got the chance to visit his home.

And with such visits being a rare occurrence, most of the time spent during those reunions were focused on catching up, reflecting back on old times, or exchanging the recent news about what was going on in each others lives.

Caleb arrived early in the afternoon at Mark's hideout, though he was supposed to arrive there initially in the morning.

He had gotten lost and confused once he hit the dirt roads, and had to be navigated over the phone by Mark on how to reach his home.

After multiple hours of instructions and some good laughs on both ends from being completely clueless at times, Caleb eventually found his way and broke through the trees— entering onto the large clearing that surrounded Mark's hideout.

As he pulled up to the house, Mark came out of the front door and wheeled his way down the ramp for a big embrace with his old friend once Caleb hopped out of the car.

It had been years since the two of them had seen each other in person, though they did write letters to one another and communicate over the phone during holidays. But this was a big reunion in the making for them, for despite being cousins, they were always brothers to each other.

After their long hug, accompanied by some tears that were shed, the two went inside Mark's home and cracked open some beers, spending the rest of the day just talking to each other.

They reminisced about the past, told old stories that the other had forgotten, spoke about the current world and the lives they were living, made a couple burgers on the stove, then headed outside onto Mark's patio to smoke some cigarettes as they continued their chat.

But it wasn't all sunshine and smiles during their conversation, as Caleb picked up on a pensive tail which hung onto the ends of Mark's words.

With the sun fully gone now, and while the stars made their first appearance above the tree-line outside of Mark's clearing, Caleb decided to address the elephant in the room over their smokes.

"So" began Caleb, sitting down in an empty chair beside his friend while lighting up their sticks of tobacco on the low-leveled patio, "We might as well talk about it. I can tell it bothers you too, doesn't it?"

Mark looked at Caleb while exhaling his smoke, "Bother? No.

But I'm sure it's been eating you alive" he said.

"Everybody feels some type of way about it, and you must have feelings about it too" said Caleb, "You've kept in touch with everyone, so I know they must give you an ear full of it since you're pretty much the only one who I still talk to."

"Sure they do, but I don't pay it much mind" responded Mark, "I understand. In fact, they all do too.

It's just the way it all went about, really. That's the reason for why most have taken a bother."

Caleb whipped his neck to the trees beyond the clearing, as a large shadow dashed across his peripheral through the woods.

"… Yeah" said Caleb, returning his focus onto Mark when nothing seemed out of the ordinary, "It's a messy matter, but I've honestly been really happy ever since I moved out the Rez.

And I feel like that's what is most important— my happiness on the matter."

Mark nodded, "Anybody would be happy to leave the Rez, Caleb. But I'm sure everyone would also agree that they'd be *happiest* if the Rez itself was better and a place where they'd actually want to stay.

It's not your fault, nor mine, nor anyone else's who lives on the Rez for it being the way that it is.

And the way that it is now and has always been feels purposeful, for sure— the conditions of it and all —but it wasn't created that way by any of us.

It was made by the government, *then* it was given to us. That's why it's the way that it is.

They've never cared about us. Never have and never will.

We all know that. And their biggest achievement since the genocide of our people and the stealing of our land and heritage, has been the way they still pick us apart during this '*modern*' time.

It truly is a crazy thing—"

During Mark's speech, another shadow— or perhaps the same one —caught Caleb's attention again as it made another dash within the tree-line.

Caleb chased it with his head, but there was no disturbance to be found amongst the trees or the surrounding shrubbery, causing him to doubt his eyes and what he thought he saw, before returning his focus onto Mark.

"More people are standing up against racism" continued Mark, "More people are voicing for equality. More people are standing up for the basics of human rights— be it a women's choice over her own body, someone's true internal identity of who they are as a person, or the right to love whoever we want through the full diversity of who we are attracted to.

Years ago, if the government wanted to allow a big company to put an oil-line through our land, it would've been a bloody fight with bullets fired at our people.

If they wanted to disregard *our* rights and *our* laws on *our* Rez, it would be a long and drawn out battle where their resources would be put against us, as well as our little funds purposefully taken advantage of to drain us dry in legal matters before it could even reach a big court where our voices could be heard, the original treaties **forced** to be respected, or maybe a news channel picking up the case to give us some more support by the people watching it all go down."

A tree branch then snapped in the tree-line, and Caleb turned his neck to catch sight of its source and sound.

At this point, he decided to keep his eyes vigil on the bordering trees of Mark's clearance, as a paranoia now began to grow within him from this stalking predator… perhaps a cougar?

"Today's different than how it used to be, but it's still nowhere near what we need and how it should be" continued Mark, "It's obvious that the world is changing.

If a big company or the government tries to build something in and/or across our land, the whole world hears about it and joins us in our fight against them.

When one of our women gets kidnapped or goes missing— and it's obvious that the one who is responsible for it or the group of people perpetrating this atrocity are not Native, but come from the blood of a colonizer— we no longer need to weep in silence about the matter. We can do something about, and more and more are willing to reach out and aid us in our quest for justice.

We can fight for justice, give voice to the life that was lost, demand action be taken, and receive support from the people who hear about it and have no connection to us outside of also being a fellow human and having a beating heart" said Mark, unfazed by the ongoing sounds that were occurring in the woods, nor by Caleb's sharp responses to them, "It's better now, but better does not mean enough. Better has yet to translate to healthier, safer, respected, and truly equal.

It's not perfect— not even fucking close. And it still has a very far way to go before we can ever say that we *finally* have an equal footing on this ground which we once roamed freely.

Maybe soon in a short time, we can say that we have our freedom, our voice, and our rights on the lands they assigned to us, as well as the lands they didn't.

But in the long run, assuming we attain that one day from this sick, twisted and oppressive world— we must still be able to be *ourselves* with that freedom and with those rights as a human being. We must still have our traditions, our beliefs, our language, our culture, our customs, our ceremonies— everything that made and makes us who we are as a people.

Though they may try, that must never be lost in the time it takes before we truly become free within our own lands once again."

"I know. I know" said Caleb, "I see the change too, and I'm happy by it.

... But I also see what little impact it has on the whole of our people and our situation.

It's nice to have hope, but it's hard to be hopeful.

And I hate that it feels like that very hope can only stem from whether the *outside* world will understand and recognize us for who we are and what we are, as opposed to it being achieved by the power and the strength that we have and show ourselves— *for ourselves.*"

Mark took a draw from his cigarette and nodded, "But the thing is… it was made that way.

Purposefully and tactically, with both eyes on the future in regard to us.

The mass genocide committed on our people was not just the biggest and most heinous act against us— it was the first one in a much bigger plan. The first step in a preconceived race against our demise, with their eyes already on the finish line."

"Mark, I hear yah" said Caleb, "But this is something that we *all* know, anyone like me or you who grew up on a Rez, or was born Native, or taught about our heritage, our ancestry, the struggles that the ones before us went through and the struggles that we ourselves shall also endure.

I know it— with all my heart —despite how much it hurts and makes me want to cry, and scream, and shout, and fight sometimes.

It's our life, and this is the journey that comes with it.

And change will happen one day, but the fight for it will continue on, everyday, until it does.

But what I wanna know, Mark, is why it was such a bad thing to everyone when *I* left the Rez?" asked Caleb.

The sound of something scraping against the trees echoed in the distance, followed by the sound of something heavy dragging along the dirt.

Caleb tried to zone in on the sound's direction, attempting to figure out its exact location and source. But he found it to be too difficult from how dark it was outside and by how thick the blanket of shadows were that amassed within the tree-line.

"... And you can't deny the fact that everyone **was** different about me leaving when I left, you just can't" continued Caleb, "It was different for you, and no one blames you or tried to invalidate your reasons for leaving.

We all understood it. No one took a second thought about it.

The accident was terrible and not your fault, and the last thing you needed was to be stuck in the very place where you lost your gift to walk on two legs— especially with how it must feel already being trapped in a chair now, forever.

And I don't want to sound insensitive, Mark, I really don't, but did I need to lose my legs too in order to be understood for leaving the Rez?" asked Caleb, his voice full of hurt and pain.

Mark gave Caleb a supportive smile, while his eyes held a mutual pain as well, "Yeah... it's not really fair for either of us, is it? None of it is.

But that's my point.

The system of this world was structured against us before we were even born.

They brought their firewater and poisoned us.

They handed over fruitless land under the guise of peace and remorse.

They gave us shitty homes and a limited space for where we can be our own people and have a rule and say over our own lands, yet don't even respect that or their own terms which *they* wrote up for this sanction of a truce.

We are still oppressed, even today, even in this very *'modern'* and *'progressive'* world— and none of that is our fault. **None of it**."

More movement and shadows danced within the tree-line, until it all stopped as a singular mass in a specific area, and remained still there for the first time, allowing Caleb the chance to set his eyes upon its exact location.

"No one was mad at you for leaving the Rez, Caleb" continued Mark, "It was because you separated yourself from us *after*. All of us; your people; your tribe; your culture—"

"—Mark…" interrupted Caleb, "Do you see that? That shadowy mass in the tree-line, directly in front of us?"

"I left too" said Mark, as if oblivious to Caleb's words or purposefully ignoring his question, "But I didn't separate.

I still talk to all of our family, and friends, and neighbors.

I help when I can despite being in a wheelchair, whether that be with money every now and then, or by showing up in person for an event, celebration, ceremony, or a protest to protect our land—"

"—Mark!" exclaimed Caleb, interrupting him again, "There's something in those woods out there!… It's watching us, it's just… watching us."

Caleb began to rise from his seat, fearful of this mysterious thing he saw in the distance, when Mark finally gave him a response on the matter.

"Sit down! And don't move" said Mark with a stern aggression.

Caleb immediately obeyed and sat back down in his seat, now noticing that Mark was also looking in the same direction, and his response was in correlation to this strange thing in the woods.

"If you stay still it'll go away" said Mark, "Don't even take a hit of your cigarette. Don't even move your lips too much when you talk. And **especially** do not stand the fuck up or move from your chair."

Just then, the giant creature that hid itself in the darkness of the woods began to poke its head out a bit more— allowing some of itself to be revealed under the moonlight for Caleb to better observe.

However, there was no terminology, definitions, or historical recordings of this thing that peeked out from the black woods.

It was like a moose… but more humanoid. Like an abomination from the intertwining of man and animal, and though its face was still hidden of any details due to the poor starlight above, enough of it could be seen to make Caleb want to turn and run in fear.

"We have much knowledge— us who roamed these lands before it became America" continued Mark with his previous speech, "Much much knowledge… about the things that roamed it even *before us.*

If you hadn't left us as fast as you did, and if you hadn't cut us all off as hard as you did, then you would've been able to attain this knowledge as well, instead of leaving it all behind as just 'scary stories' we were told as kids."

The creature let out a weird gurgling sound before releasing a disgusting and perverted howl, all while continuing to stare directly at them.

Caleb wanted to jump up from his seat and run inside the house, but he resisted this urge with every ounce of will-power in his body, under the instruction of Mark.

Mark remained motionless— almost fearless —as he kept his gaze on the creature in the tree-line.

It didn't seem to rattle him nearly as much as it did Caleb, and it also appeared as though Mark *knew* what this thing was, and therefore, was not afraid of it based on his full awareness of what it was— filling in the spot for what would've been a terror of the unknown.

"There are certain things you can't run from" said Mark, "I was forced to learn that the hard way when I lost my ability to walk, and have since been placed into a multitude of situations where fleeing was not an option I could take.

You haven't learned that yet, and so you still run from the things that aren't even a threat to you, Caleb.

Well, that thing right there… is something you can't run from.

You have to hold strong and keep your place when it shows up. Be still, motionless, and wait it out if you're lucky enough.

There are things in this world that are just as twisted and as evil as the government, and you'd do well to be aware of them both."

Tea Under the Rain

Summers were spent in Louisiana at Grandma B's.

Naomi had visited her beloved grandmother every year when the seasons passed over and school was on break.

Her mother would fly them out together, and they'd stay on Grandma B's little property where she'd hangout for half of the summer, listening to Grandma B's stories while watching her mother cook up the delicious cajun dinners she was raised on.

Her mother would only cook those warm heart-filled meals when they were at Grandma B's, while all the other time back in California, Naomi and her mother would eat out. This made these visits to Louisiana feel special and full of love— like the way the traditional family values were displayed on television.

When Naomi grew older, however, her mother stopped visiting Grandma B.

It was nothing personal nor from a change in their relationship, it was just life that made Naomi's mother more busy in the later years.

But since she knew how much Naomi loved her grandmother, and how much Grandma B loved Naomi, she would still purchase a flight for her daughter who would fly alone to Louisiana and visit Grandma B on her own.

Naomi took up the cooking and the making of those southern dishes her mother would've made and grandmother before her— using all of the local ingredients from nearby shops and corner stores for the gumbo, jambalaya, crab stew, fried catfish and okra, and so on.

Even tho Grandma B recently bought a TV so that Naomi wouldn't get too bored during her visits— since she was so much older now and her mother's absence made going out into the town a rarity due to Grandma B's old age —Naomi still preferred to sit down and stay indoors to listen to her grandmother's stories for the majority of her visits.

On this summer morning, deep in the heart of Louisiana, Naomi awoke to the delicate sound of a storm ruffling the roof of Grandma B's house as well as the leaves of surrounding trees and bushes near the property.

Because of the heavy humidity and hot summer days that consumed the South, Naomi would always sleep with her window open to flush her room with the cool breezes that passed.

Now, with a storm overhead and some rain falling down from a grey colored sky, the heat was adequately dispersed so it was no longer uncomfortably hot in that tiny house, and the humidity became filled with the fresh scent of wetted soil and of the plants breathing out their unseen pores.

With the crackling of thunder combusting above at random, Naomi made her way into the kitchen where Grandma B was already beginning her morning— her old body sat in a chair at the table while she watched the rain pour down through the open sliding glass door, while a teapot was heating on the stove.

"Morning, Grandma B" said Naomi, coming up beside her grandmother and planting a kiss on her cheek, followed by a gentle hug.

"Morning, baby" said Grandma B, hugging Naomi back with a loving smile, "I got some tea going. You want some when it's ready?"

"Yes, please" answered Naomi, taking a seat beside her grandmother and joining in on watching the rain outside.

It was so peaceful during times like this, and Naomi always knew that Grandma B had a knack for finding where and when to witness the serenity of life and appreciate it.

That same breeze that had flowed into her room when she woke now blew into the entire kitchen through the large opening of the sliding door, brushing against Naomi's skin and face like the delicate caressing hand of a lover.

Soon, the teapot on the stove began to whistle, and before Grandma B could get up to pour them some cups, Naomi was already standing and on the move to take care of it.

She pulled out two tiny cups of china from the chipped-paint cupboards, and placed a bag of earl grey tea in them both before pouring in the boiling water.

After which, Naomi brought their two cups to the table and placed one in front of Grandma B, and the other one in front of her own seat before taking her place back at Grandma B's side.

"Thanks, baby. So, watchu wanna do today?" asked Grandma B as she waited for the tea to steep, "We might have to wait out this storm before any plans."

"You know me, Grandma B. I like staying in" said Naomi, "I'll get some groceries for cooking later today, and maybe we can just go for a walk after the storm passes.

But until then, I wouldn't mind hearing another one of your stories."

Grandma B smiled, feeling both flattered and flustered, "You always are listening to my stories. You sure you're not tired of them yet?"

Naomi shook her head, to which Grandma B chuckled.

"Alright then, you know I always got some stories for yah" said Grandma B while blowing on her steaming cup, "I think with the storm we got going on right now, and the fact that I've probably repeated almost all of my stories I've ever told yah, I got a good one for this morning.

The storm plays into it a bit. A reminder of sorts— of a message from your grandfather, rest his soul, that he told me when we first met... one which I've never forgotten to this day."

"You never told me how you and Grandpa J met!" said Naomi, full of excitement.

"Oh I know, baby. That's because you were too young before.

Children get frightened easily, and I'd never want to scare my baby" said Grandma B, pinching Naomi's cheek, "And this story here" she continued, "It can rattle the bones, I'll tell yah that."

Grandma B blew the surface of her tea once more before taking a cautious sip as to not burn her mouth.

"Well, before I was Grandma B" she said, beginning her story, "I was just Beatrice. Young and beautiful, like you and your mama.

This was about 1946, and I was thirteen at the time.

Back then, the world was different, and *we* were viewed differently.

Segregation was still at play. So being a young black girl in the south, right after World War II, there weren't many places I could go out to play at or have fun like the other kids could.

So, as ridiculous as it might sound now… I went to the cemetery to play.

It was almost always empty, so no one would harass me or chase me away. And if people were there, they usually were of color since white people hardly ever buried their own dead in the same ground as ours, and the visitors usually minded their own business and kept to their tears— paying me no attention.

There wasn't much to do in the graveyard, but it was something. Better than staying in the house all day.

So, I'd wonder and explore everywhere within its gates.

I would read the names on the stones, trying to sound out the really long ones I couldn't pronounce properly back then since I was more illiterate those days.

I would climb the big centerpieces or statues of angels, hop across the grass-markers while trying not to touch the dirt like a game of hot lava, or pick up some of the flowers left on the graves just to look at them before putting them back.

All of this was just in naive, childlike fun.

It might sound like I was being disrespectful to the dead, but I was always good. I was just enjoying myself and life, and I'm sure the ones who were buried there saw it that way as well.

Sometimes I'd be so bored, I'd actually clean up around the place— blow off dust from the forgotten tombstones, or use my shoe to scrape off the algae.

There was this one big shade tree, with large thick branches that hung low and high. That was my favorite spot in the place, and I'd spend most of my time climbing up that tree and creating some imaginary world in my head. I'd even spy on some of the visitors when I was up there, as if I was some sort of secret agent from the war.

Well, the day I met your Grandfather, Grandpa J— or just Jalin back then, was on a day completely opposite to this" said Grandma B, nodding towards the storm that was going on outside while taking another sip of her tea.

"It was a bright and beautiful day, the sun high in the sky with only a few number of clouds that I could count on one hand.

It was hot, but there was this one breeze that would not stop blowing the whole time, making it feel cool like dipping in the water.

I skipped my way to the graveyard that day just as the sun reached its peak at noon, and then roamed the cemetery like usual— fun, free, bored, and innocently.

I probably spent about two hours atop that shade tree, hiding on its higher limbs… when I suddenly felt something that was… off.

I don't know how to describe it, I especially didn't back then, but the best words I can do now would be to call it a *presence*. One that was just… there.

Sort of like with bugs or animals— they don't think too much, they sort of just exist. And yet, they hold a power to themselves despite their lack of real sentience.

You know that feeling you get when a bee or wasp flies near you? Sometimes it's inspecting who you are, other times it's just going about its business beside you— and then you get that feeling from its presence being there, because deep down you know that despite the fact that you're bigger and smarter than that bug… you're still hoping it doesn't sting you.

And *that's* the worst part of it— you don't know what's going through the bug's head, or how it operates, or what it's thinking if it can even think in a manner close to yours.

You never know what you might do to piss it off and set its stinger upon you.

You might breathe too heavy, move too suddenly, or maybe just existing and being there at all is enough to make the bug angry.

Maybe the bug was already angry. Maybe the bug just wanted to sting some-one that day.

Well, that's the feeling I got… and there were no bees nor wasps around me.

So, I climbed down the tree and decided to make my way back home, because I didn't like this feeling and I didn't want to get stung.

I felt a bit more safe once I was away from that weird presence, and the idea of some bug stinging me began to fade once I reached the middle of the grave-yard— walking towards the entrance gate across the field of tombstones.

Compared to up in that shade tree, I could now see my surroundings better and would be able to see any bug that flew up on me while out in this open space. Anything that came close or near to me would be obvious under that bright daylight.

… And yet, it still happened… without a chance of me noticing it.

Something grabbed my ankles and pulled me backwards with such a fury and raging hunger!" said Grandma B, making a snatching motion with her hands.

"My chest hit the ground **hard**, and with my arms extended out in front of my head— pulling at the grass that I passed —I was taken away just like the breath I had in my lungs before the fall.

I was dragged across that graveyard, while my arms and legs and neck all got scratched up from the bladed grass and twigs on the ground, and especially from that awfully dry dirt.

Sometimes I'd be able to grab onto a tombstone to try and stop myself, but my hands would always slip on them every time like a little helpless child's would.

I was only able to really stop myself from being pulled when this unknown force attempted to drag me into a mausoleum, since the open gate allowed me to wrap my fingers fully around its iron rods.

I then looked back at the thing while I held on for dear life, and saw that it was a shadow! A literal shadow— holding my ankles and trying to pull me in!

Now baby, I'm not talking 'bout no ghost, or ghoul, or soul of the dead here. I'm talking about a *shadow.*

That's what it was, and I think they're probably different from even the devils and the demons.

I screamed my heart out until my lungs felt like they were about to burst. I cried out for help hopelessly… but no one else was in the cemetery that I could see, and my little hands weren't strong enough to hold onto that gate for more than a couple of seconds.

… My grip broke. And I was dragged down into the darkness of that mausoleum— my chin banging hard against the descending steps, rattling my brain like a bag of peas.

I was scared. I was so *so* scared as we reached the bottom of those steps where the ground leveled out even" recalled Grandma B, more so analyzing the emotions she once felt from this memory as opposed to reliving them.

"I wasn't thinking about death, nor feeling the pain from all the beating I took while being dragged all the way across the cemetery or from being brought down those rough stone stairs.

I was nothing but full of fright.

And then… I heard it!" said Grandma B, closing her eyes and placing her hands over her heart with a smile.

"A whistle! A whistle like I've never heard before!

It had the ring of a gold bell to it, and the hollowness of a mysterious horn. It was high pitch and laced with power— a power of its wielder more so than the sound itself.

I looked up immediately, captivated by that whistle which took my attention fully to it and away from this crazy situation I was in…

And there *he* was— standing high at the entrance of the mausoleum, with the bright sun at his back and a large dominant-looking hound sitting at his side, its eyes glowing orange.

The shadow must've looked up and seen them both too, or maybe that whistle of his meant more to the shadow than it did to me, because that shadow made a strange ethereal noise, as if speaking some kind of language, then immediately released my ankles and fled away into the deeper recesses of that little tomb.

'You okay?' asked the figure at the top of the mausoleum's entrance, while that large and orange-eyed hound just stared at me

'I'm pretty banged up' I answered, a simple response as you'd expect from a child despite how crazy that altercation was.

'Well then come on up and get yourself out of there then, girly' said the figure, 'You're safe now.'

I picked myself up and began to climb up the stairs, while the figure with the sun at his back and the giant hound beside him slowly became more and more clear as I emerged out of the mausoleum, and back into the light once again.

When I came out of that tomb… is the moment I saw him for the first time— Jalin.

He was the same height, same age, and the same size as me, but boy was he different.

Different than any child, or grown person, or human in general that I had ever met, still to this day.

He was so *powerful*, even back then— his soul just a radiating source of light as though he could beckon fire with it by how he made that shadow run from his whistle.

He closed the mausoleum's gate behind me, so casually too, sayin 'Let's keep that one down there, shall we? He better hope he don't come back up and run a ruckus like that again.'

While he did that, I looked at the dog— that big ole hound with its orange eyes. It looked like a cross between a wolf and a German Shepard, its fur pure black, which is why the only way I can define it is as a hound, a *real* hound.

And its eyes, its eyes held so much more behind their orange glow, like there was a power and a wisdom within them that made me more fearful of *it* than that shadow. The difference being that I feared the hound out of an awareness that it was strong— a respect of power, so to say.

Intimidated, but not in any danger of it.

'Is your dog nice?' I asked, keeping my eyes on it.

'That ain't my dog, that's the grave's dog. He's the one that watches over this place and keeps it safe, don't you know that?' he asked me.

'No, I didn't know a dog lived here' I said back.

'Now!' continued Jalin as he placed his whole attention onto me after taking care of the gate, 'My name's Jalin. What's yours?' he asked.

'Beatrice' I answered.

'That's a pretty name. I like it. Well Beatrice, what the hell are you doing here getting snatched up for?' he asked me, as if there was some common context for what had just happened, and as if I was equally aware of it just like he would be.

'I was just hanging out here like I always do and was about to leave' I answered honestly.

'Hanging out? *Here*? You do that often?' he asked, stupefied.

'Yeah' I answered.

'How can you afford that?' he asked me.

I was confused by that question 'cause it didn't make any sense to me at the time, 'Afford it?' I asked him back, equally confused.

'Wait, do you not leave any offerings?' he questioned me.

I shook my head no and said, 'I ain't got no one buried here, so no.'

'Beatrice, it don't matter if you got someone buried here or not— people are still buried here! You gotta leave some kind of gift or offering if you're gonna enter! Pennies, tobacco, and rum are always the best go-to!' he said proudly, 'I steal some change from my parents or find some in the cracks on the street. I also might sneak out one of my mama's cigarettes, and if I'm really slick, I can take a swig of papa's rum and hold it in my mouth 'till I get here!' he told me.

'Okay' I said to him, 'I'll start doing that from now on. Will that keep me safe from the shadow? I thought these types of bad and evil things only came out at night.'

He huffed a laugh and shook his head at the ground, before looking up at me and saying these words which I will never forget, 'Oh darlin, it don't matter if it's the brightest day of summer or the darkest night of winter, if the sky is raining or if the pollen is floating, it could be burning hot or utterly freezing, and you can be the only soul on the grounds or it can be packed crowded with visitors— it don't matter —because a graveyard's never bleak.' "

Grandma B smiled as she recalled that last phrase of the speech.

"Me and Jalin, from that point on… oh, that's fated love, baby. We were together ever since, and have been inseparable from each other 'till he passed away."

Naomi placed her hand over her grandmother's, "I'm sorry he passed, Grandma B. I would've loved to have met him. He sounds like a wonderful man."

Grandma B chuckled and patted Naomi's hand in a reassurance that she was fine, "Oh baby, like I said, me and him are inseparable. He's not leaving this plane of existence until I pass over and leave it with him.

He watches over me, right beside me, just over my shoulder. And we share rum on the warm summer nights, tea on the cold winter days, and we listen to music and dance in this house when the mosquitoes force us to keep our bodies movin.

And ever so often… we go to the graveyard together with our offerings, and walk its grounds in routine rounds— making sure everything is safe and sound, and nothing's acting up or where it shouldn't be, with that same orange-eyed hound right at our side the entire time."

END

B.A.D.

"Ah! Welcome back, traveler. You sure took your time, didn't you? For a moment there, I thought you may have gotten lost within my garden of terrors!

Of course, your soul is right here— safe and sound! I made sure to take good care of it and keep it safe while you were away.

Next time, bring an offering so you may keep it with you when entering my garden. Hopefully then, you may learn and grow from the tales you've witnessed in there."